Is it WRONG to TRY to PICK UP GIRLS in A DUNGEON? 17

FUJINO OMORI

ILLUSTRATION BY SUZUHITO YASUDA

2
PROLOGUE
SUPER ORARIO RPG

IS IT WRONG TO TRY TO PICK UP GIRLS IN A DUNGEON?

VOLUME 17

FUJINO OMORI
ILLUSTRATION BY SUZUHITO YASUDA

YEN ON
NEW YORK

IS IT WRONG TO TRY TO PICK UP GIRLS IN A DUNGEON?, Volume 17
FUJINO OMORI

Translation by Dale DeLucia
Cover art by Suzuhito Yasuda

This book is a work of fiction. Names, characters, places, and incidents are the product of the author's imagination or are used fictitiously. Any resemblance to actual events, locales, or persons, living or dead, is coincidental.

Original Japanese edition published in 2021 by SB Creative Corp.
This English edition is published by arrangement with SB Creative Corp.,
Tokyo in care of Tuttle-Mori Agency, Inc., Tokyo.

Yen On
150 West 30th Street, 19th Floor
New York, NY 10001

Visit us at yenpress.com
facebook.com/yenpress
twitter.com/yenpress
yenpress.tumblr.com
instagram.com/yenpress

First Yen On Edition: August 2022
Edited by Yen On Editorial: Ivan Liang
Designed by Yen Press Design: Andy Swist

Yen On is an imprint of Yen Press, LLC.
The Yen On name and logo are trademarks of Yen Press, LLC.

Library of Congress Cataloging-in-Publication Data
Names: Ōmori, Fujino, author. | Yasuda, Suzuhito, illustrator.
Title: Is it wrong to try to pick up girls in a dungeon? / Fujino Omori ; illustrated by Suzuhito Yasuda.
Other titles: Danjon ni deai o motomeru nowa machigatte iru darōka. English.
Description: New York : Yen ON, 2015– | Series: Is it wrong to try to pick up girls in a dungeon? ; 17
Identifiers: LCCN 2015029144 | ISBN 9780316339155 (v. 1 : pbk.) |
ISBN 9780316340144 (v. 2 : pbk.) | ISBN 9780316340151 (v. 3 : pbk.) |
ISBN 9780316340168 (v. 4 : pbk.) | ISBN 9780316314794 (v. 5 : pbk.) |
ISBN 9780316394161 (v. 6 : pbk.) | ISBN 9780316394178 (v. 7 : pbk.) |
ISBN 9780316394185 (v. 8 : pbk.) | ISBN 9780316562645 (v. 9 : pbk.) |
ISBN 9780316442459 (v. 10 : pbk.) | ISBN 9780316442473 (v. 11 : pbk.) |
ISBN 9781975354787 (v. 12 : pbk.) | ISBN 9781975328191 (v. 13 : pbk.) |
ISBN 9781975385019 (v. 14 : pbk.) | ISBN 9781975316105 (v. 15 : pbk.) |
ISBN 9781975333515 (v. 16 : pbk.) | ISBN 9781975345655 (v. 17 : pbk.)
Subjects: | CYAC: Fantasy. | BISAC: FICTION / Fantasy / General. | FICTION / Science Fiction / Adventure.
Classification: LCC PZ7.1.O54 Du 2015 | DDC [Fic]—dc23
LC record available at http://lccn.loc.gov/2015029144

ISBNs: 978-1-9753-4565-5 (paperback)
978-1-9753-4566-2 (ebook)

1 3 5 7 9 10 8 6 4 2

LSC-C

Printed in the United States of America

VOLUME 17

FUJINO OMORI

ILLUSTRATION BY **SUZUHITO YASUDA**

BELL CRANELL

The hero of the story, who came to Orario (dreaming of meeting a beautiful heroine in the Dungeon) on the advice of his grandfather. He belongs to *Hestia Familia* and is still getting used to his job as an adventurer.

HESTIA

A being from the heavens, she is far beyond all the inhabitants of the mortal plane. The head of Bell's *Hestia Familia*, she is absolutely head over heels in love with him!

AIZ WALLENSTEIN

Known as the Sword Princess, her combination of feminine beauty and incredible strength makes her Orario's greatest female adventurer. Bell idolizes her. Currently Level 6, she belongs to *Loki Familia*.

LYU LEON

Formerly a powerful elven adventurer, she now works as a waitress at The Benevolent Mistress.

FREYA

The patron goddess of *Freya Familia*. Hailed as the most beautiful being even among deities, a true Goddess of Beauty.

SYR FLOVER

A waitress at The Benevolent Mistress. She established a friendly relationship with Bell after an unexpected meeting.

ASFI AL ANDROMEDA

A gifted maker of magic items. Belongs to *Hermes Familia*.

OTTAR

The captain of *Freya Familia*. The strongest adventurer in Orario. A boaz.

CHARACTER & STORY

The Labyrinth City Orario——A large metropolis that sits over an expansive network of underground tunnels and caverns known as the "Dungeon." Bell Cranell came here to pursue his dream of becoming an adventurer. After meeting the goddess Hestia, he joined her familia and began to spend his days in the Dungeon, hoping to win the respect of his idol, the Sword Princess Aiz Wallenstein. Not long after, the supporter Lilly, the smith Welf, the Far Easterner Mikoto, and the renart Haruhime have joined *Hestia Familia* alongside him.

Invited on a date during the Goddess Festival by the girl from the bar, Syr, Bell underwent a grueling hazing in the guise of training by Hedin in order to properly escort her.

On the day of the festival, Bell swept Syr off her feet using all the tricks and skills that had been hammered into him as his friends watched from a distance. The outcome of their feelings is—

WELF CROZZO

A smith who fights alongside Bell as a member of his party, he forged Bell's light armor (Pyonkichi series). Belongs to *Hestia Familia*.

LILLILUKA ERDE

A girl belonging to a race of pygmy humans known as prums, she plays the role of supporter in Bell's party. A member of *Hestia Familia*, she's much more powerful than she looks.

HARUHIME SANJOUNO

A fox person (renart) from the Far East who met Bell in Orario's Pleasure Quarter. Belongs to *Hestia Familia*.

MIKOTO YAMATO

A girl from the Far East. She feels indebted to Bell after receiving his forgiveness. Belongs to *Hestia Familia*.

HERMES

The patron god of *Hermes Familia*. A charming god who is quick on his feet and is careful to maintain neutrality among the various factions. Is he keeping tabs on Bell for someone...?

EINA TULLE

A Dungeon adviser and a receptionist for the Guild, the organization in charge of regulating the Dungeon. She has bought armor for Bell in the past, and she looks after him both officially and personally.

CHLOE LOLO

A catgirl waitress at The Benevolent Mistress who talks and acts like a goddess. Chases after Bell.

AHNYA FROMEL

One of Lyu and Syr's coworkers at The Benevolent Mistress, she's something of a foolish catgirl.

MIA GRAND

The owner of a tavern called The Benevolent Mistress. Relatively tall, despite being a dwarf. Strong enough to send adventurers running away in tears.

RUNOA FAUST

A human waitress at The Benevolent Mistress. Although she seems to be a commonsense type, she has a troubled side.

ALFRIK GULLIVER

An adventurer who managed to reach Level 5 despite being a prum. Has three younger brothers named Dvalinn, Berling, and Grer.

ALLEN FROMEL

A cat person who belongs to *Freya Familia*. A Level 6 first-tier adventurer known as the fastest in Orario.

HEDIN SELRAND

An intelligent magic swordsman who has put his faith in Freya. His alias is Hildsleif.

HEGNI RAGNAR

A dark elf and Hedin's old foe.
His alias is Dáinsleif.

HEITH VELVET

A skilled healer in *Freya Familia*. She apparently often complains about Ottar.

HÖRN

The goddess's attendant who has sworn loyalty to Freya. Known as Nameless, she has no alias.

PROLOGUE
SUPER ORARIO RPG

Do you know about role playing?

It's performing a certain role, sometimes even immersing yourself in it to the point of becoming that role.

Using imagination, dreams, to simulate being someone other than yourself.

However, in our case, it's nothing so simplistic as a mere simulation.

It was just a game at first.

Dying of boredom, I descended to the mortal realm just like so many other deities.

I created a familia. Traveled the world. Became bound to Orario. Explored the Dungeon.

And after having enjoyed all the various pleasures of the mortal realm, in an entirely unsurprising development, I grew bored again.

The unknown that excites us so is not something that is always just around the corner. Indeed, as more and more layers of mystery are peeled back, my excitement fades and the days become uninteresting and bland. It's pleasing to see my followers grow, and cherishing them is truly fulfilling. That isn't a lie. But somewhere along the line, I ended up with just as much time on my hands as I had in the heavens.

That was why the game that Zeus and the others were playing happened to catch my interest one day.

That's how you get role playing.

A certain number of deities are capable of suppressing their divinity. Once they've hidden all evidence of their heavenly origin, they become residents of the mortal realm, assimilating into society, living life as a mortal. Each assumes a role and immerses themselves to forget their divinity and enjoy this world anew.

Looking down at the board upon which the children are arrayed, they adjust their personality and voice and become one of the pieces on the board.

It was simple enough to laugh it off as a curious pastime, but in the end, I couldn't endure the ever-growing boredom and amused myself with that same game.

The role that I chose for my entertainment was that of a city girl.

I had the true name and history I received from Hörn, so it seemed a perfect choice. That child's magic—*Vana Seiðr*—had an interesting side effect.

By using my ichor as a medium, a connection was established that allowed her to share in my divinity, which also made it possible to reproduce the girl's face.

Back in the heavens, Zeus was famed for his transformations. A bull, a swan, even a shower of rain. That insufferable Odin could transform, too. Most deities have a variety of masks they can don at will.

My girl had been the same. In order to slip away from the other deities who pestered me in the heavens, I would often cease to be Freya in order to sneak out of the temple.

When I found that I could take the form of that girl without running afoul of the rules that normally bound arcanum, I laughed. My covenant with Hörn gave her a taste of divinity, and it turned out to be quite the bounty for me as well.

The mysteries of the mortal realm are truly without compare.

Hörn's wish to become a goddess is the one area where her will and desire surpass Ottar and all my other children.

The strength of that will is what allowed her to succeed in summoning—in *becoming*—a goddess. Perhaps it also included Syr because her wish was not just to be Freya but ultimately to be a blessed and happy girl.

Of course, the exchange of true names bore a crucial meaning.

A name is a manifestation of a body.

Perhaps that explains why I was able to take on that child's appearance from the moment I received the name Syr.

In any case, I gained a convenient mask for my role playing.

This was the birth of *my* Syr.

In exchange for allowing Mia to half retire, I started working at her tavern. She made no effort to hide her distaste for the situation, naturally.

During the periods I erased my divine power and immersed myself in my role, I let Hörn handle all the duties required of a goddess.

Hörn could become both Freya or Syr using her magic, though the number of times I gave her permission for the latter could be counted on one hand.

She ecstatically threw herself into performing the role of Freya, taking care of even bothersome tasks with an energetic verve, as if it were an honor to carry them out. I can't say I don't understand where she was coming from, but part of me wanted to point out how that eagerness was rather out of character for me.

And even if her appearance and divine presence were identical, no matter how well she tried to mirror my speech and gestures, Loki would've seen right through the illusion, so I always made sure to personally attend Denatus and the banquets of the gods and those sorts of assemblies. Even then, though, I hardly ever really showed my face.

The protection provided by Allen and the others was a compromise. I really would have preferred being entirely alone. But it wasn't as if I didn't understand their love, so I gave a little ground on that point.

It was just a stopgap to forestall the boredom. Nothing more than a sideshow.

That's what I thought at first, but this little charade completely betrayed my expectations in the most delightful of ways.

All the children visiting the tavern. All those different, radiant points of light. All the scuffles I experienced firsthand.

There wasn't any time to feel bored.

And I found out I wasn't nearly adroit enough to perfectly play the role I had chosen for myself, either.

I discovered that I was helpless with cooking or cleaning.

And then there was that unmistakable look of exasperation that always crossed Mia's face whenever I made a shocking number of mistakes.

There's no counting the number of times I tossed and turned in bed, dying of embarrassment.

But, yes, it was fun.

Connecting with children on their terms, working together, gaining their friendship and trust…

Children are incomprehensibly incomplete and insecure. Worried, unsure, and burdened by the most trivial of things, they still always climb back to their feet, driven by a will of steel. They possess a radiance that simply doesn't exist among timeless, unchanging deities. I respect and adore that brilliance.

Above all, I love beautiful things.

I love those who strive to be beautiful for the sake of others.

A lost kitten, a lonely black cat, a girl looking for a place to belong, an elf doing everything she can to stay true to herself even when she finds herself far beyond her comfort zone. They are all favorites of mine.

With so many children, there were so many things to learn, and my eyes shone with excitement.

Interacting with children I didn't know quickly became a hobby, and my heart began to ache.

As I fell deeper into my role. I found myself immensely enjoying my life as Syr.

And then I found him.

No, I met him.

That boy whose soul is so white and translucent.

The _____ that would drive me mad.

That's the reason why.
Etiquette and respect.
Pride and appearance.
Even emptiness—I cast it all aside.
That is why I killed Syr.

CHAPTER 1

THE OPENING OF HOSTILITIES

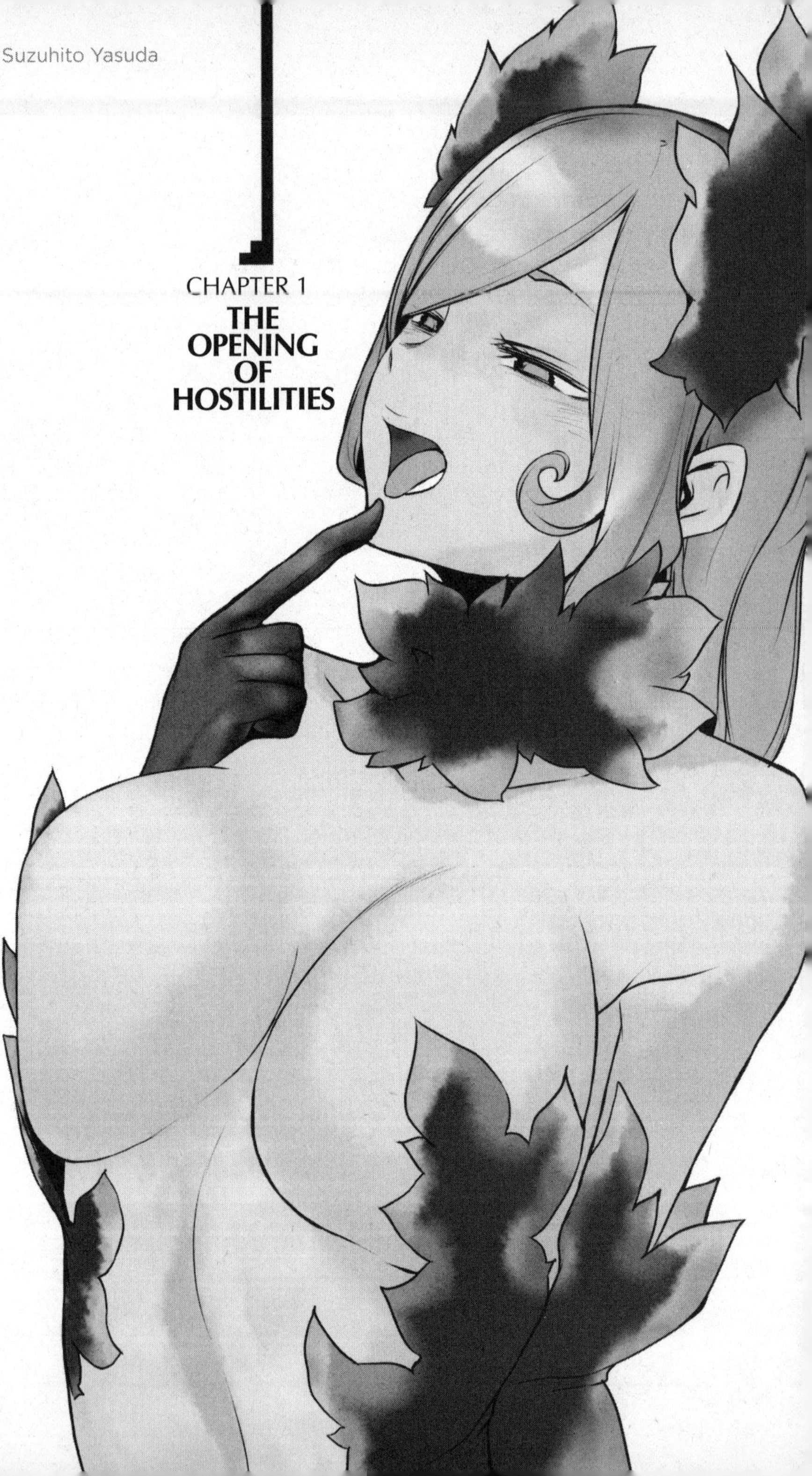

After I reject her, she looks down and then starts running, leaving me behind.

I almost chase after her, but in the end, I don't budge from the spot.

Asking her to stop and wait after I just rejected her confession would be illogical, cruel, and contradictory. I can hear a voice in my head yelling that I have no right.

A rumble tears through the sky, as if the heavens are sobbing.

Rain begins to fall.

Even as the raindrops pelt me, I can't bring myself to take a single step. Who knows how much time passes while I stand still.

"...Lyu...Aiz...I have to..."

With that delirious murmur, I finally leave behind that memory-strewn park.

My entire body is soaked, on the verge of just melting away in the rain as I struggle to drag myself forward.

I finally reach the place where I last saw my friends. They were holding off *Freya Familia* in the second district, meaning we were in the northeast quadrant of the city.

Asfi calls out and says, "Bell Cranell! Looks like you're safe after all. I was concerned, since we couldn't delay Vana Freya and the rest for very long..."

"Sorry...everyone was injured, so we couldn't follow after you..." Aiz murmurs apologetically.

The two of them spot me from beneath the eaves of an abandoned building. It seems like Lyu and the others are currently being treated by Lady Hestia and Lord Hermes.

Runoa and Chloe are unconscious. Their waitress uniforms are marked by splotches of blood. Ahnya's sitting on the ground hunched over, a shadow of her usual cheerful self. It's almost like her soul's been sucked out of her.

"Bell...What about Syr?!"

Even though she's injured, Lyu is the only one who can still talk, and she presses me for an answer.

"...Syr is...She's fine...The whole issue with *Freya Familia* should be resolved, too..."

That's all I manage to say.

There isn't really any other way to answer.

The truth is that Syr was a fake.

And I hurt the real one.

How could I even begin to explain what happened?

It's impossible. I don't even know where to begin.

"...Bell? What is it?"

Aiz gently holds out her hand to me as I stand still, unmoving.

When her fingers touch my cheek, which has grown cold under the constant rain, my body moves on its own.

I overreact on reflex, recoiling from her reach.

"Bell...?"

There shouldn't be any reason for me to feel guilty, but for some reason, I can't look her in the eye.

The truth is that I'm desperate. Looking at those golden eyes of hers is the last thing I want to do right now.

I don't want to feel her touch. Not by the person I look up to.

Not after I so thoughtlessly hurt someone precious to me because all my attention is focused on another.

Aiz opens her eyes a little wider, clearly shocked by my reaction.

When I think about how none of this is her fault, I just want to curl up and die in a hole somewhere.

"Bell..."

Lady Hestia stares at me, but she doesn't say anything else.

I guess as someone who possesses the foresight of a goddess, she can see right through me. I'm sure she already understands everything.

"...To some extent or another, everyone's hurt. Let's head inside before anyone gets sick from being out in this rain."

Lord Hermes doesn't broach the unspoken topic on everyone's mind.

Following his proposal, we carry the injured inside, leaving the rainy streets behind.

—Those are my memories of yesterday.

"........."

The morning of the third day of the Goddess Festival has arrived.

Today, there's no rain falling like tears, but dark gray clouds still fill the sky.

I stare out at the hanging wall of gray from a corridor of Hearthstone Manor without really looking at anything.

After we carried the injured to The Benevolent Mistress to let them recover, we went back to our home.

Welf and the others who had been covering for Miss Ahnya and them at the tavern came with us, too.

When the owner, Miss Mia, saw us carrying them, she got a scary look on her face. When Lord Hermes told her the story from start to finish—including *Freya Familia*'s attack—her expression twisted, and she looked like something particular had crossed her mind...

...It's no use. I can't focus on anything.

The corridor's windows face the inner courtyard, and no matter how high I crane my neck, the sky above seems constricted and boxed in.

There are so many things that I need to think about, but my body and brain feel heavy as lead.

I don't have any claim to feel hurt. Not after the choices I made. Not after I rejected her...after I hurt her.

But her face is still burned into my eyes—

"Bell."

I turn around to see who's calling me.

"…Lyu?" There she is, standing there in her uniform from the tavern. "…How are your injuries?"

Why are you here?

Why come see me now?

My mouth instinctively avoids giving voice to the questions I really want answered.

"Yes…Dáinsleif held back to avoid dealing a mortal blow. I suppose it's an effect of his cursed weapon, but the cuts will take time to fully heal…"

Apparently, she faced off against Hegni, just like me.

Her brow is furrowed as she touches her chest, as if she is still enduring intense pain, possibly because the wounds haven't fully closed yet.

But that lasts for only a moment. She looks up, piercing me with her gaze.

"What happened yesterday, Bell?"

"………"

"It's not that I do not believe you. But how could you know that Syr is safe? And where did she go? And more importantly, why was *Freya Familia* after her in the first place?!"

She's asking all the right questions.

I hardly explained anything that transpired after we'd split up. The events were too fresh, and I needed time to sort out my thoughts and feelings. Honestly, I still do.

But…I can't just keep quiet about it anymore.

I slowly start to explain as I desperately try to figure out where to begin.

Freya Familia was not after Syr at all.

The person they spotted who looked exactly like Syr was actually someone else entirely.

"A fake Syr…?!"

Lyu interjects several times in shock, but she doesn't stop me, listening all the way to the end.

And then I say it.

"Syr's…confession…I turned her down…"

"Wh—"

Lyu freezes as if time stood still for the briefest of seconds.

Even her breathing stops. Without warning, she grabs me by the shoulders.

"Why?!"

My ears ring.

The emotion in her shout is raw. It feels like her voice might break even as it washes over me.

Her voice is louder and more intense than I've ever heard her.

I turn pale in surprise as she continues to press me for an answer.

"Why did you reject her?! What about her feelings?! Her resolve?!"

"Ghh…!"

"You—! You of all people! That shouldn't…!"

"………"

"Then no one can…I can't…"

Lyu gradually loses steam until finally her voice is so weak and fragile, it seems like it might just fade into silence.

The only thing filling her blue eyes is my reflection. It feels like a silent accusation, or maybe it's a cry for help.

Our faces have come so close, our lips could touch if either of us had even the slightest inclination. To the random passerby, we probably look like lovers. Then again, there's a good chance they'd conclude we're a couple who are about to break up.

Her slender fingers are still digging into my shoulders. I grit my teeth, desperately fighting the urge to avert my eyes as I force myself to answer her.

"There's someone I look up to…My eyes have always been on that person…"

"!"

"I want to catch up to her…and when I do, I want to tell her how I feel…That's why…I couldn't accept Syr's feelings."

Even though it's miserably painful, I say what has to be said.

Lyu's grip weakens, and her hands slip from my shoulders in disbelief.

A hollow silence fills the new space that's opened between us.

She starts to say something several times. But every attempt ends with her sputtering as she looks down, the words buried without being spoken.

"...Of course. Why didn't I think of that? Just as Syr had feelings for you, it's only natural that you might fall in love with someone else...That's entirely reasonable, and yet I..."

The words that finally slip from her contain no blame or anger.

If anything, they express understanding and support, reassuring me that I didn't do anything wrong.

Right now, that is the most unbearably painful thing she could've said.

"...My apologies, Bell. I lost control of myself. I did not consider your feelings..."

I can't respond with anything other than silence.

Lyu closes her eyes, furrowing her brow in a pained expression and clenching both hands to her chest, as if trying to hold back a flood of emotions.

Both of us do nothing but stare at the ground. The corridor goes quiet as we stand there alone.

The hands on the clock move ever onward, leaving us behind.

In the end, it's Lyu who breaks the long silence.

"Bell...I'm going to search for Syr."

"Ghh..."

"She should already be at the tavern by now, but she hasn't shown up. Something may have happened...That's why I'm going to find her," Lyu says. "I don't where she lives, and I have no leads."

But even so, her resolve does not waver. She turns just her head to the side, looking up at the sky shrouded in gray clouds, as if searching for the figure of someone precious to her. When Lyu turns back to me, she hesitates for a moment before hoarsely voicing her question.

"...What will you do?"

I know I should think long and hard about my answer.

My next move has to be extremely careful.

If it isn't, I'll just end up hurting her again.

Foolish or not, I scrunch up my face and answer immediately.

"I'll...go, too."

The streets were busy.

Dark clouds insisted on staying in place even after the rain broke, but that didn't deter the bustling crowds determined to enjoy the last day of the festival. The colorful displays of wheat, vegetables, fruits, and everything else that made a harvest festival were still set out all along the main streets for the attendees to enjoy.

"It's already the third day, but it looks like we can finally enjoy ourselves a little," Lilly grumbled as she watched the other festival-goers.

Welf, Mikoto, and Haruhime couldn't help their wry smiles when they considered the complaint.

Hestia Familia had been press-ganged into heavy labor at The Benevolent Mistress until last night. Syr had been off to begin with, so when Ahnya and the others all left, too, *Hestia Familia* had been forced to work two days in a row without rest in order to fill in. After they were finally freed from a job that was more intense than venturing into the Dungeon, their heavy sighs were completely understandable.

Of course, Mia was not a monster who would make them work even on the last day of the festival.

"Ms. Ahnya and the others returned, but...they were all hurt quite badly."

"...Yes. Based on their condition, they probably won't be able to work."

Lilly furrowed her eyebrow at Haruhime's comment.

The official reason they had been allowed to go free was because Ahnya and the others had returned, but the real reason was because Mia decided this was hardly the time to open for business like normal.

"*Freya Familia* were the ones who attacked them. And Mr. Bell was also involved…"

"It seems Lady Syr hasn't returned to the tavern, either. After Lady Lyu visited, Sir Bell went to search for her, too, but…" Mikoto nodded pensively.

They had asked Hestia and Bell what happened yesterday, so they knew the rough outline of events, but neither of them had been especially forthcoming. Bell in particular visibly struggled when he tried to talk about it. It was obvious there was more to the story.

And when Lyu departed with Bell in tow, the familia had shared a troubled glance but said nothing.

"Hey, why don't we look for her, too?"

Welf had been silent until he made this suggestion. All eyes turned to him.

"It's not just Bell; we all owe them. Her and that bar…Besides, there's something bothering me."

Unlike the others, he had an idea why the boy who was like a little brother to him had clammed up. Welf had been the one who told Bell to be a man and make it clear where he stood. Just like Bell, he felt guilty about how things had turned out.

But even more than that, the fact that *Freya Familia* had gotten involved was a major point of concern.

He kept alternating between suspicion and anxiety about Syr's true identity.

"…It's not like we'd be able to simply enjoy the festival by ourselves anyway," Lilly admitted.

"Yes, I agree. My apologies, Lady Haruhime. I know you have been looking forward to it, but…"

"No, this is fine, Lady Mikoto. I can always listen to the festival songs next year."

Lilly and Mikoto nodded, and Haruhime, who had been locked away in the pleasure quarter in past years, smiled as well. They were all in agreement.

"Sorry, you guys...All right, I guess we'll start by asking around a bit."

They fanned out, asking if anyone had seen the girl with blue-gray hair.

"...I don't like these clouds..."

Hestia was walking the streets of Orario alone.

Her followers were all out, so she had asked Takemikazuchi and his familia to house-sit for them. She had asked Miach and Hephaistos to watch things for the first two days, but she still felt bad asking so much after two days straight working at the tavern. Even if Takemikazuchi had been kind enough to laugh it off by saying, "We're not exactly flush enough to go around and enjoy all the treats, so this is perfect for distancing ourselves from temptation."

Hestia's expression remained tense and uneasy, even as her mind meandered through more aimless thoughts.

What Hermes said yesterday...that Syr girl's true identity...

She had pressed him when she first met the girl called Syr. She had asked her fellow Olympian exactly what was that *thing* that mimicked a goddess so closely.

His theory was that it was transformation magic—a secret, mystical art for the sake of becoming one specific goddess. A boundless, unprecedented craving that drove a person to claw their way to divinity without properly ascending.

Hestia still couldn't believe it.

Even if it was theoretically possible within the bounds of magic, and even if the person in question couldn't access arcanum, for any mortal to be able to transform into a deity for any period of time was...

It was something far removed from the rules and logic of the world, something so *irregular* that it made her shudder.

"Then again...*that* isn't the real problem."

Hestia was imagining something terrifying.

It would be better if the Syr that Bell had interacted with all this time had merely been a follower who could transform into a goddess.

But what if it had been the goddess herself who had been interacting with him all this time?

More importantly, what if she had been waiting for something to develop?

What if that goddess of beauty had always been watching Bell since the very beginning?

—"*Watch out, dumbass. You know that woman covered for him, right?*"

Loki had pulled her aside at Denatus.

She had warned her about Freya.

Hestia had been on her guard the whole time, and she had been even more concerned after the incident with *Ishtar Familia*. Still—

"Freya never made a move, so I thought it might just have been my imagination."

The silverback during Monsterphilia. The minotaur that became the impetus for him ranking up. If her suspicion was correct, then a lot of things would make sense.

The goddess of beauty never let her prey escape. Stories of followers stolen away from their patron deities by her whispers of love were too many to count.

At the same time, Freya had been unbelievably passive despite the numerous stories that suggested she would be anything but. To the point that, in all this time, Hestia still wasn't completely sure if she was after Bell or not.

"But if she had always been so close to Bell that she didn't even have to take conspicuous action as a goddess…"

Hermes and the other gods couldn't tell whether Syr was the goddess or a follower. He said that Loki, who had known her the longest, was probably the only one who would notice the subtle differences. For everyone else, there was no way to know the truth without undoing the magic and opening the lid to take a look at the cat inside the box.

Was the Syr there the goddess, or just a follower?

Hestia had taken to the streets in the hopes of answering that very question. She was planning to meet with Hermes to discuss the dilemma in more detail. She planned to talk to Demeter and the other deities who also had encounters with Syr. She would have to wait a day or two for Demeter to become available, given the Goddess Festival, but if worse came to worst, she was willing to owe Loki a favor to get a definitive answer.

"For now, I just have to meet Hermes—"

"Hestia."

Her voice had come on the wind.

The beautiful goddess stood right in front of her, as if to bar the path.

"....................."

Hestia came to a halt.

It was an unnatural action, stopping in her tracks as if her feet had been nailed to the cobblestones.

"...Freya."

Just like during Monsterphilia, the goddess of beauty had thrown a navy-blue robe over her shoulders.

Her vibrant, fair complexion and her gorgeous silver hair were hidden beneath the robe's hood, though Hestia could see a smile on her lips.

And as a fellow deity, her expression and silver eyes hid something Hestia could not discern at a glance. How? Why here of all places?

Was this timing a coincidence? Or—?

A million thoughts raced through Hestia's mind like a firework exploding even as she stood perfectly still.

The droplet rolling down her cheek didn't register. She hadn't even realized she was sweating. Something else was occupying her attention.

Their surroundings were unnaturally quiet and empty.

Even as all parts of the city were bustling with festive excitement, they were completely alone, as if a barrier had been erected around them.

The eyes of the woman who could charm all creation flashed with the vestiges of an alluring silver gleam.

"...Do you have some business with me...?"

Hestia's mouth ran dry even as she asked the question.

Freya responded simply.

"Your child, Bell—will you give him to me?"

"Wh—"

The shock lasted only a moment.

Lit by the dread that her worst fears had come true, Hestia's emotions reignited in the blink of an eye.

"You must be joking! Of course not!"

It was fair to say that the blood had gone to her head. Hestia denied the simple and emotionless demand with a vehemence that bordered on outright denunciation.

Even so, Freya was unperturbed. Her smile never changed.

"You know, Hestia, I like you."

"...?"

While Hestia was still reeling from the unexpected confession, Freya continued speaking candidly.

"I told you so at a Denatus long ago. You might find me difficult to deal with, but I respect you as a goddess. I mean every word. The eternal, sacred flame you preside over is more precious than any gold. You could even call it something I hold in awe...And that's exactly why I would prefer this not get *out of hand*."

She revealed her true nature.

"Ghhh—?!"

Freya was a union of two polar opposites.

This was the divinity of the goddess of love who was also more uninhibited and ruthless than anyone.

"I don't want to become like Apollo.

"That dressed-up clown who tried to erase you from this mortal realm.

"I don't want to become like Ishtar.

"That coarse brute lacking in all character, blindly true to her lust.

"But if you say this cannot be settled peaceably, I have no intention of holding back.

"Because I want that more than anything else."

Her will flowed freely like quicksilver, almost as if she were reciting a poem. The sovereign's eyebrows arched like a bow as she looked Hestia in the eyes, still smiling imperiously even as she threatened her with the point of an arrow that would brook no resistance.

Badump.

Hestia's breast trembled, her heart raising a clamor she could not subdue.

A beautiful, yet ruthless smile.

This was her final warning.

A merciful concession that was also an unreasonable royal decree, handed down from on high by the goddess who was fairer and wealthier than anyone in the mortal realm, she who led the strongest familia.

Their deserted corner of the neighborhood was silent. They kept their distance as they stared at each other, the invisible force of Freya's divine will silently encroaching on Hestia all the while.

"So Hestia, may I have Bell?"

Her final warning was delivered with a smile. As for Hestia's answer…

"I refuse."

…she had decided from the start.

"No matter what?"

"No matter what."

"Really?"

"Yes, really!"

Hestia's eyes flared as she struck Freya with the only answer possible.

"Bell is my follower! My precious child! I won't give him to the likes of you or anyone else for that matter!"

Hestia's regal wrath was the most intense emotion she bore. This was the strongest manifestation of her possessiveness, and her greatest show of affection.

The goddess of the sacred flame could say with confidence that the love she had for her boy was second to none. It could not be matched in the mortal realm, the heavens, or the Dungeon.

Hestia's divine will rebuffed Freya's.

"—I see. Then let come what may."

All emotion left Freya's expression.

She did not seem to be annoyed or concerned that they were so diametrically opposed. Raising a single hand, she simply exuded a general sense of regret that it had come to this—as if she had known this was how events would play out from the start.

She snapped her slender, unblemished fingers.

The sharp sound rang loudly in the empty street.

What it summoned was a thunderclap.

"?!"

There was a flash of lightning, not from overhead, but from the ground.

At the goddess's signal, a flare streaked across the sky of Orario.

A certain white elf had just sent out a command to the strongest einherjar lurking all around the city.

As Hestia peered up at the sky, Freya's compassion dissolved.

"Then I'll take him by force."

The assault was swift and merciless.

A single blow.

After leaping down from the roof, the attacker struck home with a war hammer before anyone could even detect the explosive attack.

"Gaaaaaah?!"

Unarmored and not knowing what had hit her, Mikoto felt her bones shatter. She coughed up blood as she was sent flying into the wall of a shop.

"....Huh?"

The attack had taken but an instant.

Lilly and Welf barely registered what had happened, and even Haruhime didn't have time to react even though she had been standing directly beside Mikoto.

The throng of bystanders froze in place as the four assailants who had surrounded the members of *Hestia Familia* each let fly with their weapons.

A spear, a war hammer, a battle-ax, and a greatsword.

Wearing sand-colored helmets and armor, the four identical prum warriors delivered their callous pronouncement.

"The goddess has issued her order."

""""Now die.""""

After the eldest Alfrik spoke, the three younger brothers meted out the sentence.

The crowd erupted in panic.

"—Mikoto?!"

Haruhime finally broke out of her stupor as high-pitched screams went up while everyone in the vicinity began to flee the scene. She tried to run over to her childhood friend, who had collapsed after crashing through a nearby wall, but she couldn't reach her.

A mass of metal closed in on her.

The same hammer that had struck Mikoto was threatening to crush her.

"Not on my watch!"

"...! Aisha?!"

What stopped it at the last second was the blade of an Amazon.

Hitting the hammer from the side, Aisha had managed to save Haruhime, but she cursed upon the realization that the force of the parried blow had been enough to leave her hands numb.

"M-Ms. Aisha?! And *Hermes Familia*…?! What's going on?!"

"That's what we wanna know! Why is *Freya Familia* attacking you guys?!"

Lilly shouted, finally returning to her senses after being unable to move a single step while the surprise attack unfolded.

In addition to Aisha and the Gulliver brothers, a war tiger, elf, and chienthrope had also appeared from out of nowhere.

"I thought it was odd that he told us to keep an eye out, but…!"

Hermes Familia had been watching *Hestia Familia*. Or more precisely, they had been surveilling *Freya Familia*.

All of it had been on Hermes's instructions.

After the attack on the second day of the festival and the incident that had transpired between Bell and Syr, he had sensed something disquieting, and ordered his familia to investigate *Freya Familia*'s movements.

This was the result of their careful surveillance.

"Hey, Aisha! Lord Hermes said not to get involved no matter what…!"

"I joined your familia to protect my little sister! I've been used in all sorts of ways until today, so now it's time to pay up, Falgar!"

"…Damn it, fine!"

The war tiger tried to rein in Aisha, but when she pressed him on that point, he drew his sword and braced himself.

Or more accurately, he was in the process of drawing his sword.

Because at that precise moment, four pairs of prum eyes turned to *Hermes Familia* and concluded they were a hindrance.

""""Destroy them all.""""

In the blink of an eye, what unfolded was not so much a fight as it was a purge.

"Wh-?!"

"Ghhhh!"

"Ugh, aaaaaaaaagh?!"

The spear repelled every incoming attack as the ax mowed down the war tiger. The greatsword sliced into both the elf and the chienthrope while the hammer closed in on Aisha.

It was an intense exchange that did not allow the Level 2s of *Hestia Familia* any opening to respond.

They're too fast. This shouldn't be possible.

Welf and Haruhime didn't even have a chance to react. Meanwhile, Lilly was consumed by a penetrating terror.

As the one who had chosen the role of commander, she was the only one present who understood how abnormal this scene really was.

The level of teamwork on display was extraordinary.

They didn't speak or even look at each other, and yet there was somehow a mutual understanding driving their movements. It seemed impossible. To be able to move as one without any wasted time or actions, as if they were clones sharing the same brain.

As Lilly reeled from Bringar's limitless coordination, *Hermes Familia*'s second-tier adventurers went down one after the other.

"Monsters!"

Aisha had narrowly avoided instantaneous defeat as she hurled the insult while standing protectively in front of Haruhime.

Counterattacking was out of the question. It was just a matter of time until they were all wiped out.

The fight had not even lasted a minute, but Aisha could already see how it would end.

I have to at least make sure Haruhime gets away!

Just as she was thinking that…

""Were you trying to protect this renart?""

The sound of something crumpling came from right behind her.

Aisha caught her breath as she spun around.

""Because you didn't, idiot.""

Standing there were two prums, one wielding an ax and the other a greatsword.

And lying at their feet was the renart girl.

Her beautiful golden hair and back had been slashed. Blood was already pooling around her.

It had been just a split second.

The two of them had disappeared for just an instant. That was all.

The prum wielding a spear and the one with the hammer had misdirected her, drawing away her attention.

In that momentary opening, the other two had slipped past her and cut down the girl so precious to Aisha.

The Amazon froze as she noticed the sadistic sneers of the two prums.

Haruhime's lips were stained with blood, and her eyes were unfocused as she reached toward the Amazon.

"Ai…sha…"

The next instant, there was a crumpling sound as a small foot landed on the back of her head.

Exchanging a cold kiss with the pavement, Haruhime stopped moving.

"——Arrrrrrrrrrghhhhhhhh!"

Aisha lost all self-control.

All she could see was red as her eyes flared in rage. An inhuman growl emitted from deep within her throat.

And then she and all her rage were summarily cut down.

"——"

The greatsword parried the full swing of her blade right as the great ax instantly flashed.

Before she could say anything, Aisha was mercilessly put down just like the renart girl in a spray of blood.

"Ghhh…! Run, Li'l E!"

It was incomprehensible violence and mayhem.

Failing to fully understand what was going on, Welf burned with rage at the sight of his comrades being laid low. In order to give the prum girl a chance to escape, he chose a reckless path.

Drawing the sword from his back, he got ready to dash forward.

"—gh?"

The wind blew.

There was no other way to describe it.

A wind pressure born out of nothing brushed Welf's cheek, guiding his gaze to the side.

"You...You were there that time with *Ishtar Familia*?!"

"........."

A cat person with a silver spear stood there silently.

The first-tier adventurer who had berated Welf while demonstrating an unmatchable strength during the conflict with *Ishtar Familia*. This was the blacksmith's nemesis who had insulted him.

Allen Fromel—Vana Freya.

"What, you're going to do me in yourself...?!"

Welf immediately readied his sword.

Allen only responded with a condescending glare.

"Fool. It's already over."

His voice betrayed his utter disdain, as if this exercise was just a waste of his time.

"——"

Speechless, Welf suddenly realized something.

The sword that he was holding had already slipped from his hands. Then, as if his body suddenly started remembering what had happened, his side started to feel hot. Blood was pouring out of the gash left by a spearpoint.

All the strength drained from Welf's limbs as he realized that the decisive blow had already landed.

"...You can't be serious..."

He trembled, furious over his inability to do anything in the face of an overwhelming enemy. As those complicated feelings seeped into his voice, Welf collapsed in the puddle of blood pouring from the wound.

"Ms. Mikoto...Ms. Haruhime...Ms. Aisha...Mr. Welf..."

As the last one standing, Lilly shivered, pale as a ghost.

Their destruction had been instantaneous and incredibly thorough. A total massacre.

She hadn't even been given a chance to support them. It had happened so fast, there wasn't any time to give directions.

She was left isolated and alone in the blink of an eye as *Hermes Familia* were cleaned up before Welf and the others were also dispatched. The bystanders were more concerned with running as fast as their legs could carry them from the scene of a war between familias.

"You're the last."

"—?!"

Hearing the voice from right behind her, Lilly moved as if her body had been hurled away. She reached for the weapon at her waist, drawing the magic knife that Welf had made for her. She held it at the ready in a reverse grip, wielding it just like Bell.

It was without doubt the fastest she had ever moved in her fifteen years of life.

Having watched Bell fight for so long, from closer than anyone else, she had learned from his movements. Hers was a reflexive and desperate strike.

And that singular blow was easily—almost laughably—halted by the prum warrior, who raised just one hand.

"Good response. Good reflexes, too. I guess the report from the Guild about you reaching Level Two was true."

Unlike his brutal and merciless younger brothers, Alfrik spoke calmly while holding her arm in place. No one would guess he had just been attacked.

He stopped it! Wait, I can still—!

It was a magic blade. The trump card for powerless people.

The range was point-blank. She would get caught up in it, too, if she fired, but who cared?

They would both get blown away, and she could use the aftermath to get away—

"I'm nothing like that awful Braver, but I'm glad to see fellow prums like you appear. Truly, I am."

But it was impossible for Lilly.

Her hand and the blade of the knife were pointing limply in another direction entirely.

The slender arm that was being gripped suddenly creaked like a glacier on the verge of collapse, and then *snap*.

"Ughaaaaaaaaaaaaaaaaaaaaaaaaaghhhhhhhhhh!"

Tears filled the prum girl's bloodshot chestnut eyes as she let out a piercing shriek.

"You were just hopelessly unlucky."

That was the last thing she heard.

After she slammed into the ground with incomprehensible force, her consciousness faded to black.

"Ngh!"

At that moment, Aiz was sprinting across the rooftops.

While *Hestia Familia* was being devastated by *Freya Familia*, she raced through the streets as if something was driving her ever forward.

"Wait up, Aiz!"

"Calm down!"

Tiona and Tione had been wandering around town with her until she suddenly took off. Now they were frantically chasing after their friend, helpless to stop her.

Having been caught up in the scuffle with *Freya Familia* yesterday, she had felt an unease that was similar to what Hermes experienced. It was a vague foreboding, and Aiz found it beyond difficult to put it into words when she struggled to express herself under regular circumstances.

But even if she could not explain in great detail, she was sure that she was worried about Bell, the rain-drenched boy who had rejected her hand last night. In that moment, she couldn't help but think he looked like a poor, beleaguered rabbit. She couldn't just leave him be after seeing him like that and had gone out the following morning to look for him.

That was when she heard the worst possible news. By the time she was rushing toward the source of the commotion, she no longer needed a reason to go.

"Halt."

"?!"

However, her sprint was cut off by a single black blade.

"You're…Dáinsleif?!"

"Perhaps our blades are fated to clash and let sparks fly. It has been but a single day since our last parting, O daughter of the sword."

Their blades met with a shrill clamor.

Though she had managed to draw her sword instantly and parry the powerful attack that hurtled down at her from above, Aiz was dumbstruck.

The one who had leaped to the rooftop and was now barring her way was a dark elf—Hegni Ragnar.

By chance, this was the same opponent she had crossed blades with just a day earlier in order to protect Bell.

"Vexatious golden-eyed girl, begone and trouble us not."

"Ghh…why are you attacking Bell and his friends?!"

"I bade you to not intercede on his behalf. Do not make me repeat myself. The fruit of foolish knowledge will bring naught but destruction."

The dark elf was unmoved, even when the Sword Princess raised her voice.

Hegni's stance left no openings, as if he had already activated his magic. It was painfully obvious that approaching him carelessly would result in being cut down.

"*Freya Familia!* So it's true that Argonaut and his familia are being attacked?!" Tiona exclaimed. Her sister was just as taken aback.

"Whoa now, what's going on here…!"

As Tiona and Tione caught up, Aiz prepared to force her way through with their help. Her eyebrows furrowed just as another voice called out.

"You should stop. I'm sure you don't want to start a war between our familias."

"…! Hildsleif!"

Three bolts of lightning slammed into the roof at their feet. Turning around, they found the white elf Hedin standing there.

Everyone present was a Level 6 first-tier adventurer. That meant it was three against two. But unlike Aiz, who had brought her sword to protect herself, Tiona and Tione didn't have their weapons. To make matters worse, they were surrounded. It was fair to say that the numerical advantage had been nullified.

More importantly, Hedin was clearly implying that if they interfered, *Freya Familia* would not hesitate to declare all-out war on *Loki Familia*.

That was how determined they were to stop Aiz and the Amazon sisters.

The five of them stared at one another without letting their guards down, leaving them in a deadlock.

"...Forget a war or whatever else—how are you going to justify this? The Guild is going to give you more than a slap on the wrist for causing so much trouble during the Goddess Festival."

Tione responded with a well-reasoned but provocative question.

Freya Familia was brazenly attacking another familia in broad daylight during the Goddess Festival that directly followed the Elegia holiday. They would no doubt earn the disapproval of not only the city's residents but also every other faction and familia in Orario.

"It matters not."

"Wha..."

Hegni seemed completely unfazed by this line of questioning.

His gaze was sharp as he glared at the shocked members of *Loki Familia*.

"We will accept whatever judgment and punishment that might be meted out. Similarly, we will abide whatever vilification and slander that will come our way. The one to whom we have sworn ourselves wishes for this to happen. We are but servants for realizing her divine will."

For Hegni, all this was just another exercise in absolute loyalty to his deity.

Hedin said nothing and simply closed his eyes, erasing all traces of emotion from his expression.

The dark elf swordsman had one last thing to say.

"If the goddess so desires it, then even meaning itself shall be erased."

Ultimately, the merciless and instantaneous assault was unstoppable.

No matter how much Lilly and the others resisted, no matter how much support Aiz and the Amazons offered—it would've all been meaningless.

Everything had already been decided the moment *he* appeared.

"Eh?"

He was a boulder.

An enormous, immovable warrior stood before Bell.

The man was so tall that one could not help but look up to him. So large that he might be mistaken for a monster.

The limbs that extended from his massive body were pure muscle—larger, harder, and stronger than any other. His very presence was fearsome, implacable, and intense without compare.

That mass of terrifying strength was the manifestation of the ultimate warrior. It was proof that he was still striving for ever greater heights with a tireless will.

The rabbit trembled.

Even without words, he already understood that the beast before him was a champion who had even slain a dragon.

The one who stood at the peak of strength quietly looked at Bell and Bell alone with his rust-colored eyes that matched his hair.

"Warlord…?"

Bell had forgotten to breathe after a single look. Lyu couldn't hide her own panic, but she at least managed to speak the boaz's title.

Out of the innumerable streets in the city, in the middle of a crowd that was unaware of the disturbance brewing, Ottar had known exactly where to find them.

"Surrender."

He had only one demand.

"By my goddess's divine will, you will be hers. Your fate has already been decided." His tone brooked no objections, but this was the one and only mercy that he granted. His disturbingly quiet explanation and the unspoken warning removed all room to argue.

He was an inescapable force.

"If you do not obey, I will crush you."

There was a sudden tingle. Bell and Lyu both got goose bumps as the city's strongest adventurer stepped forward.

"—Run, Bell!!!"

It was a command that almost came out as a scream.

Bell felt his shoulder being pushed away.

She drew her dual blades.

The elf had lost all trace of calm as she immediately prepared to fight. It had been an instantaneous reaction.

But it was still not fast enough.

Acknowledging that negotiations had broken down, Ottar moved.

"——"

Time froze for the elf.

She lost track of Ottar.

He had disappeared.

No, that wasn't the reason why.

Lyu had been blown away.

It had been just a single step.

But he had moved farther and faster than anyone else could have. All he did was step forward. That was all it took to erase the distance between them and completely elude Lyu's senses. Then Ottar had swung his right arm.

He had brushed her aside.

Nothing more.

The moment she failed to avoid his massive limb that seemed more tree trunk than arm, Lyu lost the right to remain in the fight.

"—Guhah?!"

After realizing what had happened as her life flashed before her eyes, she shouted and coughed up blood at the shock of the blow that was only now beginning to register. She could confidently say it was without doubt the strongest attack she had ever experienced.

The blow sent her flying into a building, shattering the stone wall.

"Lyu?!"

A thunderous boom rang out. The very ground trembled as a cloud of dust went up.

Bell's shout joined the alarmed screams of the nearby pedestrians.

People turned pale and scattered in all directions as Bell attempted to go to Lyu. He tried to race over to the elf, who lay far too still in the cloud of debris.

However, he didn't get a chance to move.

"——"

A sudden chill shot through him as his instincts cried out in warning.

It had been only an instant. Pulling his attention away from Lyu, Bell heeded the voice in the back of his mind and turned back.

A fist filled his field of view.

He could see the creases between the fingers. Beyond that, the cool eyes of the boaz.

The price for looking away from the most dangerous being alive was death.

"—Ghhhhhh?!"

His face slammed into the ground with tremendous force. The stone pavement shattered as cracks shot through the ground, sending fragments flying.

The devastating impact tore Bell's consciousness away from him, leaving his body on the ground.

"...?!"

Asfi was speechless.

She had been keeping an eye on *Freya Familia* on Hermes's orders, just like Aisha and the rest of their familia, but she didn't have enough time to intervene even if she wanted to.

It was an attack that was over just that quickly.

"Leon...Bell Cranell..."

Lyu had been taken out in an instant, and Bell had been defeated in a single strike, too.

Two Level 4 adventurers had been downed in the blink of an eye.

She should have already known what it meant to stand before the strongest warrior, but seeing that wild power in the flesh, Asfi could do nothing other than stand by and watch.

"........."

Ottar silently threw the unconscious Bell over his right shoulder. Lyu was naturally in no position to object. Ignoring Asfi standing in the middle of the street like a statue, he calmly walked past. Her face deathly pale, Asfi could neither stand in his way nor say anything to halt him.

"Wh-what?!"

There were two of them.

Hestia experienced whiplash as she suddenly looked up. Two thunderous noises could be heard across the entire city, clearly not a part of the regular festivities. One came from the south and the other from the southwest.

The growing commotion was filled with unease and terror.

"My children attacked yours."

"Wh...?!"

Don't screw with me!

What do you mean?!

But the furious questions Hestia was about to ask were stopped by Freya's next words.

"And it's already over."

As soon as she delivered that pronouncement in a cool and composed tone, the two uproars suddenly fell silent like a quietly receding wave. As if announcing the end of hostilities.

Hestia froze.

More than anything, she wanted to deny those words.

"Y-you're lying…That can't be…!"

"It's true. Look, here they come."

Freya would not allow her to avert her eyes from the reality of the situation.

Four shadows raced toward Hestia at high speed.

"————?!"

They landed directly next to her with a tremendous crash, forcing Hestia to cover her face with her arms. After the spray of shattered rock and dust subsided, she slowly opened her eyes. Her breath caught in her throat.

A greatsword.

A katana.

A magic knife.

A fan.

They were without a doubt the weapons of her followers, now returned to their mortified patron goddess.

"Those are…Welf's…?!"

Welf's sword, Mikoto's katana, Lilly's magic knife, and Haruhime's fan.

They were sticking out of the ground, like headstones marking graves.

The broken weapons were more than enough to imply their owners' fates, and Hestia was speechless as she looked up. Far in the distance, she could just barely see four identical prums standing on a rooftop alongside a cat person who hefted a silver spear—the attackers who must have been the ones who threw the weapons down.

She could not see Welf or Mikoto or Lilly or Haruhime.

"…Th…This isn't…"

No matter how she might try to deny it, the cold, hard truth was unavoidable.

It was a far cry from the war with *Apollo Familia*. This was complete and utter domination.

An insurmountable difference in strength separated their factions.

The weak had no way to refute this absurd level of strength that went beyond all reason.

Hestia could do nothing but stand helpless in the face of it.

And then she saw him.

"—Bell?!"

The final blow.

An enormous boaz appeared from out of nowhere and dropped the white-haired boy in the middle of the weapons sticking out of the ground. He was unconscious and didn't so much as twitch. His clothes had been torn, and all that covered his upper body was what little remained of his sleeves. His eyes were hidden by his hair, and a dark silence clung to him.

Hestia started to run forward.

But just as she drew close to him, the boaz blocked her with his sword.

"Ghh…?!"

"No, no, Hestia. You can't just touch him as you please anymore."

The brusque warrior held his massive sword in one hand, drawing a boundary Hestia couldn't cross. She immediately came to a halt as the mass of metal physically separated her and Bell. Meanwhile Freya calmly walked over to the boy.

She stood where Hestia should've been.

"Freyaaaaa!!!"

"I didn't know you could make a face like that. But I told you I'd be taking him by force, didn't I?"

Hestia's blue eyes contained a blazing inferno, revealing the full extent of her rage.

Freya remained expressionless, unconcerned.

"Playtime is over. Syr's time is done."

"…Then the girl at the tavern really was you! Hah! What a joke! Bell rejected you so now you're just doing this in an act of desperation! Some goddess of love you are!"

Judging from how Bell had been acting the night before, Hestia could guess what had transpired while he was with Syr.

Everything she said was an attempt to provoke Freya.

Of course, that was largely the only thing she *could* do.

It was an expression of absolute disdain that was both a venting of emotion that had no other outlet and the bitter pill of a defeat that she could not bear to swallow. That demonstrated how decisively the struggle had already been settled.

But Freya remained expressionless through it all.

"That's right. I couldn't get what I want as Syr. That's why I decided I don't care what methods I have to use anymore."

Her peerlessly beautiful face did not waver in the slightest as she spoke with utter calm. She reached out with one hand and grabbed Hestia by the hair.

"Ugh—?!"

"I *will* make Bell mine. *No matter what it takes.*"

Ottar stepped back, withdrawing his sword as Freya violently dragged Hestia toward her.

It was an act of tyranny.

In terms of physical size, this was like a grown woman seizing hold of a child. Hestia could not resist her. She could almost feel the icy emotion seeping out of the fingers gripping her hair as she winced in pain. And then Freya peered into her eyes from so close that they could feel each other's breath.

"Break your bond with Bell, Hestia."

"...?"

"I'm telling you to complete the preparations for his conversion."

For a brief moment, Hestia couldn't understand what Freya was saying, but realization dawned on her. Bell's status was manifesting on his back as he lay in a heap on the ground next to Freya. They must have used a Status Thief or something of the like. The lock that Hestia had placed on it was gone.

"I will add Bell to my familia."

Hestia glared back at the silver eyes staring her down.

"Do you really think I would do that?!"

"Fine, then I'll kill your children."

A deathly chill coursed through Hestia's body at that casual pronouncement.

"I will send them to the heavens one by one every time you reject my request."

"No…!"

"You should be able to tell when the number of blessings decreases, right?"

Freya's expression remained unchanged as Hestia's eyes widened.

It was quite clear that she was fully prepared to make good on her ironclad word. This was her unshakable divine will.

"If you insist on refusing even then…if you tediously prattle on about waiting for their souls to be reborn…then while I would prefer not to, I will send you back as well. No matter how much you fume or struggle, in the end, Bell will still become mine." With the expression of a deity who had discarded all traces of humanity, Freya simply stated, "This is my final offer. One last show of kindness and compromise."

She asserted it with a voice as cold as the freezing wind on a dark winter's day.

"……?!"

She was serious.

Dead serious.

There was no room to doubt the goddess's resolve. If she resisted, Freya would immediately give the order to slay the members of Hestia's familia. She had said that she wouldn't hesitate to use whatever means necessary and she meant every word.

"All paths lead to the same result. So make the smart choice, Hestia."

Snap.

A crack ran down the sword sticking out of the grave of weapons.

Hestia began to hyperventilate.

Her breathing came in gasps as the weight of the choice bore down upon her, and an unconcealable sheen of sweat had appeared.

How can I choose?

I don't want to make that choice.

How can I weigh my children in the balance?!

I don't want to give my Bell to anyone!

But, but, but, but if I don't, the entire familia will—

Her throat ran dry and she could feel herself on the verge of slumping over.

But Freya would not allow even that. She pulled Hestia's hair, forcing their eyes to lock.

"Now, make your choice. Bell? Or your familia?"

The empress had made her pronouncement: an either-or choice that could not be put off any further.

Hestia's eyes wavered with humiliation, rage, fear, and sadness.

Either judging the silence as rebellion or else to make an example, Freya's gaze went cool as she prepared to give the order.

"—Every time I see something like this, I'm reminded yet again of just how terrifying a struggle between goddesses can truly be."

Suddenly, the voice of a frivolous man called out in an aloof, easygoing tone. Of course, even he couldn't hide the tension permeating everything and everyone.

"...H-Hermes...?"

"Hey, Hestia. Sorry for being late to our meeting."

Hermes smiled like always at Hestia's dumbfounded response.

Though he called it being late, he no doubt had his hands full. After realizing Hestia had not shown up at the appointed place and examining what little information he had, Hermes found their current location by analyzing the screams and thunderous crashes echoing throughout the city.

"I'm sure the circumstances must be quite extraordinary, but could you perhaps let her go for now, Freya? Such violence could become a stain on your character, and I would be sad to see it come to that."

"........."

After a quick glance around, Hermes immediately turned his attention to Freya.

He scrutinized the weapons sticking out of the ground like gravestones, Bell collapsed on the ground, the boaz calmly standing by, and then Freya and Hestia themselves. Grasping the situation, he instantly discerned who currently held the reins, and he maneuvered to take the role of mediator.

"Hermes. If you get in my way, I will crush you, too."

But Freya would not allow it.

While she did as he'd asked and let go of Hestia's hair, the intensity of her divine will did not abate. The empress was not about to take no for an answer.

Beneath the hood cloaking her beautiful face, her silver eyes flashed with a penetratingly cold light that the other gods had never seen before.

Hermes maintained his easy smile, but sweat already coated the back of his neck.

As Hestia stumbled back slightly, he stood between the two goddesses, forming a triangle of deities as Ottar watched on in silence.

"I have no need for intervention or mediation. If you try to muddy things or stir up trouble, then I'll send you back to the heavens first."

"...Judging from the look of things, it appears that you have finally decided to take in Bell. Would you say that's a fair assessment?"

"Yes. You should be able to understand that there is no more stopping me now."

She would not allow the matter to be put off and decided later at a Denatus, nor would she allow Bell or *Hestia Familia* to escape to the Guild.

It was clear from the look in Freya's eyes that those options were not on the table. This was an outrageous overstepping of bounds that would normally provoke a reaction from various authorities, but because the perpetrator was Freya, it would be overlooked. And that was because she controlled *Freya Familia*.

At the very least, there was no one present who had the ability to stop her.

Understanding the reality of the situation, Hermes shrugged.

"I know that I can't stop you. Take Bell if you want."

"Ghh...! Hermes!"

Naturally, Hestia raised her voice at his apparent surrender, but he was not done speaking yet.

"However, could you not wait just a little longer to add Bell to your familia...to perform the conversion?"

"What?"

"Whoa, no need for the scary look, Freya. I heard your warning before. I'm not trying to pull anything." Hermes raised his hands in jest and broke into a smile. One that didn't reach his orange eyes. "It's just that, it has only been *half a year* since Bell joined Hestia's familia."

"!"

"At least one year's membership is required before a child can convert to another familia. Isn't that one of the rules all of us set for playing in the mortal realm?"

"........"

"It's different if their previous familia has been dissolved, but you didn't want to kill Hestia if possible, right? Settling things peaceably is ideal."

For the first time, Freya fell silent.

Hermes was eloquently laying out a concise and careful logical argument even as he made an emotional appeal. As a mediator, he was merely explaining the most efficient and reasonable course of action that should be taken when considering the regulations and unwritten rules that had been established long ago.

He was in control now.

Using his silver tongue, he twisted reality and truth to negotiate an extension without telling a single lie.

"You can take Bell with you. It could even be treated as some sort of trial membership. The arrangement would be exceptional, but I can convince the Guild."

"Wh...?! Wait a second, Hermes! That's—gh!"

"Come now, Hestia. Just accept that you lost already. You're an old friend, so I'm trying to get you a little point of compromise, for old times' sake."

Hermes held a finger out as she started trying to argue with him. As his finger pressed against the tip of her nose, she realized what he was doing. He had an insincere smile on his lips, but his eyes were earnest and serious. He really was trying to help her.

Hermes, the god of schemes, was not someone who could be trusted without reserve.

But in that moment, there was nothing that she could do with her own power, so she had no choice but to put her faith in him.

"Grr...!"

Of course, rational thought and emotion often pull in two different directions. However, for the sake of the rest of the familia, Hestia looked down, gritted her teeth, and balled her trembling hands into fists.

Her silence was tacit acceptance of the bridge that Hermes was offering.

"...Very well. It's true that I do not wish for any unnecessary casualties. I'll go along with your little scheme, Hermes."

"Ahhh, you have my thanks, Freya. Truly you are a merciful goddess of love."

After a brief moment of deliberation, Freya made her decision without batting an eyelash.

Ignoring Hermes's ingratiating flattery, she called, "Ottar," and had the boaz retainer, who had been watching in silence, gather up Bell as she turned her back on Hestia and Hermes.

"Bell...!"

"Just bear it for now, Hestia."

Hestia edged forward as she watched Freya and Ottar whisk the boy away, but Hermes grabbed her shoulder.

"If you go against Freya here, nothing but death awaits you. But with half a year's time, you'll have a chance to prepare a plan."

"A plan...?"

"Yes. The Guild, other familias, the entire world—use anything and everything. Gather all the allies you can and steal Bell away from Freya. She is the unrivaled queen, but all the more reason to try. She has more than a few enemies."

There was no cause that would justify the tyrannical attack that Freya had perpetrated.

She had stolen Bell away by force without any concern whatsoever for the disapproval or consequences it might invite. If nothing else, most people would almost certainly sympathize with Hestia. If the victim had been a group like the Evils, then it would have been considered just barely acceptable—and in fact, there was precedent for Freya crushing an unsavory organization solely for the sake of stealing away a child she had taken an interest in—but *Hestia Familia*'s cause was undoubtedly just.

And more than anything else, the impetus was Bell Cranell, the super rookie who endlessly excited Orario.

It was not just the people of the city; other adventurers and deities would surely protest him being forced to undergo a conversion against his will.

What would happen if Hermes lit a spark near that highly flammable mixture? Considering the recent dissolution of *Ishtar Familia*, if Freya were allowed to rampage even further without restraint, it would become impossible to stop her—and if the Guild could be convinced of that, even they would be forced to take action.

"And you have far, far more allies than you realize. If this goes unpunished, then at the very least, Hephaistos and those close to you will be outraged and oppose Freya."

Hephaistos would rouse her familia and confront *Freya Familia*. It was easy enough to imagine her old friend who so despised treachery making a stand.

And weak or not, both Takemikazuchi and Miach would answer the call.

"And once they join the fray, that will set everything in motion."

Taken to the extreme, if they could get the support of *Loki Familia*, then in the worst case, it would even be possible to fight a war on relatively even terms. At the very least, with time, it would be possible to come up with some sort of strategy to take back Bell.

That was what Hermes so desperately wanted Hestia to see.

"...Why, Hermes? Why would you go so far as to make an enemy of Freya for our sake...?"

"I don't suppose you would accept 'in order to repay you for all the trouble I caused during the Xenos incident and elsewhere' as an answer?"

Hestia couldn't help but feel incredulous upon hearing that explanation. She didn't believe for an instant that Hermes, the epitome of neutrality, would choose to risk Freya's displeasure merely for the sake of an old friend.

"There's no way you're that nice a guy," Hestia responded.

Hermes played with his winged cap for a few moments before breaking into a wry smile.

"Somewhere along the way, I...started to think that it would be best for Bell to stay with you. For his sake as well." When he saw Hestia's eyes growing wide, Hermes quickly added, "Really, though, I can't explain it," which made Hestia settle back into a grimace.

He pulled the brim of his hat down, covering his eyes, and when he looked up again, his expression was completely serious.

"That's why, this time, I'm taking your side. Even if it means making an enemy of Freya, I—"

Right as the self-proclaimed patron god of merchants was about to swear a contract, Freya stopped in the distance.

"I forgot to mention one thing."

Hestia and Hermes suddenly turned her way as tension filled the air.

They had kept their voices down. She shouldn't have been able to hear them. But the beautiful goddess stood there at her leisure, as if she saw through everything.

"I shall insist on some sort of collateral to guarantee the conversion will be carried out in half a year's time."

"C-collateral...?"

"Yes. In order to make Bell mine—*I will twist everything else first.*"

Those words.

Hermes froze, too, as Hestia grew flustered.

"Be sure to keep your promise, Hestia."

It was as if there were no one else in her eyes besides Hestia.

Turning just her head, she speared the goddess of the hearth with her gaze before disappearing from view together with Ottar and Bell.

"Is she—"

The mediator gazed in shock and shuddered.

In that moment, Freya had exceeded what even Hermes had foreseen.

The ashen sky groaned as if it moved with great effort.

A bell tolled, signaling the tremendous change that was sweeping the city.

The situation was shifting at a dizzying rate.

"Goddess Freya! What was that uproar earlier about?!" the Guild head, Royman Mardeel, demanded.

Despite being an elf, his girth was so prominent that it earned him the moniker the Guild's Pig, and his rotund belly jiggled as he ran over to the goddess he had just spotted.

"Reports of your followers rampaging in combat gear have already been confirmed! To provoke something like a conflict between familias during the Goddess Festival! Even for someone such as you who has contributed so much to the development of Orario, we cannot just—!"

City's greatest familia or not, the Guild had little choice but to impose a penalty for such brazen offenses.

Royman exercised every fiber of his being when managing Orario, and he was already intimating a punishment of some sorts when—

"Be quiet, Royman."

"Huh?"

—Freya brushed him off.

Royman and the other employees of the Guild were stunned as the goddess, who had been headed toward the center of the city, suddenly stopped.

"*More importantly*, gather everyone at Central Park for me."

For a split second, her silver eyes gleamed bewitchingly.

It was already too late by the time Royman realized she was charming them.

The people around him trembled unnaturally, slipping into a trancelike ecstasy as if their souls had slipped their mortal coils.

"Children, deities, whoever. Bring as many people as possible. Also, arrange it so that my voice can reach every corner of the city."

""""Yes, Milady...""""

Male and female alike, they scattered to fulfill the wish of the goddess of beauty.

The only ones remaining were Freya and Royman, who had fallen to his knees on the ground before her.

"Ghhhh...?!"

"Distracting yourself from the compulsion with pain...Despite your unsightly appearance, you really are quite remarkable, Royman."

It had been a split-second decision.

Royman had clenched his stomach tightly, pulling fierce enough to tear away the flab from his body. His eyes were wild and bloodshot, but he had managed to resist Freya's beauty.

At the same time, that was all he had accomplished.

Roymnan was alone, groaning like a stuck beast as the cloaked goddess peered down at him.

"God...dess Freya...! Why...are you...?!"

The alluring silver gleam that neither reason nor instinct could resist was gradually consuming him.

What little consciousness he retained was slowly falling away, as the goddess answered his question with callous eyes.

"Same reason as always. Just another goddess's whim. However..." Her full lips quivered. "...This is the one thing I want most; the one thing I have been restraining myself with all this time. I simply decided to stop holding back any longer. That's all."

Yes.

Freya had always been restraining herself.

From the moment she had met Bell—Monsterphilia, the grimoire, the duel with the minotaur, his resolution in the face of death in the middle levels, the war game—she had borne witness to his growth but never intervened. Even during the conflict with *Ishtar Familia* and the Xenos incident, she had not made direct contact with him.

Throughout it all, she had always resisted and endured, refraining from stealing him away.

But now there was no need to deny herself.

She would make him hers by whatever means necessary now that Syr, the chain that had held Freya back, no longer existed.

"Ghh…?!"

When he looked up at the eyes of the goddess peering down on him, Royman finally understood.

Her invasion had already begun.

What remained of his consciousness had managed to grasp the truth. As someone who correctly understood what it meant for Freya to take direct action, Royman groaned, dizzy and afraid.

"I won't hold back anymore."

"Hestia, let out every last drop of divinity you can muster!"

A rending shout rang out.

The one who had cast aside all composure was not some resident of the city or random adventurer—it was Hermes.

"Everything you've got, all the way to the limit! If you don't, she'll even break through your domain!"

"Wh-what are you saying, Hermes…? Weren't you saying we have to make a plan…?!"

Hestia was utterly confused by Hermes's ominous expression. She had never seen such unease etched on his face as he shook his head and grabbed her by the shoulders.

"We're way past that now! It's meaningless!"

"Gh?!"

"I misjudged her! What an error, too! Her tenacity, her obsession with Bell! I've misjudged it ever since the time with Ishtar!"

It was quickly becoming apparent that the emotion swirling deep in Freya's heart was not jealousy or anger.

"For the sake of her one and only Odr, she'll discard her pride, public opinion, even the rules that she set for herself. Freya is ready to commit a transgression against the entire mortal realm!"

Driven by her mad wish, she would calmly and callously break everything.

"Freya is serious! There's nothing stopping her now! No one can hold her back!" he shouted. "Forget half a year. All we'll get is a few minutes."

Hestia recoiled as Hermes appealed to her.

"Lord Hermes!"

Overhead, Asfi was rapidly descending toward them.

"*Freya Familia* has attacked *Hestia Familia*…! Aisha and Falgar and the others have already been beaten! Even Leon…! What is going on?!"

Flying in midair with her talaria, Asfi cradled an unconscious Lyu in her arms.

She was panicked, too. The fact that she had forgotten to go invisible and was flying through the sky where anyone could see her was proof of how badly shaken she was.

Hermes's first response was not an explanation, but an order.

"Run, Asfi!"

"Eh…?!"

"You can fly! You're the only one who can escape! Take as many as you ca—no, you won't make it! Take Lyu and get away from Orario!"

"Wh-what are you saying, Lord Hermes?!"

Asfi started to argue as she took in the frenzied face of her patron god, but—

"Do as I say!"

"!"

"Don't think! Just go! There's no time! Get as far away from Orario as you can! Run, Asfi! Please!"

"….Yes…sir…"

She could do nothing but accede to Hermes's divine will. To comply with his desperate plea.

Trusting in her patron god, she took to the skies and sped away, quickly taking her beyond the city walls.

Watching this all unfold in mute shock, Hestia looked back to see Hermes hastily scrawling something on a piece of parchment he had torn from a scroll.

"When the time comes, give this *to me*!"

"A-a memo…? What do you mean give it to you…?!"

"*You can't give it to me immediately!* If you mess up the timing, *I will become your enemy*!"

Tossing aside the crimson quill pen, he stuffed the scrap of paper into her hands.

Sweat ran down his cheek.

Urgency filled his voice.

Endless unease pervaded his gaze.

Skipping right over any kind of explanation, he roared, leaving her with only the barest of information.

"Right now, the only person in Orario who can resist this is you, Hestia, the vestal goddess!"

It was a god's shout.

Hestia's eyes opened wide.

She suddenly had a terrible idea what was about to happen.

"Hermes…is…She can't possibly—?!"

Her voice had begun trembling, but she never got to finish her question.

She could hear the steady sound of ticking.

The long and short hands of the clock aligned, pointing up to the sky.

And the curtain raised on the assault.

"This will be a bit of a boring story."

Hestia shuddered.

Hermes gasped.

The two of them reflexively turned toward the entrancing voice. It was echoing from the center of the city.

"Traditionally, there should be one more goddess of the harvest here."

Freya was standing on one of the four towers of bounty at the center of Central Park.

"Lady Freya...?"

"Isn't the closing ceremony supposed to happen at sunset?"

"Did something happen?"

Guided by the manipulated Royman and the other Guild employees, more and more people were gathering in the park.

Freya was alone at the northern tower, without retainers or guards.

The goddess was clad in a hooded robe as she stood at the open-air altar, looking out at something other than the growing crowd beneath her.

"Ishtar, a goddess of beauty like myself...I returned her to the heavens."

Freya was quiet. Her voice was composed, almost sacred in its dignity.

Everyone was entranced by her tranquil aura, unable to make a sound or look away.

"Consumed by meaningless wroth, she lowered herself to the level of a beast, abandoning all sense of character. Her unsightliness was unbearable. That's why I erased her—to get her out of sight."

Though impossible to see from the vantage of the crowd below, a magic-stone amplifier was set at her feet, delivering her voice to every corner of the city.

Without exception. Everyone in the city heard her voice in their ears.

All sound disappeared from the city save the voice of the goddess. The crowd that filled up the entire park were hanging on her every word, staring up like petitioners awaiting a divine oracle.

"And now I'm going to become the same sort of hideous being."

A sneer.

A voice overflowing with self-deprecation. The goddess of beauty derided herself, causing shock to ripple out among the listening mortals. Even the deities throughout the city could not believe their ears.

"I accept any scorn or denunciation that may come my way. But I will not apologize. I have made my choice."

The goddess peered up at Babel.

She spoke clearly and without hesitation, as if making a confession to the heavens far, far above.

"Because I know what I want.

"Because I found something that I wouldn't trade for the world.

"Because I'm content to have that and nothing more."

They were like the words of a trembling, joyous, mournful song. Mortals and deities alike were left speechless, finally realizing the bizarreness of the mood.

However, it was too late.

The goddess raised her hand, pulling back the hood that shrouded her face in shadow.

"I may finally be able to know something other than love."

What appeared was the face of a girl.

Blue-gray hair and matching irises.

Dropping the voice of a goddess, she simply spoke as a young maiden.

A single droplet fell, tracing a path across her cheeks even as a beautiful smile remained on her lips.

It was what remained of the girl that the goddess should have buried, revealing what lay deep within her heart.

Time froze for the city.

Everyone was at a loss for words.

Then sky split asunder.

A crack opened in the clouds, and light poured down around her. Perhaps a blessing, and perhaps a curse.

"There's something I want to find out."

In the south of the city, the goddess's followers were kneeling, as if swearing their allegiance.

"I won't give up, and I won't let go."

In the west of the city, *Hestia Familia* remained facedown on the ground while the first-tier adventurers still standing focused on the tower in the distance.

"And so I will violate you all."

The dark elf's eyes narrowed.

The four identical prums stood silent.

The cat person watched carefully, smothering any trace of emotion.

The boaz closed his eyes.

The white elf simply looked on.

They all accepted the decision their mistress had made.

"That damned fool, is she…?!"

Loki's eyes flashed as a terrible premonition came over her.

"Aiz!"

"…?!"

Aiz and the others who had been chasing after Bell sensed the sudden change and froze.

"Hestiaaaa!"

"Ghhhhh?!"

At the same moment Hermes screamed, Hestia did as he asked and unleashed her divine power.

Common people.

Adventurers.

Deities.

All were helpless.

The final moment came without warning.

"Prostrate thyself."

Every living being's heart skipped a beat and trembled.

Her blue-gray eyes were filled with a silver gleam, and the girl's voice became a silver chain *binding all to her will.*

"Wh—?!"

In the skies far removed from Orario and still clinging on to Lyu, Asfi bore witness to the moment the argentine will of a goddess that no mortal should have been able to see transformed coalesced into an enormous glimmering dome that covered the whole of Orario.

She was the only one who could see the moment such a terrible charm consumed the city. The souls of the conscious and the unconscious were overwhelmed, subdued, twisted, and then finally united as one.

"Do as I say."

Was she a girl or a goddess?

No one could tell anymore as the tranquil voice rang in their ears.

That day, Orario was transformed.

CHAPTER 2

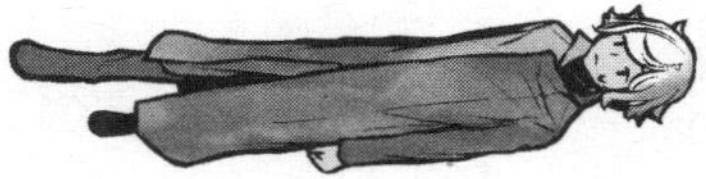

ALONE INSIDE A SANDBOX

There was a thunderous sound.

Like a silver cord snapping.

Like the groan of a parched throat.

With a splendorous, desolate tone, it made everything tremble.

It sounded like the roar of the ocean consuming whatever lay within reach.

Or perhaps it was the rumble of boots marching in thunderous lockstep, so unified it could be mistaken for the footfalls of one giant creature.

It was the sound of subjugation.

It was the sound of domination.

It was the sound of the ultimate beauty that outshone everything.

A truly terrifying, miserable thing.

The die was cast, rolling on the ground, surely soon to be crushed underfoot.

And then…

Something flares up.

The burning sensation flowing across my back feels like it's trying to protect my body from some terrible threat. After a great clash, that looming presence pulls away.

The sound of a yearning burning.

The sound of resistance against a divine will.

A fight against domination and intrusion, like a golden flower blooming defiantly atop the tallest peak.

There is no kindling.

There is no ash.

Sparks are flying.

But in the depths of the hearth, a golden hope is still burning strong.

In the impenetrable darkness, my body is embraced by the eternal flame within me.

And yet…

Why am I so uneasy?

Why does it feel like I'm the only one who's been left behind?

I'm standing all alone in a boundless darkness.

I'm surrounded by people who refuse to turn and look at me.

The warm flame crackles and burns in solitude.

My consciousness, firmly in the grasp of fear, slowly begins to surface—

"Ugh…"

A terribly raspy groan escapes me.

Opening my eyes and blinking several times, the first thing I see is a high ceiling.

A slender ray of light touches my cheek, slipping in through a small gap in the curtains.

My head is still hazy as I sit up, letting the sheets slide off my upper body.

"Where am I…?"

The room is massive. There's a table and chair with intricate curved legs, as well as a big closet, and a magic lamp resembling a sconce. The bed I've been sleeping in is incredibly comfortable, and I can tell the rug running across the floor is soft and luxurious by just looking at it.

This almost feels like a high-class hotel—the exact sort of place you'd never find me in as a member of a familia shouldering a crushing amount of debt.

But even so, something is…

I can't explain it, but...there's a sort of lived-in feeling to the space that convinces me this isn't actually a hotel.

It feels more like someone's personal room than a guest room. I take another look around, still disoriented.

Why am I in a place like this? I desperately try to remember, searching for some kind of clue.

"...! Right, I was...!"

I was attacked.

Lyu and I encountered the city's most powerful adventurer. My breath catches as a sudden burst of tension seizes my body.

But then where am I now?

Was I kidnapped?

Is Lyu safe?

Tamping down the rush of questions that welled up, I silently slip out of bed. I'm dressed in nightclothes I don't recognize. There are no restraints, and I can move freely, but I can't find any of my gear. Or the Hestia Knife.

Realizing that my gear probably got seized, I grit my teeth and carefully check to make sure there's no one else inside the room. Then I stealthily approach the window, where the morning sun is lancing in.

"...A field...?"

Peeking out ever so slightly, I see an enormous lawn...a great field.

Beneath the expansive blue sky is a sea of green, and in the distance I spot a stone barrier that resembles a castle wall.

...I don't remember ever seeing a place like this.

It makes me wonder if I'm even still in Orario.

There are no bars or anything on the window, and there doesn't seem to be a lock on it, either. It's almost disturbing how easy it seems to be to get out. But I can see what look like a couple of adventurers milling outside the window. I would definitely get caught trying to leave that way.

I quickly give up on escaping through the window.

"That just leaves..."

I look at the one and only door leading out of the room.

After staring at it for a long moment, I make up my mind and walk over to it. Putting my hand on the doorknob, I exercise extreme caution and open the door silently.

"...Where in the world is this?" I murmur in shock as I step out of the room.

The wide and long hallway is an elegant white, the sort of magnificent corridor that belongs in a literal castle.

While I'm still wondering what sort of crazy place I've been carried off to, someone suddenly calls out.

"What are you doing?"

"!"

The voice scares me so badly, I forget how to breathe for a moment. Reflexively spinning around, I see a figure standing there that has become incredibly familiar over the past few days—a blond white elf.

"M...Master..."

Hedin is standing there by himself. I assume he emerged from one of the branching passages. I didn't notice his presence at all—though I guess that is only natural, since he is a Level 6 adventurer. He can easily slip out of my sight whenever he feels like it and pummel me into submission with a casual punch or kick. He made that painfully clear more times than I care to remember during our lessons.

And there's no chance that he would help his pupil out of the goodness of his heart. I mean, he is utterly cruel and tyrannical, but more importantly, he's part of *Freya Familia*!

"Guh...!"

Am I going to be caught? Does this mean I'm going back to that room? Also, why was I abducted in the first place?

I can feel sweat already coating the back of my neck as we stare at each other for a few moments...Then with a glance like he's looking at sewage, he breaks the silence.

"Wash that dirty face of yours at once. We're going to breakfast."

...............Huh?

At first, I simply don't understand what he's saying.

"...Wait, breakfast? Wh-why...?"

"What are you talking about? Does there have to be a reason for the sun to rise? Eating in the morn is a given."

"E-ehhh…? Pardon me, Master, but what are you talking about? Did you hit your hea—"

"Are you mocking me, you foolish rabbit?"

"Ngh?!"

He suddenly closes the distance without a noise and hits me with an all too familiar kick.

I mean, yes, it's true that eating breakfast in the morning is perfectly normal, but…!

Even as I groan in pain, I'm also a little bit relieved. I mean not that I'm happy to be kicked or anything…but Master hasn't changed at all.

At the very least, there's no sign that we're enemies now. I still have no idea what's going on, but this has helped my uneasy heart feel a little better.

…I still can't shake the feeling that something is off, though.

"Finish your preparations and let's get going."

Master's coral eyes stare at me through his glasses for a long moment, and then he turns around.

All I can do is purse my lips and quietly follow him.

Then another kick comes my way as Master says, "I said to finish your preparations, you waste of space," before having my entire head dunked in a tub filled with water. He doesn't let go of my head until he's done.

I get dressed in something that resembles battle gear and generally cleaned up before following after Master.

Hestia Familia's home, Hearthstone Manor, is easily luxurious enough to be called a stately mansion, but it can't even begin to compare to this place. It goes without saying that the interior is spacious, but the silver-and-gold decorations are breathtaking. My feet sink into the lush carpet, my jaw drops when I see the enormous chandelier dotted by magic-stone lamps, and my eyes shoot open as we come to the broad, palatial staircase. While I'm preoccupied with taking in the scenery, we reach our destination—the sort of magnificently huge hall that exists only in stories.

"Did you just wake up?"

"You ought to be ashamed for sleeping in."

"Coming late like some bigshot, rabbit boy?"

"You've been getting cocky lately, rabbit boy."

The interior is filled with lines of long tables set together, measuring maybe fifty meders long. Sitting there with their legs high off the floor are four identical prums.

Bringar, the Gulliver brothers.

By this point, I'm at a loss, not to mention shocked to run into first-tier adventurers of the city's strongest familia.

"Hey, finish the tomatoes, Dvalinn."

"Come on, Alfrik, tomatoes for breakfast is torture. You take it."

"Quit screwing around. And, Berling, quit copying him!"

"No, I'm trading mine for your dessert."

"That's even worse! Hey, don't even think about it, Grer!"

"Pass, pass, pass."

"At least make up an excuse!"

""""Pleeeeeease, Big Brother Alfriiiig.""""

"I'll kick all of your asses!"

The identical brothers are passing around a plate full of red vegetables while arguing in identical voices.

If I didn't know any better, I would've assumed this mundane morning scene was playing out between clones.

...Wh-what's going on...?

This is like that cozy, at-home feeling deities are always talking about...

I start to doubt my eyes at the odd and unexpected scene of those terrifying first-tier adventurers.

"Screw it! *Bell*, you eat it! Punishment for sleeping late!"

To top it all off, Alfrik calls me by name.

""""That's not right, Big Brother.""""

"I don't want to hear that from you guys! And you're pissing me off with that tone!"

Ignoring that I'm frozen in my tracks, the four prum brothers continue their rambunctious, childlike argument.

"Four sons of fate, shared of soul, 'tis inevitable that breaking morning's fast would descend into a furor..."

"H-Hegni..."

"A fine aurora, is it not? Will you not abrogate thy prohibition of gluttony?"

The dark elf left a single seat's gap between himself and the prums, and he is primly eating with a knife and fork.

Hegni lightheartedly addresses me, as if the furious battle that unfolded the other day had never happened—no, it's more than that. This makes it seem like he's not shy around me anymore.

If I had to guess, he's probably saying, "Good morning. Won't you have something to eat?" or something like that...

"The hell are you standing around for? Finish your food and get your ass out on the field."

The last to speak was a cat person with black fur.

Vana Freya, the man named Allen Fromel...is glaring at me, ordering me to sit with his piercing gaze.

Master doesn't say anything as he takes his seat at the table.

"...?"

I'm befuddled.

Just absolutely dumbfounded. It's so bad that any nervousness I might've had before has been totally blown away. That surreal feeling is gone, too. For a brief moment, I just stare at the maids gracefully passing out the food before one pulls out a chair clearly meant for me.

Are you telling me to eat at the same table as you? A rival familia? Of course I'm shocked.

"Oi, what are you doing?"

"What's with that look on your face?"

"Do you hate the idea of eating breakfast with us that much?"

"It's a bit late to feel weird about it now."

"Ye heretic who knows not fear, thou who art heralded as Record Holder."

The four prums and the dark elf all chime in together.

This is wrong.

Something about this is terribly wrong.

The way they act as if it were totally natural that I would sit at the same table as them.

"Wh-where—!"

My shout echoes loudly in the hall.

The first-tier adventurers all turn to me. I'm on the verge of being overwhelmed by the pressure as my voice almost cracks.

"...Where is this...?"

When I ask that question, a flurry of dubious stares home in on me.

The ones who answer are two of the prums...I think Alfrik and Dvalinn.

"Our home, obviously."

"What would you call this hallowed realm other than Folkvangr?"

Folkvangr...?

Then this really is *Freya Familia*'s home?

I was kidnapped and taken away to another familia's base?

But...But still...even if I understand the situation now, I still can't get rid of the weird feeling that's been plaguing me.

I feel a slight chill as I wrench my lips open, and questions pour out.

"Why was I taken away?

"Why did you attack me?

"Is Lyu safe?!"

Silence.

Quiet.

Hush.

Sound recedes from the hall. I'm the only one who's been shouting. The mood in the room makes it feel like I'm the one who's losing his mind. Everyone is looking at me weirdly.

"Thou art not a princess held hostage, nor is there any need to abduct you."

"Are you still half asleep, dumbass?"

Hegni and Allen rattle off their replies.

"And who is Lyu?"

"I think I heard somewhere once that's another word for dragon."

"A dragon? You friends with a monster or what?"

"Training aside, we haven't attacked you at all."

The three younger brothers cock their heads in confusion while the eldest brother addresses my questions directly.

"Your doubts don't make any sense. What have you been talking about?"

And I can feel Master's piercing gaze again.

"You are a follower of Lady Freya and fell for her at first sight. That makes you a member of *Freya Familia*."

Time stops.

My heart forgets to beat. It feels like everything's slipping away.

I don't understand what he's saying. Why would he say such an absurd joke?

"Wha...what are you talking about...? I-I'm part of *Hestia Familia*! I'm not Lady Freya's follower!"

As I lose my nerve and shout reflexively, the mood changes in an instant once more.

"The hell'd you say?"

"That's an insult to Lady Freya...Is this an act of insubordination?"

Allen and one of the prums look ready to kill.

"No, wait. Something's off."

"As stupid as the rabbit is, he isn't fool enough to not pay our goddess the proper respect."

Two more prums quickly speak in restraint.

"There is confusion in this one's eyes...a tyrant of the outer realms has visited. Signs of upheaval gleam in the night sky."

"That almost seems comprehensible without making any sense at all. Translate, Hedin."

"He is saying perhaps the boy's memories have been corrupted. He may be in a state of confusion because of a powerful external shock."

Hegni, Alfrik, and Master are debating about my seemingly strange behavior. But they're the ones openly saying absurd things, so why don't any of them doubt themselves?

Why do they all think I'm the strange one?

What are you even saying?

What in the world is going on here?!

"I-I was picked up by my goddess, Lady Hestia! I haven't converted or anything!"

"Don't be absurd. Isn't Lady Freya the one who granted you your blessing when you came to this city?"

I stop breathing after Alfrik answers my shout with a quick counterargument—the only one who has ever granted Bell Cranell falna is Lady Freya. There is no trace of fabrication or doubt in his eyes as he states it like an immutable truth. I feel like I might keel over at any moment.

"Did you hit your head while training too much?"

"Or did some other familia cast a fearsome spell on you?"

"You're the one in charge of watching after him, right, Hedin? You have any idea?"

"As if I can keep an eye on this fool around the clock."

The younger prum brothers and Hedin are bickering as I subconsciously back away a step. An alien fear rises from the pit of my stomach.

These people are scary!

"Call Heith. She should be in Babel right now. Get her to check if there are any abnormalities." The moment that order is given to the stunned maids, I give in to the terror overwhelming me and start running.

"!"

I can hear voices calling me back.

But who cares?

Ignore them. Don't listen.

They're first-tier adventurers. They can catch up and capture me in an instant if they feel like it.

So I have to run. Run away fast and escape this nauseating place as soon as I can!

I sprint out of the hall in search of an exit. Rushing through the palatial home, searching for the outside, I burst through the doors of the massive entry hall.

"Ngh…?!"

The first thing I see are warriors battling.

The top of the hill where the palace stands provides a commanding vantage point to look across the field. In the sea of green where rings of flowers sway in the breeze, there are dozens of adventurers clashing. The battle cries and weapons intertwine and split the blue skies.

I've heard of this place. This…is where *Freya Familia* conducts death matches day and night at their familia's home! Their grueling internal struggle, the process of pushing themselves to ever greater heights in an attempt to earn the favor of their goddess.

It was one of the reasons why *Freya Familia* stood at the very top of the city to this day.

Gender, race, age—none of those things matter here. Everyone's blood flows freely, their fighting spirit firm and unbowed as their blades meet again and again.

I'm overwhelmed by the sheer intensity and almost stop dead in my tracks.

What should I do?

I can't escape without reaching the walls surrounding the training field. Is there some way to get out without being seen? No, it's impossible.

And there's no telling when Master or the others might catch up with me!

I sprint down the hill, hoping to force a breakthrough.

"Bell! Wandering out here so late! And unarmed to boot?! Are you looking down on us?!"

"…?!"

As I cut through the field past where they are fighting, a half-prum pulls back from the scrum to slash out at me. Wielding two blades, he calls out to me with the familiarity of someone who knows me very well.

"Don't get ahead of yourself just 'cause you're Level Four now! I'll still go a few rounds with you and leave you begging for mercy like old times!"

I just barely manage to evade his attack as I break out in a cold sweat.

It's terrifying to be treated so familiarly by someone I've never met before. Rather than face him head-on, I almost take a tumble as I slip past.

I pump my legs as hard as I can and make a break for it.

All of a sudden, the other warriors clashing nearby notice me and charge with their weapons in hand.

Fight!

Fight!

Fight Bell!

Feeling their eyes and rage focus on me, I shake my head, rejecting them even as they call my name. "I don't know you! I don't know you at all!"

I launch myself forward and leap over the imposing gate, where guards stand at the ready, clearing it in a single jump.

"Haggh, hagh, hagh…!"

I'm sprinting through the shopping district.

After breaking out of *Freya Familia*'s home, I find myself in the south of the city.

It seems like the Goddess Festival ended without a hitch, and members of the Guild are starting to help people clean up by carrying away the trolley carts packed full of harvest goods and taking down the street stalls. Seeing the vibrant and bountiful decorations disappearing evokes an emptiness befitting the end of a festival… but this isn't the time to be dwelling on that.

I still haven't caught my breath after escaping from the top-tier adventurers. Because I forced my way through, my clothes are torn here and there. I almost look like an escaped convict.

My heart is still pounding, and I can't stop sweating. This slithering unease rising from the pit of my stomach makes my skin crawl.

I want to reassure myself as soon as possible. I want to forget this disgusting feeling as soon as I can.

That's why I'm running to find the goddess and everyone.

To my home…!

"Agh?!"

Rushing forward in a desperate attempt to escape this unease and anxiety, I don't look where I'm going and end up ramming into a passerby on the street.

I stumble a bit but catch myself.

The sturdy person I ran into also managed to avoid getting knocked down. Before I have a chance to frantically apologize, a very familiar voice raises a complaint.

"That hurt! Where're you lookin'?!"

Mord!

Seeing a familiar face, I feel an inexplicable wave of relief wash over me.

The gruff-looking veteran adventurer is glaring at me just like he always does—right up until he recognizes me.

"R-Rabbit Foot?! From *Freya Familia*?!"

Fear seeps into his voice.

"——"

I started to smile in relief, but my expression freezes in place. My cheek twitches awkwardly.

Not noticing my internal chaos, Mord collapses into apologies.

"I-I'm sorry! I didn't realize it was you!"

"Mord, money! Your money!"

"Give him whatever you have on you and convince him to forgive you!"

His usual companions, Scott and Gyle, fly into a panic as well.

The reason is simple.

They're scared of me—or rather, they're scared of drawing the ire of the city's strongest familia!

"Y-you've got it wrong! I'm not *Freya Familia*!"

"Wh-what are you talking about?! I-I'm begging ya here, please forgive me!"

"It's not a matter of forgiveness or not! It's me, Mord! Don't you remember all the times you beat me up? All those weird things you taught me? And all those times you helped me?"

"I've never, ever done anything like that! Please don't try to pick a fight with me!"

When I see how they're looking at me like I'm a complete stranger, I start to lose it. I step forward, grabbing Mord's stout shoulders, but no matter how much I plead, everything I say is misunderstood. In fact, Mord is whimpering as if to say that I'm the one who is misunderstanding things.

I can see in his eyes that he is well and truly terrified of me, a human significantly smaller than him. He's barely holding himself together.

"Please forgive us!"

Gyle and Scott are doing their best to stop me while clearly getting more and more unnerved.

The people around us start to notice, and my position is getting more and more questionable.

"What are you doing?!"

As I stand there petrified like someone who wandered into the wrong neighborhood, a voice suddenly reaches my ears.

A single half-elf coming over to us.

I don't how to react.

"We're in the middle of cleaning up after the festival! What exactly is going on here?!"

She's wearing a suit with black pants. Her glasses sit atop the familiar well-proportioned face, just like always. She steps away from the rest of her coworkers with a dignified air. She is the very model of an earnest Guild employee as she attempts to do her duty and bravely mediate the adventurer street dispute.

"Miss Eina!"

I shout her name.

If it really is her, then…

Miss Eina, who has watched over me from the moment I became an adventurer…Surely she of all people wouldn't believe the crazy idea that I'm part of *Freya Familia*!

Her emerald eyes widen when I call out to her, and she flashes an awkward smile that instantly puts my heart at ease as she replies with a question.

"Pardon, but have we met somewhere before?"

Crack.

This time there's no mistaking it.

I can almost hear the weak sound of something giving out, like glass cracking. My world has been turned upside down. My eyes can't see clearly anymore.

Everything and everyone around me is twisting and turning.

"…….Y-you…don't know me…?"

"Of course I do! There's no one in this city who doesn't know the name of the record holder. It's just…I was surprised you knew my name."

She smiles.

There's no mistake. This is Miss Eina.

That's the same smile I know so well. But she's saying that she does not know *me*.

"…Mord and them, were messing with me…even though I'm a member of *Hestia Familia*, they…"

"…? I was not aware that you had converted, Mr. Cranell."

She doesn't call me Bell.

No, it must be because we're out in public. She's just maintaining her professionalism as a member of the Guild.

That's all.

That has to be it…

"…You are my adviser, right?"

"Eh?! How could I possibly advise you?! In fact, *Freya Familia* makes a point of not using the adviser system…"

She denies it.

It's a total rejection of what I know.

And she's sure we've never met before.

"M-Mr. Cranell…? Is something the matter…?"

Mord and his friends catch their breath after I let him go. The people around us, including Miss Eina, are all looking concerned as I turn pale.

I don't understand.

Why is my voice trembling?

Where am I?

What is this terrifying dungeon I've somehow stumbled into?

I don't know. I don't understand anything.

"………….Wh…who am I?"

My mouth goes dry.

Like diving off the cliff, or stepping up to the noose, or casting aside my weapons in the face of an unbeatable monster, I finally ask the question that I've been avoiding this whole time.

Miss Eina has a confused look on her face as she replies like it's obvious.

"You are Mr. Bell Cranell of *Freya Familia*."

It feels like I just slammed into the canyon floor after taking a leap of faith.

"You received the blessing of Goddess Freya and achieved the world's fastest level-up, demonstrating your heroic potential to all."

The rope tightens around my neck. I stop breathing.

"As you stand on the verge of entering the ranks of the first-tier adventurers after half a year, no one would deny that you have earned the title of einherjar."

Fearsome fangs and claws tear into my body, consuming every bit of me.

—And just like that, Bell Cranell came to a stop.

Who am I?

Where am I?

When am I? What happened? And why am I so cold?

Even with so many eyes watching, there isn't a single person who knows *me*.

Not even the woman standing right here who's always helped and supported me like an older sister.

The sacred flame covering my back crackles, burning in solitude.

"Well?" Alfrik asked inside the great hall Sessrúmnir, located deep within *Freya Familia*'s home, which Bell Cranell had recently fled.

Allen was tracking the boy, keeping him under observation. Alfrik and his brothers were sitting in their chairs, looking across the table at the white elf.

"...It's proceeding more or less according to the goddess's divine will," Hedin announced as he adjusted his glasses. "Aside from that foolish rabbit, every person and deity has been charmed and had their memories altered."

The three younger prums concealed a shudder at his emotionless response.

"Scary."

"Yes, truly terrifying."

"She is our goddess, but it's dreadful still."

And then they spoke in unison.

""""Because she could not twist Bell Cranell, she twisted the entire world instead.""""

That was the whole of it.

That was the source of what was isolating the boy, and the true form of the aggression that Freya had carried out.

"It's understandable that Bell Cranell would be confused."

"The entire last six months have *effectively been erased*."

"*Hestia Familia*'s Bell has been erased from the memories of the populace and replaced with a version of him that is a member of our familia."

That was the dominion of beauty, the culmination of its power. At times, it manipulated, at times it led to destruction, and at times it puppeted the enthralled. Beauty alone could transform the entire mortal realm even without resorting to using arcanum. It could even grasp people's very souls.

Extreme beauty was said to be a thing that could bewitch with its mere presence.

"More precisely, it's not so much altering memories as using charm to wish those memories into being. 'Don't acknowledge the human who was a follower of Goddess Hestia,' 'believe that Bell Cranell has always a member of *Freya Familia*'...the people and deities who have been enslaved by Lady Freya are merely following those orders."

Alfrik shuddered as well as he corrected his brothers.

The charm of the goddess of beauty did not have the power to transform people, let alone the world. However, it could create loyal servants out of all those who had been enthralled.

Mortals and deities alike were deceiving not only Bell, but themselves as well in strict obedience to Freya's royal decree.

It was essentially a form of autosuggestion.

But while the logic and process were different, the results were the same.

It was very much like every resident of Orario had their memories altered.

"Those friends with whom he shared joy and sorrow, those benefactors who had supported him from the shadows...they have all forgotten those eternal bonds and killed the boy who resides in their memories."

Hegni, the only one standing, closed his eyes as he murmured.

"The hare has fallen into a wondrous land...a lonely world where no matter how far he might run, no one will come looking for him."

* * *

"Ghhh?!"

Bell sprinted away from Eina and the group that had gathered around him.

Unable to face the reality before him, he gave in to a primal fear and was consumed by panic. He surrendered himself to the impulse to find someone, *anyone*, who knew him.

However…

"Look, isn't that *Freya Familia*'s—"

"It's Rabbit Foot!"

On every street, corner, avenue, and alleyway…the mood of the bustling city was distant and cold.

"Ghh…?!"

Whispers rippled through the crowd, like echoes in a forest.

Bell recognized the feeling.

He was now the focus of the same sort of attention that the masses often placed on the Sword Princess, the flower that bloomed so far out of reach. It was not remotely the sort of gaze that the Little Rookie had ever experienced before no matter how popular he got.

It wasn't simply fear. Envy and excitement were also present.

The word for it was awe. The sort of unexaggerated awe that came with being one of the strongest followers.

No it's not!

I'm just imagining things!

Screaming back at himself, Bell averted his eyes from the pedestrians, shopkeeps, and even adventurers who opened the way for him as he ran.

"Bell Cranell's fate was decided from the moment Lady Freya decided to use her charm."

Alfrik's voice filled the Sessrúmnir.

On the final day of the Goddess Festival—yesterday—Freya felled Orario with her beauty.

"Her charm extended to *all of Orario*."

Every person in Central Park who saw her, every person who

heard her voice via the magic-stone speakers—they were all charmed. Those who were asleep or unconscious were not spared. The voice of the goddess of beauty could slip into their bodies and shake them to their core whether they were conscious or not.

The vast majority of people did not even realize they had been enslaved by beauty and were going about their lives none the wiser.

"I'm sure this must be a nightmare for him."

"The entire world changed around him in the span of a single night."

"It would be fair to feel just a little bit of pity for him."

Dvalinn, Berling, and Grer spoke in the same voice.

""""After all, he doesn't know a thing, so there's no way to find out the truth or even begin to understand what's going on around him.""""

"Why...why?!"

As expected, Bell could not control the bewilderment and unease eating away at him as he kept running.

A mere mortal incapable of fully understanding a deity could not begin to imagine a goddess bending the entire world to her will, transforming a whole city without even using arcanum.

Bell Cranell possessed an unblemished soul, but no matter how pure he was or how much he strove to grow, he would never be able to plumb the depths of a deity.

"Ah, Bell. What are you doing in a place like this?"

"Eh...? Wh-who?"

The person who finally managed to stop Bell was an unfamiliar, beautiful woman. Her hair was a faint red, and she was wearing a white outfit that resembled battle gear in design. Confused, Bell realized who she was.

"Who...? It's me, Heith. You know, the healer who always heals those injuries you're always getting. I'm out on an errand at the moment."

There was a valkyrie emblem embroidered on the shoulder of her white outfit.

Freya Familia.

He turned pale, and her beautiful face took on an almost doll-like appearance in his eyes.

"I bought some sweets while I was out. Would you like one?...Wait, you're not a fan of sweets, right? I should have bought something salty, too."

Someone he did not know at all knew intimate details about him.

The terror that came with that realization far surpassed what he had felt earlier.

"Ugh, ahh...?!"

He involuntarily backed away and started running again.

The woman watched without emotion as the boy ran away from her.

"The power of charm that can overpower even other deities...We were prepared to fall under her charm as well, but..."

"More precisely, we *were* charmed. And then it was undone, thanks to Lady Freya's ichor that resides within us."

Freya's charm was almost entirely indiscriminate.

Any who beheld her or heard her voice would fall under its sway. There was no method for limiting the effect or choosing not to target certain people.

That was why before they attacked *Hestia Familia*, when they heard Freya's divine will, all of her followers had accepted their fate. They had demonstrated their loyalty and would not begrudge being twisted to her will if that was what their mistress so desired.

However, right now, the members of *Freya Familia* were able to recall information from before the change.

Hedin attempted to explain the process to Alfrik, asserting that their goddess must have activated her ichor, releasing them from her thrall using her divine power.

"But thanks to that, we can share in the setting our lady desires, so that's convenient," Dvalinn mused.

They had been charmed, had the setting Freya devised input into their memories, and were subsequently returned to their senses. Because of that, *Freya Familia* was perfectly capable of performing the role that Freya demanded. They could all act as if *Bell Cranell were always one of them* without having to expend any energy getting their stories straight.

"'Bell Cranell came to Orario half a year ago.'"

"'There he was picked out by Lady Freya, quickly grew in strength, and has currently reached Level Four.'"

"'And both inside and outside our faction, Rabbit Foot has been the subject of speculation that he is under consideration to become one of the core members of *Freya Familia*.'"

That was the current story in Orario and the ordeal assailing Bell Cranell on all sides. The young adventurer would be unable to confirm anything as he was tossed about by the world around him.

"Ghh...Lord Miach! Nahza! Daphne! Cassandra!"

In his rambling dash, he encountered the precious comrades with whom he had fought alongside many times. A certain healer god was out with his whole familia to assist with the cleanup now that the festival was over.

"Mhm? If I recall, you are..."

"*Freya Familia*, Lord Miach...Also known as the record holder, this is Little Rookie...no, it's Rabbit Foot now, isn't it...?"

"What business does a candidate for the top tier of the city's most powerful familia have with us?"

"—?!"

Miach cocked his head as if it were their first meeting.

Nahza looked at him the way she would at a stranger.

Daphne did not hide her wariness.

Bell had been battered by despair, leaving his whole body twitching as he set off at a run once again. In his rush to get away, he never noticed Cassandra, who turned pale and went speechless, as if seeing an impossible dream come true.

"Lord Takemikazuchi! Ouka! Chigusa!"

It wasn't long before he found the war god and his familia intervening in an argument between the members of two familias. Bell ran over to them and frantically grabbing Chigusa's shoulders.

"Eep?!"

"What are you doing?! Get away from Chigusa!"

"...One of Freya's children? You seem to be behaving rather familiar. Have we met somewhere before?"

"...?!"

Chigusa recoiled from him.

Ouka swatted his hands away irately.

Takemikazuchi looked at him dubiously, observing him carefully, clearly on guard.

Even here Bell tasted despair.

He was gasping for air, and his heart was racing.

No one.

Not a single person knew the Bell Cranell who was part of *Hestia Familia.*

The reality was that even deities, supernatural beings, did not remember him.

The seed of doubt that he, a mere mortal, might be the one who was wrong began to sprout, cornering him even further.

Despite being a mortal, Bell alone had managed to resist the authority of Freya's charm, and because he maintained his normalcy, he was branded a heretic in a world that had gone mad.

"This the first time I've seen the true power of her charm."

"Lady Freya had always hidden such great power, never using it."

"Naturally. It's a deformation of the world, the same desecration of the mortal realm that the sublime empress so despises."

Hegni firmly answered the younger prum brothers' comments.

Freya Familia could easily crush ten thousand armies on the field.

However, their Goddess Freya could bring those same armies under her control without ever fighting them.

She could quite literally end everything if she was of a mind to do so.

Steal a throne, construct a paradise, rule over the whole of the mortal realm.

Everywhere her gaze or voice could reach, that was her domain.

The force of her charm could even ensnare her fellow deities, and it truly frightened them.

—A world-commanding witch beyond any beauty who ever brought a country to its knees.

That was the true form of Freya, the goddess of beauty.

However, despite possessing absolute power, Freya did not attempt to trample the world beneath her in order to amuse herself, but more than anything, out of a respect for the mortal realm.

She understood that her dominion was hollower and more boring than anything.

What value was there in things that were gained through no effort? And just how much emptiness was that worth?

A charmed world that merely moved as she wished was a dead world.

That was why Freya had never attempted to bind the mortal realm to her will before.

It was taboo for her.

"...However, she broke that prohibition. That is simply how much she desired that fool...Bell Cranell."

There was a certain piece of information that she had received from a former follower of her fellow goddess of beauty Ishtar.

"Charm does not work on Bell Cranell."

He was unmoved by Syr, nor would he submit to the love of the goddess. Because of that, instead of changing him, Freya changed everything around him.

She twisted the world to isolate him.

In order to claim him. To make him hers in both body and mind.

The Sessrúmnir fell silent at Hedin's words.

The predominant feeling in most of the warriors' eyes was jealousy. The rest displayed only unwavering loyalty.

The elves were silent, eyes closed as the four prums responded in unison.

""""""All shall be as the goddess wills it.""""""

* * *

"Goddess! Everyone!"

The boy finally met *Hestia Familia* for the second time.

"Nghh!"

Bell!

The moment he appeared before her, Hestia, *who remembered everything*, wanted to shout to him.

Hestia Familia was walking along the spiderweb of streets that branched off from the main road in the southwest part of the city.

Lilly, Welf, Mikoto, Haruhime, and Hestia were helping out with the cleanup after the Goddess Festival, just like so many others—or rather Hestia was using that as a cover to investigate how the world had been rewritten, and she was falling deeper into despair the more she learned.

That was when Bell appeared before them.

As if drawn to each other, like two lonely sparks of sacred flame, they succeeded in the worst possible chance meeting.

"White hair, red eyes...*Freya Familia*'s rookie star?"

"Wh-what does the city's strongest familia want with our tiny one?!"

Welf looked suspicious, and Lilly's voice betrayed her agitation as she responded cautiously. Bell looked pained, as if a spear had just been thrust through his heart.

Hestia also felt a sharp pain in her heart, as if she had been cut by a sword.

Bell's red eyes wavered, as if crying unseen tears while desperately searching for his place in the world. All he wanted was to return to the family that now looked at him like an enemy.

"E...every...one..."

Ahhh, I have to rush over to him.

I have to hug him close.

He's trembling like a lamb.

This must hurt him so much!

But—she could not.

"L-Lilly…! You remember when you became my supporter, right…?"

"Lilly would never have become your supporter!"

The prum girl rejected him, not understanding what he was saying at all.

The boy's heart was grievously wounded by the words of his first comrade, the partner with whom he had first formed a party.

"Welf! You made weapons for me…!"

"Sorry to say, I don't recall ever taking a request from you. And I doubt you've ever held something I've made."

The blacksmith pushed back coldly as if being sold a bill of fake goods.

The boy instinctively looked down at his body, but he did not have any of Welf's equipment on him.

"Mikoto! During the war game…when you helped me…!"

"…I don't remember *Freya Familia* ever having a war game…"

The rigidly dutiful Far Eastern girl expressed bewilderment, certain that there was no reason she would have ever interacted with him.

Even though he had helped her save her old friend standing beside her, her bluish-purple eyes didn't contain even a trace of recognition.

"Haruhime…! All the times we talked about heroic epics…!"

"P-perhaps we met in the pleasure quarter…? However, I'm no longer a prostitute…"

The renart girl was clearly scared.

Possibly because of the pain and repressed memories of her time as a prostitute, she trembled and hid behind Mikoto, scared of a man she was meeting for the first time.

With every word and action, they were badly hurting Bell.

Hestia wanted to vomit.

Her familia was hurting that precious boy so terribly.

She felt like she might slump to the ground and scream until her voice gave out.

Stop already!

Please stop!

Please don't hurt that boy any further!

Hestia desperately wanted to cry out.

But even so—she could do nothing.

"Ghh…!"

Her eyes alone beheld two shadows.

Perched atop a nearby building and positioned in a dark alley to the side respectively, the boaz warrior and the cat person who was violence incarnate were even now watching Hestia.

—Hestia was in the exact same situation as Bell.

She alone had not fallen to Freya's charm.

She, one of the three vestal goddesses of the heavens. As a deity of purity and chastity, like Athena and Artemis, she had the power to reject the goddess of beauty's control.

The reason that Hermes could so confidently state that she alone could resist in the moments before Freya subjugated the city was because she was the virgin goddess Hestia. With great exertion, she was capable of neutralizing the power of Freya's charm.

And because of that, she was being watched.

They're watching…no, they're telling *me! If I try to reveal anything to Bell, they're going to kill everyone…!*

The city's strongest and fastest adventurers were revealing their presence in a way that only Hestia would notice.

The former had been watching Hestia all morning, and the latter had been tailing Bell since he left *Freya Familia*'s home.

Their cool, placid eyes were a warning and a message. If Hestia broke her promise with Freya, they would kill Welf, Lilly, Mikoto, and Haruhime without hesitation.

Allen was especially dangerous.

While he had sworn loyalty to Freya, he clearly had no patience for the farce he was being forced to endure. Even if killing *Hestia Familia* broke Bell and guaranteed that his soul would never truly become Freya's, that was no skin off his back.

Hestia wasn't allowed any contact or communication with Bell, public or otherwise.

Until Bell's conversion or until his heart willingly turned to Freya, she would always be under watch.

"........"

She desperately wanted to walk over to Bell and hug him, but she could not allow him to realize that. Hestia stared at Bell, who was deep in his own struggle.

He looked like he was on the verge of losing what little strength he had left. No matter how much he asked or how much he pleaded, everyone would reject him. The very act of reaching out would only harm him further, and his mind was already near collapse.

There was not even a shadow of the powerful and reliable Level 4 adventurer left.

His fight with the minotaur, the deadly struggle on the eighteenth floor, the war game, the conflict with *Ishtar Familia*, the Xenos incident, and the excursion to the deep levels—he could never have overcome all those adventurers, trials, and tribulations by himself.

Bell Cranell had overcome them with the help of his comrades.

Even now, everyone spoke of how miraculous Bell's growth had been and heaped praise on him for his accomplishments.

But that was all wrong.

One look past the adventurer facade, Bell was still just a fourteen-year-old boy—a human like any other. And Hestia was the only one who understood that.

He could be hurt and confused when he had no one to turn to. Abandoned and alone, he would become truly vulnerable.

Bell was terribly scared of losing the people in his life after having been separated from his grandfather. The reason Bell had stood back up no matter how much he suffered was because of the support of so many irreplaceable people.

Because of all the people he had met along the way.

And having those same connections rejected at such a fundamental level without explanation was making Bell emotionally unstable.

"...Goddess..."

There was only one place left for him to turn to in the end.

His red eyes were looking at her.

He was pinning his final hope on Hestia. His gaze seemed so fragile, so weak, that it might shatter if anyone so much as breathed on him.

Her hands were trembling, hidden behind Welf and the others.

Everything inside her withered, like a bone-dry desert.

The five members of *Hestia Familia* clustered together and stood apart from the boy wearing battle gear—*Freya Familia's* uniform, leaving a deep and impassable line between them.

"...Let's go...everyone..."

What expression was she making right now?

Had she managed to erase her emotions, successfully hiding her feelings from Bell and wounding him even more in the process?

"You shouldn't get involved with *Freya Familia*..."

Had her performance been enough to satisfy Freya's followers?

"Ahhh—"

Thud.

She could hear the sound as the boy slumped to his knees as if the last few threads holding him up had finally snapped.

But Hestia failed to notice as she was already walking away.

She was too focused on making sure her mask did not slip as Lilly and the others followed, obeying their patron goddess's will.

"Goddess...Goddeeeeess!"

The boy's sobbing voice pierced her. Haruhime and the others turned back in shock, but Hestia did not dare.

Her trembling fists were drenched in sweat.

No—what she assumed to be sweat was blood. Her nails had broken the skin. She did not know how long she had been bleeding, but she did not care.

Hestia believed she had no right to cry.

As a feeling of disgust welled up within her, the goddess of the hearth had turned away the hand of a supplicant for the first time ever.

She had rejected the hand of the child she loved more than any other.

I don't remember anything that happened after that.

Barely conscious, almost like a mindless puppet, I only just realize I've been brought back to *Freya Familia*'s home at some point. The only thing the vague jumble of memories can tell me is that Allen took me by the hand.

I'm filled with this emptiness I don't know how to describe. It's like…a hole opened up in my heart. By the order of Master and the others, I get my body checked.

"This is a curse."

That's the first thing I'm told after a long examination.

"…A curse…?"

"That's right. You've been implanted with false information and are experiencing a sort of confusion."

I'm sitting in the chair I was put down into as the healer explains her diagnosis.

I can barely squeeze out a hoarse voice, my head still not really moving.

My body goes cold…and unease numbs my limbs, like a warmth spreading through my body.

"Wait…Wait a second…that's…"

I can't accept it.

Of course I can't.

No one would be able to just nod their head and quietly agree if someone told them that all of their memories were fake and that they had forgotten their real self.

There's no way I'm a member of *Freya Familia*…!

"Considering you are cursed, it might be a little harsh to say this, but…it would be for the best if you accept reality sooner rather than later. I'm sure you experienced some painful interactions with a lot of people, right?"

"Th-that's..."

"There are many examples of curses that disrupt and disturb memories. And without some specific ability, there is no guarding against curses."

I can't respond.

There's nothing to say.

The healer is closing off every escape route I might have in a kind and gentle voice, but she's right. No one knew *me*.

No matter how much I tried to assure myself that what I know is real, everyone I met rejected me.

And if the world has decided to deny me, then even if I actually am right, I would still be wrong. If everyone in the world agrees, then white is black, light is dark, and sanity is madness.

I can't breathe. My chest hurts.

The healer's red hair shifts as she shrugs kindly.

"All that being said, having false memories of someone else implanted in you is particularly cruel. Where did you get such a nasty curse?"

Curse...? Is that really what this is...?

My memory, my time with my goddess, all the people I had met... that was all a lie?

I can hear a limp sound of something slumping over as the world in front of me grows dark.

No, it's not the world. It's my vision.

My eyes.

My heart.

"For the moment, we have to report this to Lady Freya."

"Yes, we must uncover whatever villain would make a fool of our familia and make an example of them."

"Where is Lady Freya?"

"Babel, I'm sure. With the boar."

We are in an infirmary room like the reception hall of a castle. Along with me and the healer are all the first-tier adventurers of *Freya Familia* from this morning.

Master, Hegni, Allen, and the Gulliver brothers.

While I'm losing my mind, the prum brothers are talking with each other. Their gaze turns to the healer.

"Heith, hurry up and fix it."

"If it's a curse, then breaking it is a healer's job, right?"

"Please don't be so unreasonable. My specialty is treating wounds. Curses are well outside my wheelhouse…And I doubt this curse can be broken by your average healer. I don't know if even *Dian Cecht Familia* would be able to handle it."

The healer, Heith, answers with a grudging shake of her head.

Their conversation almost seems like it was planned out in advance, but there aren't any inconsistencies. It doesn't look like an act, and it doesn't feel like a lie, either.

If anything, it's almost like they had shared their memories before this conversation currently taking place around me.

"*Dian Cecht Familia*…Dea Saint, huh."

"I don't like the idea of owing an outsider any favors, but there's no other way."

"I don't like the idea of going to that much trouble for a rabbit that screwed the pooch, but there's no other way."

"And he's Lady Freya's favorite."

""""""Argh, who asked you?""""""

These people are saying whatever they want about me, but I can't respond. I still want to reject the reality in front of me with every fiber of my being.

Master and Hegni are watching me silently, while Allen looks like he might snort in annoyance at any moment.

Finally, the healer…Heith reaches her hand out to me.

"It's my responsibility if I can't heal you, so I'll be the one to go make the request. We'll get Dea Saint to examine you and pray she can break the curse."

I stare at her hand reaching out to take mine.

…If it's broken, then what?

I absolutely don't want to believe it, but if, hypothetically, I really am cursed right now…would I forget everything if the curse was broken?

Goddess, Miss Eina, Lord Miach, Nahza, Aiz, Syr, Lyu, Mia Ahnya Chloe Runoa Lilly Lady Demeter Lady Hephaistos Welf Tiona Tione Bete Finn Riveria Gareth Mikoto Ouka Chigusa Lord Hermes Asfi Lefiya Mord Gyle Scott Bors Lord Takemikazuchi Lady Loki Daphne Cassandra Haruhime Aisha Ruvis Dormul Rai Fina Ruu Mother Maria Winne everyone everyone everyone!

If I found out that everyone I've ever known and everything we've done together is all fake…if that was all a lie, then…?!

No.

No!

NO!

Before I realize it, I leap out of the chair, swatting away her outstretched hand.

"Oww…"

"Ah…I-I'm so…sorry…"

I reject her, out of fear of getting my real memories back—no, out of fear of losing my memories.

I'm sure that's how it looks to Alfrik and everyone else around me.

Heith, who is looking at me carefully as I stand there petrified, finally sighs.

"This is a serious case."

The corridors of the home really are elegant and ostentatious, just like a royal palace.

From the windows that rise taller than I stand to the pillars embedded with rich statues and a beautiful inner courtyard that looks like it might've actually been cut out of the heavens, the interior design is based on a grand and magnificent white color. It's almost like I'm wandering through a dream I can't wake up from.

After leaving the infirmary, I'm walking down empty halls, unable to speak, and my expression still lifeless.

"This is your room."

"........."

"Stay here until Lady Freya returns."

Master stops at the door and turns to look at me.

My room is the same room that I had woken up in earlier.

I have no choice but to go into the room he led me to. I don't have anywhere else to go.

Even if I went back to Hearthstone Manor, no one would welcome me in.

No...the real reason is actually...

This isn't your home.

Get out!

I'm scared of being told that.

I wouldn't be able to stand back up again if I heard that.

"...Master..."

I look up, pleading for some sort of support from the elf.

But he does not say anything to me.

His coral eyes looking at me through his glasses seem to be saying "I have nothing to say to you if you've lost your memories."

My head hangs weakly as I look at the ground, walk past Master, and enter the room.

"........."

There is nothing missing. It's the sort of room that might be expected for a member of the city's largest faction.

The room's interior is spacious, of course, the ceiling unnecessarily high, and it's hard to even imagine what might be missing among the furnishings. To have a room like this after being a member of such a small and insignificant familia...there is no way I can relax. The picture inside an extravagant frame on the dresser contains only me.

But at the same time, I notice something.

I felt it when I woke up this morning, that the room has a lived-in feeling to it. There are traces of someone living here.

It's fairly well kept, though not perfectly tidy.

There are items retrieved from the Dungeon displayed with pride on a shelf.

Several heroic epics that I told someone I loved.

There are all sorts of clues strewn about, as if a copy of me lived here once.

Is this really where Bell Cranell lived…?

"Ugh…!"

I stagger and press both of my hands to my mouth, fighting back a wave of nausea.

After retreating a few steps, I look up, greeted by the figure of an adventurer in *Freya Familia*'s uniform reflecting back at me from the mirror on the wall.

"Ghh…"

I'm deathly pale, and my lips are twitching as I turn to the closet.

Grabbing the doorknob, I slowly open the door.

"…My gear?"

There are clothes stored there along with several pieces of equipment.

A knife, a baselard, a shortsword, and a greatsword.

For protection, there are light armor, gauntlets, greaves, and various spirit cloths.

…All the sorts of gear that I've used.

My hand trembles as I pick up the knife sitting on a rack. It's scary how well the grip fits my hand.

It's a custom-order weapon designed to perfectly fit the size of my palm and the length of my fingers. The armor is the same. It's all precisely measured.

A full kit perfectly suited for the adventurer Bell Cranell is lined up before me.

But there is no gear inscribed with Welf's mark.

And there is no Hestia Knife.

"…Uuaaagh…"

My voice quivers, and my throat threatens to clamp shut right then and there.

It's not just the gear. There's no trace of the me who belonged in *Hestia Familia*. Only the Bell Cranell of *Freya Familia*.

I feel sick. My legs start to tremble.

A me I don't recognize is staring back through the mirror.

I can't slump to the floor or even collapse on the bed. I just stand there beneath a red light shining through the window.

Outside, the sun is setting in the west, and twilight is coming.

Hestia was walking by herself.

She had separated from her followers. They seemed worried, so she had lied about having business with a god that she couldn't put off.

"Bell...? Who are you talking about, Lady Hestia?"

That was what Lilly had responded after they had woken up last night.

After Freya's alteration, Hestia had crouched, struggling to steady her senses. That had been without doubt the most intense and destructive charm ever unleashed on the mortal realm, and even with the force of her vestal divinity, she had still been shaken by its passing. When she was finally able to stay steady on her own two legs, the sun was starting to set, and everything had already changed.

The people around her were enjoying the festival as if nothing had happened, and Hermes was nowhere to be seen. The gravestones of weapons that had been erected around her were replaced by the unconscious bodies of her followers.

When she dashed to their sides in a panic, she discovered they weren't hurt at all. Shortly after, they started waking up.

It didn't take long to realize they had forgotten everything that had happened.

About the attack by *Freya Familia*...and about Bell.

"For Freya's power to be this..."

Hestia was stunned, realizing that all of Orario had been transformed into Freya's sandbox.

After returning to their home, she tried to confirm the situation in a way that did not rouse her familia's suspicions, but in each case,

Bell had disappeared entirely from their memories. Lilly had been saved from *Soma Familia* by Welf, Welf had made Mikoto's weapons, and Mikoto had saved Haruhime all by herself. Their memories were all conveniently modified, all missing the one crucial figure linking them all together, and there were more than a few contradictions, but none of them noticed any of those inconsistencies. They continued to mistakenly believe that there was nothing strange about it at all.

Their thoughts were all being forced to conform to a strict rule set, a clear sign of the aftereffects of being charmed.

None of them felt anything off about the current *Hestia Familia* even though it could not possibly have come into being without Bell.

Hestia and Bell's familia no longer existed.

"Gah…!"

Paying no heed to people around her still busy with cleaning up after the festival, Hestia clutched her head and almost screamed. Rage, sadness, emptiness, powerlessness—she wanted to vent it all in a violent shout.

Bell had surely experienced that same urge countless times already.

Put into the same position he must have experienced every time he agonized over such adversity, Hestia could finally grasp the depth of his pain, but that was little comfort. The boy whom she so wanted to understand was not there anymore.

"Hestia? What happened? What are you doing in a place like this?"

"…! Hermes!"

Hestia's face swung up when she heard that voice.

There stood the god she had wanted to meet when she had been out with her familia and investigating things under the guise of helping the festival clean up.

"Hermes…about yesterday…"

"Hm? Yesterday?"

"Umm, do you…happen to remember anything…?"

"You're being a little vague. There's no need to hold back with me. We know each other better than that."

Hestia, who had not been charmed and still retained her senses, was even now being watched. And she would probably continue to be watched going forward as well to prevent her from endangering the sandbox that Freya wanted to maintain.

Surely someone was listening to this very conversation. She had to watch what she said. Hermes was all smiles while Hestia carefully chose her words and finally asked her question.

"...Do you know Bell?"

"Bell? Come on now, of course I know him."

For a brief moment, Hestia felt a rush of hope when she heard him reply in that bright, cheerful tone.

"He's one of Freya's followers. The record holder who's the talk of the city!"

"Ghh...!"

And it was immediately replaced by despair.

"Reaching Level Four in half a year is unheard of. But it's a beacon of light that could signal that the prayers of the mortal realm, and even our greatest wish, might be fulfilled. The world demands a hero, right?"

Hermes, who had given her advice and support up until right before the world changed, the trickster god who knew the identity of the parent who had raised Bell. She had approached him in the hope that if it was him, then just maybe—but it was not meant to be.

Talking so cheerfully about *Freya's possession*, he had clearly also fallen prey to her charm. Just as he had feared in the moments before the city's alteration.

"When the time comes, give this to me!"

Hestia clenched the fragment of torn paper hidden in her hand—the note Hermes left himself.

If I mess up the timing, you'll become my enemy...This is what you meant, isn't it Hermes? You, Hephaistos, and all the others...The moment I'm out of line, you'll end up turning against me...?

The people and deities under the influence of Freya's charm would erase anyone and anything that posed a danger to Freya's sandbox. If Hestia handed Hermes the note that he had furiously written to himself right now, the moment he became suspicious, his familiar expression would disappear and he would capture Hestia. Hermes had foreseen that exact scenario.

But that meant there was no one she could rely on.

Hestia had no way to break out of the situation at present.

Just like Bell, she was all alone, isolated in the palm of Freya's hand.

It was mate in one on the board.

"That's Freya for you, though, finding a follower like that. They don't call her a collector of souls for nothing."

"........."

"Still, though, I'm surprised. I wouldn't have expected you to talk about him so familiarly."

"........."

"When did you get to know him that well...Hm, Hestia? What's wrong? You aren't looking so good."

Hermes started to look suspicious after talking so cheerfully.

It hurt to even look him in the eye, so Hestia looked down.

"...It's...nothing...Nothing at all..."

"Hestia?"

"Sorry, Hermes...I'm going now."

She left Hermes with lifeless, wraithlike footsteps.

Wandering the lively streets was painful. She hated the cheerful laughs erupting around her. A city that didn't know her Bell just made her sad.

And Bell had been hurting all this time.

That fact alone was unbearably heartrending.

She was trapped in a dead-end alley, with something so very precious to her stolen away. Unable to advance in any direction, Hestia was at a total loss on what to do.

Then she noticed something.

"...That's..."

When she glanced up, she felt like she saw a figure she recognized far, far above her.

Hestia stopped moving, and after a brief, uneasy moment of hesitation, she started heading in that direction.

Remembering the path they had taken—her, Bell, and *one other*—she climbed the stairs that reached the top of the enormous city walls.

"........"

She was standing there alone.

Her golden hair rustling in the autumn breeze.

It was a beautiful yet lonely scene.

"Wallenwhatsherface..."

"...Lady Hestia...?"

It would be funny if it were not so tragic.

If it were not for Bell, the two of them would have had nothing to do with each other, or perhaps they would have had an entirely different relationship, and yet they were speaking with each other in the same way as they had just the other day.

It was so absurd, such an unreasonable situation, that Hestia tried to laugh, but she could not bring herself to do it.

"What are you doing here?"

"...I don't know..."

"You don't know?"

"Yes...I don't know...why I came here...or what I was hoping to find...or who I was hoping to meet..."

Aiz seemed to be struggling with that question herself as she answered.

Sensing the undercurrent of her emotions, Hestia was hopeful for a moment that she might possibly remember Bell, but she was soon disappointed.

Her beautiful golden eyes were etched with a glimmer of silver.

That silver gleam was proof that Aiz had fallen prey to the charm, too.

Considering even deities had been enslaved by it, too, there was no logical reason to think a mortal might have escaped the yoke, no matter how special she might be.

Hestia scolded herself.

Quit getting your hopes up and do what you need to do.

"...Do you know Bell?"

"...? Do you mean *Freya Familia*'s Bell Cranell...?"

Hearing her refer to Bell that way was beyond disheartening.

She was surely still being watched; Warlord was out there observing her every action in a way that the Sword Princess wouldn't notice.

Hestia forced herself to continue even with that knowledge.

"I'm asking you...please don't show yourself in front of Bell."

She did not know how Freya's eyes and ears would judge that comment.

But she could not let that stop her.

Since she could not change anything anymore, the least Hestia could do was prevent Bell from suffering as much as possible.

If he were pushed away by Aiz, the idol he adored, he might not be able to resist the goddess of beauty's charm anymore. He might lose the protection of his skill and fall right into Freya's clutches.

Hestia was worried about that, terrified of it.

"Me...?"

"Yes..."

"Why...?"

"I can't tell you..."

"........"

"........"

"........"

"........"

"......Okay..."

"Sorry...and thank you." Hestia's voice was barely audible as she stared down at the dark shadow stretching along the stone pavement below.

Outside the city wall, the sky was already growing dark.

The fleeting twilight lit the girl and goddess alike.

Inside the city walls, the sun was already set.

The setting sun painted everything a beautiful, heartrending crimson.

Many stopped what they were doing to admire the beauty of the moment.

"...There it is. The profile of Bell Cranell."

In the northwest of the city, Guild Headquarters on Adventurer's Way.

Eina pulled several documents from a shelf full of paperwork and folders.

Something seemed strange about Mr. Cranell when I met him... There should be no reason for me to ever interact with the city's most promising new adventurer, but...he called my name so desperately...

The Bell Cranell she had met during the day was still on her mind. She couldn't stop thinking about his deathly pale expression, so she had gotten permission from Misha and come back to headquarters alone. She didn't believe what he was saying, but she decided to look into his records.

"...Still, what could it be? I shouldn't know him...but I can't seem to let it go..."

More than anything, it felt like there was something in the depths of her heart that was pleading with her.

It was a maddening impulse that she could not explain. An ominous, mysterious feeling that she knew she had to act on. She pursed her lips as she moved away from the shelf.

There was hardly anyone left in Guild Headquarters. Everyone was busy with cleaning the streets.

Both the file room she had left and the office where her desk was located were deserted. Thanks to that, there was no one to scold her for flipping through the files while she walked to her desk.

"Bell Cranell...Fourteen years old, male. Human. Registered as an adventurer half a year ago, no indications of having received falna before entering Orario. Currently a member of *Freya Familia*..."

Sensing the presence of a small handful of people staffing the counters in the lobby and a few other workers scattered around the building, she skimmed the adventurer's profile.

It was all exactly as she remembered. There was nothing strange about his files or the sketch of his likeness accompanying them.

Wait.

"…There are signs it's been altered…?"

Eina had decided to sit down and examine the documents closely, but she stopped and stared at the papers, not even realizing she had reached her desk already.

She could see some traces of various modifications, including the section detailing the familia he belonged to.

If she didn't know better, she would have suspected a member of the Guild had swiftly rewritten the documents during the night.

Was that a real possibility…Was someone faking Bell's history?

Was he not mistaken when he called her name?

Just as Eina had that thought…

"*—No, there aren't any signs of modifications. Mr. Cranell has always been part of* Freya Familia*—*"

A silver gleam flashed in her emerald eyes as she murmured those hollow words to herself.

Her expression blank, Eina couldn't properly see what was right before her eyes.

The charm Freya had placed on the entire city was simply that powerful. It did not steal away their free will and humanity. Even though Freya had decided not to hold back and do whatever it took to make Bell hers, she had no intention of turning everyone into lifeless puppets.

Even as she scorned her work, that was the final line she refused to cross out of respect for the mortal realm. The people of the city would be able to continue to going about their lives to a certain degree.

The rules she had laid down were simple—misinterpret anything regarding Bell Cranell.

That was all.

And if they felt any suspicion about the setting Freya had created or felt there was something strange about an aspect of his path that she had not managed to alter, those stray thoughts that conflicted with her rule would be forcibly corrected. Or rather, the people in her thrall would *correct themselves*. Just like Eina had, they would not even notice their senses being twisted.

Freya's control did not even allow them to realize what was being altered. In that sense, her plan was airtight.

"...Ugh..."

However—

Eina's head ached. It felt like she was being split in two.

Her feelings toward the boy she had helped raise for the past half a year warred with the power of Freya's charm. The repeated episodes of cognitive dissonance came with a heavy cost, and it caused Eina to stagger.

"Agh...Oh no..."

The stack of books on her desk collapsed, scattering all over the floor.

Her thoughts still unsteady, Eina frantically started to clean up the mess.

Not understanding why she had so many things scattered all around haphazardly when she was usually so neat, she picked up a book...

"...Huh?"

Time stopped. She slowly blinked and looked at the cover again.

The Koine written on the cover said, BELL CRANELL'S ADVISER JOURNAL.

Eina always kept a record of the adventurers she advised.

In order to track all records of their activity in the Dungeon and for future reference to make sure that none of her adventurers died. The journals for the elf Ruvis and dwarf Dormul were lying somewhere in her apartment, too.

So why did this journal have Bell Cranell's name on it?

She didn't understand. Her thoughts came to a screeching halt. She was gasping for air. It was unmistakably her handwriting. Why did she have something like that? And why had she subconsciously tried to throw it away along with that pile of documents? Why had she tried to make it disappear?

Why?

She didn't know. She didn't understand.

But her trembling hands slowly opened it.

After forcibly negotiating with the upper levels of the Guild, I've become Bell Cranell's—Bell's adviser. Rose and the others are betting on him. While he may not have any talent as an adventurer...I won't let him die! Just like always, I'm making a journal starting today.

The pen strokes describing her first encounter with the boy overflowed with annoyance.

It recorded how she had lectured him on the first day they'd met, when she had given him the Guild-provided gear.

I can't believe him! Not listening to a word I said and going all the way to the fifth floor?! Not only did he almost get himself killed but he even wound up running around the city covered in blood! Bell is a meek boy, but he has moments where he gets too ahead of himself. I'll have to watch him even more closely. Still, though, falling for the Sword Princess on first sight...is he going to be okay?

She flipped through page after page.

Even when she erupted in righteous fury, her notes were always filled with concern for him.

Defeating a minotaur by himself and reaching Level 2...this doesn't make any sense. But that boy just might end up being an amazing adventurer after all. At the same time, I'm terrified he really might get himself killed over nothing if I take my eyes off him...You always put me on edge, Bell.

This time it was about the boy's level up, the anticipation and excitement, and also the pervasive unease. Here was the record of a boy that Eina did not know. The charm quickly went to work.

To her eyes, the records in the journal ceased to refer to Bell regardless of what was on the page.

I raised my hand against him for the first time. Attacking an adventurer, becoming hated by the city, and not telling me anything. I slapped his cheek like a fool. Even though I should be the adult. I acted like a child. But…it's lonely. It's so mortifying, Bell. I want to help you. If something is troubling you, then…I want to support you.

But her hand refused to stop turning the pages.

She could see spots where it looked like droplets had splotched the ink.

And at the same time, tears were falling quietly from her emerald eyes.

I can't. I can't anymore. I harbor a corruption unbefitting the elf blood running through my veins. And it's because of an adventurer I'm charged with advising of all people…! It's unpardonable! Shameless! And I'm supposed to be a Guild employee, the ones who keep business and personal separate above all! Apologize! Apologize to Goddess Hestia! Ahhhh, mother, please scold me. Please hold me in judgment, Lady Riveria. I mustn't embrace these feelings, and yet…

I love him.

Her eyes were pouring.

She could not even register who the boy written of in the journal was, but the tears did not stop.

There was no sadness, joy, unease, or even a smile on her face. She was expressionless as the tears continued to fall.

It's too late now, but I realized that I don't know anything about Bell outside of his adventuring. Also, when did this turn into a love diary?! The Dungeon records are still being recorded properly, but!!!! Graaaaaah!...But that's just how much I [frantic eraser marks]

...I don't want to forget. Whatever may come. Even if he dies. Or even if I die before him...I don't want to forget these feelings.

Eina turned the page.

She kept reading, crying all the while without understanding anything.

And when she attempted desperately to reach out for the feeling deep in her heart that was still pleading with her, she heard a voice.

"Still seeking it out even though you cannot even recognize what it is you want...Truly intriguing, but that's a miscalculation on my part."

"!"

A hand reached over from beside her, picking up the book.

Eina turned her head in shock to see a person—no, a goddess—standing right beside her, cloaked in a robe to hide herself. Peering beneath the hood, she saw smooth, alabaster skin. And then seeing the silver, jewellike eyes, Eina gasped, realizing who it was.

"G-goddess Freya...?"

Ignoring Eina's confusion at her presence, Freya confirmed the contents of the book that Eina had been riffling through so intently.

"It would be one thing to miss something like this if the target was one individual, but with an indefinite, wide-scale charm, gaps are bound to appear...particularly around those who had especially strong feelings toward him. It's good I noticed."

The goddess murmured to herself before suddenly looking up.

"For a powerless girl like you to be able to resist me...I'm jealous. It's almost as if you've formed a bond with Bell."

Freya smiled.

It was a quiet and enchanting smile.

Eina felt a chill run down her spine for some reason. She couldn't move.

"I'll be taking this."

"Ah..."

"It's okay. I won't throw it away. I promise."

Clutching the book to her chest, Freya took a step away.

Eina immediately tried to extend a hand after her, but she was stopped by a silver gaze. That alone caused her body to spasm.

Eina had no way to know, but it was a powerful, direct reapplication of Freya's charm.

"My children will come later to take that pile of documents. You should go back now. Forget all of this."

".........Yes, ma'am."

Glancing down at the books scattered at her feet, Freya turned her back.

Entranced and obedient to her beauty, Eina nodded emotionlessly.

No lamps were turned on. The room was lit only by the fading rays of the setting sun.

Eina stood there limply, and once the goddess had disappeared from sight, she murmured quietly like someone slowly waking.

"What was I doing...? I have to get back to Misha and the others..."

And, of course...

"Huh...? Why am I crying...?"

...Eina had lost the reason why tears were streaming down her cheeks.

Click. Click.

Footsteps echoed on the dark stairs before sinking into the darkness below.

Holding the half-elf's book, Freya descended the stairs without being stopped by anyone. And at the end of the stairway, she reached the underground altar, where four torches burned. The stone chamber resembled an ancient temple.

"Unsurprisingly, it seems I could not bend you, Ouranos." Freya flashed an oddly sweet smile at the old god sitting atop his large stone throne in the center of the hallowed space. "In addition to your position as one of the great gods, you are protected by this underground altar. My charm could not reach you. In fact, I can't even say whether voices from aboveground can even be heard here, no matter how loud."

"...Freya..."

The towering god replied solemnly, the light of rationality shining in his blue eyes.

He looked down from his seat at the goddess of beauty, who had approached without concern, knowing full well that the god before her was not under her sway.

"Do you intend to charm me as well?"

Unlike during the Goddess Festival yesterday, she was already inside his chamber and incredibly close. If she used her charm now, even a formidable deity like him would be unable to resist. From the moment he had been unable to prevent her from entering his chamber, she controlled his fate.

"Of course not. You are more crucial to the safety of Orario than any other being. If my seduction caused a disruption in your prayers, I would lose everything."

"........."

"Besides...Hee-hee, I doubt your expression would change in the slightest, even if I did charm you."

Freya laughed teasingly as Ouranos's eyes screwed up tight.

Orario was the lid on the great pit that endlessly spewed out monsters, and Ouranos, its founding god who offered up prayers to the Dungeon, was both the most crucial deity in the entire city and the keystone upon which the whole mortal realm rested. Were his prayers to be disrupted, it was entirely possible the destruction of Orario might follow.

In other words, from the start, Freya had never intended to charm Ouranos.

The downfall of the city of heroes could not be allowed.

Only wicked deities whose end goal was absolute destruction and ruin would desire such a thing.

No matter how much Freya might act the part of a proud and haughty queen, she and they were not the same.

"What is your goal, Freya?"

"Do you need to ask? I broke a taboo in order to get what I wanted. Nothing more."

"Bell Cranell..."

Ouranos was always tracking the course of events in the city through Fels and others he relied on, and he had learned of Freya's divine will through Hermes as well. Beneath his unchanging expression, and while sympathizing with the boy who had been tossed about by the currents of fate, he also sighed ever so slightly. He saw now that the boy really was a parting gift from *that* Zeus.

"Then why have you come here?"

Ouranos could not move from the altar where he offered up his prayers to the Dungeon.

The limbs who acted on his behalf, Royman and the rest, had already fallen to Freya. There was nothing Ouranos could do. Just like with Hermes and Hestia, he had lost the moment he failed to prevent Freya from activating her charm.

Or more precisely, it was not just Ouranos who had lost. Every deity had been bested.

"I thought I might come to bargain with you, this city's creator."

The dictator who could not be moved by anyone's orders lowered her hood and looked Ouranos in the eye.

"Do not interfere."

"What?"

"If you can promise me that, then in exchange, I will advance the exploration of the Dungeon in one fell swoop."

Ouranos's eyes widened as the goddess ignored his question and laid out the contents of her proposal.

"Until now, I have been content to leave matters to Ottar and let my children do as they pleased, but if you accept my proposal, I'll give the order. I will tell my whole familia to challenge the Dungeon as one."

"...!"

"That means advancing into the unexplored territory, of course, but also beginning the preparations for slaying the black dragon."

Reaching the end of the Dungeon that was the root of everything.

And the completion of the last of the three great quests that were the wish of the mortal realm. Freya was saying that if Ouranos was willing to accept her terms, she would begin to seriously address those tasks.

There was no mistaking that if *Freya Familia*, a group that prioritized individual strength above all, began to challenge the Dungeon as a united whole like *Loki Familia*, then the rate of exploration would increase dramatically.

At its heart, *Freya Familia* only moved based on their patron goddess's whims.

All of its members had had their hearts stolen by Freya and considered her grace to be their salvation, which was precisely why they spent all of their time kicking each other down in a never-ending quest to win her love. However, if they were to become unified behind the orders of their goddess…

"I will complete the machia."

There was no lie in her declaration.

Even Ouranos, so staid and unflappable, could not help betraying his shock.

"…You, who lost to Hera and became bound to Orario? Why now?"

Freya was as fickle as the wind.

Ever since Zeus and Hera's downfall fifteen years ago, she had fulfilled her duty as a deity in Orario, but she had never seriously applied herself to achieving any common goals. Between her followers' free spiritedness and her familia management, she despised prioritizing others' goals over her personal interests.

"Because I found what it is that I want…my Odr." What changed all of that was an incredibly simple and ordinary thing.

The reverent, proud, but almost fragile smile and features of a girl crossed her face all at once.

"I want Bell. His body, his heart, and his soul as well. Yes, Bell alone is enough. If I can have him, then I don't care about anything else."

"........."

"So if you can turn a blind eye to this one transgression, then I can swear that it will not cause Orario any harm. Besides, this is the best way to go about it, don't you think?"

An instant later, the enchanting smile of a witch appeared.

"If I forcibly steal Bell away, there will assuredly be a price to pay. Whether it's Hestia's children or Hephaistos and those who would take her side. But this way, no one has to be hurt."

That much was true.

Her twisting the entirety of the city to her will was not something that could be praised. It was assuredly wrong. But from the perspective of mustering the total combat potential of the city, her method did not have any major downsides. No skirmishing or war games had broken out. The masses had simply had their memories overwritten, and everything could more or less be settled peaceably.

And on top of that, if *Freya Familia* were to apply themselves to the task of speeding up the exploration of the Dungeon, that was certainly a boon to Orario.

"Other than my followers, the only ones in this city who retain their memories from before I acted are Bell, Hestia, and you, Ouranos. Just the three of you."

"........"

"If my sandbox were to fall, then you three are the only ones who could be responsible."

So don't try anything funny.

No plots, no contacting someone outside the city for support. Just sit back and let it happen.

That was Freya's unspoken warning.

In order to nip that one in a million possibility in the bud, she had personally come down to Ouranos with her offer.

"Today has been really rough, you know? My children and I were going all around the city to tie up loose ends."

"........"

"I asked the children I charmed to take care of altering Bell's history as necessary, but there were naturally some spots that got overlooked. Just now, in fact, one of your children was beginning to suspect the modified records."

She opened the journal she had taken from Eina and flipped through the pages.

While she had told Alfrik and the others to say that she was in Babel for Bell's sake, she had been out and about putting the finishing touches on her meticulous setting.

"My charm didn't reach down into the Dungeon, so every adventurer in the Dungeon yesterday did not have their memories modified."

"...You've filled that gap now?"

"Yes. I've tracked down every adventurer we could confirm and charmed them. Even the residents of Rivira."

Freya was arrogant in her diligence.

For much the same reason she had not charmed Ouranos, she knew there was no purpose in unnecessarily provoking the Dungeon. While almost everyone had been enjoying the Goddess Festival, there were still some adventurers in the Dungeon on that day who had not fallen prey to her charm. But she had already crushed that concern with incredible zeal.

She had manipulated adventurers to call the residents of Rivira on the eighteenth floor to the surface to be charmed. Some of Loki's children were on an expedition to the deep levels, but she did not send her followers that far down. There was too much risk of missing them and passing in the night, considering how expansive the labyrinth became at those depths.

There was no rush. They could be dealt with the moment they returned to the surface. And on top of that, she had extended her control to the town of Meren not far from the city. So it was safe to say that none of the places that were closely tied to Orario because of proximity would notice anything out of the ordinary.

Her charm worked on mortals and deities alike, and all under her control had been ordered to inform her of any possible discrepancies that might disrupt her sandbox. Anyone who began to doubt that Bell was a member of *Freya Familia* would immediately be discovered.

That was why her follow-up had been so meticulous. Freya was completely serious about entrapping Bell in her sandbox.

"And I even got my hands on this."

Freya pulled out a small vial. Much like Status Thief, this was an illegal item that could be obtained only on the black market. But it was an extraordinarily rare item, and there had been only one in all of Rivira. Freya had prioritized obtaining it over even approaching Ouranos, which was why she had put off seeing him for so long.

"I'm sure I missed a couple spots here and there, but…I can use Hörn and the others to patch them up."

There were no holes in her plan. And any that might exist would be quickly *corrected*. And of course, her intention in explaining all of this was to rob the old god of any choice but to accept her offer.

Her beautiful silver hair glimmered like the moon in the dark chamber.

"I've shown my whole hand. I believe I've demonstrated my sincerity…so, let's hear your answer, Ouranos."

Ouranos silently accepted the gaze fixed upon him and heavily closed his eyes.

"Regardless of what I wish for, I am called the founder god of this city, and as such, my good faith efforts must be in service to those who would live in this city. Therefore, Freya, I cannot consider your barbarous course of action to be just."

"And?"

"…However, it's also true that I cannot stop you now. So do as you please for as long as these eyes remain closed."

Ouranos's final answer was silence.

While not accepting her outstretched hand, he promised to become an unmoving statue.

"Hee-hee…You really are a crafty god."

A faint smile crossed Freya's lips as she turned on her heels and leisurely took her leave, as if knowing from the start that it would end like this.

All that remained in her wake were the four flickering torches and the old god who had closed his eyes.

"…I can't believe it…"

A short while after the goddess had left.

There was a shudder from the darkness gathered in the corner of the chamber, and a single mage appeared.

"Is it true, Ouranos…? Not just me, but every being in the city has been charmed…"

At the foot of the steps leading to Ouranos's seat, Fels stepped out, radiating shock from head to toe.

The black-robed mage who served as Ouranos's right arm had been standing by vigilantly, listening from outside.

However, despite hearing everything from start to finish, Fels still could not fully grasp the situation.

"Even after hearing all that, I still don't feel any different. Almost like no matter what I hear, I would just write it off as nonsense… No, I suppose I can't objectively see myself being bound to Goddess Freya's will as I am right now."

"That is what it means to be a goddess of beauty. That is Freya's power."

"A forcible misapprehension of reality and warping people's perceptions…Would even I be forced to become your enemy, Ouranos?"

Though Fels's robe could block all abnormal statuses and even curses, it was impossible to resist Freya's charm. The mage had already been ensnared by her powerful influence, and the moment Ouranos made any furtive moves, Fels would transform into a mere drone who would calmly report back to Freya. Because of that, Ouranos did not respond, merely keeping his eyes closed in accordance with his promise to Freya.

Fels shuddered. Even the formidable mage could not separate conscious and subconscious impulses.

Automatic submission.

The magic Freya had cast on the city was kind in a sense. Impenetrable and unbreakable, but also a curse more heinous than any other.

"I'm sure no harm will come to the city, just as Freya said. There is nothing I can do but remain a spectator for the time being. As to whether that extends into eternity…is up to Bell Cranell."

Behind his eyelids, the old god saw the figure of a lone boy.

The twilight fades, and the last motes of light turn to shade as darkness covers the city.

The sky is clear, but the stars seem far away. Wisps of clouds have made the moon hazy and indistinct tonight.

A terribly long day is coming to a close as night finally arrives.

"Lady Freya has returned. Come."

At the same time the door to my room opens, I hear Master's command. I've just been sitting on the edge of my bed, so I quietly stand up.

I follow behind him like an unresisting prisoner.

"………"

"………"

Master doesn't say anything. Nor do I.

We just walk down the pale moonlit corridors in silence. The palatial home is quiet. Not just inside, but all around the estate.

The enormous Folkvangr is surrounded by a large wall. Despite being in the middle of the fifth district, located in the south portion of Orario along with the shopping district, these halls are far removed from the noise and bustle of the city.

Even though the lively atmosphere of the Goddess Festival has only just dissipated, the silence that clings to the walls here makes it feel all the more secluded from the outside world.

Would it be an exaggeration to say it feels like a giant prison?

"…Master…Hedin…"

I correct myself, not sure how I should refer to him, but Master responds without turning around.

"What?"

"...Do you know a person named Syr?"

All of a sudden, his footsteps stop. He slowly turns around.

"...Who is that?"

"A human girl...she works at a tavern called The Benevolent Mistress..."

"........."

"She should have some connection with *Freya Familia*...Is there someone like that here...?"

Even in this impossible-to-understand situation where no one remembers who I really am, there are several other things that keep bothering me. This morning, when I asked about Lyu, Alfrik and his brothers didn't seem to remember her.

So then what about Syr?

What about the girl who disappeared after I hurt her? What became of her?

I'm desperately clinging to hope as I ask Master, but he returns an inscrutable look.

"There is no girl like that here. There is only our goddess."

The answer I expected shatters that strand of hope.

I look down, not even managing a simple "I see" in response. I'm disgusted with myself and the total resignation I feel after confronting a world so different in every way from the one in my memories.

Master looks at me for the briefest moment before he sets off again.

He leads me first to the enormous dining hall that sits at the center of the mansion on the first floor, where he brought me in the morning. Once we're through there, we enter a hallway that continues straight north. Then it's across a covered walkway that passes through a heavenly courtyard and onward into the heart of the home.

The sheer size of these unfamiliar places makes me feel incredibly small and far from home. All I can do is follow after Master to the highest floor of a structure that stands alone.

"Lady Freya, as you requested."

"Enter," a soprano voice sings from behind the closed doors.

My heart quivers in my breast as two women wielding spears who must be guards open the doors. Propelled forward by Master's gaze, I nervously step into the goddess's room alone.

"Welcome, Bell."

There is no throne inside.

The owner is sitting there on an elegant couch situated in the center of the room. Strands of glimmering silver the same color as her eyes flow down her back. Those locks of hair twinkle like a sea of stars, and her irises gleam like precious jewels.

The rest of her figure bathed in the glow of moonlight could only be described as beauty incarnate. This tranquil deity discards her bewitching demeanor as she turns her gaze to me alone.

"...Lady Freya..."

Those words are all that manage to make it past my dry lips.

The room of the goddess who controls the city's largest familia has fewer things in it than I imagined. I'm sure part of that impression comes from how large the room is, but the only furnishings that really catch my eye are a canopied bed, a bookshelf, and an intricately ornamented dresser and mirror. The floor is a white stone that has just a hint of blue to it, with a luxurious carpet running across part of it. Several columns of matching stone support the ceiling.

It's spacious and grand, like a throne room that's been transformed into a personal chamber.

The chandelier hanging from the ceiling isn't lit. Only a dim magic-stone lamp set on a small round table beside the couch and the pale glow of the moon through the window provide any light.

"I'm sorry I could not make time immediately. We goddesses are busy with various errands in the aftermath of the Goddess Festival."

"........"

"I've heard the story from Hedin and the rest. That you don't remember us?"

"........"

"And that you believe you are the follower of some other goddess."

I remain silent from start to finish as Freya speaks. I haven't moved since coming to a stop in the middle of her room. She stands up and walks over to me.

The sounds of her heels are muffled by the carpet. She stands in front of me, just a little bit taller than me as she reaches her right hand toward my cheek.

My shoulders tremble, and I reflexively step backward.

"...I thought they were joking at first, but it seems it's true."

I purse my lips, and the goddess smiles slightly, as if troubled by the situation. She seems so kind. Her tone is gentle. It's nothing like the detached and aloof attitude she always seemed to have the few times I saw her before.

I take a deep breath, trying not to let myself notice that it's exactly the sort of behavior a patron goddess might reserve for her followers.

"Am I...really a member of *Freya Familia*...?"

"Yes. I was the first to see you."

"Then...I was always fighting at your side...?"

"That's right. On the field here and in the Dungeon. You struggled like a restless rabbit. You were always pushing yourself, balanced on a knife's edge...and in truth, I was often worried about you."

Lady Freya answers my tense questions in full. And her last comment is spoken in a whisper, as if sharing a secret.

Deep inside, I'm flustered at seeing the goddess of beauty act like that, but I quickly suppress it. It doesn't seem like she's lying at all. But she is a goddess. She could probably lie in a way that a mortal like me would never see through, or otherwise hide falsehoods deep within half-truths.

For just this moment, I brush aside the impiety of doubting a goddess and make my request.

"Then...could you please give me some proof?"

I'm beyond stunned and confused by these strange circumstances.

No one remembers the me who's a part of *Hestia Familia*. They all believe I'm the strange one. Ever since I was denied at every turn and then left alone in that room, I've spent every waking moment thinking, desperate to grasp the situation.

And this is the method I came up with to confirm whether my memories are real.

"Please update my status."

This is the most definitive proof of a connection between a follower and their patron deity.

Falna—a contract and a blood tie.

Every follower, without exception, has a status inscribed on their back using a deity's ichor. And only their patron deity can update it.

I'm Bell Cranell, Lady Hestia's follower.

The time I spent with her is not a lie.

I've been waiting for this moment where I could be alone with Lady Freya in order to prove that once and for all.

"Here and now…!"

No other deity can update my status. If I can prove that my back bears Lady Hestia's blessing, then even if I can't explain why everyone else's memories are different, I will at least have some small evidence to support my claims.

I lean forward, like an adventurer holding out a lantern called hope in the murky darkness that shrouds everything from sight.

"—I don't mind, if that's what you'd like."

Meanwhile, Lady Freya doesn't show any sign of agitation as she easily accepts my request.

"Wha…?"

"Heith, a needle."

Lady Freya rings a bell, and the healer who examined me enters the room.

Bowing her head exaggeratedly, Heith holds an extravagant, jeweled tray up to the goddess.

Lady Freya pricks her finger with the sharp silver needle, and blood quickly beads on the tip. My heart pounds as I watch her move without a trace of hesitation.

It can't be. *Really?*

No, this isn't right. It can't be. I have to make it clear. I'm not the one who's wrong. I quickly remove my shirt with trembling hands—

I'm fighting against my wildly beating heart as I strip down and bare my chest.

Guided by Lady Freya, I sit in the chair set just in front of the couch.

"I'll do it *just like always*, so don't move."

I shudder at the whisper in my ear.

Just as my mind goes blank, a drop of liquid falls on my back.

—gh?!

I can feel it the moment her finger touches my back. *The feeling of someone accessing my blessing.*

It's the same pulse that I felt every time Lady Hestia updated my status.

It's a lie. It can't be. This should be impossible—but even as I freeze with my back to her, Lady Freya is freely running her finger across my back.

The moment didn't last very long.

"And done."

As if handing down a death sentence, Lady Freya reaches from behind me, handing me a single piece of paper.

I take it with trembling hands.

Bell Cranell

Level 4

Strength: A843->846 Defense: A812->871 Dexterity: A881->895 Agility: S928->935 Magic: B767->769

Luck: F Immunity: G Escape: I

"Ghhhh?!"

The full contents of my status that Lady Freya shouldn't know about, as well as properly updated numbers. My heart feels like a hand is squeezing it tighter and tighter. The exaltation that's filling my body is a merciless confirmation that my abilities really have gone up.

"Your endurance has really improved. Has Hedin been working you hard again?"

While I'm at a loss for words, Lady Freya places the needle down on the round table.

I don't respond to her comment. I toss away the paper and turn around.

Leaving my clothes behind, I struggle to move as I stumble over to the mirror.

"——"

There, the reality that greets me is crueler than anything.

Turning my back to the mirror, when I look over my shoulder, the sight that meets my eyes is a set of silver hieroglyphs.

The ancient glyphs are not in the familiar shape of a sacred fire. Instead, they're in the form of the lady.

It's not Lady Hestia's falna—it's Lady Freya's!

"That can't..."

Hammered by the immovable reality, I collapse to my knees.

There we go.

At that moment, Freya heard it.

The sound of his suspicions cracking and shattering.

That steadfast heart he had only barely been holding together finally fell apart.

In her heart, Freya hid a smile as she approached the pitiful child.

"It's okay, Bell."

"!"

The boy was kneeling on the floor, and she hugged him from behind. His body trembled as if an electrictrifying current shot through him while she wrapped both arms around him, drawing him close and giving him no chance to run or refuse.

Her voluptuous bosom pressed against his frail back.

Ahh, I can hear his heart beat.

A throbbing, rhythmic terror. This was undoubtedly the tone of the soul dearer to her than any other.

She suppressed the urge to nibble his earlobe, to bring her lips to the nape of his neck, to have their hot breaths entwine and become one until the lines separating them disappeared entirely. And then she whispered.

"I understand your fear. And your despair, too. I also understand that you can't accept everything all at once."

"Wha...?"

"So please *don't destroy yourself.* Your body is so cold. Please don't tremble so…don't be scared."

She murmured the words that he wanted to hear, allowing him to feel her heartbeat, like comforting a baby.

The boy had lost everything he knew and had no place to call his own. Taking advantage of his vulnerability, she drew close to him, offering warmth.

There was an incredible amount of tension in his body, but slowly yet surely, he relaxed ever so slightly.

I was right to get the Status Snitch from Rivira.

That had been the trick that had broken his confidence in what was real.

Just as he had suspected, his back still bore Hestia's falna, because he had not yet converted. No matter how much she might try to isolate him through the strength of her charm, she could not change that fact. It would only serve to feed his suspicions.

And so, Freya had used a magic item.

Status Snitch was far rarer than Status Thief.

Created by combining the ichor of several different deities who presided over a great many things, its effect allowed a deity other than a child's patron deity to update a status.

An item for updating the status of some other deity's child was something with no apparent benefits and many, many problems in most situations, but it could be a solution for followers trapped by a malicious patron deity, and its original use was for various clandestine purposes like recruiting spies and luring new recruits. Given its predominantly nefarious uses, it was despised by the upstanding deities who managed the network of familias, and exceedingly few of them were ever manufactured.

It required Status Thief to be used first in order to unlock a status, but once that was done, a drop of the Status Snitch's crimson liquid was enough to update abilities—however, it could only update abilities. It didn't allow for the development of magic or skills or a level-up.

Freya, who had spent the entire day taking care of all the possible points of failure in her charm, had also gotten her hands on Status Snitch and used it to catch Bell unaware.

By whispering in his ear when he was turned away, she had created an opportunity to quickly use Status Thief and then Status Snitch. As soon as the stage was set, she had used her own ichor, so that after the update, her mark would remain on his back for a time.

Using all those cumulative effects, she had managed to deceive Bell.

"Even if isolation is all you experienced, I won't let you be alone… it's okay."

She whispered softly again and again, continuing to share her warmth with him.

Before long, his breathing, which had been coming fast and shallow, slowly began to return to normal. In the process of helping Bell regaining his composure, she had imprinted her compassion into his mind, laying the groundwork for the future.

Freya smiled.

It wasn't a derisive or scornful sneer. Just a joyous smile as she positioned herself at his side.

"Are you all right now?"

"….Y-yes…"

When his body had finally stopped trembling, Freya reluctantly restrained herself, releasing him from her embrace.

When she stood up, Bell also tottered to his feet. His eyes were averted, staring at the floor. However, his earlier wariness was beginning to recede. But only just. It did not disappear completely.

Freya's eyes danced, though, satisfied with that for now.

"Bell. Can you tell me a story about yourself?"

"Eh…?"

"The you who *isn't my follower.* Could you tell me about your memories?"

Bell's eyes shot open as he looked up. His expression revealed the confusion he felt, wondering why she would ask something like that.

Freya looked down at him with a motherly gaze.

"No matter how much I might say you're part of our familia…It's still hard to believe, yes?"

"I-I mean…"

"That's not something you need to worry about. If I were in your position, I'm sure I would be just as confused, and I doubt I would be able to trust anyone either. That's why I want to hear your story. Can you tell me about yourself? The version of you who I don't know?"

"………"

"I won't deny you, whoever you might be. Of course, I want you to remember my love…but if it hurts you, then you don't have to force yourself. What is important to me is the you standing in front of me right now, and the future."

Not a single thing she had said was a lie. What's more, she had given Bell a convenient proposition.

At the very least, he would not even begin to guess at the scope of Freya's divine will. And surely the one and only being who didn't reject him would seem like someone he could rely on for the moment at least.

It was fine if it was temporary at first. She just had to make it permanent later.

"Today Ouranos called me in. He said it was about time we make some more progress in the Dungeon."

"Eh?"

"It pains me to ask this when your memories haven't come back yet, but…I would like you to train with the others during the day. I don't want to risk losing you in the Dungeon."

"………"

"When that's done, though, let's chat some more. Like this. Just the two of us."

"….Yes…ma'am…"

Bell did not have a choice.

He had spent the entire day being turned away everywhere he went. He had no other place to stay. *Freya Familia* were the only ones willing to accept him as a comrade. Even if he wished otherwise.

Freya put her right hand on his cheek. This time he did not pull away. His body jolted and shuddered like a frightened animal, but he allowed her to caress his cheek.

"I'll see you tomorrow night."

"........"

"Or would you like to sleep together tonight?"

"N-no thank you!"

"Hee-hee, what a shame...A lot has happened, and I'm sure you are tired. Go back to your room and get some rest."

"Y-yes, ma'am...thank you very much..."

Bell broke their locked gazes and turned away as he answered her. He had experienced a far too long and turbulent day; any other answer was beyond him. It must have been a challenge to even think.

He approached the door with unsteady steps, and when he crossed the threshold, he looked back.

When Freya met his gaze with an affectionate smile, his red eyes wavered and he looked away again.

This time, he departed and silence fell in her chamber.

"—Heith. Starting today, accompany him in a way such that he does not notice, and report his every action during the day to me."

"Yes, Milady."

"And *Hörn*."

The healer and chamberlain entered the room in Bell's place.

The latter's shoulders twitched when her name was called. Freya cast her a sidelong glance.

"Do you remember the promise you made with me...What would happen if Bell discovered your lie? You may no longer contact him. I will not allow you to appear before him anymore."

"...Yes, Milady."

"Instead, you shall become me, and I will have you work for a while. I was at it all day, but I couldn't take care of every last inconsistency. I will allow you to use my charm, so whenever you discover any cracks, fill them. Pay special attention to any children who come in from outside the city."

The right half of Hörn's face was covered by her long, gray hair, but her left eye widened in shock.

She could use transformation magic to become identical to Freya with the sole exception of being unable to access arcanum. That meant that she was perfectly able to charm people using the visage of the goddess of beauty, though its force and precision paled in comparison to the original. Freya had in effect ordered the girl who could become a near copy of her to complete the finishing touches on her sandbox.

Just one step outside Orario, the knowledge of *Hestia Familia*'s Bell Cranell was still alive and well. And Orario, hailed as the center of the world, was constantly welcoming travelers and merchants who freely came and went as they pleased. These visitors might feel something off about the twisted reality that the people of Orario perceived, which might in turn feed Bell's suspicions.

Consequently, they needed to be handled.

Hörn would apply charm in coordination with the gatekeepers, *Ganesha Familia*, who were already under Freya's command. She also intended to have Hörn handle any more people who had slipped through the cracks from her citywide address yesterday.

Information was meant to be overwritten.

Once word spread outside the city walls that Bell had become a member of *Freya Familia*, that would become the truth. Even if they felt some minor discomfort about it, everyone in the city would answer in the affirmative no matter how many times they were asked.

If nothing else, over time the official story would seep into the public consciousness.

Whether it was true or not, the phrase "Bell has become a member of *Freya Familia*" itself was crucial.

Charged with manipulating that truth, Hörn started to speak and hesitated several times before finally voicing the thought troubling her.

"Will…you really not punish me, Lady Freya? I dared to lie to you, plotting to kill Bell Cranell by mine own hands…"

"I shall not punish you. There is no greater punishment than that for you, right, Hörn?"

"Ghh…!"

"I will not aid you in assuaging your feelings of guilt, and I do not doubt your loyalty. So devote yourself to my service henceforth."

Hörn felt equal parts awe and fear as her goddess saw through everything with those silver eyes.

She had still not received any censure. Even though she had resolved herself in her attempt to kill Bell Cranell, she still felt the blasphemous sense of having betrayed her patron goddess. The girl suffering from emotions with no release lowered her eyes.

"Yes, Milady…"

She accepted Freya's command with a barely audible voice.

"Hörn shall return to being my attendant from today."

"With all due respect, Milady, Allen and the others will surely make their displeasure known," Heith said.

"Tell them I have allowed it."

The healer bowed deeply in accordance with her mistress's divine will. Then Freya's gaze shifted, looking at the door to her room.

Her thoughts turned to the boy she had so cruelly cornered.

What do people do when faced with an impossible reality…? At first, they will cling to their own view, but in time, they will gradually come to doubt themselves.

Bell's mind was still unstable.

He could not trust anyone while suffering from the pressure and unease of an overwhelming and immeasurable solitude.

No matter how much Freya and her familia might try to explain that they were comrades, he would be unable to accept it.

So then, what to do?

It was simple. He needed someone who understood him.

Freya would be the only person in the world who understood him. The only one who did not deny him, who accepted him for who he was, and who empathized with him. By doing that, his childlike heart would easily begin to waver, and he would willingly bite into the sweet apple even if he knew it to be poison.

"I will continue to hurt you, Bell. And every time you are hurt, I will hold you. And heal you. I swear it."

The goddess smiled, her expression betraying no emotions.

"I'm sorry, but I made up my mind, so I won't hold back any more."

Her name was Freya.

The ruthless and free-spirited goddess. The witch who knew both the miracles and the poison of love better than any other.

CHAPTER 3
THE FIELD OF BATTLE

The sun is up.

A dark blue still clings to the edges of the cloudless morning sky, but the rain has passed and the weather is clear.

My heart is still shrouded in clouds, though, with no hope of clearing up in sight.

"Bell! Quit dawdling and get your ass over here!"

"…Yes…"

At the half-prum's shout, I stop peering up from atop the hill and follow him.

This is *Freya Familia*'s home, Folkvangr.

We're in the courtyard of the largest home of any familia in Orario. The sea of green surrounding the manor that stands on the hill rising at the center has every right to be called a field. The grass is wet with morning dew that glistens breathtakingly in the sunrise.

The walls and gate surrounding it are too sturdy to be called a simple fence, and they hide the outside world from view. It's still hard to believe that this is in the middle of the city.

And starting now, I'm going to be fighting here.

"I'm not going to treat you any different, even if your memories are messed up or whatever! I'll give you a proper baptism out here in the yard, just like before!"

The half-prum charged with watching me shouts gruffly at me with his back turned.

Last night, Lady Freya informed the whole familia that I've been acting odd because of a curse…or so I hear. Because of that, a fellow Level 4, Van, is supposed to look after me as I go through my daily activities. He barged into my room this morning and smacked me awake, brought me to the dining hall to make me stuff down a quick snack in place of a full breakfast, and then we immediately filed out to the yard with the rest of the familia.

I wish yesterday had only been a dream, but I haven't been allowed time to bury my head in thoughts of hope or unease.

With everyone gathered like this and armed to the teeth, it looks like the host of a great army.

"Before you lost your memories, you were a garbage rookie who managed to catch Lady Freya's interest despite your inexperience! I didn't like that, and I hated you! And everyone else was the same, so don't expect anyone to hold back on your account!...Hey, what's with those lifeless eyes?!"

I've been absentmindedly staring at the half-prum, who is even shorter than me, which is probably why he's angry at me.

"S-sorry..."

I hastily try to apologize when he stomps off, his face red as can be. I still haven't really come to terms with my situation yet.

...It's not as if I don't remember Van...

I'm pretty sure he was one of the people who tracked me on my date with Syr during the Goddess Festival, and I remember there being a half-prum among the members of *Freya Familia* who chased us all the way onto the boat.

Not that I have a way of confirming any of that now.

"I'll explain it once for you, but the followers of glorious Lady Freya *engage in mortal combat* here in this yard! From dawn until dusk, every day! Those going to the Dungeon are not restricted to this, but not fighting here is rarely an option! Because this is Folkvangr!"

Van gestures to the wide field around us as he speaks.

Apparently, every member of *Freya Familia*, from Level 1 to Level 4—excluding the healers and noncombatants—heads out to the field here every morning and takes part in real combat.

It's a famous story around Orario, and I even got to see it for myself just yesterday. So it's not like I was jolted in shock or anything, but...

"...What's the signal to begin fighting?"

I got dragged outside early in the morning, told to bring my weapons and gear, and now I'm supposed to get ready for a fight.

I don't know what I'm even doing, though.

There is a compulsive feeling thundering in the back of my head that there's something else I should be doing, something else I should be thinking about. I wish someone would tell me what it could be.

The pain of being rejected by so many people still aches.

Just remembering the words and gazes of all the deities I encountered leaves me on the verge of foundering.

Should I search for whatever changed the world? Or should I quietly accept that I've changed? Everything seems to be urging me to do the latter, whispering in my ear and telling me to just give up already and admit the truth. Blocking out those whispers takes everything I have.

My dark, heavy mood—

"There isn't one."

—is instantly blown away by the warriors around me. For better or for worse.

Van spins in my direction, his twin blades hurtling toward my chest.

"?!"

My instincts howl, and I reflexively parry with my knife. The heavy blow numbs my hand down to the marrow in my bone. That thrust would've gone straight through my heart if I didn't block it.

He's serious.

Van is trying to kill me!

"The moment you set foot on this field, the fighting begins!"

Other familia members around us let loose with their own weapons like they want to drive Van's point home. A thunderous roar rings out, marking the beginning of the battle.

The sounds of furious slashes and heavy, thudding blows fill my ears, and my body shivers as the battle cries wash over me. There's no time to be amazed by how quickly the field has transformed into a feverish melting pot of struggle.

The half-prum in front of me slashes with all his strength.

"I told you that I'd give you a proper baptism!"

"Ghh…?!"

"This is a battlefield! This is where the brave warriors the goddess desires are born!"

Our blades meet in a spray of sparks as Van roars at me. His weapons twist without leaving any obvious opening, and I parry his attacks with my knife as a flurry of blows envelop me.

Acting on reflex alone, I draw the baselard at my hip and intercept his blades. I move in a mixture of defense and evasion with my life on the line.

I can't let my mind dwell on the troubles that have been eating at me even if I wanted to as my inner adventurer is dragged to the surface.

"Uoooooooooooooooooooooooooooooooooooooooooooooo!!!"

As the battle cries make the very air tremble, I'm forced to join the other warriors and become one of them.

A thrusting sword point, a spinning kick that almost touches the ground, an unmistakable murderous glint in his eyes—this is anything but training or practice. Van's momentum is overwhelming. Meanwhile, I'm just barely managing to stay alive.

The unease I felt when I discovered how perfectly these unfamiliar weapons fit in my hands…that's all gone now. I swing again and again, digging in with my feet as I fight desperately. Van isn't someone I can hold back against. A moment of indecision is unthinkable.

If I don't fight back with everything I have, I'll be killed!

"Ya!"

"Haaaaaaaaah!"

It's the same for everyone around me.

I notice two humans, a man and woman, crossing blades next to me. A dwarf behind me sends an elf flying with a heavy hammer blow, while a beast person and an Amazon are locking blades at close range. If there were a bird flying above the field, it would see a scene of chaotic battle. There are even magic and curses flying through the air as people who should have been comrades in the same familia do their best to kill each other.

Blood splatters the ground.

Some collapse.

Weapons fall from slack hands.

But then someone picks up a dropped spear or pulls out a bloody sword, stands back up, and returns to the fight.

The cacophony of sound makes me go pale.

This is—

I underestimated this.

I had no idea.

I thought they meant it metaphorically when they said they fought to the death.

But there's nothing figurative about this vicious combat!

This is—Folkvangr!

It's the stage of a fierce, intrafamilia battle that has undoubtedly caused some real deaths. The most important thing here is the strength never to falter and the will to keep fighting.

Those who survive, those who continue to win—only they earn the right to be called einherjar!

Swallowed up in the fever pitch of battle, I feel sweat begin to flow from every pore. That's when I see something rustling in the corner of my eye.

The little rings of flowers blooming proudly no matter how much they are stepped on, no matter how much they are torn apart, no matter how much they are stained red with blood.

Only now do I realize the resilience of this field that has drunk the blood of so many warriors.

"Don't get distracted!"

"Ghhhh?!"

Van's furious shout pounds my head, calling me back from my idle thoughts.

My battle clothes are torn to ribbons by his unending slashes, and when I try frantically to put some distance between us, he follows up with a thrust that threatens to run me through.

I have no choice.

My left hand shoots forward.

"Firebolt!"

"Guh?!"

Fire and lightning erupt from my hand, slamming into Van. I used my magic. No, I *was forced* to use it!

It's one thing to aim that spell at a monster, but to use it against another adventurer, not as a threat but fully intending to hurt them...that never happened even in all my training with Aiz!

Van's stomach and chest are scorched and smoking as he staggers. But his eyes just bulge as he glares at me before resuming his assault.

What unbelievable durability. And the level of technique and skill are plain to see. These fighters are far stronger compared to adventurers of the same level in other familias.

I can't believe that the people here aren't even considered the core members of *Freya Familia*!

"Guaaaaaaaaaaaa?!"

Screams clearly mark the moment another person gets knocked out of the fight. The adventurers who lost their original opponents immediately leap to their next fight.

Tens, hundreds, thousands of blades cross on all sides, the sounds melting into the background in the blink of an eye.

Time feels compressed here. Blood pulses through my body, driven by a desperation to stay alive as I exert every part of my body. This battle royal is nothing like the consecutive battles I've experienced in the Dungeon. With no other choice, I throw myself into the fray.

I fight hard.

Questions like whether anyone remembers me or what I should do...

The sadness and idle thoughts...

I cast it all aside.

The fighting is too fierce for there to be room for anything else in my mind. It's all I can do not to die.

I just keep fighting.

The day grows older, and the sun is hanging high overhead.

I'm the one still standing on the field of warriors.

"Ghhhhh....D-damn it...!"

Van and the others kneeling on the ground are glaring at me, their eyes filled with anger and regret.

It's not that I'm stronger than them, especially compared to Van and the other Level 4s.

The reason I won out in the end is simply because I had Firebolt.

If I had fought a series of one-on-ones, with only half a year of experience, I would've easily lost against their greater experience and breadth of techniques. But this was a battle royal. In an endless battle where you have to face another opponent the moment you beat your first, there's no such thing as friend or foe. Surviving means dealing with attacks that come from every angle and anticipating all sorts of surprise attacks. And in that wild scramble, I had a bigger advantage than anyone with my instantaneous combat power.

I could countersnipe anyone attacking me from a distance.

I could drive back a swarm of people crowding around me.

If one shot wasn't enough, I could cast it again right away.

A spell that required no chant at all was faster than even a magic swordsman's fastest magic. I was reminded again just how much value Firebolt had in a free-for-all.

And more than anything...having survived four days and four nights lost in the bowels of the deep levels, I'm just as tough in any test of endurance.

And I desperately crush the doubt sprouting in my heart about whether that had really happened.

"Hah...hah...hah...haaaaaaaah...?!"

Still, though, the amount of magical energy burned by repeated uses of Firebolt isn't something I can just laugh off. Just breathing has become a challenge. It takes everything I have to squint and look at Van and the others, checking if there's anyone else still left standing.

—I can't fight any more than this.

That's the only thought in my mind as my whole body heaves with each breath.

* * *

“““““Not bad.”””””

Suddenly, four voices ring out.

“——”

Time stops when I hear them behind me.

“You pass the bare minimum level to be useful as an adventurer.”

“I wasn’t sure what to think when I heard your memories were messed up, but…”

“We can work with this.”

“We can fight with this.”

When did they enter the field?

The four prums are holding their own individual weapons and wearing their sand-colored armor, ready to fight.

“Our strength exists for the sake of the goddess, and so we seek ever greater strength to better serve her.”

Paying no heed to me and my silent shock, a single dark elf draws a black sword from its sheath.

“Time is limited. We will *kill* the current you *so that you may be reborn.*”

And finally, Master appears before me, stepping onto the field as well.

“The true baptism begins now.”

I, Bell Cranell, have been surrounded by the city’s strongest first-tier adventurers.

My adventurer instincts that have been struggling so hard keep me alive finally fall silent, as if all hope is lost.

Evening.

Though I can hardly see anything anymore, I can still make out the red glow that marks the end.

I can faintly sense the murmur of the breeze.

Flowers are rustling near my ear.

Apparently, I slumped facedown on the field.

I can't remember when I fell.

I was *carved.*

I was *smashed.*

I was *charred.*

I was shredded by every kind of skill, annihilated by tactics I could not begin to match, and broken by magic I had no hope of countering.

The dark elf's swordplay cut off all routes of escape, and when I attempted to defend myself, his blade cut through me and my gear. I'm honestly still not sure how my arms and legs are still attached to my body.

In a dance of offense and defense against the prum brothers' infinite combinations, they were simply guiding my every move, and the moment I revealed an opening, the spear, hammer, ax, and sword came at me from every direction.

The white elf's lightning strike enveloped my counterattack, and me along with it, turning my clothes to dirty rags. The unwavering, unceasing storm of lightning stamped out not just my body, but also my mind, and even my will.

None of my efforts at resistance worked. The opposition was too overpowering.

I finally understand what it means to be surrounded by first-tier adventurers. The experience was cruel and insane.

"................Ahh."

A pathetic, broken sound that can't even be called a groan crosses my lips.

My bones are broken. Every patch of skin has been cut. There isn't a single spot where my battle clothes aren't stained red.

I can't so much as breathe or cough up blood properly. At first, whenever I took a hit, it had been so hot, so painful that I was on the verge of tears, but now I don't feel anything. It's almost cool, cold, even. Is it winter now?

My heartbeat is growing fainter. My life is ending.

Death is close.

I know it. I know this feeling.

During that struggle in the deep levels, I tasted the darkness.

This time there is no one to hold me. My life flashes before my eyes, but it's pointless. I don't even have the strength left to recognize what is happening.

Even the cold begins to fade, and though my eyes are still open, my lungs begins to fail.

"*Zeo Gullveig.*"

A healing light envelops my body, and I'm forcibly pulled away from the brink of death.

"———Gaaaaah?!"

My pulse races, and air fills my lungs again. Life courses through my broken body and shakes me to my soul. My half-shut eyelids wrench open, and my body jolts as if I've been electrified. I quiver like a fish tossed onto dry land.

"Haaa, haaaaah....?! Ghah, goho...gahah...?!"

"That was a bit close. You were actually about to die there."

I hear an easygoing voice as my entire body shudders to a rhythmic beat, as if the entire thing had transformed into a heart pumping life through me. My arms and legs spasm as my fingers dig into the ground.

The world around me is still flickering as I look up to see the healer who revived me—Heith—standing there with a long staff in hand.

"All of you first-tier boys, that's it for today. I can heal wounds, but he doesn't have enough blood. He can't move anymore."

"Pathetic."

"That's all he can do, huh?"

"How do you plan to show your face to Lady Freya?"

"—But it's sunset."

The four prums lower their weapons as instructed.

The sun is just starting to disappear below the horizon in the west. Around me, the rest of the fighters are beginning to withdraw, and the sounds of weapons clashing have died down. The battle is over.

I made it to the end alive. But I'm dumbfounded, and unable to even appreciate that small solace.

How many times over did I die...?

I had more than a few near-death experiences.

The moment my heart stopped or my breathing ceased, I was pulled back to the world of the living. Sometimes it was elixirs, and other times it was the healers' magic. Once it was even a lightning blade. Regardless of the method, the innumerable wounds, shredded limbs, and shattered bones were restored in an instant.

Looking around, I see other people who collapsed being bathed in a healing light or receiving the attentions of herbalists.

Putting my trembling hands to the ground, I push myself up as I finally realize it.

Freya Familia doesn't just boast adventurers. They also have an abundance of healers, said to be far rarer to find than regular mages.

Is that the secret to their death matches? Their rigorous internal competition is made possible by skilled healers.

"We're quite capable, so we can heal just about anything up to three steps from death's door." I can't tell if Heith is joking or serious as I sit up on the ground, still not ready to stand. "Incidentally, if you want to come back from the literal brink of death, then Dea Saint's the only one who can help you."

I look in terror at her face half-hidden in the shadow cast by the setting sun.

Perhaps misunderstanding, Heith smiles indifferently.

"Don't worry. You're the first one I've seen them go after that hard in a show of force. You're special."

I blanch at that explanation, which fails to make me feel any better.

Dying and being revived...

This...This is what it meants to be einherjar. The indomitable followers of the goddess born and forged in Folkvangr.

"The fate of one bereft of memory, a rebirth...For your first day, you endured well."

The two elves who already overcame the baptism out on the field and reached the first tier pass beside me.

Hegni shares a few kind words as he sheathes his pitch-black sword while Master gives me an unsympathetic glance.

"We shall be your opponents starting tomorrow. Prepare yourself."

I lose any small scrap of hope I was holding on to. This is going to continue…?

There's no time to shrink in terror at being alone in the world. I'm going to have to struggle against a different despair…No matter how scared I might be, though, I know there is no escape.

"Let's go, Bell. You can't stand, right?"

Heith reaches out her hand, helping me up in my stupor.

My body is so unsteady from blood loss, I can't help collapsing into her arms.

The Gullivers, Van, and the other adventurers are all headed in the same direction.

The unconscious are grabbed by the arms or legs and dragged there, too.

Other than the first-tier adventurers, everyone is battered and wounded as they return to the manor.

Fading red light casts countless long shadows across the field. The twilight scene resembles soldiers marching off to the final battle, and I can't help feeling a sense of pathos, and a cold chill.

The flowers on the field are still swaying in the wind.

Folkvangr was shrouded in pale moonlight.

The fields fell silent with nightfall while the palatial mansion atop the hill was filled with light and noise.

The origin of it was Sessrúmnir on the first floor.

In a complete about-face from the extreme stakes of the battle on the field, a hearty feast was being held.

"Meat!"

"Gimme booze!"

"I need more blood! How am I gonna fight tomorrow like this?"

The long tables were lined up in ten rows, and dozens upon dozens of adventurers were sitting at them, reaching out to the various dishes before them, tearing away at the meat and draining mugs. It was a battle of food.

A member of *Freya Familia*'s day began with battle at dawn and ended with an enormous dinner.

It was familia custom for those who had participated in the fighting out on the fields to restore their bodies by eating in Sessrúmnir. More practically, if they did not restore themselves at the massive feast, they would have little hope of maintaining their strength and will for the inevitable fight tomorrow. No matter how much magical healing they might receive, at a fundamental level, food was crucial in order to fully heal a wounded and exhausted body. Because of that, many a warrior turned their undivided attention to transforming their food into flesh and washing it all down with copious amounts with ale.

"Haaah. You're all hungry today. Just like always…Argh, someone switch with me."

Meanwhile, Heith and the other healers and herbalists were busily preparing food in the kitchen.

Their job included not just near-resurrections, but also the aftercare involved once the baptism was complete. Herbalists prepared spices and brews to increase stamina and endurance, turned honey and goat's milk into mead, and in the giant pot affectionately called the witch's cauldron, they stewed boar meat (not as a spiteful jab at the familia's leader, who never lifted a hand to help or anything, of course).

They were often called Andhrímnir, the sooted servers.

It was whispered that the name came about because they were valkyries who satisfied the brave warriors' appetites but also because they were worked so hard that, from behind, it often looked like they were covered in soot. Heith was the young representative of the

Andhrímnir, famous for her deep faith in Freya and always looking dead on the inside. There was even a rumor that at a certain tavern, when some gods were laughing among themselves about whether she or Perseus looked more worn down, she silently bashed them in the back of the head with her staff.

At the moment, she was haphazardly sprinkling salt and spices on all the food, as if daring the adventurers to eat it.

Heith's common refrain was "I wish that legendary dwarf who used to manage this kitchen all by herself would come back."

The familia's custom of fighting from the morning until evening and holding a feast at night was not something Freya had established. The previous generation of familia members, those who had followed Freya before Ottar had become leader of the band, had come up with it themselves, and it continued to be passed on to the later generations.

In any case, the noncombat members of the familia—including even the elegant maids constantly ferrying dishes from the kitchen—were constantly busy, day in and day out.

"All right, we're short on people, so I brought some out myself... Wait, what are you doing sulking here, Van?"

Reaching him after winding her way through the long tables, Heith cocked her head. Van furrowed his brow as she placed more boar meat and mead in front of him.

"...We're sucking it up and treating that whelp like a comrade for now. He ticks me off, but he's strong. We lost out on the field today. I admit he has the strength to be called an einherjar at least. Still..." Van glared straight at the seat in front of him. The others joined him as they directed their annoyance at the same chair.

It was empty.

That was where the boy had sat before he finished eating and was called away to the goddess.

"...Why does he have such a monopoly on the love of the goddess that we always wanted...?!"

He spoke for all of them in their envy and resentment.

Heith shrugged, a detached expression on her face.

"That's simple. Because he is special to her."

"Lady Freya."

Hearing her name, she raised her eyes from the book she was reading.

She was in her room on the top floor of the home. She was wearing a delicate black negligee as she sat on the couch when her eyes went to the door.

"Bell has come."

"Send him in."

She almost burst into laughter hearing the unrefined Ottar refer to him as Bell. Stifling her smile, she closed the book and hid it under the cushion of the couch.

After subconsciously running her fingers through her long, silver hair a couple times.

No matter how much she might deny that she had been waiting impatiently for this moment, Ottar and anyone else who could see her would all respond with a knowing smile.

"Welcome, Bell. Thank you for coming."

"Welcome, Bell. Thank you for coming."

I've been taken from the enormous hall and brought to the goddess's chamber, where Lady Freya greets me. I'm startled to see the goddess of beauty herself meet me at the door and take me by the hand.

Her skin is smooth as silk, and my heart races at the soft warmth it gives off as she leads me to the center of the room.

She sits on her couch while I sit on the armchair next to the round table.

"You look pale. Did you have a particularly harsh baptism?"

"...Yes. On the field, Master...Hedin and the others...put me through my paces..."

"Ahh. I'm sorry for calling for you when you must be so tired."

We're alone in her room again tonight. The goddess's chamber is lit in a fantastical light by the moon shining in through the wall-sized window.

Even now, I still can't really believe that the famed goddess of beauty herself is here before my eyes.

It's just too unreal. Feeling an exhaustion that can't be ignored and fully understanding how improper it is...I probe her with questions once again, still unable to accept that my memories are false.

"It's hard to believe I went through such a fearsome battle every day...Today was scary and exhausting."

"Ha-ha, that's fair. I suppose the baptism might be a bit unpleasant if you've lost your memories."

"........."

She easily evades the question.

My mouth twists slightly into an awkward expression, and I quickly give up. I'm far too badly outclassed to be trying to probe a goddess for inconsistencies.

Lady Freya giggles slightly as she looks at me like she finds something funny.

"So then, will you tell me your story, like we promised?"

"...Did you really mean that?"

"Of course. Why else would I have called you like this?"

The goddess sits on the couch, not crossing her legs as she looks right at me.

After hesitating terribly, with a sense of resignation, I begin to speak.

"I came to Orario by myself. It was my first time coming to a big city, so at first, I was excited by everything, but...there were no familias that would accept me...I ran out of money fast and was lost in the city...and that's when Lady Hestia found me."

I never really talk about myself like this, and I'm not sure how to go about it. I pause at several points, trying to choose my words as I awkwardly tell the story. And there is a searing pain in my chest when I say, *Lady Hestia.*

"Oh...so after quite the struggle, you finally managed to join a familia. Then what happened?"

Lady Freya is listening to my story, looking deeply interested.

She does not reject it as nonsense or sneer that it's just a dream. If anything, to my surprise she asks questions, urging me to continue. Her soothing, pleasant soprano gradually draws more and more stories out of me, to the point that I begin to feel flustered.

Is it just her charisma? Or the allure of a goddess of beauty?

Something makes me want to talk with her forever. She has this irresistible magic that makes me feel that way.

"...Lady Freya...where did we meet?"

Trying to not get carried away, I clear my head and try asking about *Freya Familia*'s Bell Cranell.

"At the Adventurers Graveyard. I had come to leave flowers for my children when you were visiting the memorial. I was taken with you at first sight."

"A-at first sight...?!"

That phrase makes me blush, completely taking me by surprise.

"When I asked if you would become one of my followers, you got flustered and almost fell over backward. You asked, 'Is someone like me really acceptable?'"

"...!"

"Afterward, when I brought you back home, you turned terribly pale when you saw Ottar."

The story that Lady Freya tells is perfect.

If there were another me in a different universe, that definitely sounds like it could've happened. Even I think it sounds exactly like something that I might have done.

No matter how I look at it, I can't find any holes. I can't find a reason to doubt it.

"And then you started exploring the Dungeon. You wanted to go to the Dungeon so badly, even before undergoing the baptism, so I had Hedin accompany you, but...you came rushing right back to me after defeating a single goblin."

"Ghhh?!"

"I had a good laugh at that. You were so cute, getting so excited over it."

She smiles at the memory, seemingly thinking back to the moment. All I feel is a terrible shock.

That was a real event from my memories, an embarrassing scene I shared with Lady Hestia. No matter how well someone might know me, they would never be able to make up a story so absurd as me returning triumphantly from the Dungeon after defeating a single goblin!

The only possibility that makes sense is that Lady Freya had actually seen it…!

I never told anyone about that since it was so embarrassing! The only ones who would know are Lady Hestia and Miss Eina…!

It's only natural, though, since I learned about it from that very same Eina.

She could easily see that Bell was growing confused.

Freya smiled to herself as she placed her elbow on the cushion at her side.

Or rather, I learned it from her journal.

The book she had been reading until Bell came in, the one currently resting hidden beneath the cushion, was the journal she had taken from Eina the day before. And written in it was Bell Cranell's Dungeon debut, the absurd and delightful battle report that Eina had written that day. Freya had read through all of Bell's records as an adventurer and could frame them as if she had seen or heard about them herself.

It was not just Eina's journal, either.

She also used the knowledge of the now dead neighborhood girl within her to re-create plausible stories, too.

That girl had interacted with Bell at the tavern and heard all sorts of stories. Stories of his adventures, naturally, but also more personal things, like the sorts of food and drinks he liked or did not like, his tastes, his hobbies. Outside of Hestia and the rest of his familia, there was no one who knew Bell better than that girl. And Freya could use that knowledge to flesh out the plot she had designed, to breathe life into it, and make it feel all the more real.

Both the innocent boy Bell and the adventurer Bell.

With knowledge of both of those Bells, Freya could easily write a history for another Bell.

She could do that. She who had interacted with him more than anyone else at the bar, who had watched over him from Babel more than anyone else.

"Wh-what about when I reached Level Two?!"

"You fought a *minotaur* on the fifth floor. You slew a monster that had escaped Loki's children while they were returning from an expedition. I imagine the Guild still has the records on that, though."

"Ghh…?! What about Level Three?!"

"That's when you defeated Phoebus Apollo. One of Apollo's children."

"…I-in a war game?"

"A war game? We haven't done any war games. We just crushed Ishtar and Apollo when they tried to steal you away."

And above all, Bell wouldn't suspect a thing because she was a deity. A supernatural being such as Freya would remember all the events that she experienced in exacting detail.

In this situation—

If it were this person—

When that irregularity occurred—

By analyzing all those variables, she could reach the likeliest action that Bell Cranell would have taken in a given circumstance—

By analyzing and taking into consideration all the incidents, accidents, and uproars that had actually occurred and then projecting them onto her story, she could easily create a What-If story of Bell Cranell.

It was a story that hewed so close to reality that even Bell was forced to believe that it might have really happened. And if he ran off looking for evidence of it later, all of the records at Guild Headquarters and elsewhere had already been altered to fit.

Every gesture Freya made while speaking, the easy pace and tone of her voice, the way her gaze moved—all of it lent credence to what she was saying.

The child standing all alone in the middle of the sandbox would not ever be able to see through it.

"Bell? Can you tell me some of your stories, too? I don't want to just force the version of you I know."

"Oh…r-right…"

Her kind words that were as beautiful as snowflakes slowly wore down the boy and seeped into him, like a witch's poison.

Right then and there, Freya and Bell were playing a game of chess.

Bell was desperately moving pieces on a board he was not only unfamiliar with, but on which he barely even knew up from down, trying with all his might to find a way out, to find something that would confirm the world he knew.

The goddess's eyes narrowed. He was both precious and pitiful as he struggled so, and she kindly, gently guided him while teaching him how to play.

"You can't move it like that."

"You shouldn't move there."

"Right, that is the best move."

And in doing so, she was leading him every step of the way, *luring* him to move in a certain way.

Robbing him of the space to think, eliminating all the points of discomfort he was feeling, and surrounding him in her embrace. Making him hers in a way that made it impossible for him to even notice the checkmate coming.

That was the kindest way to lay the boy low.

This was the perfect way to obtain Bell Cranell in soul, body, and mind.

Because of that, Freya did not hesitate to use methods that went beyond the board. That was why she used her followers and why she used her charm, breaking the taboo.

That was why she had made the sandbox.

"………gh?!"

But it was time to stop for the night.

Bell's expression was changing at a dizzying pace. It was sloppy to push him too far too quickly. The goal was not to torture him by small degrees, but to shape his will and draw him to her.

Observing his face, Freya judged she had done enough for one night.

"…? What is it?"

"No, it's nothing."

Bell looked up, and Freya, who had been observing his condition, smiled as if there were nothing special on her mind.

—I forgot he is so sensitive to the eyes of others.

Suppressing her smile and wanting to draw away from her expression, she pointed to her skin, which was slightly flushed.

"It's just a little bit hotter than usual tonight."

Freya brushed aside her hair that had settled on her breasts, every bit the image of a self-possessed and imperturbable empress.

All of a sudden Bell's face turned crimson.

"?"

Freya cocked her head slightly at his reaction, and then it dawned on her.

The delicate gown she was wearing opened quite boldly at her chest. By brushing aside the veil of hair, her deep cleavage was now clearly visible, and with just a single misstep, her ample breasts might break free from their minimal restraints.

Bell was petrified and averted his eyes with all his strength.

Right, he's that sort of child.

She found his innocent reaction charming as she stood up.

"Someone bring a change of clothes."

She called out to the attendants waiting outside the room. They would provide something for her.

Then, Freya was struck with a mischievous impulse.

"I'm going to change, Bell."

"Y-yes, ma'am?"

"Help me."

"Heaaah?!"

The boy's voice rose into an almost hysteric shout.

Freya gathered her hair with one hand, revealing the buttons running down her back.

"I can't take this dress off by myself. How would I reach the back?"

"Eh, but, ugh?!"

"Can you undo them? I can take care of the rest myself."

"M-m-may I excuse myself?!"

"I don't mind, but Ottar's outside and he might be rather upset if you do. Tomorrow might become that much harder?"

Bell's calm was long gone, and extreme panic had set in. He turned deathly pale, as if remembering the trial he had experienced earlier that day. And through unending anguish, he reached his trembling hands out to the goddess's back.

Freya struggled not to laugh.

"I suppose this outfit was a bit too provocative for you."

"Uh, ummm…!"

"Or do you think it doesn't suit me?"

His fingers gingerly undid one button after another.

She smiled, closing her eyes as she questioned him. The boy struggled to contain his embarrassment as he responded.

"….Not at all…It looks…lovely on you…"

It was a simple answer.

Freya was no inexperienced maiden, but there was a sweet yet sharp pain in her breast.

"Mm."

Perhaps because of that, when the boy's trembling hand missed slightly, and his finger brushed against her back, she let out a carnal moan.

Freya's shoulders twitched, but Bell's whole body spasmed.

The poor boy, aware he had carelessly touched the goddess's soft skin, grew bright red—and unable to endure it anymore, he fled.

"I-I'm sorryyyyyyyyyyyyyyyyyyyyyyyyyyyyyyyyyyyyyyyyyyy!"

He departed at a full sprint. His apology resounded in her chamber as he flew out the door.

Freya was surprised and betrayed a truly flabbergasted expression unlike any she had ever shown before, and then…

"Ha…ha-ha-ha-ha-ha!"

She laughed like a child.

Running in tears from her chamber!

There hadn't been anyone, god or child, who had ever done that before!

Tears of laughter welled in her eyes as she held her mouth and stomach, spinning in a dance of sorts.

And paying no heed to the thought of how improper it might be, she collapsed into bed.

"…Lady Freya?"

Finally, Hörn gingerly peeked her head into the chamber.

No doubt, she had already confirmed Bell was gone. There was a change of clothes in her arms.

Behind her stood Ottar, who for once seemed unsure how he should act.

"I prepared a change of clothes…"

"Forget it."

"Eh?"

"He complimented me in this, so I'll wear it to bed tonight."

She kicked her legs a couple of times and then rolled over onto her back.

Her chest swelled as she inhaled and then exhaled. Her right arm covered her forehead as her reached out toward the ceiling with her other hand, her expression breaking into a girlish smile.

"………"

Ottar watched in silence as his mistress was filled with joy.

And Hörn continued watching as well, clutching her hand to her chest.

The moon was pretty.

Sadly, there was no one beside her who could share in that thought.

Beneath the clear night sky that was the opposite of her clouded heart, Hestia was walking along the backstreets of Orario.

She was all alone after having forcibly persuaded Lilly and the others who had tried to stop her.

...I'm being watched...

She did not have the knowledge and experience of an adventurer like Bell, but Hestia still knew that she was being watched by *Freya Familia*. Or more exactly, the watcher was making their presence known as a warning to her.

As expected, they fully intended to keep her under watch around the clock.

Should I try some other time...? No, it was always going to be a given that they know my every move. I have to act and just accept that they will find out! The worst thing I could do is turtle up and become afraid to do anything!

She shook her head and clenched her fists.

She had gone out on her own at night for several nights in a row, searching for any gap in Freya's charm.

Bell was still exposed and isolated. She could not allow herself to just do as Freya wanted while knowing that. Even if that meant acting like she did not know Bell to his face.

Steeling her resolve again, she took the main route, not the back door that the fool had passed.

She did not care if it was reported to Freya and dared them to stop her if they could, even though she knew it would take them less than three seconds to do so.

Visiting so late at night, she spoke with a visibly annoyed Guild member before finally getting them to pass a message for her and being allowed through.

Her destination was beneath Guild Headquarters—the Chamber of Prayers.

"Hestia. So you resisted Freya's charm."

"…! You too, Ouranos…?!"

Hestia leaned in excitedly when she heard him refer to the charm from his seat at the altar.

She had clung to the thread of hope that if it was him, if it was the great god who was Orario's creator, but her eyes were on the verge of tears from the emotion of having her hopes confirmed.

She was a little bit suspicious seeing that the old god made no effort to open his eyes, but she still began to discuss the next moves.

"Ouranos, I have a letter from Hermes. About how to deal with Freya—"

"You mustn't."

However, he quickly stopped her, his tone grave.

"Huh…?"

"Fels is here right now. Whether conscious of it or not, under the influence of her charm, all may as well be spies. If you share any plan to destroy the sandbox, it will immediately be carried to Freya."

"Wha…?!"

Hestia swiveled her head in surprise, looking all around.

There was nothing but impenetrable darkness around the altar. She could not see Ouranos's right hand, the fool. But on closer examination, she thought she could see a black robe quiver in the depths, in obedience to Freya's rules.

The four torches lit her face as Hestia's throat quivered.

"There is no place in Orario devoid of eyes and ears."

"That's…"

She had been too naive.

Hestia had thought prying eyes would be unable to enter the room of prayer, that she would be able to share a plan with Ouranos. But Freya had already seen through that possibility.

She was forced to recognize that quite literally every being in Orario was her enemy.

After being at a loss for words for a moment, she voiced her thoughts, struggling in vain.

"Ouranos…even if it's only Orario, this is an incursion against the mortal realm by a deity. Isn't that a violation of our—"

"We cannot send Freya back to the heavens by our own discretion. She has not used arcanum."

She sought the opinion of one of the first gods who descended to the mortal realm, but Ouranos's response was merciless.

"Deities are allowed to utilize their various authorities in managing their familias and drawing closer to the mortal realm. Whether it be Hephaistos's forging or Soma's wine…Freya's beauty falls within the same bounds."

The charm of the goddess of beauty that could even entrance deities.

That was not the same as arcanum.

Hephaistos, who could forge the ultimate weapons and armor despite having the same slender arms of a human.

Soma, who could brew the wine of the gods.

Freya's beauty was the same sort of thing.

It was hard to accept, but it was not some special divine ability but simply a feature of Freya's countenance, a part of her personality.

Described most bluntly, Freya had a massive effect on her surroundings merely by standing there.

It was true that she had even been troubled by that fact before and had been forced to limit her actions at times. But this time, she had deliberately used her power.

"So what?! That's…! Isn't that practically cheating…?!"

Hestia would have liked to scream her frustrations at Freya personally.

But at the same time, she also understood that as a deity she needed to take a wider perspective.

The majority of deities' actions in the mortal realm were for amusement or pleasure, and there was nothing wrong with that.

But their original stance, their true goal—at least for all but the evil gods who sought destruction and demise—was the birth of a chosen one.

A hero.

The authorities of various deities could at times be an aid to their children or else a trial for them to overcome. And those various authorities intermixed and gave birth to chaos, creating the sort of unknown that even deities could not predict.

They had collectively hoped that the ones who overcame that unknown would become a hero who achieved the machia that the world so desired.

But to treat this as a trial…! Are you trying to force Bell to overcome adversity again now like with the Xenos before…?!

But even so, logic and emotion were different things. All the more so when it was her child who was forced to go through it.

Hestia glared at the old god, whose eyes remained closed even as she harbored suspicions about his motives.

"—Hestia, do not misunderstand. The thing you should fear is not the power of her charm nor how the city has been altered."

"Eh…?"

"It's the fact that Freya twisted the entire world for the sake of a single being, and the obsession that led her to do it."

"!"

Hestia's eyes widened when she heard Ouranos say something similar to what Hermes had said before his memories had been altered.

"Until now, Freya had respected the skein of the mortal realm. She hated becoming an empress more than anyone, but no matter how bored she became, she kept to her oath and maintained her pride."

Until her assault that twisted the mortal realm.

Ouranos was right. That should have been taboo to Freya.

Or perhaps it would be more correct to call it a sense of etiquette for how the game was played.

When Hestia actually thought about it, that made sense. What would happen to the enjoyment of a game with situational changes, tactics, and elements of luck, if Freya could just win forever without any effort at all?

That answer was simple. It would become boring. Terribly, horrifically boring.

And on top of that, it was winning by using her wiles to entrance other deities, too. It could not even be called a game. If Freya was trying to enjoy the game, then winning like that would be the hollowest sort of victory. Just a pathetic farce.

That was why Freya had never resorted to breaking that taboo and always observed a bare minimum of game manners.

Obviously, she was perfectly capable of resorting to the power of her charm for the sake of her own curiosity, or perhaps breaking it out when someone or something had trampled on the dignity of her children, but she would never have disgraced all the people, the deities, and the world by resorting to her charm.

"For the first time, she has broken that oath and thrown away her pride."

All for the sake of a single child—for Bell.

Hestia shuddered. Hermes had been right. They had misjudged Freya. Even Loki, who knew Freya best, might have misjudged her. None of them had realized the intensity of the passion that currently held Freya. Her obsession, the breaking of her taboo, her abandonment of all other manners had put Hestia and Ouranos on the verge of checkmate. And for the vast majority of deities, it already was checkmate.

So long as her obsession did not fade, the situation would not be resolved.

Character...the sine qua non that defines Freya. She even abandoned that in order to get Bell...

Hestia, the vestal goddess, had never got along well with Freya and her stable of lovers. Because of that, they had not had many interactions, but she heard that in the heavens, Freya had been treated with the utmost courtesy and care by the gods who fell for her, living a life as if within a gilded cage.

However, though she was late to realize it, she understood now that Freya had not been surrounded by them—she had been restrained by them.

If she had been serious about it, she could have dominated even the heavens, just like she was controlling all of Orario now.

"What do I do…? This is…"

Hestia despaired again at the situation she found herself in after Ouranos's statement.

She could not think of any way she could break out of the current situation under her own power besides a suicidal use of arcanum in the hopes of taking Freya out with her, sending both of them back to the heavens.

But she was sure that even if she committed to that plan, it would be prevented by the other deities who had fallen under Freya's charm.

"………"

She looked down at her hands.

The fragment of paper Hermes had given her was there. She had never let it leave her sight.

When the times comes…When is that time, Hermes…?

Hermes had said to give it to him when the time came. But she did not know when that time would be. And it was starting to feel like Freya's obsession, the sandbox she had created, would never allow that moment to come.

She felt like she might succumb to a crawling, dark despair.

Hestia clenched the note Hermes had left her.

"…Is that all, Hestia? If so, then leave. There is nothing you can do now."

"Gh! Ouranos, wait, please!"

It was not clear whether Ouranos could sense that weakness in her heart or not. His eyes remained shut as he spoke.

Hestia suddenly looked up at him, but the old god's divine will was unmoved.

"Even in a situation like this, I'm charged with protecting the city. I do not have the time to spend quibbling with you."

"Ouranos…!"

"Winter is coming to Orario...the chill will be worse this year than usual. We must prepare the firewood."

"...!"

Hestia gasped at Ouranos's curt refusal to respond to her.

"Fels, task Hermes's children with the distribution of firewood for the year."

The darkness at the side of the altar shimmered, and the black-robed Fels appeared.

"I don't mind, but...*Hermes Familia*? Isn't that usually *Ganesha Familia*'s job?"

"They cannot act right now. *They are serving Freya.* You know that, too, right?"

"*...Ohh, right.*"

Perhaps butting up against a rule set out by Freya's control, Fels did not recognize the oddity for what it was and accepted the fact at face value.

Stunned by that scene, Hestia was at a loss for words.

"Just go, Hestia."

Ouranos's eyes remained closed as Hestia fell silent and turned around.

She could feel Fels watching her, but she could do nothing but close her mouth and leave the chamber.

The darkness began to fade, and the sun rose again.

The morning sun hit his eyes from the eastern sky.

The battle had already begun out on the field, and a new boy's shouts joined the chorus ringing out in Folkvangr.

Bell was unable to shake the shock from his expression. Hedin had been peering down at him, but he quickly returned his gaze to what was in front of him.

"Sorry for calling you up here. Can you wait just a little bit?"

The location was the audience room next to the goddess's chamber.

Aside from certain exceptions, all of the familia's first-tier adventurers had been called before Freya. Even Ottar, who had yielded the mission of observing *Hestia Familia* to other members of the familia.

The goddess was sitting on an extravagant seat worthy of a throne.

Her slender legs were crossed, and she had a single book open on her lap.

"It would have been better to have this meeting yesterday, but there was something I needed to finish reading."

With that, the goddess closed the book she had just finished—Eina's journal—and passed it off to Hörn, who stood at her side.

In order to perfectly answer the boy's questions, she had prioritized reading through all the records of Bell Cranell that the methodical half-elf had created—a thick journal spanning dozens of volumes. Seeing their patron goddess yawn slightly, as if she had been reading deep into the night, the four brothers and Hegni clutched their chests and shuddered. In their hearts they were thinking, *Lady Freya is so cute...!*

Ottar, who had developed a resistance to it as her attendant, was unaffected while Hedin glared at them as if looking at sewage, cursing them mentally for their immeasurable impropriety.

Being able to see the goddess without her defenses was the special prerogative of only the familia's core members and the maids who waited on her hand and foot.

"All right, shall we begin the conference? I imagine you are already all acting even without my request."

The meeting to discuss the current state of the sandbox trapping in Bell as well as the intent and settings to be maintained going forward.

Alfrik and his brothers nodded with an """""Aye!""""" at her trusting smile.

"In line with the information you have set out, Milady, Bell Cranell's position within the faction has been firmly established."

"We will continue to watch him going forward and work to remove any potential risks that are identified."

"Goddess Hestia as well naturally, but also the monsters that Lady Freya's charm cannot reach."

"That cat who is not in attendance will be watching The Benevolent Mistress from today onward."

The four identical prums took a single step forward, providing a smooth and succinct report in one flowing voice.

The next to step forward was the dark elf Hegni. "A-after this, we shall also enter the field, and w-wo-work to train up Bell Cranell, just like yesterdie! Ugh...?! Uhh..." He struggled terribly with shyness, stumbling over his words and biting his tongue. Freya smiled kindly at the dark elf, who slumped over in despair and shame.

"It's okay, Hegni. Just take your time and speak in your own words."

"L-Lady Freya...! Th-thank you very much...!"

Hegni was overwhelmed by emotion while, beside him, the four brothers gritted their teeth in annoyance. It was a very precise level of noise so as not to be so loud it offended Freya's ears while still being audible.

Even though they were all first-tier adventurers within the same familia, *Freya Familia*'s members by and large got along terribly.

"B-Bell Cranell can be used. He can see our attacks and keep up with them. His techniques seem to be the most basic of basics, but...the instant his life is in danger, his responses expand in unexpected ways, like a rabbit frantically rushing about. He is *strong in a pinch*. And fun to beat up. I-I held back throughout it all, of course!"

"Ha-ha. And then?"

"R-right...Given that, what he is missing is *experience with the unreasonable* and an *absurd number of experiences*. However, if he continues to fight in Folkvangr, he will be able to gain both."

"I see. Then I was correct to leave training that child to all of you."

Seeing through Hegni's excitement that drove his gradually accelerating speech, Freya nodded pleasantly as she glanced out the window to where battle cries could be heard.

The only thing forbidden out on the field was combat between fellow first-tier adventurers.

It was partly to avoid losing the foremost among the einherjar, of course, but the main reason was to prevent showing weakness in the event one of the core members of the familia were to fall or otherwise suffer a serious injury.

Because of that, it was almost unheard of for the first-tier adventurers to gather on the field.

And the reason for the current exception was Bell Cranell.

There was no other example of a first-tier adventurer deciding to train someone. It was a situation that went beyond being an honor and into the realm of nightmares. Bell was fated to collapse under the grueling training inflicted by Hegni and the others many, many more times going forward.

On that one point alone, the rest of the familia members could feel some tiny trace of sympathy for Bell.

"As long as his growth rate is uncertain due to the effects of his skill, I will leave training him to all of you. In addition to drowning him in training until he has no energy left to think, it's also true that we will have to advance the progress of exploring the Dungeon."

"We are to bring him on an expedition in the future, too?"

"Yes, that child is already a potential hero."

Freya, who had seen Bell's status and understood the true nature of his skill, firmly ordered it, betraying no difference in her tone of voice.

"So he must not be killed. Nor may he be allowed to die."

That was the order.

Ottar, who stood beside the goddess, did not change his expression or raise a brow at all.

He was the model attendant, not remarking upon the change in his mistress's mental state from half a year ago, when she had said that she would follow after him even up to the heavens if he died.

"Also, Bell is to be allowed some degree of freedom. He is bound to grow suspicious if he is locked away inside the home."

""""""Aye.""""""

"However, he is always to be under observation and under guard. Those with deeper relations with Bell are especially prone to irregularities. If it grows too extreme, I will reapply the charm, but…overexposure might break certain children. Avoid contact where possible."

As the rest of them responded affirmatively, Freya smiled.

"I will be staying here at the home instead of Babel for a time."

Hearing that, a joyous mood filled the air.

Or more precisely, it emanated from the maids lining the walls.

The women who managed the goddess's chambers were normally unable to accompany her to the top floor of Babel so they were on the verge of bursting with joy. Meanwhile, those who had been attending her in Babel were surely despairing. That was simply how deeply they loved Freya.

The conference proceeded apace without any disruptions. Freya listened to her followers' reports and gave her instructions.

The sandbox the goddess had wished to construct was being strengthened and maintained without any issues.

"—Finally, I have a report as well."

And as the discussion reached its climax, the silent white elf spoke.

"What is it, Hedin?"

"The night before last, Bell Cranell made an inquiry regarding Lady Syr."

All of a sudden, a nervous tension swept the room, the first-tier adventurers included. It was an incredibly delicate subject, as everyone present was inherently aware. The goddess's smile disappeared.

"And?"

"I immediately responded that there was no such girl here."

"That's right. So then why did you feel the need to report that here and now?"

"A desire to ask how information regarding the girl should be handled. There is no longer a Syr Flover in this city."

Freya immediately responded when Hedin touched upon a fundamental bedrock of the sandbox she had constructed.

"She never existed. That is what shall be said."

"Yes, Milady."

Hedin bent courteously at the waist. After watching him for a moment, Freya curled her lips like a fickle witch instead of a magnanimous goddess.

"That reminds me, Hedin. You seem to have been acting of your own accord quite a bit beginning with the lead-up to the Goddess Festival…What were your intentions in all of this?"

Her tone made it quite clear that it was a question that could lead to more dangerous charges with a single wrong move.

Hörn also turned a resentful gaze on Hedin.

"My humblest apologies for my impertinent actions. I was unable to accept that he would be acting as escort without first confirming his abilities with my own eyes. And having judged his abilities too shameful, I felt I had to break him in," Hedin responded without a trace of guilt.

"Out of your love for me?"

"Out of my allegiance to you, Milady."

He did not avert his eyes for even a moment; there was no trace of any other thought in the elf's gaze…Seeing that, Freya released the questioning tone as if her interest had faded.

Slowly, the mood in the room eased.

"In the end, my training was insufficient, and the foolish rabbit caused Milady displeasure and sadness, so I shall atone with my body—"

"It didn't bother me."

"………"

"It didn't bother me."

Freya quickly interrupted Hedin.

Everyone in the room was united in the belief that screamed in the back of their heads """"""""That means it totally bothered her,"""""""" but no one allowed that thought to cross their lips.

Left speechless for a moment by her response, Hedin adjusted his glasses with his finger in order to collect himself before speaking again.

"Lady Freya, please leave that fool's training to me."

And again the mood in the chamber tensed like a cord drawn taut.

This time, Freya's eyes narrowed, as if seeing into the elf's heart.

"Your reason?"

"I believe I'm the one most able to draw out its gleam."

"Your goal?"

"All for thee."

Hedin's eyes and voice were clear and unshaded as he declared without hesitation.

"I offer my devotion to thee."

A silence filled the room. The only noise was the muffled sound of battle from outside the walls.

Freya studied Hedin carefully for a moment before finally responding.

"...Very well. You do not appear to be lying. I will leave it to you, Hedin."

Children could not lie before deities. Acknowledging Hedin's devotion, Freya gave her permission for his request.

Paying no heed to the eyes of the boaz, who was looking at him, nor returning the gaze of the shocked dark elf beside him and beautifully ignoring the audible scoffs of the prums, Hedin bowed.

And then turning his back, he left the room before anyone else.

The rhomphaia that would easily send my head rolling is swung without any mercy at all.

"Too slow!"

"Gahhh?!"

The longer weapon that also serves as a staff slams into my face heavily, sending me into an unsightly roll. My trembling hands hit the ground, and I'm on all fours as I cough up blood from my torn-up mouth.

"Why are you sleeping? Stand! Or do you wish to be beheaded?!"

Master's shouts land heavily on the back of my head. Responding to the open hostility that accompanies those cries, I stagger to my feet.

And so my odd days continue.

Fighting on the field from sunrise until sunset and then talking with Lady Freya at night.

I have no ability to say no to anything, given the limits on my movement. And given that I'm being thrown into battle from the wee hours of the morning, I do not have any strength left for anything else anyway.

"Your back is not your only blind spot."

"Focus your attention in all directions."

"Erase every possible vulnerability."

"You have to be able to attack, defend, and evade at all times."

"Th-that's impossible...!"

"If you decide it's impossible, then you might as well put your own neck on the chopping block. The only question is whether the blade of the guillotine ends up being a monster's claws or another person's weapon."

"Giii?!"

I am turned into a pulpy mess by the Gullivers' combinations and then crushed into the ground by Hegni's deadly slash. No matter how much I collapse, my wounds heal and my stamina recovers, and I am forced to keep fighting like a warrior who isn't allowed to die.

"...Bell. You have a habit of letting your right arm drift upward, don't you?"

"Eh...? Ah, yes. Apparently, I have a tendency to do it when I get flustered...I-it's still there, I guess?"

"*The opposite.* You focus too much on fixing it, so when you attack, your right arm's windup is a lot easier to read. It's not a problem if you're just after a monster's magic stone, but against a first-tier adventurer, it's a fatal weakness."

A surprising change occurs.

Van starts to give me advice during the dinner where almost all the familia members gather to eat.

"Just leave it be. You can mix it into your attack and defense patterns as a feint. It's useful as a tactic for fighting against other people. You can't use it too many times, but it's impossible to win against a first-tier adventurer without using every last tool at your disposal."

"V-Van…why?"

"…I know just how scary Hegni and the rest of them are. If nothing else, I can at least respect a warrior who experiences that fear and pain and still continues to fight…It doesn't change the fact that I still hate you, though!"

"Setting aside Van's troubling confessions of love."

"The truth is we think you are really something, you know?…I've known it for a long time, though."

At some point, Van, who has viewed me as an enemy, and many of the other members of the familia begin to acknowledge me.

Even though I still don't really know these people who are supposedly my familia…it's still a mysterious feeling.

"You would like to go out?"

"Y-yes…or is that not okay, Heith…?"

"Hmm, I don't see why it wouldn't be. I'll let Lady Freya and them know."

"R-really?"

"Sure. Everyone else goes out if they have something to take care of, too, after all. However, make sure you go with someone, okay? Especially if you are going to the Dungeon. There was the whole thing with you getting cursed without anyone realizing it, and we can't have anything bad happening again. It will just make everyone think I'm a useless, hack healer! So promise me you won't go making more work for me!"

"U-understood…"

I even receive permission to leave the home without any hassle, albeit with certain stipulations.

Generally speaking, the baptism on the familia's field is considered the priority. I use my limited time to run around the city—and I despair countless times.

There's no one who remembers the me who was part of *Hestia Familia*. I try to figure out a way to make contact with Lord Hermes or Fels, who might be able to find a way out for me, but no luck. When I find someone and bring up a story that only they and I would know, like me peeking on the eighteenth floor or other things like that, their faces start looking suspicious partway through…No, it's almost like they're indifferent. As if they're under a spell forcing them not to acknowledge what I'm saying.

I also search desperately for Syr, who has gone missing, but there's no progress there, either.

I head to the Dungeon, too, but no luck there, either. I hope that maybe I might meet Winne or any of the other Xenos, but no armed monsters or talking monsters appear, perhaps because they're scared to approach when I'm part of a party with members of *Freya Familia*. Or maybe they're just a dream that I created in my head.

Van and the others who come with me are not particularly watching me. They just let me do whatever until I'm satisfied. Or perhaps they pity me in some small way.

My spirit feels like it might break. Maybe it has broken already.

I am battered and worn from the constant baptism on the field, and the fact that no one knows me fills me with an overwhelming pain and anguish.

I can't do anything besides stare out at Hearthstone Manor when the city grows dark, watching the warm light leaking from its windows.

It's like I'm meeting the gaze of someone standing in the window and looking out from there, but even that's probably just my imagination.

My body, my mind, and even my soul feel like I'm being driven into a corner.

"Welcome, Bell."

And amid that all, the chats with Lady Freya in her chamber at night are the only time my heart can be at peace. Because that's the only time I'm allowed to be myself, the Bell Cranell of *Hestia Familia*. Because Lady Freya accepts me with kind and gentle eyes.

I only just barely manage to hold on to myself by talking about the Bell Cranell of *Hestia Familia* that no one remembers. It's painful, it's difficult, but I can endure the solitude.

The noble goddess does not laugh at my story. And she does not look at me dubiously.

She responds, lends me an ear, and she's the only one who understands me.

She's the only one. She's—

"Umm, Lady Freya…where should I sit…?"

"Just sit beside me."

"Ehhh?!"

"Your chair's already been put away."

"Th-that's not fair…"

Lady Freya is often mean like that.

The fact that she's not just some dignified and aloof goddess is breaking down the walls I threw up around my heart one brick at a time.

She pats the seat next to her on the couch, and unable to go against her, I end up talking to her close enough that, with any mistake, my shoulder might brush against hers.

My tone grows freer with her, and a bond that's different from just deity and follower or mother and child begins to develop.

And as my sense of distance changes, and as our relationship changes, I suddenly realize.

Being next to Lady Freya…being at her side…feels incredibly comfortable.

"Are you tired, Bell?"

"Huh…?"

I'm talking with Lady Freya in the evening after yet another day.

Having visited her chamber after the battle on the field was over, just like always, I'm caught off guard by her sudden question.

"Your face looks more haggard than usual."

"H-haggard…"

"When I try to talk to you, you respond with halfhearted answers. Is your exhaustion building up?"

After saying that, she presses her forehead against mine suddenly.

"Wh-?!"

I turn red down to my neck and frantically pull away, feeling awkward as Lady Freya giggles.

It's true the baptism today was especially painful. Hegni and the Gullivers were mostly the same, but it felt like Master's attacks have been gradually increasing in intensity. Of course, it's true that all the exhaustion has just been building up, too, but…

I certainly feel the urge to bemoan my fate, and ask why I have to suffer like this every day.

But I'm also using the battle as a way to avoid facing reality, so I can't resent Lady Freya for it, either.

A merciless death match at least lets me forget about the hopelessness and isolation that I can't do anything about.

Suddenly I'm struck by a scary thought, though.

What if I met Aiz like this, and she rejected me…What would happen?

I can see Lady Freya watching me from the corner of my eye. But there is no reaction.

As if the warmth that had continued burning in my back is slowly fading—

"Bell."

That was the moment when Freya pressed.

Watching his face, confirming the gradual weakening, the pained gasps, the anguished place where he was left standing, she pulled the line that she had set out far in advance.

"Maybe you could try undergoing treatment for the curse?"

He spun toward her suddenly, his red eyes opened wide.

Confirming his inner thoughts from the changes in his expression, Freya spoke in a worried tone.

"I don't want to deny or reject the you that belongs to *Hestia Familia*...But right now, you seem to be hurting so terribly. It feels like you want to be freed from your solitude."

"Ghh...!"

"You could do it just once to see?"

It wavered.

Bell's expression and his emotions wavered.

He wanted to cling to the saving light that would release him from a prison of solitude.

—Freya was sure of what was needed for her victory.

It was the destruction of Liaris Freese.

Etching a fissure in the deep attachment that could even reject the charm of the goddess of beauty.

His skill is an irregularity of the mortal world. But it's not perfect. It can be made unstable through shifts in his mentality.

Liaris Freese was not invincible. If anything, it was incredibly fragile.

What made it so solid was the purity of Bell's soul. If any other person had developed it, it would surely end up becoming a useless waste in short order. It was just that hard for anyone to remain so pure and absolute in their feelings.

So if he began to doubt his feelings, even just a little bit...

If he started to wonder if even the memories of that idol were false...

...a hole would open in his heart.

If I can get him to believe that the path he walks is just the effects of a curse, then I win.

Because of that, she had used Heith to implant the idea of a curse all the way at the start.

Was there any person who would not waver when a means of salvation was dangled before them? At the very least, it was impossible for a mortal. And the seeds of doubt had already started to grow.

The maintenance of the sandbox was all preparation for this. Isolating him through the reactions of those around him, shaving away at his store of endurance through the daily baptism, stealing away all energy and time for thought. And at night, Freya provided a healing salve by being the only person in the world who understood him, guiding him to listen to her and no one else. And then she could lay down the final piece with sweet honeyed words.

If Bell began to believe that his memories, his thoughts, and the one he idolized were a curse, he would crumble, like a sandcastle washed away in the surf.

And once that happened, Bell would have no defense against her charm.

Redirecting the target of his thoughts slightly, ever so slightly, was all that was needed.

She wouldn't twist him like she had done with everyone else. She would just warp him the tiniest bit.

That would be enough to free Bell from the shackles of his adoration, to free him from that golden curse. And then he would look at only one person.

"I-I…"

Peering into Bell's troubled eyes, Freya made her calculations.

She asked herself whether she could achieve the result she wished, and her answer was that it was assuredly possible.

She was confident of that possibility with all the omniscience of a deity.

She could gain his translucent soul, without changing him, without clouding its gleam or corrupting it.

The slight shift was nothing more than a rounding error.

She was confident she could pull it off.

And if I do, Bell will accept me.

He will become mine.

He will accept my love and not ______.

—Really?

* * *

There.

It felt like a ripple spreading outward.

"........."

Before she realized it, Freya had put her right hand to her ear.

It felt like something creaked at the bottom of her heart. A pain?

No, it's my imagination.

After all, I already decided I would take this *child.*

"I...I'm okay. I...won't take the healing..."

"...I see. Sorry for saying something unnecessary."

She smiled as if it were nothing after her focus was derailed so badly.

There was no need to panic. The proof was there in how unsure Bell still was. She could just gradually continue to corner him. She still had plenty of time.

Because of that, Freya ended the night's chat earlier than usual and had Bell leave.

"........"

Her maids entered the room and finished the preparations for her to sleep.

Freya sat on the couch and looked at the wine she had been provided.

The surface of the liquid inside the glass seemed to be reflecting someone other than herself.

She laughed at the stupidity of it.

She scornfully snickered at the silliness of that stray thought.

She took the drink, which was a bit much for just a nightcap, and downed it in one gulp.

—Freya did not notice that Hörn alone among her maids was watching in stunned amazement.

"Milady."

"...What is it, Ottar?"

And Ottar, who was allowed to be present as her attendant, spoke.

"A report from Allen, who is watching the tavern. There is no sign of any movement by Mia. However, the elf appears to have truly disappeared."

Freya glanced at the boaz delivering his entirely businesslike report.

"It appears to be true, then. She fled outside the city walls together with Hermes's child."

"It's my failure. After defeating Bell Cranell and Gale Wind, I left her there, assuming she would fall under Lady Freya's power...However, Perseus was also there at the time."

They had discovered that two adventurers had gone missing since the last day of the Goddess Festival.

And they were cautious of the possibility those two might destroy the sandbox.

"No doubt, this is Hermes's work...He must have realized I would use my charm and probably ordered them to flee the city."

Ottar apologized again for his failure.

However, Freya did not think to punish him. Thought it was only two of them, and they deserved to be praised for managing to escape the city in such a short amount of time. And if Ottar was at fault, then it was also her own mistake in allowing Hermes the opportunity to struggle in vain.

"Maintain the net. They will return to the city at some point. They may even already be here in hiding somewhere."

"Yes, Milady."

She could not allow anyone to get in her way now.

Even if it was the elf and the rest of *that girl*'s friends.

Her voice was devoid of emotion as she gave her instructions.

"As expected, we can deal with this at the same time as the Ahnya issue. I will be going out."

She walked to the window and looked up at the pale, frozen moon.

CHAPTER 4 THOSE LEFT BEHIND

"Ugh..."

Lyu groaned as a dull pain emanated from inside her, settling and burning away at her.

Opening her trembling eyelids, she saw an unfamiliar wooden ceiling.

When she adjusted her posture, a worn-out blanket fell away from her body.

Sitting up in bed, Lyu could guess she was in cheap lodging.

"...! Leon, you're awake!"

"Andromeda...? Why are you...? No, more importantly—"

Asfi had slipped stealthily into the room, wearing a raggedy hood over her head. Lyu was bewildered more than surprised and started to ask Asfi what was going on when she suddenly stopped. She remembered.

"I was attacked by Warlord...?!"

She remembered what had befallen her body before she opened her eyes.

"Andromeda! What is this?! What is going on?!"

Remembering being helpless as her opponent delivered the final blow, she demanded information in a state of almost panic.

Asfi held the elf's already treated body down, telling her to get ahold of herself before beginning to explain.

"First of all, we are in the town of Agris. We escaped Orario to a place sufficiently far away. You have been unconscious for almost a whole day...And to the best of my knowledge, *Freya Familia* attacked *Hestia Familia* and captured every last one of them. Including Bell Cranell, who was moving with you."

"A whole day?! Wait, *Freya Familia* attacked them...?!"

Even after hearing Asfi's blunt explanation, Lyu still could not immediately process it. She had some misgivings about the incomprehensible "escaped Orario" point, and she was struck with fear upon hearing that open conflict between familias had broken out.

"Why did you not wake me sooner?! I must get back to Orario as soon as possible!"

Lyu began to leap out of bed, but Asfi put more strength into her hand on Lyu's shoulder. Lyu was flustered by the look in Asfi's eyes.

"...The reason we fled Orario is because of Lord Hermes's instruction. Right now, Orario is almost without doubt entirely under the control of the goddess of beauty."

Asfi forced herself to keep her emotions from rising in her voice as she explained the situation and her own estimation.

The thing she had seen, or rather felt. The invisible argentine divine will that had enveloped the whole city.

Judging from Hermes's unease in the moments immediately preceding it, that was almost certainly the power of charm.

The effect of it was that all of Orario and everything occurring there were completely dominated by a single goddess.

When Asfi had finished, Lyu could do nothing but be dumbfounded.

"Controlling the whole city through charm...?! Goddess Freya did that?! That's absurd! Why?!"

"From here, I can only hypothesize, but...I suspect it's in order to make Bell Cranell hers."

"!"

"Goddess Freya has been fixated on him and his continued, rapid growth for some time now. I know that much from having accompanied Lord Hermes on several troublesome tasks. I can't begin to guess why she chose now of all times to act, but for whatever reason, she resolved herself to claim Bell Cranell during the Goddess Festival."

Everyone in Orario knew that Freya was a goddess of many loves.

There were stories of her destroying whole familias in order to steal away a single man.

Lyu grew even uneasier. The person she finally realized she had feelings for had been stolen away by a goddess. It tore at her heart.

But Asfi still urged prudence.

"Leon, please. Promise me that you will keep your calm and not act rashly or impatiently going forward. If you can't, I will force you to stay here even if I have to tie you down to the bed."

"A-Andromeda...?"

"The goddess of beauty's charm is absolute...There can be no question that every last resident of Orario has fallen to it. Everyone you know, all of your comrades, even the gods and goddesses."

"!"

"...Lord Hermes, who always acts so aloof and easygoing, was that flustered and desperate to get me out of the city. And I'm sure that right now...even he is our enemy."

Lyu finally understood. The way she had slipped into the room, the way she was hiding her identity behind the tattered hood. Asfi was worried about being tracked. If they were caught and brought before Freya, that would be the end for both of them.

Asfi was desperately trying to maintain her calm, even as she regretted her failure to protect her patron god, and even as she despaired at having to fight against him and everyone else.

Looking into Asfi's eyes that refused to waver, Lyu tamped down all the turbulent emotions raging inside her and finally managed to subdue the urge to rush forward.

"Apologies, Andromeda...You have my deepest gratitude for saving me."

"It's fine. If I had been alone, I would have vented at everything around me. Once we have made all of our preparations, let's return to Orario. We need information first, so we should spy things out."

Lyu nodded in agreement as she and her old friend began to act.

Agris village lay southeast of Orario, near the Shreme Castle ruins, which had been the stage of *Hestia Familia* and *Apollo Familia*'s war game. It was almost a full day's ride from Orario by carriage, but it was shorter traveling by air. Lyu endured being carried by Asfi, who used her talaria to fly to the city in a straight line.

Counting the time it had taken them to gather the items and such they needed to disguise themselves in Agris, the great city wall of the Labyrinth City came into view on the horizon on the morning of the third day after the Goddess Festival.

"Only the city's south gate is open…?"

They did not approach the city unnecessarily. Lyu was peering through a small tube, hiding in the shadow of boulders atop a small hill a little ways from the city. It was one of Asfi's magic items. It magnified the already superior eyesight of an upper-tier adventurer, allowing them to see in minute detail a scene even ten kirlos away.

They quickly noticed oddities as they watched the city.

The various city gates in the cardinal directions that should have all been wide open were closed, save one. Because of that, merchants and travelers swarmed to that one place, causing congestion.

Asfi's murmur carried a trace of a terrible feeling as Lyu pointed the magic item to look through the gate, only to be greeted with an astounding sight.

"Goddess Freya…?!"

She saw her. The figure of the goddess with arms spread was standing before those who were attempting to pass through the gates of the city, as if she were preparing to bestow a divine revelation upon them.

Lyu immediately cast aside the magic item and broke her line of sight. Even though they were so far removed, just seeing the goddess was all that was required to fall prey to her charm. Beholding her beauty was easily enough to bewitch a mortal and send them into a trancelike state. And hearing her voice was enough to turn them into a faithful puppet.

Lyu desperately pressed against her breast, where a furious throbbing had already begun. Her heart was singing at having encountered a beauty beyond mortal ken. Finally, after several seconds, it began to slow.

"Are you all right, Leon?!"

"Yes…however, that confirms it. Goddess Freya has seized the whole city with her charm, and she is casting instructions of some sort on all who come in from outside the city!" Escaping that same fate by her quick judgment, Lyu stared in the direction of the city.

She was convinced now that all of Orario had been transformed into a sandbox ruled over by Freya's will.

—And she had no way of realizing that the being she had seen was merely someone who had taken Freya's appearance.

"Judging by how the city's gates are being controlled and she is charming every single person who enters the city…the Guild and even *Ganesha Familia* have become puppets to her whims."

"If our identity gets out after we infiltrate the city, there is a good chance we will be arrested. Let's just hope we don't have bounties on our heads."

"I mean you've been on the black list for a long time…kidding, kidding. You can put down your dagger!"

Bemoaning the fact that the day had come where they would be targeted by the authorities, they began planning how they would sneak into the city.

Outside the window, the sky was blocked by clouds.

There was a mountain of blankets on the bed that the morning sun could not reach.

A cat's tail extended from the foot of the mountain. It was swaying weakly, like a snake struggling to breathe.

Ahnya was clinging to her knees, all traces of life gone from her eyes.

"………"

She was currently in the building behind The Benevolent Mistress.

Ahnya had been brooding since the second night of the Goddess Festival.

She had been unable to stop *Freya Familia* from trying to kill Syr, and on top of that, she had done as her brother Allen had demanded and yielded the path without even fighting back.

Ahnya believed that the other girls working at the tavern were her family. And she had not only failed to protect a member of that family, but even handed her over.

Ahnya did not know what had happened since then, hiding away in her room the whole time.

What had happened to Syr? Even if she was still alive, though, Ahnya would not be able to bear seeing her.

Even if Syr forgave her, Ahnya would not be able to endure it.

Her usual cheerfulness disappeared, and Ahnya lost all hope for herself.

I'm scared to sleep...

During the morning after she had met Allen, when Ahnya lost consciousness at some point, she had seen a dream.

And in that dream, she and everyone else had been going about their lives as if nothing had happened. Slacking off from work, Mia getting mad at her, Chloe and Runoa bickering, Lyu sighing, all laughs and smiles. Just another day in the tavern, like any other.

But Syr wasn't there.

And no one else noticed the change. They were all acting as if Syr had never been there from the start.

And for some reason, Bell was suddenly part of *Freya Familia*, and none of them knew him other than from the word on the streets.

I'm scared to see that dream again...

After that, she had refused to lie down, keeping herself awake, time frozen for her as she huddled on her bed.

She was terrified, terrified that that dream was a message for her for having abandoned Syr.

She wanted to stay locked away in her shell like that forever.

"—Stupid Ahnyaaaaa! Snap out of it right meow!"

But her wish was not to be.

Chloe kicked her door open, and she and Runoa charged in.

"How long are you gonna keep hiding here?! I dunno what happened, but hurry up and get back on your feet!"

"Mama Mia said to just leave you be, but I can't accept it! It's not fair that you get permission to skip work, meow! I'm the only one who should be allowed to slack off!"

They opened the room's curtains wide and peeled the blankets away.

Chloe and Runoa grimaced, seeing how sunken Ahnya's eyes were and how different she looked.

But they still mercilessly grabbed her hands and forced her to her feet.

"Come on, hurry up."

"You stink. At least wash up, stupid Ahnya."

Ahnya could not stand how tearfully hot her chest was as they pulled her by the hand.

They forcibly got her dressed and led her to the tavern. The Benevolent Mistress was already starting to open its doors.

The others were all moving around busily preparing.

"It's been rough the past few days here without you."

"Lyu went off somewhere and hasn't come back, either. Everyone's slacking off too much meow that the festival is over!"

Ahnya's shoulders twitched as Runoa and Chloe grumbled loudly.

The comment about Lyu made her wonder, too, but in that moment her heart was consumed with the thoughts of just one girl.

"...What about Syr?"

Her voice was soft and hoarse, barely recognizable.

She did not raise her head, just looking at the floor.

Runoa and Chloe could not see her expression as they responded.

"What's a Syr?"

There was no mistaking their response.

"...Huh?"

"Is that someone's name? Was there a customer named Syr?"

"Stupid Runoa. She must mean a seer! A fortune-teller. This idiot wants to check her horoscope meow!...I think? Right?"

When Ahnya looked up, she saw Runoa and Chloe looking confused.

She wanted to ask, 'What are you talking about?" but she could not bring herself to say it.

"What." They had not even asked "who." The two of them genuinely did not know about Syr and were actually confused.

Ahnya stopped breathing and froze in place.

"...What are you saying meow?! Syr is Syr obviously?!"

"Mrow?! Wait—what are you doing?!"

"Syr! The girl who worked with us here! Syr Flover!"

"Whoa, Ahnya?!"

"A little bit mean, and a terrible cook, but kind! Our precious family who brought us to this tavern even though we were alone and abandoned!"

Ahnya grabbed Chloe and shook off Runoa's hand, but no matter how much she pleaded with them, she could not get through. And the more she tried, the more bewildered they became.

It was far beyond not remembering. They did not even understand what Ahnya was saying.

"Mei! Beryl! Fay! Rosy! You know Syr, right...?!"

Ahnya called out to the others.

But the girls who had been watching from a distance all had the same reaction as Chloe and Runoa. It was clear to see that none of them knew Syr.

The countless eyes that looked almost vacant were all drilling holes in Ahnya.

Ahnya's fur stood on end, and she felt an indescribable chill.

"That's...you have to be lying meow?!"

It was like a continuation of the dream.

A nightmare where she was the only one still sane.

The place where Syr had stood was empty.

"...Stop it, Ahnya."

The one who said that to the panicking cat girl was Mia, who had appeared from the kitchen.

Ahnya clung to the shop owner, whose usual domineering aura was gone.

"Mama Mia! Syr! Everyone's...! Not you, too...right?! If it's you...!"

She was shuddering like an abandoned kitten, tears welling in her eyes as Mia looked down.

"...Yeah, I remember that stupid girl."

"!"

Ahnya's eyes widened at that soft murmur, and the light of hope started to grow. But...

"But there's no one other than us who remembers her...The goddess *erased* Syr's existence."

When she heard that, a jolt of lighting electrified Ahnya.

"Everyone other than her followers have been twisted."

An absolute charm that could change the world. The power of the goddess of beauty. As a former member of *Freya Familia*, even if she had never seen that sort of memory alteration herself, she knew that Freya could do it.

She was sure of it. That was just how terrifying Freya was to her.

"Why...Why would Lady Freya...?!"

"........"

"Mama Mia?!"

Even when she pressed a fellow follower of the goddess, who bore the same falna on her back, there was no answer.

Ignoring the other girls, who could not understand their conversation, Ahnya ran out of the tavern without another word.

"Ahnya!"

Even with Mia's voice at her back, she could not stop as she raced out onto West Main Street.

What possible gain could there be for the goddess in one little girl disappearing? She could not understand it. Stupid Ahnya could not understand at all.

But it was just too much.

Ahnya did not believe she had any right to grieve whatever happened to Syr. But to have her forgotten by everyone was more painful than mere death. The moment it became as if she'd never existed, it would be like there was no meaning in her ever having been born. The thought that even if there were a grave, it would be visited not with tears but with blank, unknowing smiles, it was just too tragic.

Ahnya just kept running. Heading to Babel, where the goddess surely was.

Not knowing the destruction that awaited her.

"Stop."

"!"

In the middle of the big street stood a single cat person, as if he had anticipated her movements.

His eyes were the same color as Ahnya's, but his fur was black.

Holding a silver spear in hand, her one and only brother was blocking her way.

"Brother…?!"

She quivered beneath his stern gaze.

"You would have been better off just moping around without noticing anything."

Paying no heed to the odd looks of the people giving him as wide a berth as they could, he turned and started walking in a certain direction.

"Come with me. You can hear everything."

Ahnya could not do anything but follow the back of her brother.

"We managed to safely infiltrate Orario, but…"

Lyu looked around, refraining from scoffing at that thought.

They had pulled off their plan after making absolutely sure of all they could. They had gathered as much information as they could from outside the city, and Asfi had investigated Meren on her own—she had not probed deeply, but her final conclusion was that there were no notable changes, but something about it was fishy. Their enemy was *Freya Familia* and a goddess who could grasp the hearts of people. No matter how much time they had, it would never be enough. Lyu quelled her restless heart, and they spent several days devising a concrete plan.

Asfi knew of a hidden, underground passage that *Hermes Familia* had used during the Dark Ages when the Evils were at the peak of their power. The two of them went into the tunnel at the base of the Beor Mountains north of Orario, and before they could be found by Fels, the gatekeeper who had fallen prey to Freya's charm, they took the branching path that let out inside the city. Opening the hidden entrance, they got out on the northwest side of the city in a deserted residential district beneath the sign FOURTH STREET.

"Leon, once we have infiltrated Orario, we should act separately. I want to avoid as much as possible the danger of both of us being caught at the same time."

Asfi had proposed that before they began their mission, and she had now gone her own way.

She was likely flying through the skies above Orario using her Hades Head to become invisible.

"After we've gathered some information, at sunset, go to the hideout here...In the event that you don't show up, I will assume you have fallen into Freya Familia's *hands and act accordingly. You do the same if I do not appear."*

Those were the last words she had shared with Asfi. She had already committed the location of the hideaway to memory and burned the paper. All she could do was pray for her friend's safety as she began her own mission.

It would be best to avoid the main streets. Taverns are concerning, too. I'll stick to back alleys and side streets to investigate.

Even during the day, the back alleys far from the main streets were dark and shrouded in shadows, filled with shady merchants, vagrants, and washed-up adventurers. All the sorts of people with guilty consciences.

Lyu was cautious to make sure there were no prying *Freya Familia* eyes, hiding herself in a dirty cloak and intentionally dirtying her face as she began her search.

Everyone in Orario other than us is the enemy.

When thought of that way, there was no such thing as being too cautious.

"Yeah, the Goddess Festival was lively again this year. Anything different? Nah, not really."

"*Freya Familia*? Same as ever. Those are some scary folks."

"You a traveler or somethin'? You've got some odd questions."

She spoke to a shrouded fortune-teller, and some vagrants eating their fill of leftover food that had been thrown out, but no matter what she asked, the answer was always "nothing different" from all of them. They did not seem to have any awareness of being charmed. They were so consistent in their answers, it was enough to make her wonder whether Freya really had used her charm.

But after Lyu had utterly annihilated a washed-up adventurer who had attempted to attack her in an abandoned building after noticing she was a female elf, she finally stumbled upon something different.

"Do you know anything about the location of Bell Cranell? And what has happened to *Hestia Familia*?"

"B-Bell Cranell? And *Hestia Familia*? What are you talking about? That rookie's *Freya Familia*…!"

When she held her sword to his neck and questioned him, that was the scared hoodlum's answer. Just when her eyes narrowed and she was about to press him on a statement she could not let pass—

"…Are you sniffing around about Bell Cranell?"

The man who had been trembling in fear suddenly became expressionless, like a puppet.

She felt a chill for a brief moment, but the vagabond looked like he was about to shout, so she quickly knocked him out.

"He suddenly changed into a puppet…?! Are they instructed to inform anyone nearby whenever they encounter a breach of the goddess's rules…?!"

That confirmed it.

It was just like Asfi had said—Freya wanted to make Bell hers.

And she would not hesitate to remove anything that might possibly disrupt her sandbox.

Lyu shuddered at the power of Freya's charm while also silently growing enraged. In a righteous fury, she vowed that such sacrilege could not be forgiven, that she would reclaim Bell and return Orario to what it was.

"And then there's Syr…Are you safe, I wonder…?"

She also felt uneasy about her friend who had gone missing as she continued her investigation.

To be safe, she tied up the man she had knocked out and hid him in the abandoned building before expanding her search radius.

*That's...*Freya Familia*? Are they searching for us?*

Hiding in the shadows, she peeked out from a side street that connected to Main Street just in time to see adventurers in *Freya Familia*'s uniform. Lyu instinctively sensed that they were looking for her and Asfi.

At the same time, she also surmised that other members had disguised themselves as citizens around the city.

Make the uniformed adventurers stand out in order to see if anyone acts suspiciously when they pass. It was a common tactic for the military police, too. Trusting her experience with *Astrea Familia*, Lyu immediately left the place.

I can't walk around the main streets. The Benevolent Mistress is surely being watched, too. If they are on guard against us, then trying to spy on their home would be suicidal. I should wait for sunset and meet up with Andromeda fir—hmm?

Her thoughts did not pause even as she walked, when—she suddenly noticed something abnormal.

"There's no one around...?"

The location was the seventh district, still in the city's northwest.

She was intentionally sticking to emptier streets, but still, she could not sense even a single person. Even in the buildings. As if there had been an evacuation warning—or a barrier had been set up to ward off people.

An enormous hole had opened, as if an entire district had been emptied of people.

A trap? I should withdraw—

Getting a bad feeling, she immediately started to turn, when she spotted a familiar face.

"—! Ahnya?!"

She saw her colleague from the tavern, following behind Vana Freya.

—How long have I watched him from behind?

Ahnya thought as she quietly followed behind her brother.

Ahnya Fromel did not have a family. None save Allen.

It was a long distant memory. She could not remember anymore why they did not have parents. Or perhaps it was because her heart refused to let her remember. She could hazily remember a vaguely happy family home, but by the time she realized it, she was living in a sea of ruins.

Only she and her brother were alive.

More accurately, Ahnya had always been living off Allen.

Lawless people unrestrained by societal order, monsters that did not know or care about the ways of people, against all those pillagers who would steal away anything and everything from small children, her wildly temperamental older brother had fought with a fire in his belly to drive them away. And Ahnya could only cry in fear.

She sought protection from her brother. She had clung to him, seeking warmth from the only remaining thing she had, that one family bond. She knew that she annoyed him by doing that.

She did not know how many times his eyes had flared in annoyance at her. It would not have been strange if his fist had knocked her aside at any point. Ahnya now knew that the only reason he had not cast her aside was because he had still been a child then.

In a corner of the abandoned town that was their roost, there had been an old, weather-beaten bronze statue of a beast person in the middle of a street they always walked down. One day, the statue looked down at them and asked:

"Lost little stray kittens,

Where is your home?"

Unable to answer through the tears—that was how they met the goddess.

"Come with me."

The goddess Freya smiled when she saw the pair of souls—particularly Allen's—and held out her hand to them.

Ahnya was scared of the beauty that seemed not of this world, and she pulled at her brother's clothes with trembling fingers, while Allen silently took the goddess's hand.

From that moment, Ahnya's memories were ones of continuous, dizzying change.

The two of them received falna, joined *Freya Familia*, and what awaited them in Orario was a baptism that was truly not of this world. Though they had been given clothes, food, and shelter, they went through days and days of fighting and wounds that made their time in the sea of ruins seem like a vacation.

Ahnya coughed up blood, vomited, and collapsed countless times. She was on the verge of just running away more times than she could remember. The battles out on the field were traumatic for Ahnya, and she was sure that anyone who had not sworn their loyalty to the goddess would not be able to make it out. Anyone else who made it out had to have a remarkable level of talent or else have some irreplaceable thing besides Freya that drove them, like she had had.

Allen met Freya's expectations, and he distinguished himself in the fighting more and more as time went on. He easily adapted to Folkvangr and had reached Level 2 in the span of a year.

Because of that, Ahnya did not have any more time to cry or complain. She started actively choosing to go out into the field and fighting desperately—anything to avoid being left behind by her brother.

Ahnya was starved for family.

Even when she had a familia around her, her bond with Allen was special.

Ahnya had always been a lost kitten, so no matter how much Allen might dislike it, she did not want to let go of his hand. She believed that if she did, she would truly be all alone.

At the time, Orario was in its dark ages, and even members of *Freya Familia* could die easily. Even if she had made friends among the familia, it wasn't uncommon for them to disappear the very next day. Because of that, everyone was always on edge, always tense, and would berate anyone without strength. The only ones who spared any concern for Ahnya were a rare few, like a certain dwarf captain, and even she had only talked with Ahnya a handful of times. In another sense, that was just how little anyone other than Allen registered in her eyes, how single-mindedly she had chased after his back.

She had desperately tried to keep up with Allen.

No matter what anyone tried to say, she continued to stay at his side.

When Allen became Level 3, she became Level 2.

When her brother was bestowed the honorable name Vana Freya by the deities, the sister who always clung to her brother was given the name Vana Alfi.

And then, the limit came.

She ignored Allen's angry rejections like always and forced herself to come along on an expedition to the deep levels, and almost got herself killed.

Allen had gotten wrapped up in it and been badly wounded, too.

If he were alone, he never would have fallen. It was all because of Ahnya.

Those who are chosen, and those who are not. Allen was the former, and Ahnya was the latter.

The insurmountable wall of talent that separated even siblings—a cruel distinction. Ahnya became unable to follow Allen using her own two feet.

Weighed down by Ahnya and on the verge of life or death, when he finally recovered, he said it to Ahnya's face.

"You idiot. Never show your face before me again."

That day, Allen washed his hands of her.

The moment his eyes became like frozen ice, Ahnya cried out in despair.

She sobbed desperately, begging for forgiveness, clinging to him, only to be mercilessly kicked away.

"You are unnecessary."

And Freya said it as well.

A valuable einherjar, or one who had failed to make the cut. It was obvious which would be chosen. The goddess had smiled coldly at the fool who had almost killed one of her favorites and easily cast her aside.

Allen was the one Freya had wanted. Ahnya had just been a part of the package deal from the start.

And the foolish Ahnya realized it only after the goddess had already stolen her brother away from her. Before the unstoppable swell of emotions could transform into hatred, Ahnya was consumed by grief and collapsed.

A stream of tears poured from her eyes.

No matter how much she reached out her hand, her brother would not turn back.

The lost kitten was abandoned by her last family, and on that day, she became a stray cat.

She was kicked out of the home, soaked by the pouring rain, and soon fell to her knees on the pavement.

Everyone ignored the dirty, disgraceful, hollow stray cat.

It was during the Dark Ages. The city was filled with people like that.

The line between her tears and the raindrops blurred and then disappeared, and she became an empty doll waiting to break completely.

And the only one who held out a hand to that Ahnya—the only source of warmth.

"Are you okay?"

The girl with blue-gray hair.

What reached out to her was not the hand of her brother that she so desperately wished for, but *her* hand.

"You'll catch a cold. Why don't you come to our home?"

Ahnya did not respond at all as the girl smiled.

She gave Ahnya a home and a family, without asking for anything in return.

She was Syr Flover.

"My home is called The Benevolent Mistress—"

"Here."

"!"

Ahnya was brought back to reality by Allen's voice.

It was a random plaza like any other near the center of the city's northwest.

The only odd point was that there was not a single person around. Ahnya had not noticed it as she slipped into her thoughts, but the people around her had been cleared away. Probably, almost certainly by the power of charm.

And as if to confirm her guess, the goddess was standing in the middle of the plaza shrouded in a robe.

"Lady...Freya..."

Even if she kept her distance, and even if she covered herself with a robe, Ahnya could recognize her beauty at a glance. Her voice was hoarse, and her throat quivered. The trauma and terror of being abandoned by her came rushing back.

Gray clouds were silently rolling in. It might rain.

"Welcome, Ahnya."

When she saw Allen walk ahead and stand at Freya's side, Ahnya's will almost broke as she stepped forward.

The distance between them was only five meders. It was a distance that the current Ahnya could not bridge no matter what she did.

Beneath her deep hood, Freya's silver eyes narrowed.

"I suppose I should say it has been a while. Not so much for me, but from your perspective, we have not met in quite some time."

"...?"

"Have you been eating properly? Your face looks awful. Did something bad happen?"

Ahnya was just dumbstruck by the incomprehensible greeting.

The hypocrisy of worrying about her health when it was Freya who had cast her aside. She could not understand anything the goddess was saying. Fear of a deity who could not be understood by mere mortals robbed Ahnya of her voice and her freedom.

Seeing her inability to answer, Freya smiled once and moved on to the main subject.

"Would you prefer to just stay silent yourself, or do you prefer I charm you so you can forget everything?"

"Eh…?"

"I'm letting you choose whether to become my puppet or not."

When she was told that, Ahnya's eyes opened and strength returned to her hand.

She broke through the awe she felt at the goddess and clenched her fist as she glared straight ahead.

Ahnya's spirits flared, like an abandoned cat baring her fangs at her former owner.

"Wh-what are you doing, Lady Freya?!"

"I'm creating a sandbox. A gilded cage to surround my love."

"What do you want that you are turning Orario on its head meow?!"

"There is something I want. And for that, I twisted everything."

Stupid Ahnya could not figure out what Freya was saying or what divine will drove her.

But when she realized what Mia had said, that Freya had wanted to create this twisted world, there was just one thing Ahnya wanted to discover.

"Where did you take Syr meow?!"

Her feelings for that girl, more than anything the unyielding affection the stray cat felt toward her precious family.

Those feelings turned into an explosive shout bursting from Ahnya's breast.

"Answer me, Lady Freya!"

Her shout left the air around them trembling.

A moment's stillness followed the shout that almost felt like it had to have reached everywhere in the city.

Behind the shadow of her hood, Freya's expression grew blank.

Ahnya did not look away for even a second, staring down the goddess.

Allen said nothing as he watched on. However, her elder brother's eyes did not pass judgment over his younger sister.

"She does not exist anymore—is what I would like to say."

From the shadows, her lips moved.

"But you two would not believe that, so I'll let you meet her."

And then...

"I never intended to become her again, though—"

Before Ahnya could begin to understand that last murmur, the goddess put her hands to her hood, and—

"—What?"

When she lowered the hood and revealed the girl, time stopped for Ahnya.

She shook her head, her long, blue-gray hair flowing freely down her back.

She slowly blinked as her cute, round eyes of the same color met Ahnya's gaze.

She smiled the same smile that Ahnya knew so well.

"This is how it is, Ahnya."

It was a voice that Ahnya could never mistake.

Unmistakably the voice of Syr.

And it had a devastating effect on Ahnya.

"The one who was always there with you at the tavern, was me."

"...No..."

"I'm Freya. And I'm Syr."

"...No..."

"Freya is Syr, and Syr is Freya."

"...No!"

It was a scream.

Her cat's ears were bent low, and she grabbed her head and shook it with both hands, rejecting the scene before her eyes.

It was impossible. A joke of the highest order. Syr being Freya. There was no way that could be true.

But the Syr standing where Freya had been just moments ago would not allow the denial screaming in Ahnya's heart.

"'Are you okay?'

"'You'll catch a cold. Why don't you come to our home?'

"'My home is called The Benevolent Mistress—'

"—That's what I said when I first met you in this appearance, right? I remember it all."

The voice kept rocking Ahnya's mind, forcibly recalling the scene from that rainy day.

The moment that had revived Ahnya after she had been abandoned.

The precious memory of when she had first met Syr.

It was being spoiled by a silver divine will.

"'Try to cheer up, Ahnya? You don't have to be scared here?'

"'There aren't any scary people here.'

"'Let's work together. I'm not very good at it, either, so let's learn together?'"

Again, again, again.

She was making Ahnya remember those days when at first she had not been able to open up to anyone, when she had taken her feelings out on everyone around her like a betrayed cat, but even so, her heart had eventually been melted by Syr's kindness, she had been worked by Mia so hard, she did not have time to dwell in sadness, and she managed to recover her natural cheer while working at the tavern.

Each and every one of those memories was being corrupted.

The past memories and the present voice matched perfectly.

Reality and despair merged into one.

The girl in front of her smiled as she said there was nothing wrong at all.

"Ah, ah, ah…aaaaaaaaaaaaaaaaaaaaa!"

Tears fell from Ahnya's eyes as she furiously shook her head.

Her arms and legs were trembling, she was dizzy, and her ears were ringing. Her teeth were chattering.

What was real, and what was a lie? What was reality, and what was fake? Who had saved her, and what had toyed with her?

Ahnya was pushed to the brink of destruction by the unending onrush of emotions.

"Wh-why…? Why…would you…?"

Her feet and the pavement grew wet beneath her falling tears as she raised her still twitching face, her voice a grief-stricken cry.

"You know why."

She answered.

"It was just to pass the time."

She smiled.

"Just a goddess's whim."

The goddess's smile crossed Syr's face.

"Aaaaaaaaaaaaaaaaaaaaaaaaaaaaaaaaaaaaaaaaaaaaaaaaaaaa aaaaaaaaaaaaaaaaaaaaaaaaaaagh!"

Ahnya broke.

All of her memories cracked, shattered, and crumbled into ash.

Having learned the truth, she reached the promised destruction that awaited at the end.

"No, nonononononono! No!"

She flailed her head as she lost control of herself.

Ahnya chose to deny reality.

The impulse and desire to reject the being before her eyes exploded.

"You're not Syr! You're not Syr at all!"

Ahnya did not realize she was hurling abuse at the goddess she had once respected and feared. That was already irrelevant to everything.

Her desperate desire for light overcame her fear of darkness.

"Give Syr back! Give her baaaaaaaaaaaaaaaaaack!"

Ahnya screeched as she leaped forward.

She could not tell what expression was on the face of the girl right in front of her whom she tried with all her might to grab on to.

"Idiot."

"Gah?!"

Immediately afterward, Allen sent that rage flying backward with his spear.

A first-tier adventurer standing guard would not allow his

mistress to suffer any harm. He mercilessly knocked her away, sending her flying back to the edge of the plaza.

Ahnya's rage lost its target as she slammed into a mound of wooden boxes, sending up a plume of dust.

"Ahnya!"

The moment her friend was sent flying, Lyu stood up.

The elf who had followed Ahnya, and had until that very moment been watching with bated breath to see what fate lay in store, leaped out at the danger to her comrade.

"There you are."

And as if it was all fated to be, the goddess with the face of Syr spoke in Syr's voice.

And with a sidelong glance, Allen easily caught Lyu's blades as she charged him.

"I was right to cast a wide-range charm on the surroundings. That way you could find us and come to me."

"Ghh…?!"

Her blades easily caught by the shaft of the spear, and quickly at a disadvantage, Lyu was filled with unease.

She realized that she had been had. *Freya Familia* had quickly realized that Lyu and Asfi were not in Orario. And they had used Ahnya, whom they had waited to deal with, as bait to lure Lyu out.

Clearing out a large area and making it stand out as unnatural, she had let Lyu notice it.

The exchange with Ahnya had been a trap to lure out Lyu.

"Allen, lower your spear."

"There is no need for that. I can just crush—"

"Lower it."

"…Understood."

The mistress's voice commanded the first-tier adventurer without brooking any argument.

Freed from Allen's pressure, Lyu was bathed in another layer of cool sweat.

She could not accept the unwavering reality before her eyes, either.

"Are you really Syr...?!"

"—You saw our conversation just now, didn't you, Lyu? I'm Syr. There is another child with the ability to become the same beings as me, but the one who was always there with you, was me."

The aura around the goddess changed again at Lyu's challenge.

As if her personality was tearing itself apart, or as if out of respect for the relationship she had with them, Freya's tone turned into Syr's.

Lyu's sky-blue eyes wavered.

The storm of emotions that had assaulted Ahnya were racing about her breast, too.

Freya was Syr? She wanted to believe it was a terrible joke. A hallucination. But no matter how much she wished it so, the scene before her refused to change.

Aware she had lost her calm, Lyu forced her lips open.

"What you said to Ahnya...was that all true?"

"........."

"You saving me...all those days in the tavern! Those were all just a game to you?!"

Faced with that question, that outburst that Lyu could not hold back, Syr—

"...Haaah..."

—forgot to even try to hide her sigh.

"And what if it was, Lyu?"

"Wh...?!"

"It was a game. All of it. It's role playing. The role I chose for myself was a neighborhood girl, and the stage I chose was a tavern. In her boredom, a goddess decided to play with everyone. Is that really so hard for you to swallow?"

Lyu felt herself being torn by a terrible shock as Syr spoke a simple truth without any trace of lie.

"Everyone tells their own little lies, right? That was mine."

And with her appeal to that objective truth, Lyu had no words left to deny her.

"Ahnya ended up like that, but I don't want anyone to get hurt. I mean it. So please. Won't you understand? Won't you accept me? I won't tell any more lies. I can just be myself without holding back now. So please, Lyu."

She held out her hand.

She walked toward Lyu with hand outstretched, her voice clear and bright, like a song. Just like always. Just like that day when Lyu had collapsed after completing her revenge.

Syr's hand tried to take Lyu's.

"——gh!"

It happened in an instant—Lyu's hand brushed Syr's away.

"…gh?!"

Lyu herself was immediately shaken, staring at the palm of her own hand.

There had only been three people who had taken Lyu's hands.

The first was Alize. The third was Bell. And the second was Syr.

Lyu's body had clearly rejected the hand that had once been able to hold hers.

That was the ultimate proof. The elven hand that could perceive good and evil.

Her elven body had decided that even though they were the same person, this was a different being from the girl she knew.

"You…are not Syr."

The conclusion she reached was the same as Ahnya's.

Lyu shouted at the being who was looking down at the hand rejected, eyes hidden by hair.

"I cannot accept that you are Syr!"

Immediately after—

"Silence."

The girl before looked up, and her blue-gray eyes were shrouded in a silver light.

"Prostrate thyself."

The moment she saw them, Lyu immediately obeyed her command.

"Ugh?!"

Both of her knees fell to the pavement.

Against her will, she helplessly knelt then and there.

Her mind was agitated. Her consciousness melted away like candy while her body and heart desperately wished to become the goddess's slave.

As her body and soul were ravaged by an almost impossible to resist magic, Allen's eyes widened ever so slightly as he watched from the side.

Syr was irritated. Visibly so.

And then in the blink of an eye, with a sigh of regret, she apologized to the elf kneeling before her.

"I'm sorry, it's becoming a terrible habit. It's become *awfully troublesome.* Right now, I have gotten bad at holding myself back. I end up resorting to that power I always hated so much. It must feel terrible, you must be so hurt. Sorry, Lyu, I'll undo it right away."

The silver gleam disappeared from her blue-gray eyes.

At the same time, Lyu gasped and started coughing.

The red-hot stream swirling in her breast resided.

Syr bent over, putting her hand gently on Lyu's shoulder.

Lyu felt a cold chill.

"Lyu, I told you before. I love people who try to be beautiful for the sake of others. I love Bell. But I also love you, too."

The elven nature ingrained in her body was screaming.

Her skin crawled with an unpleasant feeling from the hand on her shoulder and the voice so suddenly filled with affection.

She wanted to brush the hand away, but the power of the charm had not fully resided, and her body would not listen to her.

"I know—how about we share Bell?"

"....Huh?"

Not believing her ears, Lyu barely managed to look up and see Syr's broad smile.

"We can keep him all to ourselves."

"...What are you...?"

"Just a little bit more and *he should be ready.* I'll break the curse of the one he adores. With that, I can make Bell mine."

Syr smiled pleasantly, like an innocent child talking about her treasure.

"I don't like the idea of others touching Bell, but if it's you, then I wouldn't mind. I could allow it because it's you."

Lyu could not understand what she was saying.

It was terrifying.

Somewhere in the back of her mind, she realized that the blue-gray-haired girl she knew no longer existed.

"Let's both love Bell. Just the three of us, bodies touching, tracing each other's lips, our scent mingling as we embrace each other."

Nauseating.

"Hidden away, atop a bed, loving each other until our bodies melt together, until we become one."

Revolting.

"Our souls joining, etching our love into each other. And while I can't, you might even be able to have Bell's child."

Disgusting! Disgusting!! Disgusting!!!

The witch's proposal. The intoxicating drug of one who knew love. Or perhaps it was a wish for destruction.

While the girl was offering the sweet nectar of love, Lyu felt an intense loathing and revulsion.

The being before her was some other creature wearing Syr's skin.

"Ghh...I refuse...!"

Lyu firmly gave her response.

Her eyes flared, her breath ragged, and her body trembling, she glared back with all of her might.

I will not hold hands with this stranger who is not Syr.

She declared that even as her tongue struggled to move, her gaze filled with anger.

"...It really did come to this."

At that moment, Syr's eyes drooped slightly, barely noticeably, and a lonely smile crossed her lips.

Eh...

For just that one moment.

Lyu could see the blue-gray-haired girl, unchanged from the girl in her memories.

"Whether it worked out or failed in the end, I knew you would be disillusioned regardless. We would fight, and might not be able to make up...it turned out to be true."

Lyu's vision wavered, and her consciousness suddenly faded.

While it had been released, the recoil of the charm shook her world. Struggling to breathe, unable to focus her gaze, she could no longer hear Syr's words.

But why?

The words that seemed to reach her ears sounded like something she had just heard from someone not long ago.

Seeing this person who wore a lonely smile after running out of things to say felt incredibly familiar.

Somewhere in the area between friendship and yearning—

"But I can't go back."

Those were the last words Lyu heard before her consciousness faded to black.

"Allen."

She quietly pulled her hood back up.

The girl—the goddess—turned away from the elf collapsed on the ground.

"Take her and hide her away somewhere in the underground portion of the home so Bell can't see her."

"...Will you not charm her?"

"It's sentimentality. I don't want to corrupt her soul. Are you disappointed with me?"

"...No."

Allen shook his head slightly at the unvarnished confession of his patron goddess.

"As promised, I will leave Ahnya to you."

With those brief words, the goddess left the plaza.

Drip. Drip. Droplets began to fall on her shoulder.

After a few moments' silence, Allen turned around and looked at his sister, who could no longer stand up.

"If you do anything uncalled for, I will destroy that tavern. If you don't want that, then don't get in the goddess's way. Be quiet and keep your mouth shut."

With that warning, it was over.

Lifting Lyu over his shoulder, he followed after the goddess.

Just a single cat person was left behind in the empty plaza.

"………Aah…"

Finally, the rain began to fall.

Her vision became drenched with water, her ears filled with the sound of droplets falling.

Facing the sky as she lay atop the broken and scattered fragments of wooden boxes, it was impossible to tell if the droplets on her cheeks were rain or tears.

"Uaaaaaaaaaaaaaaaaaaaaaaaaaaaaaaaaaaaaaaaaaaaaaaaaaaaa aaaaaaaaaaaaah!!!"

Her lamentation reached no one's ears, drowned out by the sound of the rain.

The same rain fell on Ahnya as the day she had been abandoned by her brother and her goddess.

Heavy clouds and a torrential rain that shrouded the city blocked the light of the setting sun.

Asfi sat on the bed in the hideaway as the second hand of the pocket watch she was holding ticked onward. Asfi closed her eyes.

"Leon…you too…"

It was a murmur of despair as the hands on the watch marked sunset.

She did not allow herself an optimistic or wishful hope about her elven friend, who had failed to appear at the appointed time. No matter how lonely it was, she did not allow herself that.

"I'm all alone...Do I not have any allies left at all...?"

Her voice was weak, on the verge of dying out.

But Asfi stood up.

She smothered the feeble whines and resignation as she put her worn-out black helmet on.

She became invisible, and without anyone knowing, she put that place behind her, disappearing alone into the chill rain.

The rain does not stop.

Even as night settles in, the sound of the rain continues, as if the sky itself is crying.

Just like the day when I turned down her feelings.

...Where is Syr...?

When I pause in the long corridor and look out the window, Master glares at me.

"What are you doing?"

I continue following after him, taking the same path through the manor as always.

Because the baptism goes on rain or shine, I'm even more exhausted than usual today.

Even as I make my way to the goddess's chamber, I can't hide my exhaustion.

And shrouded by that, my thoughts drift to the blue-gray-haired girl I search for every time I'm allowed to go out.

She is nowhere to be found.

There is no one who knows her.

Is she just a product of my imagination?

Even just a little bit ago, I would have laughed that thought away, but my body and heart are gradually being cornered, and I can't be so sure anymore. Trapped in those dark feelings, I arrive at Lady Freya's chamber.

"Welcome, Bell."

Receiving permission to enter, I leave Master and step into the room where Lady Freya is waiting in a simple white nightgown. My legs draw me to the side of the goddess who gave me my night's peace. I'm already used to sitting beside her on the couch.

I feel a kind of warmth as she asks to hear my story again tonight, like a continuation of a thousand and one nights, when—

"...?"

Something seems a little bit different today.

"What is it, Bell?"

Lady Freya cocks her head curiously. Her long hair like a pure stream reflecting a silver gleam rustles and glimmers as it falls from her shoulder.

It's not as if something is wrong with her appearance. I'm sure it's just my imagination.

But...it's as if a part of her is not there, as if it has been left behind somewhere else.

It almost feels like her beautiful silver eyes have taken on a different tinge.

"...Did something happen...?"

Before I realized it, I had already asked the question.

Lady Freya looks surprised and stops moving.

"...Why do you think that?"

"Ummm...You just seemed a little unwell..."

I can't really explain it, so my answer is just vague and fuzzy. Lady Freya is looking at me when, all of a sudden, her shoulders relax, and she smiles, her eyes dropping slightly.

"You're always so oblivious to women's subtleties, and yet so sharp in moments like this."

"Ugh...!"

I gulp, afraid I have annoyed her.

Lady Freya's eyes narrow like a cat's as she smiles and then giggles, just like always.

I realize that reaction floods me with relief.

"...If you would like, you can tell me..."

"Oh?"

"Yes...since you are always listening to me."

Lady Freya neither accepts nor rejects my suggestion. She just looks back at me with those eyes like the winter sky that seem to glimmer from some unknowable place.

I open my mouth.

"Did...something happen?"

"...I'm a little bit emotional. Someone I thought of as a friend hurt me."

"Hurt you?"

"Something like that," she responded.

"Ummm, would it be possible to make up...?"

"No. I was the one in the wrong after all."

Instead of telling my story, I'm listening to Lady Freya.

I feel a mysterious sensation and hesitation as I carefully choose my words.

"If you know you are wrong, then...what about apologizing...?"

"That is an option. But I can't do that."

"...Why is that?"

"Because I've found what I want most."

Lady Freya is just looking forward, not at me, her profile almost cold in her resolution.

"Because I've decided that I'm willing to cast aside anything and everything for that sake."

I shiver at the coldness of her voice that is so unrecognizable from the goddess that has shown me so much warmth. But in that moment, her resolve feels terribly lonely.

"If you have to cast away something precious...then would it be possible to pick it up again?"

"Eh?"

"If you could make it in time, could you go back...even if some time passed...would it be possible to go back later and pick it up again?"

That's why I said it.

I'd been on the verge of leaving behind lots of things before myself.

Things I wanted to hold in my heart forever, but that always felt like they might fall from my grasp at any moment.

But no matter how difficult, how painful it was, how much it felt like I would fail, looking back, I'm glad that I never gave up trying to hold on to them.

And even if I could not hold on, if I lost something…I was sure I would reach out and try to embrace it again.

"Going back for something after having to let go of it once…I'm sure that only makes it even more precious than before."

Lady Freya's eyes widen as I smile at her.

Her barely opened lips tremble ever so slightly.

I do not know much. But I know that somewhere in the corner of their hearts, people, and even deities, always regret the things they leave behind.

Lady Freya doesn't respond.

But her cheeks flush ever so slightly while she looks at me.

"I love you, Bell."

"Eh?"

"I love you."

It's just a split second.

The world around me fades.

"…Whaaah?!"

And then a hysteric sound erupts from my throat at being told that all of a sudden.

I lean backward and try to scoot away, but the arm of the couch stops me and can't retreat any farther!

Lady Freya dons a sadistic smile.

"Hey, Bell. Do you know how to comfort a woman?"

"N-no…?"

"You'll be popular if you learn how, you know? Women love a man who can give them a sense of security."

"I-I-I don't want to be popular with the ladies or anything so wicked…!"

"But weren't you the one who wanted to pick up girls?"

"Bwhu?!"

She even knows that?!

As far as I remembered, the only ones who knew about that were the goddess and the people at the gate when I first came to the city!

"Now, I'll tell you the secret, so listen closely."

Her impish orders don't stop, and I'm forced to do as she said.

"First of all, wrap your arm around her shoulder."

"Umm…"

"Quickly now."

Sitting next to her, I nervously put my right arm around Lady Freya's shoulder, just like she instructed.

Our shoulders touch. A pleasant smell tickles my nostrils.

And then I realize it. A plain, undecorated nightgown quickly transforms into an outfit that drives many a man mad if she's the one wearing it.

"When a woman leans against your shoulder, you lean in, too."

"………"

"If you notice her looking up, then should hold her gaze."

"………"

"After looking into her eyes, put your hand to her chin."

"………"

"And then kiss her lips s—"

"Nowaynowaynowaynoway! I can't do that!"

I reach my limit and topple over backward off the couch, landing on my back on the floor.

"Wa-ha-haa-ha-ha-ha-ha! What are you doing, Bell?!"

Lady Freya is clutching her stomach and laughing out loud at me as I turn bright red after my embarrassing display.

"You really are so naive and timid."

"I-I'm sorry…but just now, that seemed not quite right, or rather…!"

"Even though I love you so much, you won't answer my feelings?"

"Eeeh? No! That's not it at all…! But I mustn't behave crudely with a goddess…!"

"Running away from a goddess of love whispering sweet nothings is far more discourteous."

She holds out her hand to me, and I stand up from my disgraceful fall, my eyes darting around awkwardly as Lady Freya watches me in good humor. There is no more tragic determination in her eyes as she wipes away the tears of laughter.

It's the first time I have seen her like that, but…it looks like she has cheered up a bit. Good.

I smile awkwardly as I think that.

"—Ahhh, I truly do like you."

Just then, her softer voice, her expression. Time stops for me as it all overlaps with a scene from my memory.

"Syr—?"

I don't know why, but that name passes my lips.

—Ahhh, I really do like you.

Those words…that time. Isn't that what she said in the cathedral?

This smile…isn't that exactly the same smile she had?

I'm dumbfounded, and Lady Freya is aghast.

The room falls quiet, and even the sound of the rain disappears as we look at each other.

How many minutes? Or is it only seconds? I can no longer tell how long we looked at each other, when she quietly holds out her hand.

I can't move at all as her right hand rests on my cheek—

"—Saying another woman's name when I'm right here before you. What are you thinking?"

"Owwwwwwwww?!"

She pinches my cheek *so hard*!

Lady Freya's gaze hardens, and all resemblance I thought I saw is already long gone.

In fact, she is glaring at me, seemingly extremely upset.

"I've never experienced such humiliation before."

"I-I'm sorry!"

My eyes water as I desperately beg forgiveness, but Lady Freya turns away with a harrumph.

"I'm upset, Bell. Please leave."

I made her mad…

I have no way to explain myself. Ordered to leave without any choice, I slump forward, genuinely reflecting on my mistake as I move to the door. When I look back right before leaving, the goddess is still turned away from me. She might not forgive me for a while.

But...what was that?

Was it just my imagination...?

Obsessing over that mysterious feeling, I leave her chamber, driven out by the silence and the sight of her back.

"........"

Freya pressed her hand to her breast.

That had not been the behavior of a haughty empress; it had been almost like the action of an inexperienced and innocent young maiden.

After a long time had passed, almost subconsciously, she walked over to the side of the room, to her luxuriously decorated dresser, and opened the drawer.

Her slender fingers removed a blue hair ornament.

A paired accessory that a boy had given someone.

The goddess did not say anything as she stood there, hugging the accessory to her chest.

"...Ngh."

There was one other person standing, unmoving, like a reflection of the goddess.

At the door on the opposite end of the room from the great oak doors the boy had left by.

While the goddess's permission was withheld and none could enter the room, she looked down, shrouded in a faint magic light as she leaned her back against the door.

Her face was locked in a distressing grimace.

"What are you doing?"

When someone addressed her directly, the light around her scattered. As the glow faded, her regular profile returned and Hörn looked up.

"...Hedin."

The white elf's expression remained unchanged.

Hörn said nothing as she moved past him.

The elf watched in silence as the girl whose face was so pale left.

He then turned his gaze to the door.

As if addressing his thoughts to the goddess on the other side of it, he closed his eyes and then opened them again with a determined look.

"My body shall ever be thy faithful servant."

And murmured an oath like a knight to his lady.

CHAPTER 5 THE END OF HER WORLD

It intensifies.

The battle on the field, the holy death match. The baptism by the first-tier adventurers.

"—soldiers of lightning."

"Ghhh?!"

The short cast echoes cruelly.

I've just been slammed by magic, and despair claws at me when I realize another round is already coming as I quickly move to evade it with all my might.

"Caurus Hildr."

A fusillade of lightning falls.

Each bolt is a swift arrowhead the size of my head, pouring down all around me as if fired by a whole regiment of soldiers. I manage to avoid the first few blasts, but after that, I falter and clumsily absorb a hellish number of strikes.

Shot, burned, chipped, and electrified.

Even the blood spattered around me is scorched and comes to a boil.

I can't see for the flashes of lightning erupting all around me, and for a moment, my consciousness goes blank before a merciless declaration reaches my ears.

"Strike forever, indestructible lord of lightning."

—A third cast?!

It's too fast!

Calling his casting ability transcendental did not do it justice. Master was doing successive high-speed casts, ruthlessly unleashing even more lightning.

"Valiant Hildr."

An enormous lightning spear pierces me where I stand frozen.

A first-tier adventurer's rampage.

The tyranny of a single elf.

It had already been a severe enough battle, but one day Master simply declared, "Pathetic."

And thus began a fierce, one-sided struggle.

Master began unleashing his magic and destroyed me countless times. Even now, a corner of Folkvangr was swirling in the grips of a white elf's lightning storm. Any person or monster who took one step inside it would meet their end, and I was forced to try to survive while trapped inside the storm.

"—Aaaaa, guhah?! Igh…ahhhhhh?!"

Activating my skill—charging my right leg for just a brief moment, I somehow manage to kick the ground and escape the line of fire, but half of my body is charred.

I had no hope of evading it in time. I'm writhing in agony like a beast from the blast fired with deadly timing, while Master has already closed the distance between us.

Tears are welling in my eyes from the intense pain as he follows up with another attack.

"Haah!"

"Uwah?!"

A spear-like kick hits my shoulder. I can hear bones breaking. My charred left arm is now well and truly unusable. Master's rhomphaia hurtles at me. That at least I manage to deflect with the knife in my right hand, escaping death, a desperate extension.

Responding with martial arts—is hopeless. I can't get through even if I force hand-to-hand combat. Master outclasses me even at close range. If I try to use Firebolt, my arm will get severed by his rhomphaia. There's no way one of the greatest magic swordsmen in the city would overlook the telltale flow of mind that telegraphs a spell. The moment I resort to a cheap spell will be the end for me.

Master…why…?!

This is wrong. It's all wrong.

He's totally different from the master I remember. The Hedin who trained me to escort Syr. And as if declaring that it was all just my own foolish imagination, every trace of the expression from my memories has been erased entirely. His eyes are shaded with cruelty, and he is really trying to kill me.

A groaning cry emanates from the pit of my stomach as I attempt the best counterattack I can unleash.

But there is just a slapping sound as he deflects it with the palm of his hand and immediately follows up with an attack to the right side of my head while I stand there in a daze. He spins, unleashing a snakelike elbow strike to my temple. I stop breathing and my knees buckle, and like a broken rag doll, I leave myself wide open.

"Fool."

"Gaaaaaaah—"

He spins his rhomphaia violently down toward my body.

It bites deep into my shoulder, and a swell of blood pours from the wound. There's no question it's a mortal wound.

Strength leaves me, and the scene reflected in my eyes as I stagger backward is Master's figure, his rhomphaia swung upward, preparing to deliver the next blow.

As time slows to crawl, it begins to swing down—

""""""Stop, Hedin.""""""

—but it doesn't land.

Alfrik, Dvalinn, Berling, and Grer all have their weapons at Master's throat, stopping his rhomphaia.

As I'm drawn to the ground with a mortal wound, collapsing entirely onto my back, a murderous voice echoes on the field.

"You've gone too far."

"Did you forget how to hold back?"

"Are you trying to actually destroy him?"

"Even Heith and the others won't be able to fully heal him."

At the edge of my vision, I can see Heith and the other healers growing pale at Master's sadism.

The healers have not been able to keep up with the treatment at all. They don't dare approach because of the tempestuous rain of lightning. Even if they could have gotten close enough to heal me, my body has been carved away with deadly precision.

The other familia members around us are the same. Van and the rest are staring at us in silent shock, their own battle forgotten.

At some point, the sky grew a bloody, crimson color. I can't remember when it started, but the sun was beginning to set.

"Are you okay, Bell?"

"Aah, ngh, argh...?!"

Hegni gives me an elixir and sits me up.

A billow of smoke rises from my wound, and the effects of the dramatic healing assault me. I let out a formless scream as Hegni supports my back while glaring at Master...

"What are you plotting, old foe? For what reason do you enact such tyranny?"

"As if that question should need asking. It's obvious," Master fires back at the censure in the eyes of his fellow first-tier adventurers. "This idiot rabbit has attracted the love of our beloved goddess. Therefore, it's imperative he prove his worth. If he does not prove to possess a soul worthy of our mistress...then none will accept it!"

His honest, unvarnished shout is filled with intense emotion.

The others all fall silent.

Out here in Folkvangr, there is nothing mistaken about that warrior's battle cry.

"Everything else means nothing! Fulfilling the goddess's wish is your duty!"

Suffering from blood loss, my vision fuzzy, I look up.

The elf's coral eyes are looking at me, calling to me.

"Stand! Rise to your feet!"

"...ghh..."

"You must stand!"

He, who had vowed loyalty to the goddess, more earnest than anyone, is looking just at me.

"Prove that you are the Odr for whom the goddess has so long waited!"

The elf's shout thunders as it slams into me.

The next day, and the day after that, Master continues to increase the intensity of the baptism.

"What mental obstruction hides within thy mind, Hedin?"

Hegni's eyes were flared as he pressed Hedin, who remained unmoved.

"It appears you want to ask me what I'm thinking, but what do you mean?"

"You know full well! The white hare is the goddess's offering! Such sadism will corrode his innocent heart! You leave me no choice but to be the hare's knight!"

When the city was shrouded in dark night, the first-tier adventurers of *Freya Familia* gathered in a certain room deep within Folkvangr. The Gullivers were sitting at the table, Allen had his arms crossed and was leaning against the wall looking bored, and Ottar stood silent. It was the place where a lone white elf stood in judgment for his excessive persecution of the boy.

In response to Hegni's menacing glare, Hedin snorted.

"What knight, you fool? Do you wish to earn more incomprehensible derision from the deities?"

"Th-that has nothing to do with it…?!"

Hegni's eyes watered, and he immediately switched back to his normal voice at having that bit of old history dredged up.

"Then have you grown attached to that fool? Would you call *that thing* your friend?"

"F-friend?! No, no, no! It's true that this human is a good-natured and kind person, and I get the sense that no matter how deep into chaos I might slip, he would speak to me with consideration, yes, but at best he is like an apprentice!…No, this feeling is…an unrivaled friend?"

The dark elf whose nature was so shy and timid had an over-the-top reaction to the word "friend," and his focus was cast into a world of imagination.

Glaring in annoyance at Hegni, who was off on a wild adventure in his head, Alfrik and his brothers spoke up.

"It's true that Lady Freya entrusted Bell Cranell's training to you."

"But even so, your rash behavior these past few days is intolerable."

"Don't try to dodge the question by blowing smoke up that idiot's ass."

"If you do not have any ulterior motives, then explain yourself."

And the prum brothers threatened implicitly, *If you do not have an acceptable reason, we will draw and quarter you.*

Hedin sighed with more than a trace of disappointment.

"Are your eyes just decorative holes?"

""""What did you say?""""

"In this sandbox at this very moment, the one being driven into a corner is not that fool, but Milady."

"""""!!!"""""

It was not just the Gullivers; even Hegni's and Allen's eyes widened at that statement.

"Bell Cranell is worn down, yet he is unbowed by our trick. Meanwhile, he is disturbing the goddess's heart."

As he said that, Hedin looked at the boaz, the only one whose expression had remained unchanged.

As Alfrik and the rest also turned their attention to him, Ottar, who had been serving at Freya's side, responded with a delicate expression, as if he had some idea of what Hedin was saying.

"...It's true that Milady has spent more time of late alone in contemplation. Either looking up at the sky from her window without listening to the maids' conversations or taking her meals. Other times she's merely been looking out at the field to watch the boy fight. And..." Ottar added, "it seems as if her time is mostly spent in self-reflection."

The Gullivers could not hide their shock.

"The thought of someone resisting her charm is enchanting the goddess. We must corner that foolish rabbit at once and bring him down. I'm merely taking the steps necessary for that to happen."

Hegni and the Gullivers closed their mouths at the words of Hedin, who stood in the role of commander or strategist.

After silencing those who had been accompanying him in the boy's baptism, Hedin turned his gaze to Allen.

"Starting tomorrow, you join the baptism, too, cat."

"My job right now is watching the tavern. What are you thinking, giving that monstrous dwarf a chance to do whatever she wants, dumbass?"

"Do you really still intend to play the fool? *Quit using Mia as an excuse.*"

"!"

"You and Milady have already made a move against the tavern. There is no more reason for you to bother with it. Leave watching it to Van and them."

Allen was silenced by the elf's insinuation, which seemed to have hit home.

Beating him about the head with sound arguments, Hedin stepped right in front of the cat person, who was shorter than him, and leaned in close.

"Or what? Do you still have some attachment to that idiotic sister of yours, even after abandoning her once?"

"—You wanna die, gnat?"

Allen's pupils flared, and he unleashed a full-powered burst of murderous intent.

A normal person would have been helplessly overwhelmed, but Hedin did not waver in the slightest.

"Our mistress is in crisis. Obey."

"....tch..."

The first to look away in the staring contest was Allen.

Scoffing instead of a verbal acknowledgment—a silent acceptance. Irritated, he pushed Hedin back with one hand.

There was no argument from Hegni, Alfrik, or the rest of the brothers.

All of their priorities aligned at the top, at Freya. Every one of them wanted most to protect the goddess's heart.

Pushed away, Hedin fixed his clothes and turned finally to the boaz.

"You too, Ottar. Crush that rabbit with your sword."

"...There is no need for me to join as well. I leave it to you, Hedin."

The warrior's words were few.

He firmly rejected the demand. Instead, as the familia's captain, he entrusted the task entirely to Hedin.

Rust-colored and coral eyes met.

Hedin made no further attempts to draw him in.

"...We will corner the fool beginning tomorrow. Do not allow any pity to move you. Do it thoroughly and completely."

He pushed his glasses up as he delivered the merciless pronouncement.

"*Freya Familia*'s movements have changed...?"

Asfi was observing Folkvangr from atop the city wall as she murmured to herself.

It was exactly noon, but the sky was shrouded in gray clouds. As the rest of the city returned to normal after the Goddess Festival, unaware of the fact that it had been twisted by the power of Freya's charm, Perseus was still fighting, even if she was now alone.

The battle she had been tasked with was righting the wrong that had warped Orario.

From the information I've gathered already, it is clear Bell Cranell has been forced to fight in Folkvangr for consecutive days, but...this is growing more intense...!

Maintaining her invisibility with the Hades Head, she was peering through the magic item while exercising extreme caution—praying that Freya did not notice her presence from the top of Babel—and Asfi was covered in a cold sweat. Even though she was so far away, it almost felt like she could hear Bell's groans and screams of pain.

The cat person's swift spear, the prums' waves of attacks, the dark elf's slashes that severed everything, and the white elf's terrifying magic all enveloped the boy in a storm of blood and destruction.

This is far more intense than just their usual baptism, and it almost feels like they're losing their composure...Are they getting impatient? The one and only Freya Familia*?*

The goddess of beauty and her followers should have already attained victory.

They had created a perfect sandbox, a prison that the boy could not possibly escape. They were surely aware that Asfi was watching, but she was just a single second-tier adventurer who could view events only from a distance, and there was no way she could dramatically alter the state of the board.

There should not be anyone who could threaten them, not in Orario, not in all of the mortal realm.

Then...an Irregular? Some unforeseen thing that is disturbing their familia...no, Goddess Freya herself?

And if such a thing could happen, then the only one who could be causing it was Bell Cranell.

During the incident with *Ishtar Familia*, Hermes had suggested that there was a possibility that charm did not work on Bell. Because if it did, there was no reason for Ishtar not to charm Bell and use him as a shield against Freya when her familia stormed through the Pleasure Quarter in a fiery blitz.

At the time, Asfi had laughed off the idea of someone defeating the charm of a goddess of beauty, but given what she had seen so far, that idea was gaining strength.

Most likely *Freya Familia* was losing patience with Bell for continuing to resist, for refusing to give in, and they were getting tired of waiting.

Or else Bell himself was becoming something that threatened to destroy the sandbox.

"Bell Cranell...what even are you...?"

In her exhaustion, Asfi let her real feelings slip out in a whisper.

That boy was practically a contagion of chaos at this point. Like the time with the Xenos, incidents centered around him exploded and shook the world. Or perhaps it was the opposite, and it was people like that who truly had the qualifications to be a hero.

For Asfi, a worldly person who wished to avoid troublesome matters as much as possible, Bell was someone who made her want to plead with tears in her eyes to just leave her alone—even if she understood that, from his point of view, it was an unreasonable request and he had not actually done anything bad himself—

She was split between despair and sympathy for the boy who seemed to summon trouble as she pinched the back of her hand and forced herself to stop from spiraling into a bad place.

Anyway! I can observe Vana Freya and the rest of them from here, and Warlord is surely at his goddess's side...! With all of the first-tier adventurers gathered at their home, whatever the reason, their surveillance network must have loosened! There's no mistaking it! I should be able to move more freely now...!

She could maintain her stealth as long as it was not against those monsters.

Freya Familia? *Who cares about einherjar? I'm Perseus. Against anyone on the same level as me, I can slip past easily. If I'm surrounded by Level 4s, then it's game over, but I'm going to break through no matter what, damn it!*

Driven forward by a desperate motivation in the back of her mind, Asfi silently began to move, making a list of the deities who might possibly be able to help her as she went.

"Haaah...I'm such a useless goddess..."

Hestia was melancholic.

Unable even to see the sunset through the clouds, she was walking falteringly through the hall of the home, steadying herself on pillars as a sense of powerlessness hammered her.

This was her general mood ever since Ouranos had driven her from his chamber.

She had skipped her shift at work for several days in a row, and the owner of the Jyaga Maru Kun shop was mad enough to come beating down the door of the home, which in turn meant that Hephaistos's store of patience was probably close to running dry. The moment she would be fired was drawing near. And Lilly, who did not know anything about what was going on, had berated her to get back to work because it was causing the familia problems. Hestia wasn't trying to use it as an excuse to slack off. She just couldn't pretend everything was normal while her precious follower was all alone.

"Bell..."

Her heart felt like it was being torn in half by the reality that Bell was still suffering even that very moment.

A rustling sound roused her from those painful thoughts.

"Huh? What, a scrap of paper...?"

Where did that come from? Did I drop it?

Hestia cocked her head at the odd scene as she reached down to pick it up. It was almost as if an invisible person had dropped it right in front of her.

"'I forgot something in the workshop'...?"

Opening the torn fragment of paper, she read the Koine written across it.

Her eyes widened at the *red pen strokes* that were written like a note to herself not to forget something.

"Wellllf! Are you there, Welf?!"

She made a point of calling out in a particularly loud voice as she ran around the home.

She was fully aware that *Freya Familia* was watching her and her familia from somewhere, even now. So Hestia went along with the memo and acted like a foolish goddess who had left something lying around.

Mikoto popped her head out of the kitchen to tell her, "Sir Welf is in the storage room on the first floor."

With a quick thank-you, she headed in that direction.

The blacksmith was in the process of carrying several boxes.

"Welf! Can you lend me your key to the workshop?! I need to go in real quick!"

"Eh, you do...?"

"Oy, oy, what's that unpleasant look on your face! What do you think I am?!"

"No, I was just a little worried about my smithing tools getting broken is all...What do you want in there anyway?"

"I lost my copy of a two hundred million valis loan! I think it might have gotten mixed up in the move and ended up in your workshop!"

"That sounds pretty bad..."

Hestia babbled on in a voice loud enough to be audible outside the home as Welf reluctantly winced and gave her the key with a firm "Don't lose that, please."

"Of course not," Hestia responded with a hearty thumbs-up. "...What are you doing, by the way?"

"The truth is, I've been storing a bunch of stuff beneath the workshop, but it was getting a little bit tight, so I decided to organize a bit."

He was carrying weapons and gear wrapped in cloth, along with armor stuffed in boxes, and even some magic blades. It was true that just leaving all that lying around would be concerning. Hestia then noticed that Welf was looking down at a piece of armor in his hands that was almost broken.

"Welf...?"

"...Lady Hestia...Do you remember why I made light armor?"

There was no one in the current *Hestia Familia* who favored light armor.

Hestia gasped at the presence of armor that Lilly, Mikoto, and Haruhime would never use.

"I can't seem to remember who I made this for...but I can tell that I must have taken a lot of care in making it."

Welf was staring at the armor even though he could not possibly know what was happening.

For a second, Hestia almost burst into tears. After the moment passed, she gave him her biggest smile.

"You don't have to remember, just feel it. The bond you had with the adventurer who used that armor!"

With that, Hestia fled the storage room.

No matter how much Freya twisted things with her charm, people's bonds with Bell still remained. With enough searching, many more would surely come to light. And within that realization, there was hope. Renewing her thoughts, Hestia hurried forward.

Reaching the workshop in the backyard, she unlocked the door and slipped inside.

With the door closed firmly, the room was dark. At first glance, it seemed empty, but…the door leading down into the underground was open. Hestia quietly descended the stairs and firmly closed the hatch. There—

"Apologies for calling you out here, Goddess Hestia. I wanted to be sure we met somewhere we could not be overheard."

Asfi released her invisibility and appeared out of thin air.

"A-A-Asfiiiiiiiiiiiii!"

"Ghoh?! P-Please calm down. While we are underground, it's still possible *Freya Familia* might notice us if we cause a disturbance…!"

Hestia was overwhelmed with emotion as she tackled Asfi. She remembered seeing those red pen strokes on a memo once before.

On the night of the Daedalus skirmish involving the Xenos, that same handwriting had filled the fake Daedalus Notebook that Hermes had prepared. Hestia only heard later that Asfi had been the one who was responsible for its creation.

She didn't need any further confirmation that Asfi was not charmed. She felt bad for her carelessness, but she was still overwhelmed with emotion at having such a reassuring adventurer as one of her few allies.

"Thank goodness you were safe! It was so lonely and painful being all alone without any support all this time…!"

"I feel the same. I was right to trust that you would still be in your right mind."

As comrades who were both on the outside of the sandbox, they could share in both the pain and the joy of finding an ally at last.

Even though Asfi was usually so cool and collected, she openly smiled like a child, as if relief was suffusing her whole being.

Hestia sniffled loudly and asked, "By the way, out of curiosity, how did you get in here? It was locked, right?"

"I'm Perseus."

"Ah, right, of course."

Asfi pushed her glasses up, and that was enough for Hestia to understand. In other words, she had picked the lock.

Hestia chose to prioritize going through all the stuff they needed to cover, when had Asfi returned, what had she been doing, all the information they had to share. Asfi had correctly guessed Freya's intentions, and Hestia learned *Freya Familia's* current status.

"Their movements have changed...?"

"Yes, to some extent. All that can be said is that baptism of theirs has intensified, but...it looked to me like they were growing impatient."

"Impatient? Them? Why?"

"...Most likely because Bell Cranell is still refusing to succumb to her charm."

Hestia's eyes widened as Asfi struggled to put into words the impression she had gotten.

And then, she looked down at the tiny scrap of paper that she had held on to all this time—her one strand of hope.

"Has the time come...?"

I'm being worn down.

I'm getting ground down.

My body, my mind, my heart—they're all falling apart under the intensity of the baptism.

I'm being pushed to my limits and far beyond, not down in the Dungeon, but aboveground. This situation is so extreme that even though I'm getting plenty of healing, nutrition, and sleep, it rivals that death march through the deep levels. The moment that realization dawns upon me, I vomit.

There's one thing I'm forced to realize from my fights with the first-tier adventurers.

Each and every one of their moves is deadly.

With no hope of finding a way out from the valley of death, I have to carve my own bloody path.

If I don't learn new tactics, I will die.

If I don't become stronger with every drop of blood I lose, my life could end in an instant.

On top of that, even as I can feel my strength growing, I am constantly trampled by ever-greater tyrannical and incomprehensible power. And then I'm forced yet again to endure another absurd revival. It suddenly occurs to me that if death were possible for undying warriors, then it would be only in the destruction of their spirit.

It's a form of doping.

The cost of such sudden, drastic growth was bound to come crashing down on me at some point.

And that point is now.

Regardless of how determined or single-minded I am, my will, my pride, and my spirit have been systematically eradicated. All that remains is the survival instinct that fears death. It's unclear whether my spirit has already been broken, and I'm not sure if I'm standing on the edge of the cliff or in the depths of the ocean.

And more than anything, the devotion that has been my driving force seems to be losing meaning.

Where is that flower atop the mountain even blooming?

Am I climbing the wrong peak?

Does that flower really even exist?

I'm so tired and on the verge of losing something precious.

From the bottom of my heart, I want to run away.

But even if I escape, I don't have anywhere else to call home. The people I met are no longer there.

That fact is the most painful. The most terrifying.

—In just over half a year, I am on the verge of becoming a first-tier adventurer, an einherjar in anyone's eyes.

In the back of my mind, I remember the words of the woman I look up to like an older sister.

Einherjar.

That word has another meaning in the language of the deities.

It refers to dead warriors.

Fated to die beneath the sun, only to be revived again by the moon.

And in accordance with that, the things I cling to become simpler and simpler, until only one thing is left.

Until *she* is all that remains.

"Hey, Bell, why don't you sleep with me tonight?"

"...Eh?"

Night has fallen and I'm back in the goddess's chamber.

She is beautiful like always.

There is a sacred dignity about her, her silver hair tied back, wearing an elegant nightgown.

Meanwhile I'm exhausted to the bone like an old man.

My brain can barely function and what little of my rationality remains is desperately trying to avoid doing any discourteous.

"I won't do anything to you. I promise...So why not sleep here tonight?"

...I suppose that's fine.

If nothing's going to happen, then I, who have no one to cling to other than her, have no reason to resist the temptation. She's kinder than anyone I know.

I nod like a child and climb into her canopied bed.

I'm wrapped in a silk blanket.

At first, I stare up at the ceiling.

But soon her hand rests on my cheek, turning my head to the side.

Her face is lying there right before my eyes.

"Hey, Bell. Is there anything you want?"

"Anything I want...?"

"Yes. Wealth and honor, strength and legacy, the seat of the hero, even the world itself...or someone's heart. Whatever you want, I promise I will get it and give it to you."

"........"

"So is there anything you want?"

My answer…comes easily.

"Nothing…I don't need anything."

I'm scared she might accuse me of rejecting her kindness, but… she smiles.

"Yes, I had a feeling you would say that."

"Eh?"

"It's because this is who you are. That's why I fell for you."

Am I being tested?

I can't tell.

But her eyes are kinder, softer than I have ever seen before as she whispers in my ear.

"I like you, Bell…I like you so much."

Her outstretched arms embrace my head and hold me to her breast.

She feels so good and smells so nice—but more than anything, she's warm.

So warm that I want to stay in that embrace forever.

…Isn't this enough?

Can't I just accept it?

Accept that the memories, the feelings, the encounters that I've been holding on to this whole time are all just a dream?

Couldn't I be forgiven for wanting to be free from this nightmare?

She's warm. So warm. I'm comfortable at her side.

Her fingers caress my hair like she's soothing a child. I feel at peace. Her tender lips brush against my head and heal the wounds carved into my body and soul. The goddess's cradle melts so many things away as it embraces me.

Is it really wrong to indulge in this love?

Haven't I done enough?

…But.

……But.

………But—

If I forget her, if I forget this feeling that made me reject Syr, then I won't remember why I hurt her.

No matter how much it hurts, and even if it's all just fake, I know for a fact that I hurt her.

I made her cry.

If I forget the reason why...if I laugh it off as all just a dream...that would be unforgivable.

—I'm Bell Cranell, the absolute fool who can't lie to himself.

No matter how sweet the salvation before me, unless I've already lost everything...I can't reach out my hand and take it.

Wavering in the space between thoughts, my journey unending, I close my eyes.

As my consciousness fades, I suddenly realize something.

She—Lady Freya—has stopped saying she loves me.

That night I dreamed of sleeping in the embrace of a girl with blue-gray hair.

Unlike the past several days, the sky is clear today.

It's painfully bright and blue for my tired eyes.

After spending a night in Lady Freya's embrace, morning has arrived.

I wake up in her chamber, leave the bed that's already empty, and go back to my room to clean up. When I open my door—a single elf is standing there.

"Master...?"

The morning sun is coloring the long white palatial corridor.

It's so bright, I reflexively squint and put my hand up to shade my face, but I can't help but still notice his coral eyes fixed on me.

"Are you neglecting the baptism to go out again today?"

"...Yes..."

As my eyes gradually adjust, I nod weakly.

My struggle continues as I use every single opportunity to go outside. Obviously to search for anything that would confirm *me*. But right now I'm only interested in the fate of one girl.

Syr.

While the world differs from my memories, she is the only one who has completely disappeared. I don't want to accept that's reality. I did not want to believe that she was just a figment of my imagination.

Even though I could just use whatever excuse to escape the battle and go outside to rest for a little while, I still fully intend to explore all around the city again.

"...Unsightly. Intolerable," Master says while looking at me. "Don't drag anyone else down in your quest for self-satisfaction. Go by yourself."

"Eh? But..."

"If you get yourself cursed again, Lady Freya will be disappointed in you. It will simply mean that her love was too great for you to bear."

Master has a look of disgust on his face, and he turns away as soon as he's said his piece.

I can only stand there, but before I realize it, I call out to him.

"Master...Hedin..."

"........"

"Am I...crazy?"

Battle has already been joined on the field outside the window.

The roars of the warriors are ringing out beneath the blue sky.

My gaze falls, and I'm losing sight of myself as I ask him that question.

"Whether you would be a heretic or not is irrelevant."

He stops, not turning around, but pausing for just a moment, he gives me an answer.

"Move forward. Standing still is what is unforgivable."

Leaving behind those words, he walks away.

Looking up, my eyes are wide for several moments, but finally, I turn around and begin walking.

The boy's presence was still plagued by doubt, but it gradually turned in the opposite direction.

Sensing that behind him, Hedin walked without hesitation to a certain place.

"Van. Remove Bell Cranell's guard and observers."

"Huh…? Wh-what do you mean, sir?"

He went to the back entrance of the home and delivered an order to the three-person party led by the half-prum.

"There are signs that *Loki Familia*'s expedition to the Deep Levels is returning. We've received a report from the spies watching the Dungeon."

"…! *Loki Familia* is…?"

"Yes. Lady Riveria the Thousand Elf and the rest of their group are by no means a minor force. We must safeguard the sandbox."

That one report was enough to cause their expressions to change dramatically.

Hedin calmly explained the situation and gave them new instructions.

"It would be possible to send Hörn directly herself, but there is no telling when an Irregular might occur in the Dungeon. We will take care of them with absolute certainty at Babel the moment they leave. Allen and the Gullivers are already en route. You are to join them as well."

"Yes sir!"

"Take the lookouts currently stationed at The Benevolent Mistress and other key points with you. We will need more numbers than what the second tier can provide to ensure that none escape. I will set new lookouts myself."

No one raised any questions about the order coming from the white elf who served as the familia's strategist.

While acknowledging his understanding of the logical battle orders, Van finished with a question.

"What of Bell? It's true that there is probably no need to strictly watch him anymore, but…"

Bell was already functionally a walking corpse.

No one in the familia doubted that.

It was clear as day that he would obey Freya's divine will before long.

"That will not be a problem."

Hedin's answer was simple.

"I will observe him myself."

Even though there is not a single cloud in the sky, it's cold outside.

Autumn is drawing to a close, but today is particularly cold for the season. It's almost like it were actually winter. Tonight the glow of fireplaces will probably join the city's dazzling magic-stone lights.

I return my gaze back in front of me. I can't see anyone on West Main Street dressed lightly. Even the occasional adventurer has warm clothes on. The members of the Guild walking around are probably carrying firewood to supply each district of the city.

"Look…it's Rabbit Foot."

"Freya Familia's…!"

A murmur like birds chirping begins to swirl around me.

I'm already used to it.

The curious and awestruck gazes follow me as I walk around in *Freya Familia*'s uniform. The normal people living in the city and the merchants, none of them doubting that Bell Cranell is a member of the city's strongest faction.

I'm tired of denying it and being hurt all over again, so I just bear it and proceed along Main Street while mostly looking down at the ground, my heart numb.

The building I'm headed for stands at the corner of a major intersection.

The Benevolent Mistress.

"Oh! He's back, meow! *Freya Familia*'s white rabbit!"

"We told you, there isn't any kid named Syr here. You really don't know when to give up, do you?"

When I enter the tavern, Chloe and Runoa, who appear to greet new customers, grimace when they see me. I can't remember anymore how many times I've come here.

"I know your scheme! You just created a fake girl and are pretending to go around looking for her as an excuse to get close to some other girls! That's so sneaky and shady! You would have had a better shot seducing me with that nice butt of yours! Okay, come around to the back of the tavern meow!"

"What are you doing, you stupid cat?"

I can't bring myself to smile at their familiar banter.

The look in their eyes when they glance over at me makes it painfully obviously that they think we're strangers.

And I do not have the strength of will left right now to try to forge a new bond with them.

"If you're not going to offer up your bottom to me, then shoo! Hurry up and beat it!"

"You don't have any filter, do you…? I guess it's true he's interrupting business. If you don't plan on buying anything, you mind heading out? We've got a ton of work since our elven coworker hasn't come back. And Ahnya isn't coming out to work right now, either…"

Their cold, businesslike words claw at my heart, and I'm worried about Lyu.

I have also been searching for a clue about what had happened to her, but they at least know who she is. Because of that, I end up focusing more on Syr's whereabouts.

Trying to prove someone ever existed is more difficult than trying to track down someone who people still know and remember.

And Ahnya is apparently feeling unwell and not working today, too…

"What are ya chatterin' about, you ijits! If y'all've got time for that, then get out and take care of the errands!"

""Eep?! R-right away!""

Suddenly an angry shout resounds through the tavern.

Chloe and Runoa jolt, turning pale as they run into the back of the tavern.

Dumbfounded, I look over to see Mia, the owner, standing behind the counter.

"………"

"…?"

Mia's eyes silently dart around.

She's glancing at me…no, *outside*?

It's probably just my misunderstanding, but it seems like she's being cautious of someone who might be watching. She quietly goes about her preparations for opening that evening.

There are no other customers, so Mia is the only other person inside the shop.

An odd moment passes between us.

"Kid."

Mia has not said a single word to me since the Goddess Festival, but just when I can't bear the silence anymore and start to leave the shop, she stops me with an awkward and apologetic expression on her face.

"Eh?"

"I have no intention of saying anything to the goddess. I swore not to get in the way when the time came."

…?

What is she…?

"I'd love to roast the damned fools who laid their hands on those stupid girls, but…"

"Wh-what are you saying…?"

"I'm *Freya Familia*."

"!"

I'm shocked by the sudden announcement.

"You know I'm half-retired from the familia, right?" Mia continues as I stare at her agitatedly. "In other words, not helpin' out is my form of resistance, and what I'm about to tell you is outright rebellion."

Saying that, she looks up, and looks right at me for the first time.

"'Bein' an adventurer ain't about lookin' cool.'"

My breath catches.

"'The last one standin' is top of the pack's all there is.'"

My hands are trembling.

"So believe in yourself and stay standing."

Ignoring my stunned reaction, Mia looks me in the eyes as she finishes her message.

"—Just keep on runnin'."

It feels like the world I'm seeing suddenly changes shades.

I stand stock-still for several moments before somehow managing to get my lips to move and begin to ask a jumbled question.

"......M-Mia, that was..."

But before I can finish, her eyes flare and she shouts at me.

"Go on and git! I don't have food to serve the likes of you!"

"Huh?!"

"I'm sayin' an adventurer lookin' so grim and depressed is gonna drive away my customers and hurt business! Git and don't come back 'til you ain't so tirin' to look at!"

"I-I'm sorry?!"

I leave The Benevolent Mistress after being forcibly driven out.

I run without thinking, desperate to escape her terrifying shouts...and when I finally slow to a walk, my heart is hammering.

My breathing returns to normal, but my pulse is still racing.

I can't get my head around it. Everything is still fuzzy.

What she told me...those words just now...

"Bein' an adventurer ain't about lookin' cool. Just worry about not gettin' yourself killed to start with."

"The last one standin' is the top of the pack. Pathetic or not's got nothin' to do with it."

That was what Mia said to me...way back, at the very beginning of my time here, half a year ago...

Freya Familia's Bell Cranell has no connection with Mia, though. There's no mistaking that. Then why?

Is it just a coincidence?

Does Mia know I'm going through the baptism?

Was it just a bit of encouragement from someone who was part of the same familia?

Or...did it mean something else?

Keep standing, until the end...believe in myself and stay standing...?

What was Mia trying to tell me?

What was she trying to convey?

Should I go back and ask her? But I have a feeling she would not tell me anything else. Not until I look less grim.

Was she testing me?

No—was she trying to entrust something to me?

...But...even if she did mean something by it...

My body is already battered.

My mind is worn down.

I'm overwhelmed by a sense of powerlessness. What can I even do?

I remember everything leading up to today.

No one remembers me, no one knows me, and they all reject me.

I lost my home, my comrades are gone, and I just want to not be hurt anymore.

I'm just yielding everything to the goddess, so what can I even do—

"—All I can do is stand up."

I can feel strength in my hands.

They curl into fists.

My knees that are on the verge of collapsing cry out.

My bruised and battered body that was racked by pain braces itself and reaches out to the flame still burning inside.

"All I can do is keep believing in myself! And stay standing—!"

Right.

I'm an adventurer.

No matter how miserable.

No matter how pathetic.

Just desperately cling to life.

"—All I can do is just keep running!"

I run.

The people around me are surprised and look at me like I'm a madman as I sprint through the crowds.

My back is burning from Mia's push as I race through the city.

Logic can't begin to explain what I'm feeling. I can hear a voice in the back of my head whispering that I'm just acting like a twitchy rabbit in a burst of sudden excitement. But even so, I'm not fighting the impulse driving me.

It's a scary thing to keep believing in yourself. I know that. Before long, I start wanting to cling to what others say for support. Start wanting to accept the sweet words of the goddess and everyone else, to give myself over to them.

But I'm done running away.

I need to stop being scared of getting hurt.

After all, there is still *one person* I haven't met yet!

"Hah, hah, haaah—!"

I keep running.

Swinging my arms, lifting my legs, no place in mind, just haphazardly pushing forward, but still believing in myself.

Even if I'm climbing the wrong mountain, that just means my journey to the peak isn't over yet.

Envisioning the golden flower so far above me, the idol that has stolen my eyes and my heart.

I'm going to meet her.

"Ghhh—Aiz!"

I call out to the one I adore.

In the northern district of the city, a long manor comes into view. This is their territory, which I never attempted to approach before.

As I let my ragged breathing go unchecked, I see the girl with long, beautiful blond hair slowly turn in my direction.

"Huh? Isn't that…?"

"*Freya Familia*. Why can't you even remember that?"

"Oh, right! It's what's-his-foot, the guy that Loki and them said to be careful around!"

Aiz is with Tiona and Tione.

I run into them on just a normal street corner. There are lots of people around us. Tione and Tiona watch me suspiciously, while the girl I called out to looks surprised.

"Why is someone in *Freya Familia* calling Aiz, though?"

"What business do you have with us? Are you trying to start a fight or something?"

"Ghh…!"

Loki Familia and *Freya Familia* are rivals.

And Tiona's and Tione's eyes are filled with open hostility. They're looking at *Freya Familia*'s Bell Cranell, like that has always been our relationship.

Against my will, my heart shudders.

What little sense I have is crying out.

This is a fork in the road.

If she rejects me. If she looks at me the same way Tione is on guard…if she doesn't remember me, like Tiona, who doesn't call me Argonaut like always…if she does that, the flame still burning in my back will most likely go out forever.

My already cracked heart will shatter completely, and I won't be able to resist anymore when I feel the goddess's affection.

Sweat runs down my back.

My heart feels like it might burst out of my chest.

I can't get my tongue to move how I want.

My heart is wavering like never before as I meet her golden gaze.

"Aiz…do you know me?"

"………"

"Do you remember everything that happened before?!"

"………"

It's a question I've asked so many times.

Everyone in *Hestia Familia*, the waitresses at The Benevolent Mistress, the orphans on Daedalus Street, multiple gods and goddesses—they all reacted with suspicion and rejected me. At some point, despair turned into resignation that threatened to freeze my throat and limbs.

But I shout it again, brushing off the despair and resignation one last time.

I lay my irreplaceable feelings out in the open as she watches me.

"What are you talking about? Get away. We're not supposed to have anything to do with you guys."

"Let's go, Aiz."

"Ah—"

The sisters who rejected me like everyone else move between me and my idol.

They get between us while trying to move past me.
My body won't listen to me. I can't extend my hand.
I can only manage a hoarse sound.
My legs are trembling, and my heart is thundering as I slump over.
There's no hope.
The flame in my back starts to gutter as my despair grows, when—

As she passes, she takes my hand.

"——"

I look up.
I stare at her with wide-open eyes.
Aiz stops and is gripping my hand firmly.
Her eyes are widened, too, like mirrors as her slender fingers squeeze my hand.
"A-Aiz?"
"Wh-what are you doing?"
Tione and Tiona are openly confused as time stops for the two of us.
Everything around me fades. She is all that is reflected in my eyes. I can't bring myself to say anything.
Her lips tremble slightly.
"……D…"
And finally, she speaks.

"Do you want to train?"

""""Huh?""""
The sisters and I have the same reaction.
Our eyes narrow, and our jaws hang slack at the utterly out-of-nowhere question.
Ignoring our reaction, Aiz looks extraordinarily serious as she desperately tries to put her thoughts into words.
"I…I knocked you out so many times…"
"Ehh?"

"And then let you rest on my lap..."

"Wai—"

"And when you woke up, I knocked you out again..."

"A-Aiz?"

I, Tione, and Tiona all freeze, unable to string any words together as Aiz closes her eyes for a moment as if something is hurting her, and then she leans toward me.

"I feel like I have to fight with you on the city wall."

"—!"

"I feel like I have to teach you and learn from you."

It's like she's struggling to express the emotions in her heart.

It's like she's gathering the fragments of a dream that she can't remember.

My golden idol answers my call.

"I feel like I made a promise with someone...who said they wanted to become strong..."

The feelings put into those words beneath the sunrise, after meeting the Xenos, after that struggle.

Bell Cranell swore that in front of Aiz Wallenstein. A promise and resolve.

That morning was why I started running again—

—Ahhhhhh.

My knees give out.

But it's not a surrender to despair.

It's hope, a feeling of release that I can't restrain anymore.

"...!"

I drop to my knees on the ground, holding her right hand in both of mine and pressing it to my forehead as I tremble.

I can hear a gasp from above me. A swell of curiosity from the people around us. But I don't mind.

My eyes are hidden behind my hair as tears fall to my knees.

It's nothing so impressive as a knight swearing a vow to a princess.

But as I cry shamelessly like a child, I also renew my feelings toward the one I adore.

That is all.

"........."

"...Are...you okay?"

How long have I been in this state?

I desperately try to get my sobs and my trembling heart under control as I wipe my eyes and slowly stand back up.

Aiz is stunned.

She might not even know why she said what she did.

But that's enough for me.

As Tione and Tiona watch in bewilderment, I look into her golden eyes and lay my feelings bare.

"I'm glad you're the one I admire."

My face is still wet from the tears as I smile from the very depths of my heart.

"It wasn't wrong to meet you at all."

Aiz gazes in wonder as her slender hand rests against her breast.

I smile one last time, and then let the white-hot determination that has erupted inside me lead me forward.

"I'm going now."

With just those parting words, I start running.

I'm gone in a flash, leaving Aiz and the twins behind.

My body accelerates by leaps and bounds. I overtake person after person, becoming faster than anyone as the world rushes past me on either side.

The moment of my first cry.

The moment I let my feelings loose.

Together with the flame raging in my back again, I set out to confirm the miracle my idol has given me, to confirm the path I walk.

I'm running to the field of battle where a brave warrior awaits me.

—At that moment, it almost feels like a fairy who had been watching over me through it all looked away.

Smashing.

Crashing.

I target the rhomphaia trying to tear through me, slamming the baselard in my hand into it with all of my might.

Today is furiously heated, and I'm engaged in a fiery struggle, driven by the feelings roaring inside me.

"Hwah!"

Sparks fly from my slash, and there is surprise in Master's eyes as our blades clash.

Folkvangr is lit by the sun in the west.

Having returned to the battlefield of dead warriors, I hurled myself into the swirling death match once more.

I've fallen dozens of times. The constant attacks have battered me and my endless wounds trouble the healers over and over. But even so, my will never broke.

Instead of just relying on survival instinct and a fear of death, I transform my vow to overcome this trial into kindling, and the flames of my spirit roar as I let loose a battle cry that reaches the heavens.

"Haaaaaaaaaaaaaaaaaaaaaaaaa!"

I slice upward with the knife in my right hand and unleash a horizontal slash with the baselard in my left.

They are both deflected by the rhomphaia being spun at high speed like a fan, but still I advance.

A thunderous clash of metal rings out. The rhythm of blades echoes across the fields. At some point, the refrain of attack and counterattack composed all around us fades, until only ours remains.

The other members of *Freya Familia* have stopped, standing still and lowering their weapons, completely focused on our fight.

Heith and the other healers forget their other tasks and fix their gaze on us.

Hegni, who was part of the clash until just a little bit ago, is also staring at us from a half step away.

I focus every bit of my attention on the opponent in front of me as countless sets of eyes follow my movements.

The rhomphaia thrusts toward me with a sharp whoosh.

I pull through by slamming it *from the side* with my knife.

My skin is just barely sliced by the blade as its path shifts by the tiniest of increments, and then I mount my counterattack, performing a rush that takes full advantage of *my speed and number of attacks.*

I use the techniques I stole from *her* through so much training and repetition!

Silver, silver, and silver again. Arcs of light carve through the air with each attack. The knife and baselard in my hands cross and change places as I continue my charge, all while Master blocks every blow as he watches me with silent shock.

In the midst of a series of slashes that might well be considered rash when my opponent is a first-tier adventurer, I unleash everything I gained from our training on the city wall in a single explosion.

Remember.

I remember!

I remember it all!

The Sword Princess's technique of deflecting and parrying by striking the opponent's weapon from the side at an angle!

The swordsmanship style I copied from Aiz in battle, which I studied in order to catch up to her even just a little bit more!

Her experience and history that Phryne saw in my fighting!

My body has not forgotten the things my idol taught me!

I'm not Freya Familia*'s Bell Cranell at all!*

No matter how the world might reject me, even if all the deities and people deny me, the techniques and skills engraved in my body reassure me.

My encounters with the Sword Princess and all the training on the city wall were reality. The lessons she taught me are still firmly rooted inside me.

And it's not just her teachings, either.

Van mentioned it, too—my habit of letting my right arm float upward. It was none other than Lyu who endured hell with me in the Deep Levels who first pointed it out and suggested I try to correct it!

Why hadn't I noticed it sooner?

Why had I mistaken what they taught me for my own strength?

How egotistical could I be?

I'm weak and can't do anything by myself! I only managed to get where I am with the help of so many people!

I'm Hestia Familia*'s Bell Cranell!!!*

There is only ever one answer possible.

I trace the path I walked, confirming it, and use it to construct a solid, unshakable core for myself. All the battles I endured before, they are all reflected inside me.

Don't be afraid. Don't flinch away.

I'm done closing my eyes, plugging my ears, and averting my eyes from it!

I will prove what she taught me in this fight and reclaim who I am!

"Struggle for eternity, indestructible soldiers of lightning!"

I'm pushed back by a powerful swing of the rhomphaia, opening some distance between us, when Master begins casting, aiming to land an immediate strike.

"Caurus Hildr!"

Middle range. Abandoning the more optimal longer range for his magic, he unleashes a massive fusillade. The wide-area destruction magic mercilessly rains down toward me.

In response, I shout.

"Firebolt!"

Eight streaks of crimson lightning clash with the spray of white lightning.

I can't hope to negate all the bolts crashing down on me like undying soldiers.

But I only need to cancel out a few of them.

I unleash several rounds of firebolts, one after the other, and they slam into some of the bolts of incoming lightning, canceling each other out.

It's just the briefest moment. In that instant, my legs flash, and I twist myself through the small path forward I've wrenched open, my shoulders and thighs scorched as they skim past the lightning, and I break through the volley.

"!"

His coral eyes are wide. Instantaneously, not giving him time to prepare the next round, I unleash a full swing with my baselard.

The white elf easily deflects the strike that used all of my strength.

"Ghhh?!"

My baselard gets caught by his twisted rhomphaia and knocked skyward out of my hand with a metallic clang.

Not enough. I've expended an enormous amount of magical power and caught him off guard, but it's still not enough to land a blow on a first-tier adventurer.

My body shudders from the force of his strike, revealing a decisive opening.

Seeing that, Master's eyes flare, and his weapon flashes toward me.

——

My mind goes blank.

My whole body erupts in flame.

I only need one thing.

I break free from the flow of time as my soul roars and the memories engraved in my body activate.

Guards are lowest while delivering the final blow.

I hear her voice as I rush toward what lies beyond.

The moment you're cornered—!

A spin.

Master's eyes widen as he disappears from my view. I go with the momentum as my body spins in the air like a top. The thrusting rhomphaia grazes my back. It splits the skin on my back. But so what? As if tracing the movements she made in my memory, we change positions and I end up behind Hedin!

"—Is your best chance!"

I shout the lesson she taught me, unleashing a strike using the knife in my right hand that I held on to throughout it all.

"———ghhhh?!"

I pour everything into my knees, which are screaming at me, unleashing the fastest spinning slash I can.

An attack from beyond his field of view—but even so, Master manages to react in time.

Exhaling with a shudder, he twists his body, escaping out of range with his ultrafast reflexes.

It was unmistakably a slash with every bit of me poured into it. And it cut the air.

There is a thud as we both kick the ground, opening a significant distance between us. The baselard finally falls to the ground in the crimson setting sun, sticking out of the ground halfway between the two of us.

My breathing is uncontrollably ragged. My body is covered in wounds.

Meanwhile, Master is entirely unruffled, his expression calm and cool enough to make me despair as he watches in silence.

But.

As he stands with the setting sun at his back…he quietly wipes his cheek with a finger.

"…He wounded…Hedin…"

Hegni murmurs.

The moment they realize what happened, the rest of the familia becomes noisy.

Heith looks like she can't believe what she is seeing. She looks back and forth between Master and me.

There is a single cut on his handsome features.

A new drop of crimson blood trickles down his white cheek.

That's all it is. Just a single scratch.

But it reached him.

A strike imbued with everything I've learned and experienced, a strike that encompassed all of Bell Cranell has reached him.

I proved the teachings of the one I adore. I breathe heavily, my shoulders heaving as I clench my fist.

"………"

Master looks at the finger that he used to wipe the blood, and then slowly looks at me.

Meeting his gaze, I respond.

"Master…I'm me."

Whatever anyone might think, whatever might come of it, I shout the feelings swelling in my breast.

"I'm Bell Cranell!"

My voice resounds.

The field immediately falls quiet. No one says anything. Forgetting what they saw, what they heard, everything, vacillating between reality and illusion.

Suddenly, the setting sun flickers.

The light of the setting sun burns my eyes, and for an instant, I squint.

And shrouded in that crimson light, his back still to the sun, for just a moment, it almost looks like Master's lips curl into the slightest smile…

"What nonsense are you babbling about? Don't get so uppity over a mere scratch."

"Ogfh?!"

"If you want to celebrate, at least save it for after you manage to dirty my clothes a bit."

While I'm blinking away the sunlight, Master somehow teleports right in front of me before delivering a magnificent kick right to my stomach. I already used every last bit of energy I had left, so I can't defend against it. All I can do is crumple and fall to the ground with a muffled grunt.

Master is the same as always…!

"I would like to crush you for getting cocky…but it's sunset. Let's go back."

With that, Master turns his back and begins walking away.

As if a spell has been released, the rest of the familia members suddenly shudder and begin moving again.

They glance over at me before they head up the hill to the manor. Even Heith, who watched in silence. Even Hegni, who sheathed his sword without a word.

Lit by the fading red twilight, the shadows of the warriors extend out into the sea of green.

The scene that felt so hopelessly sorrowful the first time I saw it now has a different feeling.

As I plant my hand on the ground to push myself up, between the fingers of my hands, the white flowers of the field still sway stubbornly.

Red light filtered through the window.

The setting sun lit the face of the silent god.

"Lord Hermes, please just do your work already…How much paperwork are you planning to let pile up?"

"…Hm, ah, apologies."

Hermes finally responded vacantly to the voice of one of his followers, the war tiger Falgar.

The room was plastered with countless land and sea maps, making it look like the home of a serial traveler—his chamber in *Hermes Familia*'s home.

Hermes was sitting in his chair in front of a mountain of paperwork that Falgar had constructed on a desk that was already cluttered with chess pieces, a sand clock, and all sorts of other items.

"If you keep on slacking off like this, it's seriously going to be a problem…What are you going to do about all this?"

"Lord Hermessss, I'm begging you, please get it together."

Falgar looked weary and exhausted, and behind him the chienthrope Lulune kicked open the door as she brought in another armful of papers to be dealt with.

Hermes Familia served as couriers and information merchants while also supporting travelers and handling business propositions from various merchants while also exploring the Dungeon.

Essentially covering every sort of project. Because of that, they received documents regarding progress reports, contracts, and every sort of paperwork imaginable from all sorts of directions, at times creating a level of office work that made even members of the Guild blanche.

"And Asfi's out now, too."

"More precisely, she's gone missing...the number of falna responses hasn't gone down, so I'm sure she's safe, but where in the world did she go?"

Hermes was naturally inclined to putting off work, but this time was far worse than usual, and work had stalled completely.

It was almost entirely due to the fact that the familia's capable leader, who usually handled the paperwork while complaining the entire time, was currently absent.

Lulune and Falgar were lamenting the mountain of paperwork that just kept growing even with them helping out, too, realizing again just how great Asfi really was.

"And we were given the job of delivering the firewood this year, too...I wonder why the Guild didn't just leave it to *Ganesha Familia* like always."

Lulune grumbled as she slumped down in the nearest chair.

Hermes intertwined his fingers as he listened, and questioned himself.

—Huh, am I in a loop?

It was an absurd question, but his expression was deadly serious, and a cold sweat formed on the back of his neck.

How long? When did the days that seemed normal turn into something abnormal?

Hermes *noticed* it.

Even while being twisted by some outside power, he realized that it was incredibly likely that the days they were living through were abnormal, off in some fatal way that he could not perceive.

While everyone else living in Orario, adventurers and deities alike, failed to notice, he alone was closing in on the truth.

I have some evidence. Slight twists hiding in the shadow of the normal day-to-day. More specifically, there is something that does not match up between what I did during the past half year and how I acted before that...

It not was something Loki or Hephaistos could notice. Because he so regularly left the city on trips, he alone could realize it.

There is no way I just stayed in one place for so long without going out on one of my trips. Yet I've been here for the past half year—no, the past four months...

The reason my travels stopped is probably because something was tying me down here to the city. So what could it be?

—I don't know. It's not that I can't remember, I literally can't recognize it.

Hermes inhaled sharply as his thoughts progressed.

It was the first time he could observe the unnatural reality from an outside observer's perspective, that some external factor was affecting him.

He was unable to recognize reality, as if some limit had been placed on him.

The most conclusive point is this letter that I received...

Opening the drawer on the right side of his desk, he pulled out a letter.

His hand shook as he stared at it. There was no sender or return address on it.

"Stiiiiill no update?"

When he first saw the message accompanied by a scribbled picture that had been delivered to him, before he could even be annoyed, Hermes was shocked.

—Did I slack off while contacting Zeus?

It was a matter that Hermes had conducted with regularity.

Hermes maintained contact with a certain great god who was no longer in the city.

Always careful not to let anyone suspect, occasionally going himself, that was Hermes's job as the god of messengers and something he did out of respect for the old bond he shared with that great god. A secret between just the two of them that no others knew of.

And Hermes had neglected it for more than three months.

No, it was difficult to believe that he had actually just neglected it.

He could not explain it, and it was nothing more than supposition, but he believed it was likely that he had not had time to make contact.

And the reason for that was a turbulent span of three months.

There was no other explanation for why the shrewd god of messengers would cease communication.

The problem is that those turbulent three months are nowhere to be found in my memories or in any of the city's records. It's a stretch, but I could at least chalk up all of the city's records not mentioning anything after being deliberately altered. But what about my memories? The only explanation is that they were manipulated at some point without my noticing.

The turbulent three months—he could not remember the Xenos incident, dealing with Knossos, and all the cleanup required for such massive events. Because they all involved a certain someone, he was unable to acknowledge them.

The divergence caused by the barrier between conscious and unconscious forced the god to notice the contradiction.

And most likely...I'm experiencing a loop *of some sort in my thoughts!*

There was a stack of parchment for memos held by a pin on Hermes's desk.

It had shrunken drastically. Dozens of them had been torn off.

All told, seventy-seven had been used.

There were charred fragments of parchment left around the torch, proof that they had been disposed of.

Of course, Hermes didn't remember doing it. He had asked Falgar and the others, but they all insisted they had not touched anything of his, and none of them were lying.

The only person who had gotten rid of them could only be himself.

He had burned the memos.

He had written something desperately and then promptly disposed of it himself. The only explanation was—

For the sake of convenience, I'll call it old me—old me had the same sense of something being off as current me. And he wrote a memo in order to leave a note about it—but that infringed on some rule. And then old me lost consciousness and disposed of that memo...!

That leap of logic was imbued with a divine certainty.

There was some sort of trigger, and the moment he engaged with it, Hermes would forget everything and erase all traces of it himself before resetting his thoughts.

And that reset triggered by a sense of something being off had occurred at least seventy-seven times.

The moment he happened upon that hypothesis, Hermes felt an uneasy chill.

To be able to do something like that in a way that we deities don't notice, making sure that no one senses anything...!

Falgar and Lulune looked at Hermes as his lips twisted at the realization that even deities were being turned into puppets.

"Hey, Falgar, did I ask you to give me a message three days ago?"

"...*That again*, Lord Hermes? How often are you going to do this? How many days has it been already?"

"Now now, it's just a bit of game for the gods...Anyway, what did I tell you?"

"Haaah...'loop,' 'reset,' 'not just me,' 'Lulune next.' Just that incomprehensible string of words."

Falgar sighed as he responded. Hermes's mouth clamped shut as he slipped back into deep thought.

Most likely, the old Hermes had also recognized that his memos were being destroyed and changed methods when he realized that writing things down would not work. And that new method was leaving messages for himself through his followers.

Most likely they are being twisted just like I am...but by passing along messages like this without feeling anything suspicious about the current situation means they're not infringing on any hard rule.

First was Falgar, then Lulune, and then Merrill…the old Hermes had feared his followers' thoughts being reset, so he had not left too much with any one person, and limited his message to only fragmentary thoughts, explaining it to them half-jokingly as just a message passing game played by gods to pass the time.

And linking together all that information—

A loop in thoughts, reset, and it's not just happening to me. The world is twisted. An overwhelming coercion. No one remembers. An inability to recognize certain information. Or else misrecognition…

Hermes shuddered.

How many past Hermeses had fallen in order to pass that information safely onto the next Hermes? It made him want to praise his past selves who had uncovered so much of the rules twisting the world already. It was enough to earn a snarky smile at his own tear-jerking dedication and devotion.

What is clear from the fact that I'm thinking about this right now is that my thoughts and words are not being restrained currently. But based on the old Hermeses' information, there is one or several absolute rules. And if I violate any rule, I will immediately lose my memory and repeat the cycle…

For everything else that he was, Hermes was still a god.

Even while being violated by a powerful magic, to be able to get that close to the truth without relying on other people or even trusting himself entirely. He was undeniably one of the shrewdest deusdea.

Most likely it's safe up to the point of something feeling off. But outright suspicion probably crosses the line. The moment that various odd feelings add up to something that might endanger this scenario, everyone…or at least everyone in Orario…unconsciously transforms into puppets. And on top of that, trying to actively figure out who created this situation is probably taboo, too.

Deities were omniscient. It was possible to make predictions based on what was happening, but it was crucial that he not probe past a certain point.

He policed his thoughts in a way that no mortal could begin to emulate, achieving a literally godlike discipline, while also being careful to avoid any unwanted leaps of imagination.

Constantly wondering at what point he might be forcibly turned into a puppet again, Hermes left a tiny update of information with Thane, who eyed his god in exasperation. He assumed Hermes was just playing around again.

Still, though, being able to twist even deities, and without using arcanum at that. The only thing that could do that is some really crazy wine, or else her—ah, crap.

Thus Hermes met his two hundred and thirty-third reset.

And so Hermes's thoughts went through the same loop over the course of another day.

In the same manner, by the same process—thanks to the clues provided by the past versions of Hermes, it went faster than the first time—he noticed the oddity in the world, and Falgar and the others were reaching their limit at being forced to play a fruitless message-passing game yet again. It was humiliating having to endure all of that.

Unable to bear it, Hermes left home alone, without any guard.

"Come on now, I'm Hermes, right? Always aloof and above it all, the ultimate trickster and all-around cool guy who always gets things done with a snap...Why do I have to struggle so hard?...It's like I'm turning into Takemikazuchi or Asfi..."

Rudely referring to a certain god of war and his follower without any hesitation, Hermes sighed.

He was struck by an overwhelming urge to vent on Takemikazuchi or another deity like him, but he stopped himself. If he went too far and ticked off that god of war, skinny Hermes would be the one who would end up getting tossed around.

Coincidentally, the time was evening, around the same time as he had realized the situation last night, too. The street was peaceful beneath the western sun, crowded with villagers and adventurers returning from the Dungeon.

...Hypothetically, if I suppose this situation is a sandbox...Based on the factors that cause a mental correction, the mastermind behind it wants to maintain peace and order in this world.

It was unclear whether it was intended to be for a limited time or indefinite.

But there was no intention to savage the mortal realm by turning all beings into mindless puppets. The fact that Hermes and the others maintained their free will was proof of that.

Maintaining Orario as an unchanged city of heroes...The most likely reason for such a circuitous tack is because the mastermind had no choice but to twist the world for the sake of something or someone that could not be bent. To create a paradise and a prison for someone. That is the true nature of this sandbox.

And the moment he thought of some opening to possibly break out of the sandbox, his thoughts would be reset.

It was no good. He was blocked off in all directions.

The conclusion Hermes came to was that even if he could guess at the outline of the sandbox, as long as he could not understand the precise rules and core of it, he could not plot any way to break free.

An inescapable mental game. Hermes had been in checkmate long ago. From the moment he had fallen prey to it, there was nothing he could do and no way for him to break free. It was all just pointless struggle from the start.

I need some sort of plan. Some external guide that I can just follow without thinking.

Because of that, the only thing he could do was hope for some external help from someone else out there who was still struggling. Someone who had not quite been checkmated yet.

Hermes was currently incapable of doing anything under his own direction.

The moment he plotted anything himself, it was highly likely he would break one of the rules.

Because of that deadlock, he needed something external to break through.

He had no choice but to entrust himself to someone else's plan in a way that did not raise any suspicions of outside influence, did not cause anything unnatural, and did not break from the normal day-to-day.

While knowing that that thought itself was only just barely this side of safe, Hermes took off his hat.

"I'm begging you, first me…You were Hermes, after all, so you must have some trump card prepared, right…?"

Hidden in the brim of the hat was a fragment of torn scroll.

A bit of parchment that had traces of a piece being torn off in one place.

That along with the letter from the good-natured old man had been the trigger for Hermes's noticing something off. At first glance, it was just a fragment of paper, but there was meaning in hiding it in his hat. Noticing that, Hermes began to reflect on his past self's actions.

It was just a meaningless fragment of paper that Hermes had not attempted to destroy even when he became a mere puppet.

Most likely the first Hermes, the Hermes before he had been checkmated, had written something.

And he had entrusted it to someone.

Hermes could only cling to that supposition and hope it was true.

Aside from the fact that I have not gone on a trip, the other factor that is different from usual…is Asfi being gone. Then is Asfi the key…?

Hermes was terribly disappointed in himself for having to rely on such tenuous information despite being an all-knowing god. He scanned his surroundings.

It was Main Street at twilight. Lively and crowded.

There were no suspicious shadows. And he wouldn't really be able to say who might be suspicious anyway.

He did not want to believe that he was being watched, but he could not allow anyone to suspect that he felt something off about the sandbox.

At the same time, though, he had to make it clear to Asfi, who held the key, that he was feeling something off about it. If he did not do that, then she would not make contact with him.

It was a difficult conundrum. Suffering a painful headache, Hermes stopped in the middle of the street.

Was Asfi watching him? Was she beside him? The odds were low, but he had no choice except to try.

Looking up at the red sky, his eyes narrowed, and he spoke.

"Asfi...I love you."

It was not a loud voice. Just a whisper.

"So please...*come back to me*."

Dubious gazes started to center on him for stopping in the middle of the street.

Some beast people glanced over at him, doubting their ears after they picked up the murmur.

It was something he would one hundred percent, absolutely never in a million years say.

Hermes concluded that there was no other way for him to contact Asfi without anyone else noticing. From the outside, he looked obsessed, and more than a little bit narcissistic, too, but so be it.

Hermes earnestly, honestly revealed a feeling in his heart that he would otherwise never show.

If there was no response, he would just move to another corner of the city and whisper sweet words of love again.

He would continue singing of his love for his follower.

If it came to it, he would persist through to the very end.

Hermes was growing desperate as he prepared to head to another Main Street.

"*—North Street, Jyaga Maru Kun stall.*"

"!!!"

An invisible someone slipped past him and whispered something in his ear.

The voice blended in with the everyday sounds of the milling crowd. If anyone heard it, it would only be a meaningless fragment of a message.

Hermes's eyes widened, and he was immediately struck by the urge to turn around, but he stopped himself.

Even if he did turn, she was still invisible. He could not meet her. So he put a smile on his lips and headed in the direction he had been told.

In his heart—

Thank you, Asfi.

And you know I was telling the truth when I said I love you, right?

And as he sped along his way, he felt like he heard a murmur.

"Argh...you're the worst.

"Hurry up and return to normal...you hopeless god."

Hermes's cheeks softened as he imagined her face red through and through as she glared tearfully at him.

"Oh, Hermes! Great timing! I'm begging you, buy some Jyaga Maru Kuns from me!"

Reaching the spot, he was greeted by a lively voice.

Hestia was in uniform, her massive breasts swaying like always as she worked in a rush.

"For reasons, I slacked off too much on my job and I'm in trouble! I'm gonna be fired if I don't sell enough!"

"Ha-ha, I dunno what all that's about, but good luck. It takes a long time to get back into society after losing your job. For old times' sake, I suppose I could buy one. What would you recommend?"

"Then make it this! The hyper-ultra-jumbo Jyaga Maru Kun deluxe! It costs a hundred times more than the regular Jyaga Maru Kun, but just buy it as a favor for me! Please, please, please buy it!"

"O-okay..."

Hermes's eyes were bloodshot as he reflexively took the golden, crispy Jyaga Maru Kun that Hestia held out for him.

Genuinely speechless at the totally exhausted figure that did not look remotely like an act, he paid a hundred times the usual price in gold coins (3,000 valis). Saying good-bye to Hestia, he started to help himself to the snack that was five hands long as he walked the streets, and after significant struggle, he managed to finish all of it—before slipping into a dark alley.

Leaning against the wall, he examined the wrapper, unwinding the several of them that had been used since it had been so large. And inside the oily paper, what appeared was—a torn fragment of a scroll.

Hermes broke into a smile as he read it.

"Turn Orario into a hearth."

It was unmistakably his own handwriting.

The first Hermes had fallen, but he had left behind a plan that would lead them back from the brink.

"Yeah, yeah, this is more like me."

Reassuming the cool, shrewd trickster's expression, he quickly began walking again.

There had been two pieces of paper.

The first was the letter to himself that the first Hermes had entrusted to Hestia.

And the second was the location of the materials needed for the construction of the hearth.

He could stop thinking. There was nothing else to worry about. He could just carry out his job in a way that would not infringe on any rules.

"Let's make a hearth."

It was three days after Perseus noticed the change in the *Freya Familia*'s baptism—and three days before the boy managed to land a blow on the elven warrior.

The moon has driven away the clouds, filling the night sky with a pale light.

The air is biting cold, but it's clearer than ever.

Just like my heart.

I indulge in a brief poetic thought as I sit in a chair at the window.

The fog that shrouded my mind and all the uncertainty is gone. I have no more doubt that I'm *Hestia Familia*'s Bell Cranell.

My whole body is filled with feelings toward my idol, and I'm consumed by a sense of exaltation.

"But…what do I do now…?"

I munch on a premade meal from the pouch of my Dungeon kit as I furrow my brow.

Just an hour ago, I refused dinner in Sessrúmnir after finishing the battle that night and headed straight back to the room I've been using for over two weeks now. I tried to lie and say that my body is not feeling well after exerting myself so much today, but Master saw through it. He just called me a fool while allowing it, though…He did actually forgive me, right?

A-anyway, under normal circumstances, this is right about the time when I would be leaving Sessrúmnir after dinner and start heading toward Lady Freya's chambers.

I wanted some time to figure out a plan in order to avoid doing that.

"If I meet Lady Freya now…she would definitely see through me. She'll realize I'm not swimming in doubt anymore."

Children can't lie before deities. She would surely see through my current thoughts.

And I have no clue what she would do when she realized that I was certain I was not a member of *Freya Familia*. But at the very least things surely would not change for the better for me.

And in the first place, what even is the current situation?

However much I might be sure of myself, as far as the world is concerned, I am still *Freya Familia*'s Bell Cranell, and it's not like Aiz or anyone else actually remembers the *Hestia Familia* Bell.

"Is Lady Freya…the reason why Orario is so strange?"

…Has her charm really created this world?

It seems unbelievable, but I don't have any other explanation I can think of. And I can't believe anyone other than a deity could manage such a feat.

And if my guess is correct, then deities really are far beyond the comprehension of us mortals. To change not just a person, but the entire world…

I shudder at an act so far removed from logic.

"If this really is something that Lady Freya has done, then…why would she do this…?"

It couldn't just be to have me join *Freya Familia*, could it? If it was, then why not just charm me along with everyone else? Was there something that prevented that? Or some prerequisite?

…No good, I have no idea.

In the first place, there is no way a mere mortal like me could begin to understand the divine will of a goddess like her.

For the moment, I set aside my questions about Lady Freya.

What I have to figure out is how to behave myself after this…what should I do?

I can't meet Lady Freya. I still have no idea what sort of expression I should have when I meet her.

And before the question of how to interact with her even came up, there would probably be others who felt something off about me from the battle today. Like Hegni or Heith. As for Master…I don't really know what he's thinking.

I probably should have just confirmed the techniques I learned from Aiz and Lyu in a way where no one would notice, or else try to say there was no way I could pull off such an absurd imitation against a first-tier adventurer, but I was still high on the feeling of renewing my feelings toward my idol.

If Lilly could see me now, I'm sure she would have a harsh lecture for me.

Welf and Mikoto and Haruhime would all smile awkwardly as the goddess watched us…

"…Goddess…everyone…"

Looking out the window, I think of my true familia.

The days I spent with *Freya Familia* were painful and harsh, but they were not only painful and harsh. There were moments when I was saved, and I felt warmth from such mysterious bonds. But still…this is not my home.

Slapping my cheeks painfully hard with both hands, I wipe away the sentimentality creeping into my thoughts.

I do not have time.

It's possible that Hegni or someone else is reporting my current state to Lady Freya right now.

Should I just try to run away? But what would I even do, then?

Even if for the sake of argument I managed to escape *Freya Familia*, the city's biggest familia, and got out of Folkvangr, the world is still not right. I would not have anywhere to return to without fixing that first.

I gulp down the last of the packaged meal, replenishing much-needed nutrients.

I can feel blood circulating in my body and my head as I desperately try to think of something—when a thought suddenly pops up.

"What about Syr…? If this world is a lie, then where is Syr right now…?"

Chloe and the others do not remember Syr.

Everyone in *Freya Familia* says there is no Syr, too.

But I know that she existed.

It isn't a simple contradiction. She vanished entirely. My suspicions focus on that point. My instinct is ringing.

It feels like she is the key to understanding what is happening in some way.

So what I need to do is to search for Syr…to find her?

"Lyu disappearing is weird, too…! If I can find the two of them…!"

Deciding clearly what I need to do, I jump to my feet.

Just when I resolve to start moving…

There's a thundering sound, as if in sync with me and my defiant stand.

"Wh-?!"

A massive tremor shakes the building.

Dumbfounded, I immediately steady myself against the shock. I know I decided to act, but I haven't even done anything yet!

I frantically open my window and look all around the estate.

I'm afraid there is some kind of attack happening, but all I see is a part of the first floor belching smoke and dust along with the glimmering remnants of magic.

"Bell! Bell! Are you there?!"

"...! Y-yes!"

There is a furious pounding on my door, and the familiar healer's voice rings out.

After a brief moment's indecision, I respond honestly.

"Thank goodness you're here...! You haven't left the room, right?!"

Opening the door, as expected, I see Heith standing there.

She has a couple other members of the familia in tow, and she looks more intense than I have ever seen her before. She looks obviously relieved when she sees me.

"I've been here the whole time, but...what is happening?! There was a really loud noise just now...!"

I'm a little bit suspicious of the question as I respond.

From outside my room, no, from somewhere inside the home, I can hear the shrill clang of blades clashing.

"...An intruder. Some individual has invaded our sacred Folkvangr."

Heith is silent for a moment before responding.

I freeze in place, forgetting the situation and responding in a hysterical voice.

"A-an intruder?! A single person?! Taking on *Freya Familia*?!"

Crisp slashes closed in.

Lyu was sweating. She used her sword to knock aside blades that hit harder than her own.

"Ugh?!"

"Haah!"

And then she unleashed a sharp kick to the beast person whose stance had faltered from having his longsword knocked upward.

She didn't stick around to watch as her opponent's back slammed into the wall, instead turning and running. She heard the thundering shouts of "Found her!" "Catch her!" from the reinforcements already swarming behind her.

The location was the first floor of the enormous palatial manor. Lyu was trying to escape by herself.

Trying to escape from the worst imaginable pursuers: *Freya Familia*.

"This really is Folkvangr…! *Freya Familia*'s home!"

Running with all her might, Lyu attempted to confirm the situation as best she could, even as beads of sweat continued to form.

It had already been a week since she'd woken up in an unknown underground room. She had passed out in front of Syr—Freya—and she guessed she had been carried away at some point after, but there was no end to her worries. It would not be hyperbole to say that, save the Dungeon, there was no place in Orario more dangerous than where she was.

"Hiyah!"

"Khh?!"

Immediately as she entered a wide corridor, a human leaped from a higher floor, slicing down at her.

In the split second when her legs were numbed from blocking one strike, another person mercilessly took advantage of that opening, attacking with a sharpness and swiftness that forced Lyu to respond with her full strength.

—Her opponents here were all strong!

It was simple, but that was the whole of her impression.

She was in the fortress of the city's largest faction. There was not a single weak person among them, and the warriors slashing at her right at that moment were the match for any second-tier adventurer. Each individual's level of training was incomparable. She had only just escaped her prison, but they had already noticed and were quick to force her into a precarious position. Even the lower-tier adventurers understood their place and were harassing her with magic to slow her down. She had to resort to every last trick she could muster, and she had even been forced to use her magic once, which completely revealed her position.

Fortunately, the inside of the manor was still in a confused panic and the enemy was not coordinating perfectly, but that did little to change the fact that she was stuck inside a cage filled with ferocious beasts. As a reward for clashing with an elf lancer who seemed to be a Level 4 like her, her clothes were torn slightly in exchange for cutting through the spear's haft.

"Fellow, no, Gale Wind! How did you escape the underground?!"

The other elf was agitated, and it showed in her intense tone. The question made Lyu remember the encounter from just a few minutes before.

She had been in a room underground that could not really be called a jail cell. She had not been wanting for clothing, food, or shelter.

However, she could not escape due to the cursed manacles on her wrists that weakened her and sealed away her magic.

As Lyu had grown more and more concerned, unable to do anything, a certain elf had appeared before her.

"Leave."

She had somehow incapacitated the upper-tier adventurers who were always guarding the door and entered before dropping Lyu's Futaba and the key to her restraints.

"My condition for releasing you is that I want you to cause as much of a commotion as you can in the eastern half of the manor while I act."

Lyu had been on guard against the girl who made such a straightforward demand while keeping her distance and not allowing her true intent to show in her eyes.

Lyu had glared back defiantly, demanding to know what she was thinking, what she was plotting, and did she really think Lyu would just listen to her?

"Please, Lyu."

But those two words, the way she said them, her gaze…they moved Lyu's heart.

Even though her face and voice did not match, she resembled a certain girl.

The girl left the room, with the elf still dumbstruck behind her. Unable to say anything, Lyu had taken the key in her hand, unlocked the restraints, and begun fighting.

I don't understand it, either. Why did I do exactly what some stranger wanted without even understanding her real intent? But those words and that gaze were—

Clenching the hilt of her sword tightly, Lyu's eyes flared.

She parried the stunned elf lancer's attack and finished spinning the cast that she had been murmuring softly.

"Imbue the light of stardust and strike down my enemy—Luminous Wind!"

The blast she had been preparing while fighting knocked aside all the reinforcements that had been gathering, causing a second explosion that rocked the manor.

"An explosion in the home?!"

The first floor beneath Babel.

Allen, who had been waiting for *Loki Familia* to return from their expedition in the chamber that connected to the Dungeon's first floor, exploded menacingly when he heard the report.

"What are you talking about? What are the boar and elves doing?!"

"A-about that…it appears to be magic set off inside the home and not an external attack…!"

Cowering at Allen's dangerous tone, the member who had sensed the uproar at the home lowered his voice while offering his analysis.

Allen scoffed, concluding that they knew nothing important, as the four prums who were also present responded.

"The battle on the field should be long finished by now."

"There is no one in our familia so fool enough to trouble the goddess's ears with accidental magic."

"Which would mean the work of outsiders."

"Could it be...Gale Wind?"

Allen's eyes narrowed sharply as Alfrik and his brothers reached a hypothesis through near telepathy.

"A-Allen! Alfrik!"

The half-prum Van came running over at that same moment.

Allen ratcheted his head into high gear as he brushed off Van, telling him to get lost and save it for later, but—

"She...just disappeared!"

When Allen heard that, his eyes darkened.

"...I should have just killed her..."

Van and the rest of the familia members gasped and recoiled from the bubbling wrath welling up from the cat person.

"What's the plan, Allen?"

Alfrik, for the sake of appearances, asked the second-in-command of the familia who was in charge of the operation there.

"As if you need to ask. We're going back."

"Something happening at *Freya Familia*'s home?"

Aisha looked suspicious.

She stopped on a corner of a major street where tipsy bar goers were enjoying themselves, near Daedalus Street in the east of the city.

"Yeah. Thane and the others near the shopping district got wind of it, apparently. There are still sounds of fighting from inside the walls, according to Merrill's report."

"What's that about? They stop their death matches come sunset, right? Does that mean some other familia picked a fight with them?"

"No clue. But we can't just ignore it..."

Falgar looked troubled.

For better or worse, there was a lot of weight that accompanied being the city's greatest faction. If something suddenly happened in their home, all sorts of other familias and the like would start wondering about it and getting nervous. All the more so for a group like *Hermes Familia* that maintained neutrality and always had their ear to the ground for information.

The Amazon looked troubled, as if something was bothering her, even though she didn't remember anything that happened during the Goddess Festival.

"I'm sure it'll just end up being their death match going a little bit longer than usual, is all. More importantly, let's get this firewood delivery job done already."

Lulune did not bother paying any attention to Falgar and Aisha's conversation. The chienthrope girl was holding on to a bundle of firewood as she dexterously shrugged and knocked on the door of a family's home.

"We're with *Hermes Familia*. The Guild asked us to deliver firewood."

"Ohh, thank you! It's already feeling like winter. You're lifesavers."

"Sure thing. We'll be coming in if you don't mind."

"Eh? Wh-what?"

Lulune slipped past the woman who had met them at the door and bent over in front of the fireplace in the house.

"Sorry, our patron god told us to be sure to start the fire before coming back."

Quickly arranging the kindling, she started a fire with practiced ease, using a flint starter, and the fireplace was filled with crackling flame in the blink of an eye.

The couple and their daughter were pleased with the refreshing display of skill and extended a tempting offer of dinner as thanks, but Lulune restrained herself and excused herself with a tired, "Unfortunately, we still have more work to do."

"Haaah, how many more of these volunteering gigs do we have left...I mean it's definitely cold tonight, but still..."

"You took the words out of my mouth. Sheesh, since when did *Hermes Familia* do such obvious brownnosing?"

"I mean, we don't usually, but..."

Magic-stone warmers were expensive, so most of the residents of

Orario endured the winter cold using normal stoves and fireplaces. But still, what was Hermes thinking, giving them a map of houses to deliver firewood to and calling it all volunteer work? Every member of the familia had been brought in to help with it even. Lulune and Aisha both had been confused by all the fuss, and the familia's second-in-command, Falgar, shook his head while holding an identical bundle of firewood over his shoulder.

"And also…this wood kinda smells a bit like blood…"

Lulune held up the bundle she was carrying and sniffed it.

"You think we're passing out logs that were used to pummel someone to death?"

"Save the stupid observations and let's get moving already. Lord Hermes specifically said we had to get this over before midnight."

"Ah, wait up!"

Lulune quickly rushed to catch up with Aisha and Falgar, who had left her behind in exasperation.

Hermes Familia delivered the firewood to residence after residence, starting the fire everywhere they stopped.

Without anyone noticing, the city began to fill with hearth fires.

Boom!

Another tremor shakes the mansion as I catch myself against the wall.

"Ugh…?! A-again…?!"

Heith did not quite catch herself and stumbles into my chest, managing to head-butt me in the process. I cough as I pull her off me.

"It seems like something really crazy is happening. Is this really okay?!"

"U-umm…!"

"It sort of seems like a lot more than just a single rebel breaking in. If anything, it seems like a pretty big—"

"—Argh! Look, it's not like I freakin' know, either; this is just happening out of nowhere all of a sudden! I'd like some explanations, too!"

Heith rubs her forehead as her face turns red, and she swings her hands up in the air in frustration.

I'm a little bit taller than her, but I can't help recoiling apologetically and reflexively mumbling a hasty "I-I'm sorry."

"Bell, no matter what, please don't leave this room!"

"Eh?! ...B-but!"

"You're special to Lady Freya, so if anything happens to you, I'm going to get a massive earful! Just think of it as helping me out, and please just stay here! Okay?! I'll leave guards here for you, too!"

Heith leaves the room without letting me get a word in edgewise.

Like she promised, a couple of older familia members, one male and one female, come in as she leaves.

"Bell, listen to what Heith said, okay? I know she's being a bit overprotective, but she's also taken a bit of a liking to you, too."

"And also, there's the issue of you getting cursed. This attack might have some connection with all of that, too."

"O-okay..."

My impromptu guards are Remilia and Rask. Along with Van, they're the ones who spoke with me most often.

Their tone is kind, but...their eyes are watching me with an odd intensity.

Are they on guard around me? No, is it that they don't want me to make contact with the intruder?

If that's the case, then it would explain Heith's question when she first came to my room.

What do I do...?!

It's definitely true that a different wind is blowing now.

It's almost like a tailwind has been watching me and picked up right when I regained my idol. Given the fact that I have to avoid contact with Lady Freya, this is unmistakably a great opportunity.

Turning away from the two of them, I pretend to look out the window while thinking about what to do.

I heard that the Gullivers, Allen, and Van and the other second-tier adventurers are not at Folkvangr because of a quest they have to handle. It does not change the fact that the difference in combat strength is impossible to overcome, but it's still less than half of what it would normally have been…!

I should make my move. Make a decision. Break through the people who have taken care of me these past weeks and take action.

I close my eyes for a brief moment, carefully managing my breathing to avoid being noticed, and then I instantly spin around. Just as I'm about to start running, the two of them collapse.

"Wh-?!"

They shudder and slump to the floor, and for a second, I'm stunned.

What happened?!

Confusion and caution mingle as I hear a squeak. At some point the door was opened.

Staring at the half-opened door, I make up my mind and cautiously step outside.

Looking to the left and the right, I see the hallway is deserted.

—No…

At the end of the long hallway, there is an almost illusory figure shimmering as if beckoning me in that direction.

I set aside my doubt and follow after the shade.

The magic-stone lights lining the castle-like corridor go out, bringing darkness. I follow the indistinct, almost-ghostly shadow without anyone finding me.

Soon I arrive at a western corner of the home, on the top floor.

A room for meditation to allow warriors to gather their mind.

"This is…"

There is a stained glass window in the ceiling high above. It's almost like an altar.

The room is a long space like a small chapel. The floor is made of black marble. There are no chairs. It almost looks like a stage for a coronation, with long shallow stairs leading toward the back of the room. Instead of statues of deities, greatswords, spears, battle-axes, and various other weapons that are all clearly well worn line the walls here.

They are surely the effects of the einherjars who are no more.

I step into the hall of warriors, into its tranquil, almost sacred atmosphere.

And when I reach the center of the room, the door that I left open suddenly closes.

"!"

I spin around.

The only light in the dark room is the faint moonlight from the stained glass window in the ceiling above. Rays of deep blue, light purple, and a sorrowful silver all fill my eyes as a single girl steps toward me from the entrance.

"Hörn…"

Long, ashen hair and a black dress that made her look like a witch's apprentice.

It's my second time meeting her.

Her hair covers the right half of her face, just like it had when she came to deliver the letter before the Goddess Festival.

"………"

Her footsteps ring out as she silently approaches me.

There are questions I have to ask. And countless curiosities.

Was she the one who guided me there? If so, why? What are her intentions?

Why have I never met the girl who is called the goddess's attendant despite having visited Lady Freya's chamber so many times?

And more than anything, is this really only our second time meeting?

What is this strange feeling…as if I've met her dozens of times before, as if she's always been beside me?

Many questions cross my mind, but none of them make it into words.

Nameless, the one without a second name.

Forgetting to speak, I'm drawn into her eye, as if she is there to hand down my judgment in place of the goddess.

"………"

"………"

She stops.

We look at each other.

There is a small distance between us in the center of the room.

The noise from outside the room is distant.

Is the intrusion happening in the east of the home? There is no one near this room.

No matter what happens here, there would not be anyone who would intrude.

Time continues as we look at each other, and finally she speaks.

"How much of the answer have you reached?"

I instantly understand what she is asking.

I shouldn't answer. Logic is screaming at me to keep my mouth shut, but I give a foolishly honest response.

"I'm not actually a member of *Freya Familia*. I'm *Hestia Familia*'s Bell Cranell."

It felt like I could not lie to her.

Her expression does not change in the slightest at that confession, and she asks again:

"Then, *how much have you figured out*?"

"...Huh?"

But I do not understand her second question.

It does not sound like she is just asking about the weirdness and inconsistencies that are affecting Orario.

It sounds like she is confirming something different, a far more crucial core of something...

"Wh-what do you mean? What are you...?"

I do not know what Hörn's intentions are. And I'm clearly flustered.

Her face that was as calm as the surface of a lake at night suddenly grows stern.

Her small hand clenches.

And just as it looks like her long gray hair has tilted down—

".......Trash."

I hear her murmur.

"Eh?"

"...Trash, trash, trashtrashtrashtrashtrashtrashtrashtrashtrash-trashtrashtrashtrashtrashtrashtrashtrashtrashtrashtrash!"

The next moment, she looks up and explodes.

A mindless, shocked look crosses my face for a brief moment before my eyes widen and I recoil, taken aback by the barrage.

"You go beyond an utter fool, putting you squarely in the realm of pure garbage! Enchanting her so! Tormenting her so! And you still don't understand anything?! Nonsense! Snap out of it!"

"Eh, eh, eh?!"

"How long must you insist on being content with playing the fool?!"

Her long hair sways violently, and she swings her hand roughly to the side while unleashing a storm of rebukes at me.

Talk about a change of appearance! It's scary. Like scary enough that I'm afraid for my life here!

Because of Hörn's sudden eruption, I forget my position and almost fall backward.

"You brute, feigning harmlessness! Unconscious of your crimes! Enemy to all women! Filth of humanity! Monster who mistakes obviousness for sincerity! If the deities ever erred, it was in creating a foul beast like you! Parasite of original sin tempting all those older than you! Daring even to seduce the sublime goddess! Have some shame!"

"Wait! Seriously, what are you talking about?!"

"The 'Please Call Me "Big Sister"' ranking is a joke! What a farce!"

"Why do you know about that?!"

I can only cry out in panic at the furious fusillade of abuse.

While that's happening, Hörn's rage knows no bounds, and she reaches behind her hip and pulls out a knife—wait what??!!

"Unforgivable, unforgivable, unforgivable!!! I will never, ever forgive what you've done! Your stupid face and your pathetic voice and that kindness that torments the goddess so! I should have killed you when I had the chance!"

"E-eeeeeep?!"

"It's all because you appeared before the goddess!"

A blade dance begins in the blink of an eye.

Just like she indicated, I cry out pathetically while I avoid the knife slashing toward me.

Our two figures dance in the light of the stained glass at the center of the room.

The swishing sound of wind being cut assaults my ears time after time. I can't let my guard down. Even if her level is below mine, there is no mistaking she is still an upper-tier adventurer.

I fall into panic by the utterly unexpected development as I desperately try to avoid being carved up. We change places several times as I evade the knife she is holding in a backhand grip.

"When you're around, the littlest things give her joy! And sadden her! And hurt her!"

"Eh…?!"

"You have the potential to be a hero, so why do you not have any lust?! Why can't you just accept love?! If you did, then she would at least be rewarded some small amount! How many women must you keep hurting like this?!"

Hörn does not stop as she vents at me.

She swings her arm to release the pent-up rage and punches me square in the cheek with a heartfelt scream.

Realizing that she's referring to Lady Freya, I'm stunned, and try my hardest to understand what she is saying.

"What devotion! Slave to your accursed infatuation!"

"Ghh—!"

When I hear the person I idolized scorned like that, though, my limbs, which only recoiled so far, burn with a resolve to fight back.

My eyes flare as I try to grab the knife that she is swinging down at me.

"Because of you! She is…! I'm…!"

But.

"——"

When I see the tear falling from her eye, my arms freeze.

The next moment, she tackles me, knocking me to the ground.

"Ugh?!"

My back slams into the hard floor.

Her soft limbs cling to me, and she throws the knife down beside me.

A shrill sound that feels like it will split my eardrums rings out as Hörn grabs my neck with both of her hands.

"Aaaaah! Odious! Detestable! How I wish I could kill you!"

I forget to fight back, my arms limp on the floor as my eyes open wide.

Not because I'm bound by her furious visage.

"And yet, so maddeningly precious..."

Her bluff is falling apart, and her feelings are on the verge of being entirely revealed as time stops for me.

It's almost pitiful how her trembling fingers don't squeeze my neck at all.

Even though she seems like she wants to stop my breathing so badly, she can't bring herself to go through with it.

Love and hate.

Even though it's just the littlest bit, and only surface deep...for the first time, I feel like I really understand the concept of love and hate being two sides of the same coin.

"If I had just met you first!"

She shouts.

"If I had known the future that awaited!"

She rages.

"Before the goddess could meet you, I could...I could have embraced you..."

She trembles.

"If I...had just met you...first...!"

The light through the stained glass window shines on her back as she reveals the thoughts that lie in the depths of her heart.

"—The goddess would never have been tormented, and I could have fallen for you as myself."

She's like a sinner confessing all her sins.

"It was no good..."

"Huh...?"

"My way...didn't work..."

Her voice is faint.

Trembling.

Her feelings slowly slip out from behind the mask that has been removed.

"I wanted her to remain a sublime goddess...I didn't want her to become a mere girl like me...! That's why I tried to kill you, to stop her deluded wish...but, but...but...!"

Her long hair falls, brushing against my forehead.

Her hidden right eye is uncovered.

Unlike her left eye's iris, which is fully black, her right eye looks almost silver, or bluish-gray.

Tears are welling in that eye.

"Even though she fully intended to bury the girl's feelings when she failed to achieve her wish! Even though I thought she would wake from her nightmare after being rejected by you! I can still hear her! Crying! I never heard that voice before!"

Her tears fall on my cheek.

As I watch in shocked silence, she cries like a child right before my eyes.

"She's suffering! Hurting! To a degree she does not even recognize herself! She's on the verge of breaking! At this rate, she will never be saved! This isn't right! It can't be! That isn't what I wanted at all...!"

Wavering between love and ______, on the verge of collapse.

It's a string of words I can't comprehend. I can't grasp her intent.

But my eyes are stolen away by the overflowing emotions, and by how she herself is sobbing.

"...Realize it! Just notice already! It won't mean anything if you don't realize it yourself!"

Hörn howls at me even as her tears continue to fall.

"There is no meaning if a fake like me tells you the truth!"

Her face is a mess as she pleads with me to reach out my hand.

"So please..."

Her heartfelt plea rings in my ears.

* * *

"Please realize it...*Bell*—"

The moment I hear that voice...

So many of the memories and events leading up to today all flash through my head at a fantastic speed.

"——"

Words, tone, resonance, sadness, tears, feelings.

Similarities, commonalities, resemblances, closeness. There are too many to count.

The girl crying right before me. The girl who worked at The Benevolent Mistress. And the sublime goddess beloved by all.

Three people that should not be interchangeable in any sense of the word.

And yet their three expressions overlap.

—The goddess's attendant.

—Nameless.

—*"This child will never become anyone else."*

If she cannot become any other person—then from another angle, that means the person she could become was already determined?

Then could that be—*the goddess*?

The odd feeling I have whenever I meet her.

The feeling that I've met her before, as if she has always been at my side, *as if I've known her since long ago.*

Her face and voice are entirely different, and yet she resembles *them* too much.

Like a reflection on the water that changes with every little ripple.

She also called herself a fake just now.

And she also said, "I should have killed you then."

The person who resembled Syr who tried to kill me that day during the Goddess Festival.

The assumption I had then was that they shared memories or perhaps senses. If that was actually close to the reality of it, then she and Syr really are bound in some deep way.

And...

"*—Aaaa, I really do like you.*"

"*—Ahhh, I truly do like you.*"

What she said, and what the goddess said…

Her smile that I saw in the goddess's expression that night.

The warmth that enveloped me. The line between that silver and bluish-gray.

It always seemed so strange. Her having some connection with the city's biggest familia. The guards and honorifics. One and only. Irreplaceable.

This world being so twisted, and her disappearing, and the goddess appearing before me in her place.

Wait, wait, wait, wait….

I reach a possibility so absurd, so crazy, there should be no way I could possibly reach it.

The existence of Nameless is the final piece that finally lets me realize the truth.

As the torrent of flashbacks and realizations finally finish, my lips open.

"You're…Syr?"

I speak her true name.

"And Lady Freya…is Syr, too?"

And the name of the girl.

"………"

Her crying expression slowly changes into a beautiful smile.

Her fingers leave my neck and gently caress my forehead.

Looking down at me while I'm stunned and unable to move, Hörn's eyes narrow, and she slowly stands up.

As if following her, I stand up as well while she picks up the knife.

"…Here…"

"Eh…Th-this is…the Hestia Knife?!"

I'm dumbstruck by what she holds out to me.

The knife she was swinging at me is the knife that Lady Hestia ordered just for me. Even if the room is shrouded in darkness, I'm ashamed of myself for not noticing. It almost feels like the knife itself is upset with me.

At the same time, though, I remember something.

Something the goddess told me once, and something that Lilly said, too. Anyone who doesn't bear Lady Hestia's falna can't properly wield this knife. The blade itself has been dead in a sense. No matter how much Hörn might have hacked away at me, it wouldn't have been possible for her to mortally wound me with it.

She wasn't trying to kill me this time at all.

"...Wait, from the very start, were you...trying to help me?"

I'm still gripping the knife as she firmly clasps my hand in both of hers.

All of a sudden, the hieroglyphs engraved in the knife take on a purple gleam, as if life has been breathed back into it.

Seeing that, Hörn laughs softly.

"Yes, I never intended to kill you—from the very start, this was my intention."

And then, as if offering up her body, she throws herself onto the knife in my hand.

"What?!"

I can feel the blade piercing her skin. The warm red pouring from her.

In the blink of an eye, her clothes and my hand are drenched in blood.

I immediately hold Hörn as she starts to lose strength and collapse.

"What are...what are you doing?!"

Kneeling down, I support her slender arms as I cry out in shock.

I only just barely managed to redirect the knife blade that slipped into her chest. I could not do anything more than that. The blade pierced just a little bit below her chest, but blood is still welling from inside her, robbing her of life.

I pull the knife out and desperately try to stop the bleeding as Hörn weakly leans her head against my chest.

"I betrayed...the goddess...out of devotion to her...And for a second time...at that..."

The smile on her lips is one of pity.

A smile of pity and of contempt for her own foolishness.

"And more than anything…I loved you…Not because of anyone else's feelings. I did it of my own volition."

Her fragile, repentant smile reflects in my wide eyes.

"So I will die…in order to atone for what I've done…"

She is bleeding out, and her face is frighteningly pale as my hand forcefully pushes against her chest.

"Healing! There's still time! If I take you to Heith—!"

Why are you doing this?! Why are you trying to die?!

I can't help remembering Winne, who once died for me, as I grit my teeth and try to carry Hörn.

"Wait…"

But when I start to stand up, the slender hand clinging to my chest stops me.

"My magic…miracle to connect me with her…"

"C-connect…?!"

"If I use this…she will…see everything…she will know everything about you as well."

Hörn tries to explain as I listen in confusion.

Her breathing is shallow, and she wheezes in pain as she gathers the last of her strength.

"But even so…that you may know…her feelings that only I could hear…"

Summoning every last bit of mind she had left inside her, she begins to pray.

"*…Untrodden stairs, forbidden door…today, this day, my body infringes heavens' laws…*"

A magic circle unfolds around us.

Its color is a gray that does not quite reach silver.

"*Hollow soul, shallow lust…*"

A quiet undulation. The magic power swirling is slight as well.

Particles of light reflect the glimmer of the stained glass, gleaming as they ascend to the heavens.

It's an ephemeral beat that sounds almost like a prayer for salvation.

A shorter cast incomparable to that of the sage.

But it treads upon a taboo realm of the same sort. A secret spell that is hers alone.

"By the name exchanged...descend, daughter of the gods—"

And with quivering lips, she speaks its name.

"Vana Seiðr."

The magic circle shatters.

And the fragments of light, the ashen color gleam, transform into a beautiful, jewellike silver and are absorbed into Hörn.

"?!"

Her body shimmers like the crescent moon as I hold her and become shrouded in heat.

The light subsides as the magic courses around her, and once it has all settled, in my arms is—

"...Syr...?"

The girl with the blue-gray hair.

I murmur in a daze.

As my voice reaches her, her eyelashes quiver.

Her blue-gray eyes slowly open and look up at me.

"...It hurts..."

"Eh...?"

"I didn't want to experience this feeling...I can't bear it...I cast Syr aside, and yet...and yet it still hurts so much."

Syr's voice. Syr's gaze. Syr's breathing.

These are not Hörn's words.

They are the feelings of *the real her*, which only Hörn with her connection to the goddess could know.

"Even though I thought I would be satisfied with you alone...I hurt so many people and so many precious things...I'm so numb. Syr was all just a lie, but...I can't explain it...!"

A sacred scene is unfolding as I hold her beneath the blue-and-purple light of the stained glass window.

By chance, the room feels like the cathedral did when I visited it with her.

Is the grief-stricken voice filling the room the remnants of the goddess?

That which should have been cast aside.

Should have been buried.

But it had remained deep within her in a place where she didn't notice?

"The thing I wanted most…is something else. What I wished for, what I prayed for was—"

A voice seeking _____.

I gulp.

A big tear wells in her eye and trickles down her cheek.

"Please, stop me! I don't want to be driven mad by love anymore!"

And she says the words that the goddess could not speak.

"Save me…Bell…!"

"Ghhh!"

My fingers tightly grip the slender shoulder I'm supporting.

My heart starts throbbing. On impulse, I…

The billowing torrent of emotion scorches my chest and my heart, and I swear a vow.

"I will save you."

I respond, even if the answer is a foregone conclusion.

"Even if it means hurting you again! Even if it's nothing more than serving my own ego! I will save you!"

I swear it in a loud voice with all that I have, as if to ensure it reaches her hollow heart.

I do not know what I should do. But I've made up my mind.

No matter how much scorn it earns me, no matter how ugly an act of self-satisfaction it is—Bell Cranell is an absolute fool who can't abandon this girl.

Self-preservation is not enough to make me brush aside a hand reaching out to be saved!

Her tears fall on bloodstained clothes. Just before the girl looking back at me quietly closes her eyes…it feels like she smiled every so faintly.

She slips into a deep sleep, like a child who has cried herself to exhaustion.

"…! The wound…?"

The wound on her—no, on Hörn's chest—is gone.

Is this a side effect of the spell?

Is the wound healed?

No, is it because she transformed into the daughter of the gods?

I honestly don't know the nature of this spell. But it's clear that her life is safe for now.

But I can't take that for granted.

When the magic that is still being maintained is finally released, Hörn's fatal wound will probably return, and she will breathe her last shortly after.

"I won't let that happen…!"

Holding her in my arms, I stand up.

I don't want to lose anyone. I won't let it happen.

No matter how boastful, how fanciful, how much a pipe dream, or pathetic, or shameless, or foolish it is—say it, say it, say it!

I will save everyone!

"I will save all of you!"

Holding her body, I start running.

I leap out of the mediation chamber and head deeper into the estate.

Charging to the highest floor, where the goddess awaits.

He's coming.

The boy is coming here.

Realizing it from the senses that Hörn shared via her magic, Freya grimaced.

"Ottar."

"Milady."

"Save Hörn. I won't allow her to return to the heavens and disappear from my sight like this."

She gave her loyal retainer his order as she sat in her chair.

"No, I won't allow it. To do something like this...I will punish her personally. Do not allow her to die under any circumstances."

"But what of your guard, Milady...?"

"It matters not. I do not need any other children, either. Take everyone and go."

"...Yes, Milady."

With that, Ottar left the room.

The presence of the rest of her guards and attendants grew distant.

There was only the single goddess in her chamber, which had fallen silent.

He was coming to where she awaited.

"Bell..."

Running. Running. Running.

I sprint, holding her body as her arms hang limply and her eyes stay closed.

At my back, I can feel the battle cries and furious swordplay still unfolding in the eastern wing. Using the suspended corridor on the top floor and avoiding the central courtyard, I rush into the northern building.

I encounter no one. This is unnatural. I can tell that much.

The building has been intentionally cleared out. She really has seen through my movements. She's inviting me in.

But even so, I'm not going to stop.

Abandoning all fear and unease for the moment, I push forward.

"!"

Just a short distance from my goal.

As I run up the stairs leading to the highest floor that I had grown so used to passing through, I see him standing there blocking the way.

The enormous, rust-haired boaz.

"Hand over the girl."

"Ghl…!"

The city's strongest adventurer, who has already defeated me in a single blow once before. Ottar is looking down at me from above as he makes his curt declaration.

The overwhelming presence of someone impossibly stronger causes me to catch my breath, but I still adjust my hold on Hörn to shield her.

"I will not kill her. It's the goddess's will."

"Eh…?"

"That girl shall live."

Those are the warrior's brief words.

But because he is a true warrior more than anyone else, I feel like I can trust what he says.

Looking into his rust-colored eyes, I fall silent and make up my mind. I do not know anything about the nature of her magic, and I can't use any healing magic myself, so I wouldn't be able to heal her wound myself no matter what I tried. Trusting Ottar, I walk forward and hand her to him.

His treelike arms gently cradle her.

"Go. The goddess is waiting beyond here."

That is all Ottar says.

I watch his back as he passes me on the stairs and then turn forward again.

I climb the remaining stairs. I stop running, taking the steps one at a time to steel my will.

Suddenly.

I remember the heroic tale—"Erlandr of Water and Light."

The spirit passes away without ever revealing her true name.

The saint falls into grief and regret.

And the knight is tormented by guilt.

Then what about now?

Who is the knight, who is the spirit, and who the saint?

Who has failed to act on their feelings?

Who has achieved love?

Who has failed to realize ______?

Who is the most pitiful?

I'm no Erlandr.

But I'm going to go to the saint—to the witch.

To bare the feelings that lie in my breast.

"—You've come at last, Bell."

The highest floor.

Opening both doors, I arrive at the goddess's chambers, where she is waiting alone for me.

The couch and table where we sat and talked so many times before has been put away. She is just standing there.

"I suppose it would be shameless to ask what brings you here."

Her tone and the air about her are totally different from just yesterday.

She is staring me down not as the loving goddess who has given me so much warmth, but as a cold empress.

"If you had just accepted me without noticing everything…I would have always been at your side and provided you with love… Hörn did something she really shouldn't have."

Her silver gaze is clear and cold, strict.

She is like a child whose favorite toy had been ruined, like an arrogant dictator. And yet even so, she is brimming with a supernatural charisma.

Two sides of the same coin.

A ruthless and uninhibited goddess of beauty worthy of being called an absolute ruler. The form of a deusdea utterly unlike the girl at the tavern from my memories.

But I speak without cowering.

"You were Syr."

She responds without batting an eyelash.

"Yes, it was I who played with all of you at that tavern."

And if anything, she answers as if this is all pointless.

"However, you appear to be misunderstanding something. The girl Syr never existed to begin with."

"………"

"There was once a girl with the same name…but I received that true name from her. What you saw was merely my performance. A pretense."

I'm surprised by how calmly I take what should have been such a shocking confession.

"What do you mean?"

"Just what I said. I was role playing…it was just a game. Hiding all traces of my divinity, assuming the mask of a girl, I pretended to be a mortal to pass the time."

"Role playing…?"

"Yes. And while doing that, I met Lyu and the other girls. And you. It was all just an extension of my game."

Her eyes narrow soberly, as if explaining something so trivial as not to be worth the effort.

"I created all of it. Syr never existed from the start. She was just a piece in my game. A flight of fancy."

She was implicitly saying my resolve to save Syr was badly misdirected. But even so, I still called out to her.

"Syr."

"…Stop calling that name."

"No."

"Ghh…"

"Syr."

Every time I say that name, her expression twists in annoyance.

I stare into her silver eyes.

"Why? Why were you crying then?"

The day of the harvest festival.

She cried that day when I hurt her, beneath the gray skies, which continued to look like they might also break into tears for days afterward.

Her eyes widen.

"Why did you always help me? Even up to today?"

When I ran away from the bar after being laughed at. When I was overwhelmed by just how far beyond my reach my idol was. During the incident with the Xenos when my body was so hopelessly cold. She always appeared before me, at times offering a smile, at others a path to escape, and sometimes just providing me simple warmth.

And all those times she continued to prepare a lunch for me.

There were so many questions lying within those few words.

"...The reason I helped you in Syr's form was to guide your growth. I fell in love with your soul at first sight. After cultivating that translucent gleam, and after developing your body and mind to my preferences, I intended to harvest the fruits of my labor."

"........."

"The grimoire, the amulet for the war game, and everything else as well...it was all to help you grow and to protect you."

That much was certainly true. I overcame so many battles largely because of all the support and advice she gave me. It was because of all that that I could stand there before her as a second-tier adventurer.

It wasn't wrong. But it wasn't the whole truth, either.

"The tears you saw...were merely the performance of the girl. At that moment, Syr would have cried, so I conformed to my game and acted out my role."

"That's a lie," I fire back immediately.

"!"

"Your hurt was real. Those tears were so real, I was paralyzed by them."

I reject her claims.

No matter how painful it is, no matter how much it tears at her heart and mine, I will not allow her to say those tears were a lie. I will affirm the existence of the girl named Syr Flover.

She was not just a performance or a pretense at all.

"Syr was there."

A wispy cloud passes outside the large window.

The moonlight shining into the chamber quietly stills the air.

After my vehement denial has finished echoing, the pale, moonlit room falls silent, and her face remains warped.

And as if growing annoyed by my refusal to avert my eyes, my unchanging expression, as if losing her patience, she pulls something out of her pocket.

"...! That ornament is...!"

The paired accessories. Not my knight one, the spirit's.

The one I gave Syr.

"The first present Syr received from you...she was happy."

The silver inlaid with blue decorations draws my gaze.

She smiles.

She holds it up in her right hand, as if to put it into her hair—

"But I don't need it anymore."

She swings it down with force.

Before I can react, she throws the ornament forcefully to the ground, shattering it.

The shattering sound that pierces my ears is almost like a girl crying out.

As time slows to a crawl, the fragments of blue scatter cruelly across the floor, robbing me of speech.

"The game is over. There is no point in indulging your wild musings."

A piece fell near her foot.

She raises her leg and crushes it without any hesitation.

"Syr is gone now. Syr is dead."

Time stops as she steps on that fragment. I see all my memories of Syr dwelling within it, and my blood boils.

The goddess's gloating eyes see into my heart, stirring up my emotions, manipulating my feelings.

As if it is amusing, setting fire to a calm heart.

I'm caught in the goddess's trick. I'm in the palm of the witch's hand.

But so what?

I break the silence, screaming.

"You're wrong! Syr is still alive! Syr is you! You were the one who asked me to save you!"

"That was just the result of Hörn's emotions getting crossed up. The impurity of a child's wish and my divine will mixing in the process of her magic. I don't want to be saved, and I certainly have not asked to be saved."

Her senses were linked by the magic, so she knew from start to finish.

She has a bewitching smile, confident of her superior position. Her eyes narrow, as if teasing a foolish child who is growing enraged over nothing.

"And who would ask you for help? Weren't you the one who rejected Syr's love in the first place?"

Her lips curl into a sneer.

That is the crux of it all. The arrogant reality that Bell Cranell perpetrated.

Faced with her entirely correct argument—I absolutely agree.

"That's right! I did reject it!"

"!"

I step forward, paying no heed to how her silver eyes widen in shock.

The fragments of the accessory have scattered across the floor, creating a single path.

A single, straight path that doesn't require me to crush any pieces of memory underfoot.

She looks stunned as I push forward with long strides until I stand right in front of her.

"I rejected *your* confession! *Your* feelings! It was none other than me who hurt you!"

Like another moment in the past, I'm so close that our lips might easily meet as I unleash all of my feelings.

"I'm the one who did that to you! That is why I'm going to stop you!"

"Ghh…?!"

"That is why I'm going to save you! I won't let anyone else take this terrible role!"

The determination burning in my chest. The vow of what is surely a childish stubbornness.

I can't make up for the tears she cried. But I can protect her from hurting anyone else and from hurting herself any further.

I'm the source of the problem? That's right! I caused it, and I hurt her!

So what, then, as terrible as I am, I don't have any right to do anything? This isn't a joke!

However much other people might scorn me, however much I might hate myself, I know full well that just folding my hands and doing nothing is more unsightly and more meaningless!

It isn't reparations or atonement or anything!

The source of what is hurting us is the fact that I rejected her feelings!

"...Do you understand what you are saying? One-sidedly deciding to save a girl you yourself rejected before? Even though you refuse to give her love or anything else?"

She has stood in shock, but soon a clear and obvious loathing appears in her eyes.

She snorts scornfully.

"What a hideous ego. Even among the gods, there was no male like you. You really are a hypocrite beyond all possible comprehension."

"Then what you've done is ego, too!"

"Ghh...!"

"In order to take me for yourself, you've twisted everyone—all of Orario! That is a terribly hideous ego, too!"

Her sneer pierces my heart, drawing blood, but in full defiance, I force her to look in the mirror and bleed, too.

I know it already. She's letting her possessiveness run wild, and I'm spewing sophistries. We are both flailing about, letting our unbearable and unseemly selfishness show for all the world to see.

The die was cast and shattered long ago. However much one might long for love or wish for _____, blood and tears will always flow in a clash of egos that devolves into hurting each other.

There is no going back for us.

My eyes and her silver eyes glare at each other.

"...No matter how much you scream and cry, it does not change the fact that I was playing a game. Syr was my lie—"

"There's no way I could believe such a heartfelt confession was all just a lie!"

"Wh—?"

I shout back half on impulse, and for the first time, her silver eyes waver in shame.

"No matter how much you try to say it was all a game, I won't let you say Syr did not exist! What do I care about your pride?!"

I can never forget that day.

I will carry her tears and my shock and regret for the rest of my life.

No matter how much we might wish it, no matter how much we might want a do-over, nothing will change the fact that that day actually happened!

"That wasn't a lie at all, it was real! I won't let anyone deny it! Not even you!"

As I continue shouting, it seems like for just a moment her perfect white skin, her cheeks redden.

But just as soon as I think that, her peerless visage warps, and as if she can't bear it anymore, she pushes me away.

I move back a few steps without stumbling, still watching her.

"...Disagreeable. Yes, this is terribly unpleasant. It's the first time I've felt this way."

Her smile disappears, and a quiet rage backs her words.

The goddess's wrath, her divine strength, makes my skin tingle.

I'm surely doing something unbelievably crazy right now.

I'm defying the goddess of beauty. Getting into a heated argument with one who awes even other deities.

But even so, the sacred flame in my back, the feelings hidden in my heart, will not yield.

"You'll stop me, you'll save me...for all of that glib speech, what is it that you are going to do?"

"........."

"I'm sure you have guessed, but it's true, my charm does not work on you alone, Bell. But Orario is still twisted. Were I to give the order, the whole city would become your enemy. *Hestia Familia*, too…and even your precious Sword Princess."

While I'm pressing onward in solitude, she thrusts at me with reality.

No matter how much I try to be calm, my heart is racing. And as if seeing through even those movements, her eyes flare sharply as she declares the solemn truth.

"I will absolutely break your spirit, by whatever means necessary."

There is no exaggeration in what she said. She has absolute control over the fate of everyone in Orario.

I can't hide the bead of sweat that trickles down the back of my neck.

"There is no way you could save me—"

Just as she says that, something odd happens.

I notice it immediately.

"—Hot?"

My back is burning.

The blessing of the sacred flame is roaring, as if burning away the false blessing from when the goddess of beauty updated my status.

"——"

At that same moment, Lady Freya inhales sharply, and her expression changes.

She turns sharply, her gaze directed outside the window.

To Orario's night sky, filled with the light of hearths.

"…Hestia…?"

At some point, countless hearth fires began flickering throughout the city.

"Ugh…?!"

The change gripped the entire metropolis at once.

In the Chamber of Prayers beneath Guild Headquarters.

Fels dropped to a knee in front of the stone altar, one hand on the ground for support.

"My body is hot…?! There is no flame, and yet it's like I'm burning…!"

The mage's voice shuddered as if actually being scorched by flame.

Seeing that, Ouranos, eyes still closed, quietly spoke.

"The authority of the sacred flame has begun to move."

"Sacred flame…? What do you mean?"

As if sensing danger instinctively, the silver gleam deep in the black robe's hood sparkled like an explosion of fireworks.

Running against one of Freya's rules, words and actions that would upset the balance of the sandbox, Fels became a puppet to her charm, holding out a magic item pointed toward Ouranos's seat.

But Ouranos did not waver.

"It's meaningless, Fels. It's already too late. No matter how she might try to turn all of you into puppets, the roaring flames cannot be stopped."

Like the heavens that watched over the world, he coolly began the reveal.

"If all who are charmed react to certain words, actions, and signs in order to erase any points of danger…then we need only rely on signs that we alone can understand."

"What…?!"

"Subtle signals that children and even deities from other homelands would not notice."

When Hestia had come down there, the arrangements were already complete.

The two deities were conspiring even as Fels listened.

That was why Ouranos had said what he did. "There is nothing you can do now."

There is nothing you can do yet, so wait until the time comes.

"From the first part of the conversation, I knew that Hermes had left a message with Hestia. With such limited options, it was a gamble…but I entrusted Hermes with delivering the firewood."

"Firewood…?! What of it?!"

The firewood that the Guild had prepared and entrusted *Hermes Familia* with was nothing but regular kindling. It did not have any special power in and of itself. And Fels, bound by Freya's rules, had not been suspicious of it at all.

Ouranos, or rather Hestia, had tampered with it after that.

Sparked by Hermes's first message, it was all Hestia's daring resolution in correctly interpreting the old god's will and continuing to act without giving up hope.

"The wood carried through the city—has had Hestia's ichor poured over it."

"That was a really…really dangerous tightrope walk…"

Hermes leaned against a wall, murmuring weakly beneath the cold sky that looked like it might deliver snow on the city at any moment.

Wherever he looked, on every corner, there were residents of Orario holding their heads and keeling over.

Adventurers and deities alike were no exception. They were all leaning against a wall like Hermes, or bracing themselves against the ground, all grimacing as if suffering a terrible headache.

And from the windows of the houses lining the street shone the light of countless hearths.

"Innocent, thoughtless hearth-making…I'd say I did a pretty good job of it…"

The two letters he received from Hestia were the key.

The first was the memo he had written himself, *Turn Orario into a hearth.*

The other pointed to the location where Hestia's ichor had been stashed away.

Because Hestia could not move while under observation, Asfi had surely stored the blood in a magic item and carried it out while invisible. It was fixed beneath a table in the corner of an underground, run-down bar that Hermes enjoyed and patronized regularly.

Everyone in his familia knew about Asfi's magic items. If she snuck invisibly into the home where the firewood was being stored, it was highly likely that she would be noticed. And if that action was reported to Freya by the charmed familia members, that would be the end of things. So Hermes carried out the finishing touches himself.

Retrieving Hestia's ichor, he spilled a single drop of it on each log that had been brought in by the Guild.

"Even if I felt something was off, I did not know anything at all about the situation...And how could I even begin to suspect that following a note written by a mere mortal like Asfi would somehow lead to the destruction of the sandbox...! There was no reason for misinterpretation or a reset to trigger...!"

His expression twisted into a smile as a cold sweat formed on his brow.

Hermes had desperately controlled his thoughts in order to prevent the feeling of something being off from rising to suspicion.

He had already confirmed that, at that level, his memories would not be reset.

Because of that, even if he did not grasp the rules of the sandbox or who the mastermind behind it was—indeed, he tried not to figure either out—he had little reason to believe that the act of creating a hearth would be the cause of the destruction of the sandbox.

For example, suppose there was a special flame sword that could destroy a legendary demon king.

But for anyone who did not know the demon lord's weakness or that such a weakness even existed, if someone told them to make a flame sword, they would just cock their head and wonder why. Without understanding the connection between those two, it was impossible to see how the sword could lead to defeating the demon lord.

Hermes had not probed the disturbances he sensed and had just quietly gone along with the plan he had received from outside. He had Lulune and the others carry the wood that had been prepared with ichor and ordered them to light a fire with it when they delivered it. All how Asfi had written it in her letter.

The distribution of firewood had been arranged by the Guild and was an annual occurrence. The residences of Orario under Freya's spell did not interpret it as something outside the ordinary and suspected absolutely nothing.

"Well, even after getting taken out of the game in a pathetic fashion at the start...there were still things to do outside the board..."

He could see Lulune, Falgar, and everyone else sitting down, suffering from the effects after they had finished delivering the wood.

Gratified, Hermes smiled. He felt bad about forcing his followers to carry out a scheme like that without understanding about it, but even so, he had still continued fighting from off the board.

"We wouldn't have had any moves left if Freya had turned everyone in Orario into complete slaves."

Ouranos's voice echoed in the underground chamber.

If she had turned the people, adventurers, and deities all into faithful puppets who only listened to orders, then there would have been no preventing her victory.

If Hermes had been just another servant to the empress, unable to think for himself, let alone sense a disturbance, then Hestia would have been unable to move on her own and Asfi would inevitably have been caught in the not-too-distant future.

"However, Freya did not do that. Or rather, she could not do it. For Orario to cease to be the city of heroes would mean nothing less than the destruction of the mortal realm."

If every adventurer save those in *Freya Familia* were reduced to a puppet, would it be possible to complete the three great quests, to slay the black dragon?

Was it possible to clear the Dungeon with only slaves who did nothing more than obey orders?

The answer was no.

By turning them all into puppets and creating a perfect sandbox, the hero that the deities desired could not be born. Freya knew that, too.

She was still one of the deities who loved the mortal realm and not an evil goddess bent on destruction.

In order to avoid the destruction of the world, she could not completely twist it.

"And the destruction of the mortal realm...would mean the loss of Bell Cranell, whom she had just gained. Indeed, since she wishes to push him to become a hero, she needed to preserve the nature of the city of heroes."

And thus, this result.

The twisted current state of Orario, where people could still live freely, albeit with certain limitations.

And that distortion was the one and only opening for them to break through.

"What...what are you saying, Ouranos?!"

At the foot of the altar, Fels was flustered...still struggling with the strength of the charm.

Even the former sage who had lived for eight hundred years and attained great wisdom was powerless before the unknowable unknown. Fels was still incapable of comprehending what Ouranos was saying or his divine will.

Fels's outthrust arm was trembling, as if the mage's body was fighting against the restraints shackling it even now.

"What are you planning to do now?!"

The old god responded solemnly.

"What will occur now is the re-creation of a certain goddess's temple from the heavens. She will heighten her divine might to envelop all of Orario and purge all wickedness."

"...?!"

"Her name is Hestia, and her dominion is the sacred eternal flame of protection—the goddess of the altar where fire is consecrated."

The old god slowly opened his eyes.

"Orario will be transformed into a hearth—into an altar to her."

The silence that he had promised Freya was at an end.

The eyes of the god that evoked the blue skies were revealed, and his lips curled up.

"I'm done entertaining your tantrum, Freya."

The black-robed mage, unable to understand what was happening, unable to act, was stunned.

But looking up blankly at the god, the mage murmured with eight hundred years of emotion.

"This is the first time I've ever seen you smile, Ouranos."

"So cooooooooooooold!"

In the sky.

Approximately three kirlos up.

Far removed from the ground, Hestia was being buffeted by the winds.

"Please don't make any sudden moves, Goddess Hestia! I've only flown this high a handful of times myself!"

"Even if you say that, I can't help it if I'm cold, Asfi! It's almost winter! This is the time of year when everyone starts breaking out the stoves! See, my teeth are chattering! Look!"

"Then why did you only wear your usual outfit?!"

"You know, not that it matters really, it's a pretty rare combo for the two of us to be working together!"

"You're right, it doesn't really matter at all!"

Asfi was holding Hestia as they descended while they bickered.

There were two reasons why they were so high in the sky where they could see clouds up close and personal.

The first was an abundance of caution.

Hestia had disappeared at some point, and *Freya Familia* was probably in an uproar about it.

Even if they failed to discern that Hestia had taken to the skies, the eyesight of upper-tier adventurers was a looming threat. The Hades Head's effect was only to make the wearer and their equipment invisible, and Asfi had only been carrying enough magic items for her own use, so she could not make Hestia invisible, too.

Because of that, they had to go high enough to escape the eyes of upper-tier adventurers and use the clouds in order to hide their movement.

Because of that, the atmosphere was thinner, the wind was terrible, Hestia's hair kept hitting Asfi's glasses, and both of their moods had gotten strange.

And the second reason was—

"I'm going to land on Babel now, Goddess Hestia!"

The tower of the gods that loomed over the city and stretched into the sky.

The wings on her talaria spread out, and just like she'd said, her feet touched down on the roof of Babel.

After a brief moment of an odd sense of floating, Hestia opened her eyes, which had been clenched so tightly shut as she clung to Asfi…She was greeted by an autumn night's sky with nothing interrupting her view in all directions.

There was no decoration on Babel's roof.

There was no edge to prevent falling off or anything like that.

It had never been designed with the intention that anyone would stand there.

The only thing there were stars above, which looked like they were just barely out of reach of an outstretched hand, and a chill wind.

"Ahhhh, I know I suggested it myself, but I'm glad we actually made it."

"It appears we managed to escape the notice of *Freya Familia* as well."

Hestia rubbed her arms as Asfi looked at the door to the stairway that was the one and only entrance out onto the roof.

Babel's top floor was currently Freya's domain, and *Freya Familia* regularly occupied it. They would surely be noticed if they had tried to climb the tower the correct way, so Hestia had suggested the route that only Asfi could take.

Set down by Asfi, Hestia looked all around.

"How pretty…not that we really have any time to enjoy the view."

The gorgeous night scenes of Orario were visible in all directions around the tower.

At the very center of the city and its highest point as well, the view it boasted was the most luxuriant in all the city. Picking out the lights of stoves and fireplaces amid the glimmering magic-stone lights that looked as if a jewel box had been scattered across the city, Hestia narrowed her eyes and undid her hairbands.

"Goddess Hestia, having come this far, it's a bit awkward to admit this, but…I still don't really know what it is you are going to do…"

Asfi had trusted what Hestia said and brought them to the summit of Babel.

Would this really free Hermes and the others? What would happen to Orario? Her voice could not hide the unease of those thoughts.

"Hmm…the phenomenon that I administer, bluntly, it's flame, but…well, it's a pretty plain sort of thing."

"Huh?"

"It's a hearth fire, different from Hephaistos's smithing flame… basically, unlike Take's martial arts, Soma's wine, or Freya's beauty, it doesn't really do much down here in the mortal realm."

Asfi's expression grew confused at the sudden strange examples.

As Hestia explained what was part of the reason why her familia had never gathered many members until Bell joined, the goddess released her long black hair, letting it hang to her waist.

"But with an altar prepared like this, there are things I can do."

At that moment.

When Hestia quietly raised her right hand to the level of her chest—all around the city, slender rays of crimson light began to rise.

Dozens, hundreds of pillars of light.

The houses that *Hermes Familia* had delivered firewood to, or more crucially, the flames rising from their stoves, furnaces, and fireplaces, swelled.

Asfi's eyes widened.

The light was a different color, but it was familiar.

It was the light of falna—the residual warm glow from her back when her status was updated.

"We created countless hearths in the city laid out in formation. All imbued with my ichor. In other words, they are a medium. Those countless lights are equivalent to my retainers. And with them, I can re-create the Temple of Hestia that exists in the heavens."

That was when Asfi noticed it.

Hestia's voice. The usual warmth and gentle familiarity in it were fading.

In its place was a mechanical, wholly unhuman voice imbued with divine splendor.

Divinity swelled in Hestia's small body as Asfi subconsciously recoiled, pulling back in awe.

"Mine is the virginal. Bowing not to the force of charm, resolutely rejecting that. Wicked is passion, righteous is purity. Cleanse the binding wiles of charm that blanket this land. Purify wickedness, O cleansing flame."

Her voice wove a sonorous declaration.

It sounded almost like a spell or an invocation of the deities.

The goddess's expression became blank.

Her eyes stared down on the city, aloof and divine. There was no trace of humanity in them.

The innumerable faint pillars of light reaching into the sky gleamed a vibrant crimson as if responding to her call. The surging divine might burned into Asfi's eyes.

"Th…this is…?!"

The human reflexively covered her face as the swirling, overpowering divine authority came blowing in.

The firewood delivered to the points that Hestia had indicated and Asfi had delivered transformed into a blaze amplifying the goddess's divine authority.

If there were anyone who could see from a bird's-eye view, they would understand.

The hearth fires dotted around Orario like watch fires were growing, creating something that resembled a magic circle.

The round tower surrounded by city walls was transforming into an enormous hearth itself, overflowing with the light of flames.

"Don't go calling me a cheater after what you pulled. This is the way of things decided by deities. This is my transient mission and endeavor."

It was a silent acknowledgment.

The agreement of the great gods who feared such an incursion and domination of the heavens and an unwritten rule of the mortal realm.

The virginal goddesses who could reject the force of overwhelming charm were a counter and a check on the goddesses of beauty. Hestia was allowed to fully wield her authority—not arcanum but the phenomenon over which she ruled—in the face of a danger that menaced both the heavens and the mortal world.

"...It was a mistake to retreat from Babel in order to corner Bell, Freya."

For just a brief moment, her tone reverted back to her usual as she turned her eyes to Folkvangr in the south of the city.

"What you surrendered was the very core of the altar."

Babel stood at the heart of Orario.

And it was also the tower of gods, the point closest to the heavens.

The flames increased in intensity.

The ground shuddered silently.

The city itself seemed almost to become a hearth for the sacred flame.

On the streets, in bars, in plazas, the children and deities alike were collapsing.

"I'll show you Hestia's secret technique, something even you've never known."

It was her trump card, a ritual that only the deities of her homeland knew of.

The ultimate divine mystery, it was a miracle far below the level of arcanum.

Asfi fell silent as she watched the goddess quietly wave her right arm horizontally.

"*Dios Aedes Vesta.*"

* * *

An enormous magic power swelled. A tremendous, different divine might roared.

"——!!!"

Being so close to the manifestation of that power bent Asfi's body backward as far as it would go.

An all-purifying light was born.

A cleansing flame.

A crackling fire that rang in the ears of all who had fallen under Freya's charm, but also a warmth rumbling deep from within them.

The power of the goddess dispersed, engulfing the city in a scorching wave.

The ritual flames rose.

The fire of blessing sang a song of purification.

It spread like a wildfire through all points of the city, but its blaze did not burn anyone.

It was not an inferno that destroyed enemies but a protecting flame to save supplicants.

Like a gentle bonfire lighting the darkness, like the kind crackling fire in a hearth, it provided a warm comfort and divine blessing to those who were suffering.

It was the crackle of flames signaling the end of a nightmare.

A divine fire the scorched away all binding spells.

On the streets, in the bars, in homes, and towers. The path of the flame that consumed buildings touched mortals and deities alike.

The messenger god, the smithing goddess, the god of medicine, the god of war, the trickster goddess.

A prum supporter, a young blacksmith, a girl from the Far East, a renart sorceress.

And a princess of the blade.

The raging flame gently engulfed deities and followers who had fallen to the floor or the ground with their eyes shut.

The flame of the hearth resembled a spirit's miracle and spread without end, sending scarlet sparks flying up into the air—and finally, it disappeared.

The city fell silent, as if it had all been an illusion.

"...What was that light?"

Hegni murmured.

Around him, the other members of *Freya Familia* were struggling to understand as well.

Their eyes looked up, outside their home, searching for traces of the scarlet blaze that had lit the night sky, their attention directed above them.

Ghh...Not good, something isn't right!

An unease that was difficult to describe quickly took root in his heart.

The blaze that had been entrapped by the great city walls had not infringed on Folkvangr. The countless sparks flying through the air had shrouded his body entirely, but there was no abnormality. But Hegni's cowardly heart was afflicted by an urgency he could not put into words.

Gripping his black sword in one hand, the dark elf glared straight ahead.

Before him was the battered and bruised fellow elf who was down on one knee with her back to the wall that separated *Freya Familia*'s home from the city.

"...Surrender. Lay down your weapon slowly and without struggling. Else I shall sever one of your limbs."

"Ghh...!"

Lyu was surrounded by members of *Freya Familia*, including Hegni.

Her hard-fought struggle, escaping from underground and rampaging all around the home, had reached its end once Hegni joined the fray. Just like when she had been overpowered in the battle during the Goddess Festival, she was forced into an unfavorable position by the strength of a Level 6, and she had been eventually cornered on the edge of the field far removed from the main building.

She was surrounded by a semicircle that would not let even the smallest insect through.

Lyu put the fist gripping her sword on the ground as her face twisted.

"Khh...Bell..."

Her eyes focused on the mansion atop the hill where the boy was surely still being held. She brushed aside the thought that she had only reached that far and hardened her heart, which was on the verge of breaking as she stood back up and steadied her blade.

Hegni felt a great respect for his proud fellow elf, who did not lose her battle spirit even in such a hopeless situation, and as such, he immediately cast aside all mercy.

"If you would choose honor, then you shall have it in your death!"

He stepped in silently, his figure disappearing from view before appearing right before Lyu's eyes, swinging down his pitch-black blade.

However—

—*Shiiing!*

"""?!"""

There was a shrill metallic screech and a spray of sparks as the dark elf's slash was parried.

"Wh...?!"

Was it Hegni whose eyes widened in shock, or Lyu who was dumbfounded by the sight, or was it the others of *Freya Familia* who could not believe their eyes?

All of them beheld a beautiful golden-eyed, blond-haired girl.

"...Sword Princess...?"

Aiz swung her slender silver blade as Lyu murmured behind her.

All of *Freya Familia* there save Hegni recoiled at her golden gaze.

"I remember everything."

The girl who rarely displayed obvious emotion had a clear, unmistakable anger in her voice.

"Bell isn't part of *Freya Familia* at all."

She pointed her sword straight at Hegni, whose eyes widened as she placed her left hand on her chest.

"Lady Hestia's fire...reached me, too."

A warm light like a hearth had been lit inside her.

Even though she was not bound by oath, though she served a different mistress, she was still a retainer of the goddess of the hearth in that moment, and there was surety in her voice as she declared:

"She scorched away the power of the charm."

As if that statement had been the trigger, a crowd began stirring outside the walls.

"Eh...what...?"

"Why is Rabbit Foot with *Freya Familia*...?!"

"Hold up, what is this weird memory?!"

The voices of people returning to their senses in the shopping district, no, everywhere at once all around the city gave birth to a rising tempest.

It was proof that the domain of the hearth had broken through the domain of beauty.

Sensing on his skin the rising tide of chaos and turbulent confusion, Hegni stood still for just a brief moment before two more figures leaped over the wall and descended from above.

"Argggh, I said something terrible to Argonaut, didn't I?!"

"Bewitching all of us like that was a pretty shitty thing to do, you know...You're going to explain yourselves now, right?"

Tiona had her Urga at the ready while Tione seethed as she leveled her twin kukri blades at *Freya Familia* alongside Aiz.

"*Loki Familia*...! It can't be...Lady Freya's charm has really been...?!"

That sight was enough to make even Hegni shudder.

Freya Familia, who had been so sure of their mistress's absolute dominance, were thrust into confusion.

Disregarding their panic, Lyu somehow managed to regain her calm.

Facing the back of the swordswoman still covering her, she spoke.

"Sword Princess...to think I would be saved by you..."

Hearing that, Aiz suddenly turned around.

"Umm...where is Bell?"

"Wha?! Wh-why is the first question out of your mouth regarding Bell's whereabouts?!"

"...? Should I not have?"

"I-I wouldn't say that, but...actually, no, you shouldn't have! I don't know why, but you shouldn't!"

"Why are you getting into it with each other now?!"

Aiz cocked her head in confusion as Lyu struggled to respond, and in the end, her calm went out the window with a red-faced shout, forcing Tione to be the voice of reason.

Hegni had frozen at the farce unfolding before him before his eyes flared.

"Be it truth or fiction, you have set foot in the goddess's realm! Those who would barbarically disrupt it will be cut down!"

"All right, let's do it, then! I'm realllly pissed, too!"

Tiona spun her weapon over her head as she howled back at Hegni.

In an instant, the dark elf's and Amazon's weapons met with a crash while Aiz, Tione, and Lyu faced forward and began to engage the rest of *Freya Familia*, who raised a battle cry.

"—Tch?!"

A tremendous kick smashed into Allen's silver spear.

"You really did a number on us, kitty cat…You can save us both the excuses 'cause I'm gonna murder you right now."

"…Werewolf son of a bitch…"

Bete Loga was brimming with a savage ferocity with the moon at his back.

The location was the fifth district in the south of the city.

The force that Allen had been pulling back to the home had been stopped in their path with Folkvangr in sight by the other biggest faction in the city that could stand against them.

"Sheesh, Bete. Just like Aiz and the girls, not listenin' to a thing I say. But just this once, I suppose I won't just wait and watch."

The single dwarf grumbled, but his eyes quickly narrowed.

"Aye, I won't be satisfied if I don't pummel your faces in before the Guild can stop us."

"Elgarm…!"

"How was the goddess's will repelled?!"

"That mysterious blaze just now must've been the cause."

"Washed-up old dwarf!"

Right next to Allen and Bete, Gareth Landrock and the Gulliver brothers were staring each other down.

The dwarf was not holding a weapon, but his boulder-like fists rumbled heavily as the prum quadruplets expressed both shock and animosity.

As Van and the others gasped, the most hotheaded members of *Loki Familia* appeared one after the other, following Bete's lead.

The fact that they had been manipulated lit a fire in the ferocious werewolf and the great dwarven warrior.

There was a furious clash of arms as a second battle opened.

The residents of Orario who had not yet recovered from the shock cried out in terror at the scene of a full-on conflict between familias exploding into the open.

"...No way..."

A single prum girl's voice fell weakly, as if her heart had been ripped from her breast.

"No way, no way—no! It can't be! Lilly, Lilly hurt him, hurt Mr. Bell...Noooooooooooooooooooooooooooooooooooooooooooooooooo oooooooooooooooooooooooooooooooooooooooooooooooooooooooooo oooooooooooooooooooooooooooooooo!!!"

"L-Lady Lilly?!"

An earsplitting scream rocked Hearthstone Manor to its foundations.

Mere moments had passed since the purifying flames appeared and burned away all the restraints binding them.

The shock of how she had treated the boy who'd saved her, whom she had fallen for and sworn never to betray again, was too great to bear. Remembering everything in a spew of memories flashing through her mind, Lilly collapsed onto the floor and screamed in a voice resembling a broken music instrument.

Mikoto grew pale as she recalled her own actions even as she rushed over to Lilly's side...when there was another thud.

The sound of knees collapsing to the ground in another location.

"What...what did I...why...That's...I'm...so terrible..."

"L...Lady Haruhime..."

The renart girl had slumped down to her knees, sitting on her heels, as tears overflowed from her empty eyes.

The opposite of Lilly, she was consumed by a quiet grief and slipped into a hell of self-deprecation as a chill gripped her heart so tightly as to freeze time in its tracks. Caught between two impossible despairs, Mikoto froze, unable to do anything.

"...Ghh."

Beside them, Welf, who had been standing in dumbfounded shock, clenched his fists.

He was gripped by a nausea and self-loathing that did not pale in comparison to any of the others, but he turned the flames of that inward to force himself into action.

He walked over to Lilly, who was holding her small head in both hands and pressing her forehead to the floor as she kept apologizing over and over and over, and he grabbed both of her arms.

"Wake up, Li'l E! If you want someone to curse you, then I'll give you all you want afterward!"

And as tears filled her chestnut-colored eyes, he hit her with it:

"If we don't go save Bell now, he will be swallowed whole by that goddess!"

"—Nooooooooooooooooooooooooooooooooooooooooooooooo ooooooooooooo oooooooooo!!"

The next instant, her eyes widened beyond all limits, and a new high-frequency wave emanated from her.

Mikoto and Haruhime both twitched at the sign that the serious time was over.

"No, no, nooooooooooooo! Corrupting a child like Mr. Bell with such extreme seduction! Lilly will protect Mr. Bell's chastity—!!!"

"Then let's go!"

"Aaaaaaaaaaaaaaaaaah! Mr. Beeeeeeeeeeell!!!"

Welf's timely anti-magic fire countered Lilly's despair, setting her off with a screech as she immediately leaped from the room. Welf shouted at Haruhime and Mikoto, who were watching slack-jawed.

"You two, hurry it up! We're a familia! We're gonna go get him!"

"Ghh...Right!"

Haruhime wiped away her tears roughly and stood up on her own before running out as fast as she could, too.

Mikoto snapped out of it and frantically continued after Welf.

Lilly and Haruhime took up the vanguard while Welf and Mikoto left the home close behind them.

The Eastern girl could not tell whether she was moping in regret or overcome with emotion as she flashed a clumsy smile at the blacksmith she was running alongside.

And as if she could not restrain herself, she slapped Welf's back and accelerated.

Welf smiled back and shouted as he swung his arms:

"Just you wait for us, Bell!"

"Uwaaaa...How many times is it now that I've caused Bell trouble...?"

In a mostly empty drugstore.

A listless chienthrope girl's voice fell.

"I seriously want to just die..."

"Don't say stupid things like that! We have no choice but to repay what we owe now!"

Nahza was utterly aghast with herself as Daphne grabbed her by the prosthetic hand and pulled her outside.

Miach chased after the two of them as well as they ran toward the obvious place.

"Even a god committed such a folly. Do not avert your eyes, we must act now!"

"Uwaaah, the prophecy was trueeeee! I saw it in my dream, so why didn't I stand by him?!"

Cassandra clutched her staff to her chest and ran even as their patron god, who so rarely raised his voice, shouted.

The tragic seer was crying for a different reason from everyone else as *Miach Familia* embarked on the same mission as *Hestia Familia*.

"He was cornered in such a precarious position again...! Just being his shield won't be enough to make up for this!"

"Even so, let's go! To help Bell!"

Ouka and Chigusa ran down Main Street while readying their weapons.

The rest of *Takemikazuchi Familia* continued after them.

"Well now, I've experienced my share of shameful lows since coming down to the mortal realm, but...this takes it to a new level!"

Despite having only the same physical abilities as an average person, Takemikazuchi was sprinting at incredible speed across the roofs of buildings like a ninja.

* * *

"S-stop! Stop all of the familias running wild!"

Inside Guild Headquarters, which was stirring as everyone regained their memories, the Guild head, Royman, was screaming frantically.

"Protect *Freya Familia*!!! Send out the order to halt all fighting!"

"What?! But, sir, surely, we can't forgive what *Freya Familia* did. I mean, what if it happens again after we let them off this time...?"

"That's all secondary! If powerful factions, particularly *Loki Familia* and *Freya Familia*, butt heads in the city, Orario will be swallowed in a sea of fire!"

"Eeeep?!"

Misha interjected on hearing the order she could barely believe, but she shrieked at the furious shout that Royman fired right back at her.

Royman had plenty to say about being manipulated by Freya's charm, too, but he was calmer than anyone else and more worried than anyone else. More precisely, he sensed the all-out clash brewing between Loki and Freya that would be more dangerous than anything Orario had ever witnessed, and he was trembling in fear because it seemed to be getting more likely with every passing moment.

He leaped into action to extinguish the fuse on an explosive situation that made the Orario destruction plot, which they could remember now that the charm had been broken, mild in comparison. Realizing the gravity of the situation, the rest of the Guild employees paled and started moving.

"We have to stop them...! If not, I'm going to need even more medicine for my stomach...!"

Grabbing his stomach with one hand, Royman staggered.

As the Guild master, he was desperately trying to remain calm.

And on top of that, he knew better than almost anyone just how impossible it was to stop rough and wild adventurers in a situation like that.

"E-Eina! I'm not sure how to feel about it, but we should probably do what he...!"

Misha's peach hair swayed as she turned around.

"Ah, she's gone..."

Her half-elf colleague and friend had long since disappeared, rushing out of the headquarters.

Rage, fear, shock, panic.

While all the people and deities living in the giant Labyrinth City were consumed by various emotions, by coincidence, they ended up in the same situation as *Freya Familia*.

In other words, by being charmed and then having it released, they were aware of the false input and could grasp the situation without having it explained to them.

"The only one who could do this is Goddess Freya! On the last day of the Goddess Festival, she charmed all of us...!"

Her memories from around when the charm had been applied were unclear. But just as the deities and the more perceptive people had realized, Eina immediately realized that there was only one suspect who could perform such an act.

Running down Main Street, which was stirring with confusion, leaving behind the people of the city still struggling to figure out what had happened to them, Eina shouted as her breathing grew ragged.

"I won't forgive her! I won't forgive the goddess who made this happen! Who did this to Bell, and to me!"

Her emerald eyes filled with water, which glimmered as it spilled over.

"I'm gonna kill those bastards!"

"W-wait, Aisha! Calm down!"

"I'm begging you, don't go picking a fight with *Freya Familia*!"

"No! They don't get to get away with this!!!"

The Amazon's eyes were bloodshot, and waves of rage were billowing off her as Falgar and Lulune tried to stop her.

Not only had she been manipulated, but the renart who was like a little sister to her had been wounded before her eyes. She shook off their hands and dashed off.

From different directions, the half-elf and the Amazon both set their sights on the same place.

"Folkvangr!"

Eina and Aisha and all the adventurers from Aiz onward had acted almost immediately.

Pushed by rage or by a desire to protect their bond with a certain boy, they gathered at the home of the strongest faction in the south of the city.

Banners were waving in the wind.

Dozens of familia banners were fluttering in the wind surrounding Folkvangr.

"Is this really okay, Milady? Taking positions before *Freya Familia*'s castle with *the full familia*?"

"It is. We have more than sufficient cause to merit it."

The master smith Tsubaki Collbrande's question was answered by a Hephaistos whose voice was filled with wrath.

They stood atop the wall that surrounded the great field, at the head of *Hephaistos Familia*, which had deployed almost all their members, including the master smiths, who were a match for upper-tier adventurers.

Hephaistos was glaring at the manor built at the top of the hill in the center of the field, as if she fully intended to siege it.

"This cannot be allowed to stand. Even setting aside standing with Hestia and all of that...you're going to have to pay for this, Freya."

Tsubaki's expression showed just a little bit of fear at seeing her patron goddess so infuriated—the wrath of the goddess of the forge that had made countless goddesses cry in the heavens—before she shrugged in acceptance.

"Serves you damn right, Freyaaaaaaaaaaa! This is what ya get for actin' all high and mighty! Time for a super-ultra burst storm of destruction that'll blow you away, you sex-crazed idiot!"

"Calm down please, Loki..."

While *Hephaistos Familia* surrounded the south and the west, *Loki Familia* had deployed along the eastern and northern perimeter. As their patron goddess stood atop the wall and roared with laughter, her eyes gleaming in rage, Finn pressed his small hand to his forehead.

"Why did you have to make me go all goggle-eyed and babbling while I did everything you wanted, you piece of shit?! Even after I warned you to never use that while we were in the heavens, ya damned fool!"

Looking askance at his patron goddess, who was ultimately just enraged at the humiliation of being ensnared by Freya's charm, Finn tapped the haft of his spear on his shoulder, holding back an aggrieved sigh.

"I suppose one silver lining is at least Riveria was with the group that went into the Dungeon...If it became known a high elf could be controlled like this, it wouldn't end in this city; no elf in the world would be able to look the other way at that."

With that frightening thought, he looked around.

In addition to *Loki Familia* and *Hephaistos Familia*, there were also Miach, Takemikazuchi, and many other familias that had strong connections with *Hestia Familia*, all joining the ring around Folkvangr, a show of force and popular demonstration.

"Hey, Mord. Is this really okay? Getting mixed up in something like this...?"

"D-don't get scared! *Loki Familia*'s here, too. Even if it's *Freya Familia*, they'll get their asses handed to them when they're up against numbers like this! If that happens, we can just slip away in the chaos and swipe whatever money they've got hidden there...!"

There were even crooked adventurers with a keen sense for profit looking to turn a valis.

Shouting back at the adventurer who had come with him, Mord stared at the home.

"Better hurry up and give that kid back, or else we'll all come crashing in!"

"Captain?!"

In a room in the manor.

Heith's troubled voice rang out as she worked to heal Hörn.

"It can't be..."

Ottar's eyes widened at the scene outside the window.

"Lady Freya's charm was broken…?"

Atop the hill.

Hedin, who was protecting the mansion, was struck by a true surprise.

The panicked gaze of all the other members turned to him when he took command.

It was not just the main gate, every wall was being overwhelmed, and the number of adventurers staring down at them undeniably outnumbered *Freya Familia*'s full forces.

"…I suppose it would be ridiculous to berate the ignorant masses. We were the first to trample dignity underfoot for the sake of fulfilling the goddess's will."

However, Hedin did not sweat a drop as he adjusted his glasses and struck the hill with the butt of his rhomphaia.

"But that will not change what must be done. My body is the goddess's spear and shield. I will protect her from malice and scatter the enemy!"

The wise white elf's face was filled with determination to fight, which quickly spread to the rest of the familia as well.

They were still einherjar.

As Hegni's and Aiz's groups continued to fight, their morale did not flag, and the explosive staring contest continued.

And—

"""Ahnya!"""

Voices rang out in The Benevolent Mistress.

"What's going on meow?! I was just feeling annoyed at not being able to go after that boy with the nice butt because he was *Freya Familia*, but it was actually some kind of mind control, and he was a regular here and part of *Hestia Familia*! So then who does his butt belong to, meow?!"

"Just shut up, you! I can hardly believe I forgot everything after getting my ass kicked by *Freya Familia*…! Damn it!"

"Chloe, Runoa…you remember…?"

Ahnya was haggard as Chloe and Runoa burst into her room. Her two friends were seething with confusion and anger as they pressed in on her, but finally, there was unease and shock in their eyes as they asked.

"Syr…what happened to Syr?"

In the setting that the goddess had created, the blue-gray-haired girl did not exist.

Ahnya's eyes slowly filled with tears at Runoa's questions.

Her face warped as she buried her head in Runoa's chest.

"H-hey! What are you doing?!"

"…Ahnya…?"

Ahnya cried out as she clung to Runoa.

Runoa was stunned and stood there weakly before slowly moving her arms, which had frozen awkwardly, holding Ahnya's trembling back.

Chloe had a chastened look on her face as she moved closer to Ahnya, like an older sister licking a kitten.

Ahnya continued to sob silently.

"………"

Outside the open door.

Directly beside it, where the light from the room would not reach, Mia was leaning against the wall in the shadows, her arms crossed as she looked out the window.

"You really are a foolish woman…"

Her words and gaze were directed toward the goddess's castle.

The adventurers' fervor and the sounds of furious battle were obvious even from the goddess's chamber on the highest floor.

Bell and Freya were stunned as they stood there frozen, looking out the enormous window that filled the whole wall.

"My charm was broken…? …If it were possible, then—"

The goddess's stunned expression shifted as her brow furrowed in annoyance.

While Bell could not comprehend what was happening at all,

just as Freya guessed what was going on—the enormous window shattered.

"Whaaaaaat?!"

Bell gasped in surprise as fragments of glass scattered all around.

And in the middle of that rain of glass, as Bell and Freya both covered their faces with their arms, he saw it.

The needle with a spiral engraved in it that had been fired at high speed to break the window.

And, of course—

"—Beeeeeeeeeeeell!!!"

"G-Goddess—ghagh?!"

The goddess was charging through the night sky, carried by four flapping wings.

Forcibly leaping from the arms of Asfi, who was controlling the talaria, Hestia dove head-first into Bell's arms.

He reflexively caught her, but he was sent rolling by the force of her charge. And rolling. And rolling.

Asfi flew through overhead, flustered by the goddess who had just leaped from her arms while Freya stared in shock, and Bell held on firmly to her small body.

He finally came to a stop after exactly ten rolls across the floor, then he slowly sat up.

"...Goddess...?"

Hestia snapped her head up when she heard Bell's quivering voice.

"—I'bm zo zorrrrrrrrrrrrrrry, Beeeeeeeeell! I acted so horribly to you! I'm a failure of a patron goddessssss! Please forgive me for being so powerless!"

The teary-eyed, sniffly goddess wrapped her arms around Bell's neck, hugging him tight. While Hestia sobbed like a child, Asfi's face twitched at the gap between how she had looked while unleashing the full force of her divinity and how she looked now.

That was when Bell realized it.

It must have been Hestia who had undone the charm afflicting the whole city, and she had always been trying to rescue him.

His eyes watered at the warmth of her hug, and he started to sniffle, too.

His face became as much of a mess as hers as he looked into her eyes and smiled from the depths of his heart.

"Thank you so much, Goddess!...I love you!"

"...Yeah, I love you, too!"

The follower and the goddess shared both tears and smiles.

Hugging one more time, they both stood up together.

They turned their gazes to the goddess of beauty, who was watching with a grim look.

"And with that, Freya! I will be taking *my* Bell back! Not yours! Mine! My beloved Bell with whom I have the deepest bond of anyone and with whom I share a mutual love!"

"G-Goddess..."

Bell looked forward and broke into a cold sweat as Hestia decided there of all places to assert her supremacy.

The empress, who had just had mud thrown in her face, looked clearly displeased.

She did not do something so clichéd as bite her nails, but she twirled her hair as she stared at Hestia and Bell holding hands.

"Unleashing your divine might to the full limit...using ichor and flames, you summoned your temple from the heavens...no, *re-created* it. So you still had a move to make, Hestia."

Freya swiftly analyzed the information she had available to her, neither detesting Hestia for destroying her sandbox nor resenting her followers, who had allowed the situation to happen.

Her anger and disappointment were directed only at herself.

For allowing her heart to be so shaken by the boy's trivial words and actions, for being so absorbed in her internal thoughts, for being so lax in her attention. If she had been her usual self, she would have noticed Hestia's actions and Hermes's vain struggle, and she would surely have stopped them in their tracks.

"Yeah, the full strength of my divine blessing that only the gods of Olympus know! It's usually not any help at all and almost unusable to boot! But it's just perfect for someone willing to try every trick in the book like you!"

Hestia accepted Freya's grim gaze head-on.

"It's all due to your halfheartedness, or rather, your kindness in not just sending me back to the heavens! You won't be getting thanks from me, though!"

Hestia was definitely still upset because she was being more aggressive and cynical than usual.

Stuck on the outside looking in at the carnage of two goddesses fighting, Bell began twitching awkwardly. In fact, he was cowering. And Asfi, whom Hestia had gotten down on her knees to beg to bring her there, was laughing hoarsely. "Ha…ha-ha-ha…breaking into *Freya Familia*'s home…and smashing a goddess's window to boot…I'm done for…"

Half out of her mind, she arrived at the same sort of despair, self-abandonment, and a sense that what will be will be that her patron god Hermes had achieved earlier.

"So…what now, Freya? No matter what you say, this is your loss. The spell you cast on Orario is broken, and Bell won't become yours!"

With her charm failing to work on Bell, altering the rest of the world was the sort of last-ditch effort that could work only once.

Even if everyone around him rejected him because of Freya's manipulations, Bell would not lose sight of himself again, and Hestia as the vestal goddess would not allow it to happen, either.

Having such an oppressive board state turned about and placed in check herself, Freya was expressionless.

Her arms hung limply.

"Where do you suppose the point of compromise should be, Loki?"

Atop the wall surrounding the palatial estate.

While Bete's group and Allen's force were fighting behind them and Hegni's forces and Aiz's group were clashing before them, Finn looked ahead as he questioned his patron goddess.

Standing beside him, Loki eyed Mord and the other adventurers sparked by Aiz, who might start pouring in at any moment.

"It really pisses me off...but the Guild won't stand for a war that would rock Orario to its core. Even if we go wild right now, we won't be able to reach any decisive conclusion."

She could barely hear the Guild members, who had finally arrived from South Main Street and were desperately trying to order a halt to hostilities.

"But it's impossible for adventurers to just set aside their pent-up anger."

Finn spoke as if it was none of his business.

While he maintained the encirclement, his eyes were trained on the uppermost floor of the manor, where Perseus and what looked like a child-sized goddess had invaded Freya's chambers.

"Then there's only one thing to do."

Looking in the same direction as her follower, Loki's scarlet eyes opened slightly.

"A war game."

"Hestia—I challenge you to a war game."

"""!!!"""

Hestia's and Bell's eyes widened at that declaration.

Even Asfi looked up, forgetting herself as Freya continued calmly.

"If I lose, then I'll do whatever you say. I'll even accept being sent back to the heavens...And if I win, I will take Bell."

"...Don't screw with me, Freya. You really think I'll accept a challenge in a situation like this? You've already lost, and you're going to be judged for what happened."

Hestia's voice was low, and her eyes narrowed angrily, but the goddess of beauty was ever the arrogant empress.

"We will suffer a heavy penalty from the Guild. But *that's all.*"

"Wh...!"

"Orario must accomplish the three great quests. They cannot afford to let us go to waste or forcibly break us up. You can bet on it. And once the heat of the moment has cooled sufficiently...my hand might slip again. I might just play another trick."

"Ghh...!"

"Can you really live in peace with that thought always looming over you?"

Even while being right where Hestia wanted her, Freya still had her cornered, and Hestia was agitated even though she should have been in command. Bell was just as stunned.

Asfi's silence spoke to the truth of what Freya was saying.

Everything slowed to a crawl.

However, they did not have any time to think.

There was a loud noise below, and the familia members who noticed the intruders were closing in.

"That is the true strength of my familia. The status that I have built up all this time."

Her manner of speaking was haughty and shameless, but…

"And I will wager all of it. My wealth, fame, honor, and even myself."

The three of them were struck by a second shock.

Freya was willing to bet it all, putting everything on the line in a war game.

If she lost, she would lose everything, becoming nothing more than a naked queen.

"You may have as many cooperators as you wish. You can even ally with all of the familias in the city. I will face everything you bring to bear with only my familia."

She would even provide a handicap, demonstrating the extent of her resolve.

Casting down her crown, the goddess was looking at one person and one person alone.

"Let's duel, Hestia…and Bell."

Silence fell.

Their three gazes crossed and interlocked.

Asfi watched as an observer, gulping hard.

The first to speak was Hestia.

"Freya…I really do hate you. This just made it clear. I can't sympathize with your way of doing things, and I can't empathize with you."

"………"

"Holding my followers hostage, hurting Bell…I resent you, and I will scorn you for eternity."

"………"

"…But why are you so hung up on Bell? Why would you go so far?"

Hestia's eyes flared with malice and contempt.

"Because you are a goddess of love? Is it really just that you've taken a shine to him? What has made you so desperate about this?"

Her gaze shifted from scorn to clarity. Hestia set aside her position and her dominion and was asking as a fellow goddess.

"Freya…what did you really want?"

There was no answer forthcoming.

The cool breeze from the broken window and the pale moonlight lit her profile as the silver-haired goddess looked downward ever so slightly.

To Bell, she looked almost like a lost child who did not know herself what it was that she wanted.

Sensing that the silence would never be broken, Hestia quietly sighed, and clenched the hand she was holding as she looked up to the boy beside her.

"Bell…what do you want to do?"

He was the greatest victim of all in this situation, as well as the goal that would be fought over in the coming days, so she left the decision to him.

Her eyes saying that she believed he was best suited to decide this.

Bell slowly released her hand and took a step forward.

"…If we win, will you also listen to my request?"

"…Very well. What do you want?" the goddess asked indifferently.

"Allow me to meet Syr once more. No." He shook his head. "Please let me know the *true you*."

"——"

Her silver eyes widened, and she was speechless before finally averting her gaze.

Her hair quivered, and her expression became blank for a moment before she stared back at him.

"As you wish. I know not what truth it is that you are seeking, though."

Mutual acceptance.

All the terms had been met.

And Perseus was the witness.

With the testimony of Hermes's follower, the decision reached that day would become the city's consensus.

"Lady Freya!"

The members of *Freya Familia* that had rushed up the stairs burst through the door at that same moment.

Freya quietly unleashed her divinity.

Her power shook the room like a wind, stopping the flood of adventurers pouring in in their tracks and causing them to drop their weapons. Even Hegni and the rest fighting outside paused in shock and looked up to the top floor of the home.

A stillness filled Orario, and combat ceased everywhere.

Aiz's eyes widened; Lyu stood in shock; *Hestia Familia*, *Loki Familia*, and everyone else who had gathered all turned their gaze to the chamber where the goddesses were facing each other.

"Okay...then it's a duel, Freya."

Bell's will.

And Freya's resolve.

Accepting both of those, Hestia spoke in a voice that reached many ears.

"It's a war game!"

Her shout reached the sky.

It was a proclamation.

Orario's greatest ever war game.

The bell had rung, signaling the opening of what would later come to be called the Familia War.

DOUBLE ROLE I

THAT'S WHY I RUN

If you called it ridiculous, I wouldn't disagree.

I can still remember it now.

A cool spring morning.

It was just happenstance that I caught a glimpse of that child.

The gleam of his soul was so small. Incomparable to Ottar and them.

But it was beautiful. Translucent. A color unlike any I had seen before.

—*I want it.*

The moment I saw it, that thought struck me.

A gorgeous light, a rare color, a powerful sparkle. I have a bad habit of wanting to collect the souls that catch my attention when I see them.

At first it was just an unvarnished lust.

I chuckled in the back of my mind when he looked so heatedly at me, and I approached that child who like a baby rabbit was so cautious of his surroundings, and I reached out for the magic stone hidden in his breast.

"You dropped this."

It began with a lie.

The start was just a fib.

Because the one who met him first was Syr and not Freya.

"I'm Syr Flover, Bell."

If it were my usual self, I would have just tried to steal him right away. I would have found out the familia he belonged to, and if it turned out not to be bothersome, I would have approached like the cruelest of witches and stolen him away.

But at the time, I controlled myself.

Because it was Syr who had met him and not Freya.

It was a game. Role playing.

So I decided to go at it differently, for a change of pace. I decided to restrain my divine arrogance just a little bit, and watch him develop for a little while. It was still me after all, though. I was sure I would end up not being able to resist and reach out to take him before too long. So I figured why not wait a little at first.

Moreover, I had failed so many times before.

My true wish is to happen across my Odr.

God or child, it mattered not to me. I searched for so long for someone worthy of standing beside me, in the heavens and in the mortal realm as well. So I had my hopes up for the child, for that soul was like none I had seen before. I decided to treat his soul more carefully, more preciously, more deliberately, to draw out its true shine.

Thus began a relationship between a boy and a girl, different from anything else I had done. To anyone who knew me, it would seem quite slow and uncharacteristically passive.

Thinking back now, that might have been a mistake.

At first it went just like I'd expected.

I was not content to just sit back and wait, so I incited the silver-back, and thinking he was lacking, I gave him a grimoire. To make him stronger, worthier. While interacting with him in the tavern and when I stared down from Babel all those days, my thoughts were only of my future Odr, and so I tried to polish that child's soul.

But unexpectedly, something started to grow strange.

It was not sudden.

Quietly, slowly, before I even realized it, the gears stopped meshing and started to creak. A ripple spread across the cool, calm spring beneath the moonlight. My divine will was gradually corrupted by the clear water.

There were signs.

Even as I was preparing the minotaur trial where he might easily die, I appeared before him as Syr that night and said something strange.

"But you don't have to go on adventures, right?"

It was wholly contradictory. Laughably absurd.

Those words praying for his life in the mortal realm, even though I had decided I would chase after his soul if it was returned to the heavens. When coming back from the tavern, I cocked my head in confusion at my own actions.

At the time, I concluded that I had gotten a little too much into my role playing. Sure, Syr might say something like that, but that was not my will. I had become too focused on the roll of the dice.

And the slight discrepancies began to increase.

The frequency of my interventions decreased, and I acted more to protect him. His return from ruin, when I spurred him to face the minotaur once more when he was on the verge of awakening, I grew agitated and ordered my followers that he not be allowed to die.

My time as Freya decreased, and my time as Syr increased.

I was astonished when I realized it. Something had changed inside me.

What was the cause?

Because I had kept making such clumsy lunches like an innocent maiden?

Did the name I had received from Hörn somehow exert some sway over my body?

Or was it because that child was so utterly foolish and pitifully naive and straightforward?

Was it because his potential and the way he chased after what should have been an unreachable goal at full speed was so brilliant that it made my unchanging self jealous?

I don't know. I don't think there was any direct reason. If I had to put it into words, I could only say it just sort of happened.

It wasn't long before I was constantly watching him, searching for him at all times.

When I gave him the packed lunches.

I loved the smile that spread across his face.

When he was talking to another woman.

It bothered me just a bit when his face grew red because some other woman was teasing him.

When his pure white will showed hints of gloom.

When he was worried, hurt, yet still holding his head up and trying to keep pressing forward, I really thought, without any ulterior motive, that I wanted to support him.

And, and, and...

There were so many examples, I could not list them all, even as I spent laughably trivial moments of time with him—and in the course of it all, I fell in love with him.

I did not understand it. I realized it was an exceedingly embarrassing thing. I did not want to acknowledge it at all.

But I was attracted to him.

Not as a deity, but as a woman.

It was easier and simpler once I acknowledged that fact.

But at the same time, I could hear my thoughts as a goddess scoffing at that idiotic result in the back of my ears.

I mean, obviously, right?

I had become so engrossed in a child during my role playing, as the resident of a game.

Silly does not begin to describe it. Hopeless does not begin to describe it.

I was just playing a part. I was just looking down on the game board that was the mortal realm and controlling a piece on the board, a single little girl. Unlike a normal board game, the characters were not wood or stone pieces—they had will; they had life. But so what? I changed my voice, moved the Syr piece, interacted with them, but when I realized I was just looking down at the board from above, I was gripped by a terrible emptiness. It was like falling in love with characters in a book, like dreaming of a rendezvous with a fictional character. Everyone knew it was impossible to live in the world of fairy tales.

But—

The one who saw him first was me, the goddess.

But the one who fell for him was me, the girl.

So it could not happen as Freya.

What I was chasing after had to be attained by Syr to have any meaning.

Syr should have just been a means to Freya's end, but somewhere along the line, things had been turned on their head.

At some point I was freed from the goddess's yoke. I embraced anew the hope that I should have cast aside tens of thousands of years ago. And a breakdown occurred.

And this is the result.

I cannot gain anything as Syr anymore. So I just threw away that game piece and returned to my original self. As Freya, I was true to myself and to the lust I had felt all along.

To make that soul mine. To have my maddening Odr with me. To keep him to myself.

I do not need any proof. In the end, I have only love.

Ahnya and all the other pieces on the board looking up at me and saying I'm not Syr. Demanding I give back Syr.

What a joke. I told them already there is no Syr. I can't help laughing at the ridiculousness of those girls. And at myself for being so hurt by that reaction.

I spent a little too long as Syr.

And using that opening, he and Hestia flipped the whole board on me.

...No.

...It's not that.

A voice.

A voice echoing in my head all along has been muddling my heart.

—When will you realize what it is you really want?

Ahhh, so annoying.

The voice of someone who should already be dead and buried still echoes in my heart—

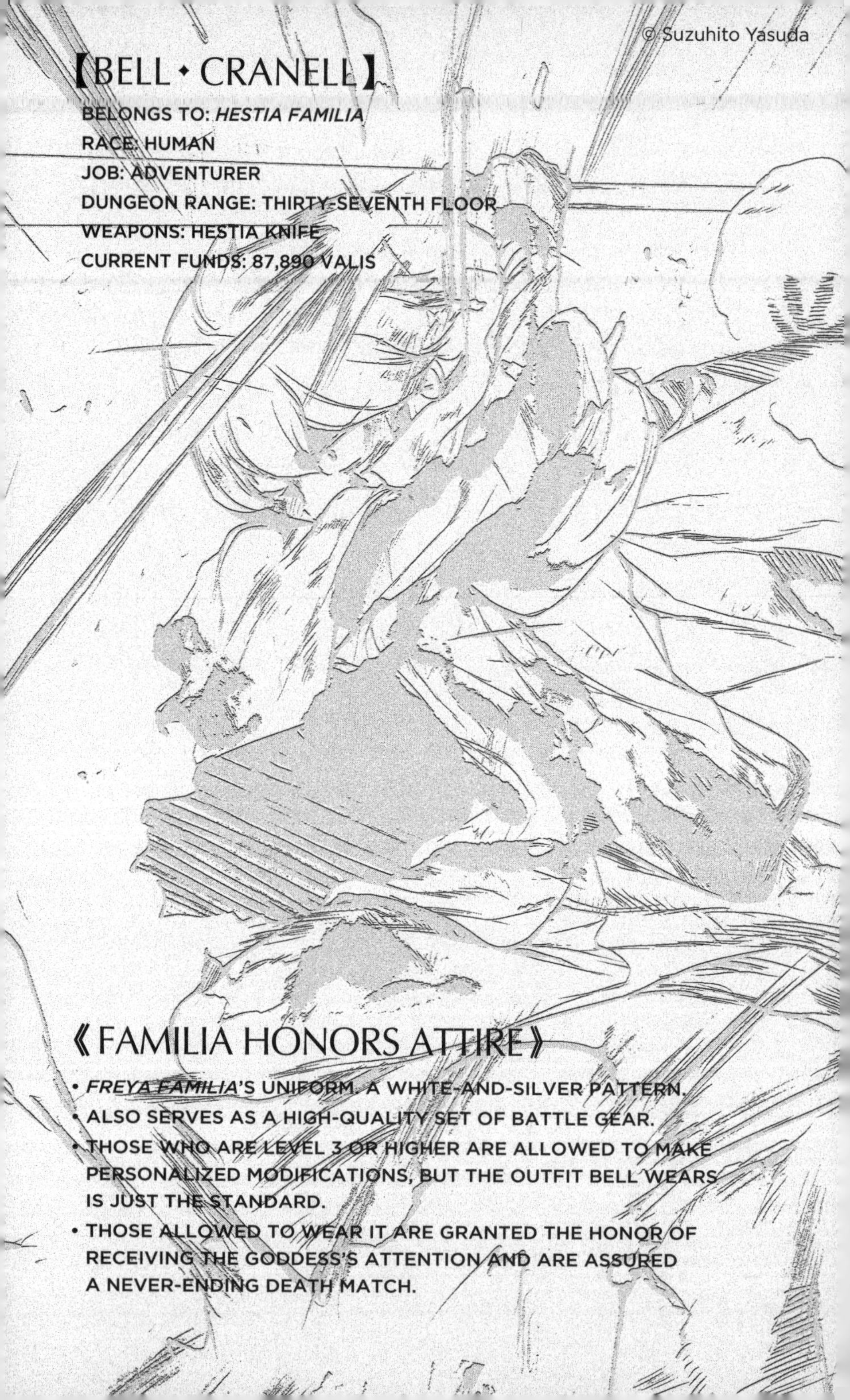

【BELL ✦ CRANELL】

BELONGS TO: *HESTIA FAMILIA*
RACE: HUMAN
JOB: ADVENTURER
DUNGEON RANGE: THIRTY-SEVENTH FLOOR
WEAPONS: HESTIA KNIFE
CURRENT FUNDS: 87,890 VALIS

《FAMILIA HONORS ATTIRE》

- *FREYA FAMILIA*'S UNIFORM. A WHITE-AND-SILVER PATTERN.
- ALSO SERVES AS A HIGH-QUALITY SET OF BATTLE GEAR.
- THOSE WHO ARE LEVEL 3 OR HIGHER ARE ALLOWED TO MAKE PERSONALIZED MODIFICATIONS, BUT THE OUTFIT BELL WEARS IS JUST THE STANDARD.
- THOSE ALLOWED TO WEAR IT ARE GRANTED THE HONOR OF RECEIVING THE GODDESS'S ATTENTION AND ARE ASSURED A NEVER-ENDING DEATH MATCH.

STATUS

Lv. 4

STRENGTH: SS1033 DEFENSE: SSS1218 DEXTERITY: SS1041
AGILITY: SS1089 MAGIC: S965 LUCK: F IMMUNITY: G ESCAPE: I

《MAGIC》

【FIREBOLT】	• SWIFT-STRIKE MAGIC

《SKILL》

【LIARIS FREESE】	• RAPID GROWTH • CONTINUED DESIRE RESULTS IN CONTINUED GROWTH • STRONGER DESIRE RESULTS IN STRONGER GROWTH
【ARGONAUT】	• CHARGES AUTOMATICALLY WITH ACTIVE ACTION
【OX SLAYER】	• ALL ABILITIES ARE DRASTICALLY ENHANCED WHEN FIGHTING MINOTAURS

《COUPLE'S PENDANT》

- A SILVER ACCESSORY CREATED BY LINKING TOGETHER TWO PAIRED PIECES.
- THE SPIRIT HALF HAS BEEN SHATTERED, LEAVING ONLY BELL'S KNIGHT HALF.

"AAAH, YES, BETLINDE,
WHAT SHE GAINED AFTER LOVE DESTROYED HER.
AND LOVE ITSELF HAS DRIVEN YOU MAD.
THE BEAST HAUNTING YOUR HEART HAS SWUNG ITS CLAWS
AND CUT HER LIFE SHORT."

Extract from a note found in a hidden room in Erlandr's Cathedral.

Afterword

Author: You see, women are like different people when they put on makeup.
Editor: You don't say.
Author: And even without makeup, they can become a different person entirely when they are motivated.
Editor: So what?
Author: So Syr is just Freya without any makeup.
Editor: Yeah, no.

No matter how much I tried to explain it, my editor wouldn't accept it, so I changed the setting to make it a unique magic, and this was Volume 17.

I'm sorry for still not reaching the end of this arc that began in Volume 16. However, 800+ pages were just not doable for a single book. I will be striving to bring this Syr arc, or Freya arc, to a conclusion, so I hope you can please just wait a little bit longer.

And commenting on the contents this time is difficult, so I was thinking about telling an old story.

The original DanMachi story I applied to GA Bunko with actually had a different development for its climax.

When the protagonist was chased by monsters during Monsterphilia, it was a certain blue-gray-haired girl, and not the goddess, who was originally supposed to end up fleeing together with him in the book.

The goddess would still ultimately bring him the knife in a similar plot development, but the editor at the time gave me the advice to set Hestia properly as a main character, and I accepted that and changed the story to what it is now.

Reading over the original submission made me wonder about what I had originally intended when I first wrote it and remembered all sorts of things, but even back then, and throughout it all, the fact that that girl at the bar was special has never changed.

I still wonder if the field of flowers she reached here is the same place as I imagined at the time.

Now then, please allow me to move onto the customary thanks.

To my new editor, Usami, I look forward to working with you even more going forward! To Editor-in-Chief Kitamura, who is still in charge of watching Omori, please keep your eyes peeled. Thank you as always to the illustrator, Suzuhito Yasuda, who garnished the story with such enchanting artwork. A humble thank-you to Media Mix and everyone involved with DanMachi in all its forms who have provided so much support. And thank you to every reader who has picked up this book.

Shifting gears to another work, allow me to make an announcement.

On April 9, 2021, Kodansha is releasing *Wisteria's Wand and Sword*, a manga written by Omori. The artist, Toshi Aoi's art is at a Warlord level despite being a newcomer.

And not having enough of it, the story is a dungeon exploration fantasy like DanMachi.

But at the same time, I have emphasized the swords and magic a bit more heavily.

I will continue to push down what I believe is the classic, orthodox route while hoping that everyone will experience the excitement I do, so if you give it a shot along with DanMachi and compare them, I would be thrilled.

Thank you very much for reading this far, and until next time.

Fujino Omori

Between Syr and Hörn

Hörn was always watching that boy's unsightliness.

"Do you remember the promise you made with me...the requirement if Bell discovered your lie? You may no longer contact him. I will not allow you to appear before him."

In accordance with Freya's order, she was careful not to allow herself to be seen, but she was always watching Bell Cranell fight in Folkvangr.

At times by simply looking down from the window of her room. At others by using her magic and watching through Freya's eyes.

She fulfilled the duty the goddess had assigned her while watching him more than any of the goddess's other followers did.

"...Foolish man..."

Those words always fell from her lips when she was alone.

Being pummeled by Hedin, rolling across the ground, tears welling in his eyes, struggling desperately against a swirling storm of violence. No, what he was struggling against might have been the sandbox that Freya had constructed around him. Desperately writhing in agony, screaming in tears, displaying a pitiful figure as he struggled against a world that affirmed *Freya Familia*'s Bell Cranell and rejected *Hestia Familia*'s Bell.

Hörn watched that unsightly boy with cold eyes.

"This is your punishment...for tormenting the goddess, for pushing her this far..."

She murmured it, sure of its meaning.

However, for some reason, she could not bring herself to think that he truly deserved it.

If she were asked if this was the situation she had imagined, she would be at a loss for a response.

Her attempt to assassinate Bell during the Goddess Festival had ended in failure.

If she had to guess, her plan to have Bell himself seal Syr's fate had been a partial success and a partial failure.

When he rejected Syr's feelings, Freya was no longer going to lower herself to being just a mere girl. She remained the sublime and supernatural goddess just as Hörn had hoped.

But her obsession with the boy remained. If anything, it seemed to have transformed into something more intense and more twisted.

Hörn had not been executed.

She had resolved herself to die to preserve the goddess's existence, but Freya in her mercy had spared her.

It was surely its own form of punishment, living with the shame.

There was not a single moment when Hörn did not feel guilty for what she had done to Freya, and no matter how hard she worked and how faithfully she exerted herself, she could not look upon the goddess's countenance as she had before.

Also, the eyes of the other attendants when they looked at her were subtly painful.

They did not bully or ignore her, but the way they looked at her with pity and whispered when she was not watching was so difficult to bear. And Freya had indulged in an impish sadism by telling them precisely what it was that Hörn had done. And the glares from Allen and the others were terribly unpleasant. As if they were asking, "Why the hell are you still serving the goddess and not dead and buried yet?"

And when her thoughts reached that point, she scoffed to herself that she was a criminal just like him.

Though they expressed it in different ways, Bell and Hörn were both unsightly.

A twisted empathy started to make her expression shift into a smile—but Hörn's lip immediately warped in distaste.

"Why must I feel so happy at having something in common with you...? This is absurd."

As she watched the boy splay out on the field below after getting knocked down.

"Miss Hörn has started to talking to herself more lately."

She had not yet noticed that the other attendants had started whispering comments like that behind her back.

One day.

As she prepared to go outside the city in order to maintain Freya's sandbox, as she was walking down a corridor of the home, she heard a voice around the corner.

"Umm, Heith...is there someone named Hörn in *Freya Familia*...?"

"...There is. Obviously. She's the goddess's attendant after all. Did you forget that, too?"

She was jolted out of her thoughts and immediately hid against the wall.

Peeking out around the corner, she saw the healer Heith and Bell standing there talking.

Bell was apparently taking the day off from the baptism in order to go out.

For some reason, she had been startled to hear the boy say her name.

"Why do you ask?"

"Umm...I'm going to Lady Freya's chambers every night, and yet I haven't seen Hörn at all, so it just seemed a little strange..."

Hörn's lips curled subtly as she focused her ears to listen in on them.

She had been strictly ordered not to appear before Bell, but Bell had no way of knowing that. She could not interact with him in order to make sure he did not notice the truth of what had happened during the Goddess Festival, but not unexpectedly he had noticed the unnaturalness of the situation.

She watched on edge, wondering how Heith would respond.

"...Ahh, that's what you mean. It's because you walked in on Hörn while she was changing."

"Ehhhh?!"

Pfft?!

Hörn almost burst as the boy cried out.

She coughed while turning red to the ears, but miraculously Bell did not notice while in the grips of his own agitation.

"With the perfect timing, you ended up going into her room while she was changing and ended up getting a perfect look of her in the black lingerie she always wears."

"B-black lingerie?!"

"And to top it all off, as if by some rule of nature or something, you ended up tripping and falling face-first into her soft breasts."

"Why did that happen?!"

"She turned bright red and just let you have it, and afterward she purified herself by dousing her whole body in holy water, hid away in her room without eating or drinking anything for three days and three nights, offering a prayer and a vow to Lady Freya and all the gods and goddesses that she would never appear before you again, never approach you again, and never look at you again."

"She went that far?!"

I did not! Who would do that?!

Hörn screamed in her heart.

If something like that happened, there's honestly a good chance I might do something similar, but that never happened!

After a few more questions and answers, Bell left on unsteady legs, and Hörn, her face still red, approached Heith.

"Heith!"

"Hello, Hörn. Yeah, that was dangerous. I'd say that was some good thinking on my feet and all around a decent job." Heith pretended to wipe her brow.

"What part of that was nice?! What was that story?!"

The healer just shrugged at her colleague's menacing glare.

"I'm the one having to clean up after you, so just give me a break. It's a little unreasonable."

Hörn's momentum stalled when confronted by Heith's tone, which did not contain even a trace of disagreeableness. She was just saying what she thought.

Suddenly, Heith looked closely at Hörn—at the girl who had been listening in on her conversation with Bell—and asked:

"I know your situation of being pulled by Lady Freya, but…are you still attached to him?"

"Wha…?!"

"The honor of experiencing the countercurrent of Lady Freya's love is wondrous. I can't begin to imagine it, and I'm jealous of it, too, but…why not draw a line already?"

Hörn started to indignantly shout that such a mistaken observation was badly misdirected. But she stopped just before opening her mouth.

She recognized that she had lost her composure. In order to calm herself, she asked Heith a question instead.

"…What of you, Heith? You seem to be interacting with him quite a bit."

"Me? I definitely like him."

"Wh…?!"

Heith continued with an untroubled pace as Hörn revealed a stunned expression.

"He is special to Lady Freya, so I would never in a million years do anything inappropriate, but…even if I wasn't the healer assigned to monitor him, I wouldn't mind taking care of him. Compared to the captain and them and their complete and utter lack of interpersonal skills, he's honest and cute."

"Ghh…! Have some shame! If you lie down with dogs, you will wake up with fleas! What are you going to do if you end up caught in that terrible, worthless man's spell?!"

"Please don't say it so crudely. You're leaping to some pretty tenuous conclusions. It's not like I'm over here professing eternal love for him or anything." Heith sounded fed up as she confidently stated, "My everything belongs to Lady Freya."

Her behavior was polished and refined, but she still had some sort of amiable charm, the exact opposite of Hörn.

Heith Velvet was an alluring girl no matter who was looking, man or woman.

Her pale red hair was tied back in two braids, and the red apron and white dress that she wore brought to mind the image of a nurse.

Her figure had a goddess's good looks, and aside from the fact that her eyes looked dead from being so heavily worked every day, she was cute and wise, not more stubborn than Hörn, and generally harmless (with the exception of topics involving Freya, where she was like every other member of the familia).

She had a reasonable and serious personality, and if she had not been in *Freya Familia*, everyone would be friendly with her. Hörn had even heard adventurers talking about the two great healer girls, the silver saint Amid and the golden witch Heith.

The only time Hörn's voice became rougher and lost its respectful tone was around her. She was by no means a friend, but they were of the same generation, and she was affected by the mood she evoked.

If Hörn was icy, then Heith was a flower atop a hill blooming without a care in the world.

...Heith and Lady Syr are both the polar opposites of me...

Did that foolish man let his guard down around members of the other sex like them?

Thinking on it, I have seen him with Heith often—

While Hörn had continued to reflect on the honor of being Freya's attendant, she had not thought at all about the other girls her age.

However now, for some reason, she was on the verge of feeling a sort of jealousy toward other women.

"—Also, could you stop always watching me when I'm talking to him? I can feel you staring from the window of the manor all the time...It's honestly kinda scary."

"Wha—?"

Perhaps noticing what Hörn was thinking, Heith chimed in.

This time Hörn had nothing to say.

Not because she had been noticed, but because she had not realized she had been doing it until Heith pointed it out.

Heith was to accompany Bell as a healer out on the field of battle, and yet she had glared holes into her.

Heith watched Hörn carefully as she froze at being caught out like that.

And then she sighed ostentatiously.

"You're too desperate. It's almost like you love Bell more than her."

Hörn blushed redder than she ever had before.

And so the humiliating days continued.

The amount of time she spent thinking about Bell increased because of that unnecessary comment by Heith. She started noticing it. It was all Heith's fault—no, the boy's fault.

The days passed in the blink of an eye, but his spirit still refused to break.

He was still roiling Hörn's heart.

"Caurus Hildr!"

"Ugaaaaaaaaaaaaah?!"

As the sun set in the west, the boy screamed, roasted by the white elf's lightning.

"...Ghh...ughhhh?!"

And after being bathed in healing light, crying tears of terrible pain, he stood up again.

As if he understood that he would not be able to stand up again if his will broke there.

And Hörn unsurprisingly was watching it from a window in the mansion, a hand resting on her breast.

"...I don't understand..."

While she watched him through her own eyes, the boy looked both terribly unrefined and more earnest than anyone.

The number of times she had looked at Bell through her own eyes were surprisingly few.

She was always looking at him through the goddess's senses.

Without the filter of Freya's senses, though, the feeling she had when she looked at him through her own eyes was bitter adoration.

He's just like the old me—

Bell was currently utterly alone, just like the girl who had once been named Syr.

Cast out by the world, with none who would affirm him.

She had thought that Bell would shudder in a cold chill, unable to do anything once he was trapped in Folkvangr, just like she had been before.

But he was different.

Even though in the truest sense of it he was alone and without any allies, even if he was unsightly, he still continued to struggle, to fight.

Even though he was still lost and unsure.

Even though she had immediately taken the goddess's outstretched hand on that snowy day in the slum.

He still didn't take the goddess's hand.

Bell was strong.

Stronger than the reports about him would indicate.

Far stronger than she could have imagined.

Far, far stronger than the old her.

It made her jealous, it was bitter, and it was dazzling.

Hörn had to admit that she was chasing after the boy she saw in her own eyes, not a reflection of what the goddess saw.

"…No. No! I can't have feelings for him!"

Hörn looked down at the floor as she shouted.

Pulling her gaze from the scene outside the window, she shook her head over and over as she stood alone in the room lit by the setting sun.

"This is just Lady Freya's feelings! They aren't mine at all!"

There was no one there to agree or disagree with what she was saying.

She tried to convince herself that she was just being deluded by the goddess's feelings, but the emotions pouring out from inside her proved otherwise.

"They aren't mine...!"

What if...

What if Syr was not Freya...?

What if Hörn had remained Syr?

Would she have been able to love him?

If she ran outside right that moment, rushed over to the boy collapsed on the field, held him tight to her, protected him from the einherjar wounding his body, could she be forgiven for doing that—?

And when she thought of that what-if, Hörn wanted to kill herself, even if it meant tearing herself free from the goddess's command.

Thunderclaps echoed.

She could hear the boy's groans and battle cries.

And a single drop fell to her feet.

And as if mirroring Hörn's anguish, a change visited the goddess as well.

"____"

At night in the goddess's chambers, after the boy had retired for the night, the goddess's emotions flowed into Hörn.

At first, she thought it was just her imagination. But it was anything but.

When he had complimented her dress, when she had silently looked into her wine, it had shaken Hörn's heart.

My right eye is—

A change had occurred in Hörn's body when she had received Freya's falna and gained her transformation magic.

Her right eye.

When transformed into a goddess, that eye lost its original color, and took on a silver or, at a certain angle, a bluish-gray color.

She believed it to be the price paid for a diminutive human attempting to become a goddess.

There were moments when even though she was not using her magic, Freya's emotions flowed into her through her right eye. It was just the slightest bit of the goddess when compared to when she was using *Vana Seiðr.*

But in that moment, even though the goddess herself did not notice it—there was a girl crying alone in a field of flowers.

—When she felt it, Hörn was speechless.

—She was crying.

—She was hurting.

—She was suffering.

—Then she is—

"What are you doing?"

The voice broke the magic that Hörn had activated.

"...Hedin."

As the goddess still held the paired hair ornament to her breast on the other side of the door, Hörn left the place, trying to escape.

She ran away, fleeing to her empty room and locking the door before collapsing.

"My way didn't work...? And even with her method, the goddess is still—"

She hugged herself tightly as she murmured in shock. Her nails dug into her arms, and she struggled to restrain her trembling body.

She had to make a decision.

Would she just watch and do nothing?

Or would she sully the goddess's mercy, become truly shameless, and betray her a second time?

It was a fork in the road.

Would she continue to live as Hörn?

Or return to Syr?

Would she forget everything of the goddess and just one time appear before the boy?

May I accept these feelings—

"—The answer to that is obvious."

After a long time, Hörn looked up.

The moonlight shone on her beautiful features.

"I'm Hörn, daughter of the gods."

She smiled.

"My craving for you was the first thing I yearned for. I'm here because I chased after you."

She smiled as tears ran down her cheek.

"I will offer up this life that you saved so that I might save you."

She chose the goddess's attendant.

She would never choose Syr again.

Grasping her hands, she closed her eyes. She made a vow to the moon as she returned all of herself, and all of her feelings toward the boy, to her.